RISING

A STATE OF THE UNION NOVEL

First published by Primal Instinct Publishing
2023 Copyright © 2023 by Nelle Nikole

First edition
ISBN: 979-8-9878508-0-0
Cover art by MiblArt
Editing by Emma Jane of EJL Editing
Map by Cartographybird Maps

RISING

A STATE OF THE UNION NOVEL

NELLE NIKOLE

WORLD OF RISING

You've come to the right place if you're a reader who craves vivid imagery and immersive worlds. Scan the QR code below to discover the world of RISING and its characters.

    P.S. Don't forget to hit download on RISING: Origin Stories, a collection of three short stories following Amaia, Reina, and Tomoe's journey as they share their stories of struggle, survival, and strength.

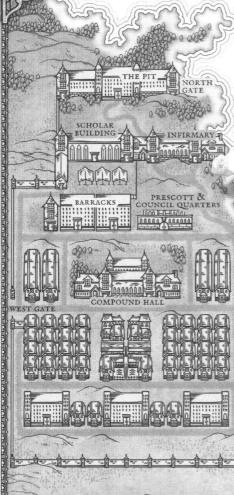

MONTEREY BAY

THE PIT
NORTH
GATE

SCHOLAR
BUILDING
INFIRMARY

BARRACKS
PRESCOTT &
COUNCIL QUARTERS

THE KITCHENS

WEST GATE
COMPOUND HALL
THE
GARDENS

THE ARENA

ENTERTAINMENT
SQUARE

SOUTH GATE

THE MONTEREY
COMPOUND

STATE OF THE
UNION

THE
EXPANSE

THE COVERT
PROVINCE

TRANSIENT
NATION

THE ATLANTIC OCEAN

The spark of evolution can come from anywhere. Science just has to give it a chance.

CHAPTER

ONE

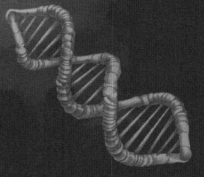

AMAIA

Everything was just a theory before the bombs went off. That's the thing about science. You can only prove so much without a doubt. Until chaos erupts.

I considered myself a woman of science once. Fact over fiction, or opinion any day. Guess they were right about how life can change in an instant. For thousands of years, humans placed ourselves at the top of the animal kingdom, thinking we were better than all species.

There was a show I'd watched years ago. One of the main characters had stated that the only difference between us and them was opposable thumbs and the ability to have complex language. For a long time, I internalized that.

Thought about it to the point it made my head hurt. He wasn't wrong. If anyone cared to pay attention to the outcome of Chernobyl outside the cancer and outward appearance of the mutated animals, the ridiculous theory on the end of humanity wouldn't have been a theory at all. They thought humanity would be brought to its knees.

Well, evil doesn't die easy. Humanity is … resilient.

Turns out some of us are immune to radioactive bullshit. It's literally in our DNA. The strong ones. The ones Darwin gushed about. The ones that would persevere, no matter the circumstances. The resilient. Some of us have a magic green thumb, some a knack for all things fire, others water. Others possess a scary amount of accuracy with anything that could be considered a weapon. I should know, I'm one of them.

Then there're The Pansies. Though the words amused me, it wasn't the official name. Some say "respect the dead" or whatever. I say to hell with it, they aren't really dead.

Just something else.

Something that borderlines both humanity and beast. An impossibly perfect balance of light and dark. They still think, just not the same as us. They walk and run with impossible speed and grace. The fundamental difference is that they fucking reeked like the dead, and eat human flesh.

I was twenty-two when it all happened. Fresh out of university, working at some soul sucking company. It was miserable but paid the bills. As good as life could be for a young girl in the U S of A. The perfect fiancé, the ferocious pup, a core group of friends, nice car, well-funded parents. As a child I'd told myself there was no chance in hell I'd ever be one of those people that spent their whole life behind some stuffy desk. Perhaps I'd spoken the wrong thing into existence.

That was five years ago. A different lifetime. My biggest problem went from mustering the energy to cook for the fourth time that week after a tough workout class, to chasing some asshole out of our territory or clearing a field full of Pansies.

It helps clear my head, anyway. I'd always told Jax it's good for people to see the General out in action. Leading from beside them, as one of them. Within them. But the truth was, it helps me get out all the pent-up aggression from living in such close quarters. Enclosed settlements had that effect on people. Big enough for everyone to have their own space, small enough for everyone to know each other and spread your business when there was nothing else to do. Despite it being thirty-thousand people deep.

More times than not, it felt akin to a prison. Like someone was just waiting for a spark to set everything ablaze into flame, then kick the dirt over it and move along, pretending nothing ever happened. Rumors ran rampant throughout The Compound all the time about settlements reforming, joining as one to take over with a military state of mind. Forming some sort of sick alliance with The Pansies.

"Amaia." *Urgh, one day.* For twenty-four hours, I'd asked for a moment of respite. Told everyone to find a hobby outside of bothering me. "Maia. Maia, wake up. Seriously, what the hell, get up!" I breathed in once, soaking in the last few moments of the warm sun heating my russet skin.

"I'm not asleep. Get off me." I shrugged one of my best friends off. God, she could be persistent.

She was usually the type to respect others' privacy when asked, not wanting to encroach on any boundaries. *This better be urgent.* I opened my eyes to her pale, olive hued skin and dark brown hair.

"You're drunk. God, unbelievable. I shoulda known. Moe was willing to bet she saw you take off with a bottle, but I didn't want to believe her. Said it must be extra water, and you'd gone off on one of your hikes. You're really something you—"

I rolled my eyes and cut her off before her loud voice could ring anymore, rattling my brain.

"I'm not drunk, Reina. I'm simply relaxing my mind, soaking up a moment of peace." We'd spent weeks out securing our borders, the uptick of attacks concerning. I sat up and quickly scanning the old abandoned golf course, now littered with tall grass and patches of trees.

It nestled me between it and the cliff. Most people would never close their eyes in such a precarious situation. Pansies were quick and efficient when they went in for the kill. There'd been many times where someone excused the snapping of a branch as a deer, just to be wrong, and to only have a cliff as an escape route.

Yeah, I could see how that would make people uneasy, but I was just as lethal, just as efficient as they were. Even if I was half out of my mind thanks to the bottle of tequila now half empty at my side. Most apocalypse shows I saw insinuated a bottle of alcohol or drugs would run dry thanks to those trying to take themselves out of the equation. The writers clearly had no imagination.

If the world was going to shit, best believe man would find a way to continue their escapism.

My eyes narrowed as I took in the sadness on her face. Despite her job, she never let much break her even demeanor. She'd claimed it was to help keep her patients calm, but even as General, I wasn't sure how she could be so *on*, all the time.

The position I held didn't give me the luxury of feeling things. Caring, sure. Dedicated, always. But being emotional was never an option. Which meant I needed to shed the emotions somewhere and why I'd tried to make my peaceful day once a week a priority. Yet somehow, it always ended up ruined.

"Amaia, it's Jax," she huffed. "There's been an accident."

I sprang to my feet, taking off towards The Compound, not bothering to see if Reina could keep pace.

CHAPTER

TWO

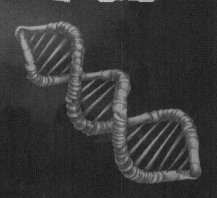

AMAIA

The coastline was a blur. My feet trying their hardest to keep up with the pace my brain desperately wanted me to move at. Rocks shifted loudly at my rear, and I could only hope it was Reina doing her best to follow behind. I didn't have time to cover my tracks carefully on the way back. If some opportunist were this close to the wall, they'd be right in earshot of The Pit, anyway.

After spending months out on the road without a watch or clock, I needed nothing more than the sun to tell time. If I wasn't too far gone from my rounds earlier, it was near 3 p.m. The smaller kids would be receiving their Sunday classes, which usually came with a lot of high-pitched screams and a series of ouches.

One mile turned into the next. The cliff side turned to trees, giving way to an old suburb, letting me know Jax wasn't too far off. I kept steady and jogged towards the North Gate.

"Open the gate," I breathed. Someone who didn't know me would mistake it as a shy request, rather than the lethal demand it truly was. The guard, Riley, yelled at the others to hurry. The urgency behind his words showed he was as agitated as I by whatever caused the delay.

"General Bennett, please. Prepare yourself." His brown skin matched the warmth in his eyes.

Pity.

I hated pity. Scoffing, I squeezed through the small crack of the gate that had already opened, hands wrapped around Reina's clammy wrist. We matched pace. Composure now fully in check, as we pulled our shoulders back, chin high, and walked into the Infirmary.

It was settled between The Pit and the Scholar Building, for obvious reasons, but now that I was here, my curiosity caught up. *What kind of accident? It was just a routine patrol with new recruits.*

We purposely set out a path that had minimal Pansies. Wanting to give them time to adjust to the speed and unnaturalness that was sure to catch them off guard in their first few encounters, especially within an organized unit. While The Compound accepted new citizens all the time, they rarely had the same training that could guarantee survival of our home, just enough to get by and survive. Most times, when they showed up on their first day, they'd come in thinking they were a hot commodity. Always thinking their fighting stances were perfect, or they're qualified to hold a gun.

It's usually quickly discovered that just because they can fight and hold a gun, doesn't mean we should let them. Only after they passed a series of tests supervised by Jax, or me, could they go out into the field for the first time. From there, based on skill, intelligence, mutation, and general assumption of their ignorance, they're put on assignment. Everyone fulfills another role once a week on a monthly rotation in order to stay fresh should the situation come to worse.

Reina kept quiet. This had to be bad. It took a lot to silence her and she let little slip. Taking a deep breath, I pushed open the door to the Infirmary. It was silent, all eyes turned to me. Soldiers were everywhere. All fifteen beds in Unit A were filled.

I passed by each bed, soldiers muffling their cries of pain. Weakness is not taken kindly in a world like ours. Most people felt some kind of pain day in and day out. You get hurt and you shake it off or you get left behind.

It's the reason, despite the population, we only had three hundred medical beds on standby. We typically reserved the beds for soldiers. Children next if their prognosis was positive. Nothing that didn't require around the clock care was permitted. They typically instructed everyone else to hit the Apothecary for a remedy they could use at home. There was also the option of requesting a home medic, or hope they had friends and family with healing aspects of the water elementals.

The Compound must survive at all costs. That was the rule. Being one of the most successful within the territory, others often sent emissaries here for training and guidance. Our rule is part of how we survived in this messed up world. Five years after the world went to crap, and we're practically a fully functioning city in the 1800s.

Perhaps that's why no one ever challenged our ways. If you can't contribute, then you're gone. Everyone has a role to play. If you can't or don't want to do your initial assignment, then you better hope you have another skill to fall back on.

It smelled of puss, iron, and something sharp. Something toxic. The soldier on my left, not any older than twenty, was missing a foot. *Sad. I remember him from his test last week and if my memory served me right; he was a pretty promising fire elemental.* His blond hair shifted as he readjusted himself, uncomfortable under my gaze.

To the right of him, another soldier bit down on her bruised lip to avoid screaming, her arm bent at a disgusting angle. I nodded at her. *Respect.* Prescott, leader of this place, had told me from day one to always pay attention to brave women. They shape history.

Cold air hit my face as we moved into the lab, one of the regulated areas of The Compound since the air elementals used it for controlled experiments. Reina's personal lab, office, and sleeping quarters were in the back.

Even at a young age, her intelligence stunned many. For a ranch girl from Montana, she sure knew her shit. She claimed her mother passed a lot of knowledge as a livestock veterinarian and it gave her a great background, but she often undersold herself. When she first arrived, she spent a lot of time heads down in the books, trying to understand her mutation and how it could help others. Something she continued when our other friend, Tomoe, had arrived about a year later.

Reina tapped the hard wooden door twice before opening to her sleeping quarters. Tomoe sat slumped over Jax, her tattooed arms covering his pale chest. I froze. This was worse than anything I could have imagined.

Jax's shaggy auburn hair was plastered to the side of his face. Clumps of blood distinct in its tone of brownish red. Pale. He was ghostly pale. Not in the way most people would go pale with years of no sun. No. He was pale in a way that could only mean death was coming and not far off. Every breath he took sounded painful and hollow, followed by a small whoosh of air.

My eyes continued to scan his body. His slim shoulders were rigid and barely lifted with every breath. Good God. In my years as a General, never had I seen a wound like the hole in his chest. It was less of a hole and more of a crater. How he'd survived long enough to make it onto Reina's bed, I wasn't sure.

Hot, salty water streamed down my face uncontrollably. My love. My friend. Laying there, so absolutely helpless, the antithesis of the bouncing beam of a kid I'd met years ago out on the road. I had to look away. Refusing to let myself fixate on his body any longer.

"Henry did what he could to patch him up," Reina whispered from the door. "I've removed fear and any levels of discomfort from his body to prevent him from going into shock. Try to give him a chance at healing, but, there's nothing else we can do Amaia. The wound is too deep. His body has to fight to do what magic cannot. I'm sorry."

Sorry? I wanted to laugh. Sorry didn't cover it. I wanted answers, but I found I wasn't yet ready to ask those questions.

I took in his face again, this time realizing his nose was bent at an awkward angle with dried blood crusted underneath. His labored breaths allowing me to see two of his teeth were missing as well.

My chest shook as I took another deep breath, daring to take in the rest of his appearance. I noticed his navy cargo pants were tattered and blackened at the ends, tugging at my mind to place the smell from earlier. The crisp clothing of everyone involved. *What the hell was this?* It couldn't be The Pansies. They didn't coordinate complex attacks that required tools that created fire, nor did they possess any magic. The smell was more than just something burning, it also contained the toxic tinge of chemicals.

"What happened?" I demanded.

"An explosion," Tomoe mumbled, shaking off the vision she'd succumbed to. "Maia, I. An explosion, I'm so sorry."

My ears rang. I laughed. Belly hurt, full throttle laugh. "Sorry? Why does everyone keep telling me that?"

I lost more minutes to laughter until my core couldn't take it anymore. Moe stood up and moved towards Reina, who had inched closer to me. The same worry lines plastered on her face.

"Don't you touch me, Reina!" I shrieked, "You let me feel this. Do not touch me." More minutes of silence rang out. "Sorry is the person who will answer for this. Get everybody to The Pit. Bring Harley."

I fell across Jax's nearly naked body; the order consuming what adrenaline I had left. My tears cascaded faster than the rain now falling against the window. I watched as they filed swiftly out of the room, leaving me alone with a nearly dead soldier. One hand slid over his torso, finding any part of skin on display while the other rubbed the spot where I held his heart every time he tried to take my anxieties as his own.

My legs trembled, holding in the tears that came in waves crashing against my inner defenses, *still. Be still and breathe. Remember who you are.* I braced myself to rise from my knees, and adjusted my disheveled clothing. I glanced back at Jax one more time, then wiped my tears as I watched my reflection in the mirror behind the bed, and walked out the door toward The Pit without looking back.

CHAPTER
THREE

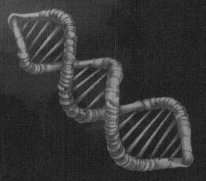

AMAIA

I swiftly made my way back through Unit A, ignoring every glance that came my way and doing my best to maintain my composure. Perhaps that was the only thing keeping me from crumbling. That my strength and willingness to persevere is what kept them all going. Hoping for better days.

Pushing through the doors to the courtyard, I let the heavy rainfall soak me as to hide the few tears I let slip. Entering my quarters, I quickly changed to my Pit clothes, pulling on my black cargos and t-shirt. My fingers shook, making it difficult to tie up the laces on my combat boots and wipe off the dried blood from my last rounds outside The Compound. Strapping my gun to my belt, I strode towards my bathing quarters to inspect myself in the mirror. This time pulling my tight jet-black curls from my messy bun into a low military style one instead. Tonight, I wouldn't play any games. If someone did this to Jax, then the chances of them having other things planned towards leadership around The Compound were high.

While I couldn't rule out if this was a personal attack towards our relationship, I also couldn't shake the feeling that this was some political power move directed at Jax's position as my second. Which also meant I could be next.

Pull yourself together, Amaia. Grieve later, get answers now. God, I needed a shot to get me through this. It wouldn't make anything better, but damn, it would help. *Reina.* She must have gone through my things before me after finding me out near the cliff, given my stash under my clothes in my hamper was gone. *Sober, it is then.* I thought to myself as I made my way towards the door and grabbed my matching black cargo coat on the way out.

My fire magic lit up the torches surrounding The Pit. What was usually dirt and gravel turned muddy from the consistent rain that fell, giving the now gray night sky an even more ominous appearance. One by one, soldiers stumbled out of both the barrack side of The Pit and the Infirmary. I strode towards Moe and Reina, who were chatting in hushed tones in the shadows.

"Tell me about the vision."

Moe jumped, not having sensed me come up behind her. "What?" she said, looking at me with eyes that always appeared to be seeing right through you.

"Tell me about the vision you were having when I walked into that room. I need to know about the explosion," I said. "Tell me everything."

Reina shifted uncomfortably, trying to decipher if she was going to have to step in or separate us. We both had tempers when challenged and sometimes things became rather destructive.

More times than not we just settled things out in The Ring like decent human beings, but sometimes things were damaged that probably shouldn't have been. Especially after a few drinks. This wasn't one of those times, though. I knew the difference between defiance of leadership and protection of a friend.

"Amaia." She tried to warn, then surrendered to the plea in my eyes. "They were out on the trail when Jax thought he scented something off in the wind. He told Seth to keep moving and fell back since he couldn't determine what exactly it was that was off."

Tomoe's eyes glazed over as she channeled the vision to tell me more. She was one of the strong ones that had unusual control. If she focused and wanted it bad enough, she could pinpoint a vision of her choosing no matter past, present, or future. Visions came through as memories of a person who lived through the event. Most lit-heads didn't possess enough power to determine what was in the past, what would happen in the future, or what was happening in real time. Let alone through the eyes of the person of their choosing.

As far as we all knew, Tomoe was one of three in the territory that could, and even then, the closer to the person she was, the stronger she was in pulling a vision. If the relationship was weak, then inaccuracies arose.

She came to from the vision, her eyes becoming as focused as they could appear. "A soldier in front of him stumbled, walking funny. Then another. He figured they may not have the endurance, so he turned them back, since they weren't too far from The Compound yet. Then the explosions went off."

Explosions? Plural? Her sudden shift in tone with the last sentence was enough to let me know she wasn't telling me the full picture. "I am giving an order as General to tell me the entire vision Tomoe. Not as his partner, not as his friend. His and your General. Tell me *everything*."

I felt Reina's powers sending out feelers and shot her a glare to back off. I knew she wanted to ease the tension, but this wasn't the time. Moving a step closer, I closed the gap between us even more. "The Compound could be in danger if what I think is true. I need to know everything, every detail." We stared eye to eye for a moment, tension heating the space in between us.

Tomoe was a badass, and I wouldn't doubt her ability to put on a proper show just because she spent most of her time in books. "You only *need* to know details that will help us sort this out. You *want* to know the rest, so you have an excuse to do whatever it is you're about to do and justify it as being right. There's a difference and for you to think Reina and I can't decipher which is which, especially after the way you probably downed a bottle of tequila, what? Two hours ago? Is quite honestly insulting."

The tension rolled off, her eyes softened. I could tell she wanted to hug me, but in my position, it wasn't possible at the moment. I allowed my posture to relax and willed her to continue.

"When the soldiers turned back, one of them got startled and was heard calling out to someone right before the explosion went off. I couldn't tell if he was calling out to Jax or someone ahead of them on the trail since Jax's back had turned. That was just the first explosion. He was tossed deeper into the trail, but he was able to get up pretty quickly. He heard someone calling out for him specifically up near Seth. His ears were ringing, but he pushed himself to keep forward, fearful something had happened to Seth. Then the second one went off and he was flung again. When he came to, there was a branch through his chest. But he wasn't laying near any trees. He was thrown into the field on the other side of the trail. It goes black again right before his next memory of Seth hovering over him. That's who brought him back. He sprinted here with him in his arms and alerted the rest of the medics and the standby unit to go out and get the rest. The gory details of the in-between are not relevant. Please, do not ask me."

Selfish. I was selfish for forgetting for even a moment how close Tomoe and Jax had gotten. They sparred together every morning at dawn until breakfast. It was their form of therapy. They didn't talk, just sparred, and then sat and ate next to each other quietly, lost in their trauma. No one knew much of Tomoe before this, just that she'd been through a lot and probably seen even more. She was alone for months after everything happened to her family. Thought she was alone in having visions, had called it a curse. And Jax, only I knew about Jax's past. It wasn't worth repeating, not if you wanted to sleep at night.

I reached out for her arm and gave it a squeeze before turning around and moving towards the center of The Pit. All eyes went on me and silence took over. It wasn't because they feared me, no. It was from respect to knowing I would do whatever it took to keep them all safe. Even if it meant taking things to the extreme, otherwise what was the point of me having all this power? At least, that's what they all assume. No one ever cared to ask if I enjoyed all the responsibility.

Maybe it was time to show them all why they *should* have just a little fear. Without respect and fear, a great General can fall. I'd seen it first hand. That, and incompetence.

Glancing around, I took in every face of every soldier, meeting each of their stares from the tip of my nose. Sighing, I closed my eyes and took a deep, unbeknownst to them sobering breath and opened my eyes displaying the glowing red color of flames that now took place in my iris. Sticking my hands out in a circular motion, I encased the inner part of The Pit in flames, raising them into a wall reaching eight feet high with me dead center. They tried their best to hide their fear, but I didn't need Reina's powers to sense what hid in their core.

"I'm only going to make this offer once," I stated, choosing to focus on Riley.

He tilted his head in silent response, the only comfort he could offer at the moment. I trusted him with my life, and him with me. There was no genuine fear of me for him, making it easier for me to use him to focus my energy on and do what needed to be done.

I'd only allow the best of the best to man the gates. The fact that I chose him to run the most important one, the one that provided direct access to our forces, meant he was truly one of our top men.

"If you have any information about the incident today, I urge you to step forward. Now. I will not make this gentle offer once. After that, there will be consequences for silence. We know what happened today was not an accident, nor was it an unplanned attack by some roamer out in the woods. There will be no display of mercy in the next few seconds." More silence. God, I was tired of the silence. "No one?" I said, scanning the crowd again once more. "Going once, going twice. I won't count to three." The world stopped, and a smirk pulled at my lips. "Very well. Seth, Harley please."

Reina's brother Seth appeared first in his usual jeans and cowboy boots, sporting a black tee that was now soaked, showing off his sinewy muscles from a lifetime of ranch work. He wasn't a bulky man, but he was threatening enough. Especially with his height and the two pistols strapped to his belt and the other attached to a thigh holster right above his knee. His olive skin, slightly darker than Reina, mottled soft freckles lined underneath his eyes down his cheeks. His blue eyes swirled fiercely. A sea during a summer storm, fully displaying the anger of a downed friend. His brass knuckle rings closed in on the silver chain link attached to Harley's collar.

On a normal day, I'd run up to her and smother her in kisses while doing nonsensical baby talk. But not here, not now. Now was time for work, and like the good girl she was, she knew that.

An engagement gift for me in my past life, my baby sat at a whopping eighty-five pounds of muscle. Big for a Doberman girl, which made her practically perfect for an apocalypse. Harley let out a menacing deep growl that was deep enough to scare off a large bear. Her drool only symbolized her thirst for violence. With the flames still going but lowered, I took in the faces of more soldiers, who now showed clear signs of discomfort.

The flames, the weapons, the dog, and my backup, I'm sure they were experiencing sorts of sensory overload. The perfect time to find our weakest link. A soldier near the back who I deemed a bit too shifty caught my attention as he stole glances between me and Harley. He lifted his head as if sensing someone staring and nonchalantly scanned for a quick exit.

"The thing about situations like this is, they take a lot of coincidences to end up as an accident. And I find myself as being someone that believes in, how does that saying go, Seth?"

He looked at me, eyes still dancing, and smirked. "No such thing."

I smirked back. "Yes, no such thing as a coincidence. Thanks to Tomoe, we were able to see what Jax, unfortunately, cannot tell me himself at the moment. It was rather enlightening and helped me put some things into perspective. You see, when I went to give Unit A a visit earlier, it reeked of chemicals. And you know what fire magic mishaps don't have? Chemical stench."

Whispers broke out as I glanced over towards Reina and Moe, who were monitoring the crowd, trying to see what I couldn't. Moe gave me a sharp nod, showing that she understood where I was headed, and she agreed.

"But bombs do."

The soldier I hadn't stopped watching from earlier sucked in a quick breath, head swiveling towards me, his eyes meeting my own. His eye whites became visible on all sides and his brows shot up in a straight line for less than a second, but enough for me to fully register what he was about to do. He backed up two steps and turned. But not before I could summon my own little demon.

"Harley, bring him to me." And she took off.

CHAPTER

FOUR

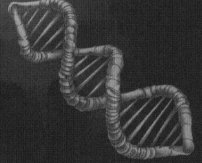

AMAIA

Harley bit into his arm and dragged him over towards me, blood dripping down her black coat. The soldier cried out in pain as sweat slid down his face, meeting tears inspired by genuine fear. Good. The side of my mouth upturned, proud of my display of power. That wasn't even half of my tank, not even a quarter.

I locked eyes with Riley, who nodded slightly acknowledging my quiet request, and slipped off into the shadows, pulling his hood over his shoulder length locs.

Glancing back at the soldier as if I were bored already. "I remember you. Tell me, Carter, right?"

"Caleb, ma'am," he replied in almost a snarl. I didn't appreciate the disrespect, not in front of all these people.

"Carter it is," I said even-toned, "So tell me, Carter, how a recruit reject ended up out on patrol after I personally told you that you wouldn't be joining my units?"

If he sweats anymore, he might give the rain a run for its money. "I-" he stammered, glancing over my shoulder towards Harley, who Seth was now reattaching to her chain leash.

My fingers snapped in his face, calling his attention back to me. "*I* am right here Carter, anything going on behind me isn't worth losing the opportunity of a spared life. I assure you."

"I suggest you focus on the General, *Carter*." Seth came up from behind me, standing side by side. His eyes narrowing, focused on Caleb.

Caleb's lips pulled upwards as if disgusted by Seth. His mouth moved faster than his brain, stumbling out a response. "I spoke privately to Lieutenant Brennan and asked for another chance. He told me he would think about it."

Interesting, as Jax usually ran these things by me. Everyone has off days. There were times we saw something within a recruit, and if they pushed and showed enough want for it, we'd grant them another opportunity to showcase their talents. But never without discussing it with each other first, not when it came to our troops. Everything was transparent and to be agreed upon. If there was no trust within leadership, soldiers would fall. That's how history had always proven.

"You expect me to believe that with your poor display of competence and skill in almost every category, you impressed someone as respectable as *my second* to consider giving you another shot? And why would he waste his time on such a charity case?" I said, gesturing up and down his body as if I was unimpressed.

"Lieutenant Brennan approached me this morning, telling me I had one more shot to show him I was worth something. He told me someone close recently reminded him to him of how far he'd come. That if no one gave him a chance, he wouldn't have made it to—"

Seth cut him off, "So then why use your chance to prove yourself, to blow half the unit into burger meat and the other half unable to be worth anything to our troops outside of sitting at the watchtowers? This doesn't seem like something one man, especially one that lacks any substantive value, could pull off on their own."

I glared at him. Everyone here was of value. As long as they pulled their weight, their position didn't matter to me. Watchtower, border patrol, one arm, no legs. Didn't make a difference if the job was able to be done right. He knew that.

Caleb took a step forward and spat directly on Seth's face. Before it had a chance to start dripping down, Seth pounced.

If anyone was more prone to violence than me, it was Seth. He'd probably be my second if he didn't enjoy manning the Stables so much. A true Montana cowboy through and through. The number of resources we saved by sending him and his crew out to secure the outer border was insane. They were fast and efficient. The fact that he also possessed the Scholar gene and could communicate with me mind to mind made my work as General even easier. If Seth found an issue of concern, he'd instantly alert me and I'd send reinforcements out faster than whatever the threat was could clear the area.

Caleb tried to stand up from Seth's initial shove and swung a powerful right hook. *Impressive.* He sure didn't exhibit this on his any of his tests. *Maybe he did have an off day.*

The crowd became rowdy as shouts of excitement rang out. I rolled my eyes, typical. They'd spent the last month on edge, fighting off herds of Pansies that somehow kept breaching our outer borders. They'd already overtaken a smaller settlement a few hundred miles north. The news made people anxious, to say the least.

Seth met Caleb's second swing halfway. Invigorated by the attempt to challenge him. It was Seth's turn to swing, his movements were quick, catching Caleb in the gut. He threw another, this time clocking him directly in the mouth. Blood gushed down Caleb's nose onto his chin.

"Seth, enough," I snapped, "I need him to be able to talk."

His temper, I should say, is probably the second biggest reason he didn't serve as my lieutenant. Anger led to impulsiveness and impulsiveness only gave way to sloppiness, and sloppiness got people killed.

Seth circled around him, cornering him in a way as Harley lingered on the side of us all.

"Please." Caleb's face was bruised and blood reddened, eyes pleading.

"I just want to know who helped you. You worked with a Scholar or Tinkerer, right? They created the bomb. You don't know how to do that, I assume. But you used your fire magic to ignite them? Tomoe, is this one of the soldiers that were turned around? At any point, was he out of view during the vision?"

Tomoe stepped forward, separating herself from the crowd. She studied his face with a heavy gaze. "Yes, he went out of view when the first soldier yelled out in warning right before the explosion."

Caleb fell to his knees and grabbed his punctured arm. "Please, my brother and his wife. Their safety was threatened. I was told to do this, or they'd be escorted outside the borders. His wife is eight months pregnant, I couldn't allow it. You have to believe me, please. I am an honest man in a bad situation. I worked as a social worker before all of this. Please."

I sensed the truth behind his words, though I possessed no gene that would let me know for certain. "By who? Who threatened you?"

He looked into my soul. Such sad eyes. He didn't speak. The soldier in me told me he wouldn't say. Not with his family's life, presumably still on the line. Sure, I could torture it out of him, but I wasn't yet ready to set that standard with my units. Not on public display.

Besides, there were worse things in this world than anything I could do here. Not as we tried to return to some semblance of civilization. Prescott wouldn't be happy if this one move dismantled everything he'd worked hard for. This place of retreat we had all worked to establish.

Riley had returned and gave a slight nod as a signal that things were now in place. I had walked into The Pit with two options in mind. Depending on his words, I would take my pick at his consequence. I guess I was going with the latter.

"Riley, open the gates."

"Wha- what? No." His voice cracked.

"I've revoked your citizenship at the Monterey Compound, effective immediately. You may not say goodbye to your friends or your family. You may not return home to collect any of your belongings. An air elemental and an armed guard will escort you somewhere outside the borders. You will not be told which direction you are being moved and you will be provided a compass to find your next home. I hope you didn't miss dinner amid this chaos, as you will also travel with no food."

The crowd that had been silenced previously murmured once more. This was as merciful as I could be without appearing weak. When you're a woman, most mercies were taken as weakness. I rather found the ability to see past the BS and find the human inside to be a strength. People can surprise you if given another chance to prove themselves, and in this world, owing a life was everything. Strategic on both ends.

"Consider this a mercy, Caleb. May luck be on your side." Turning on my heels, I grabbed Harley and cut towards the part of the crowd where Reina and Tomoe stood, walking in between them as they followed on my heels.

I kept walking towards my office and lounged out on the couch. I was exhausted, and I needed just a second. Once the strength came back to me to open my eyes, I was greeted by Reina's face, blood red from anger. Tomoe stood at her side, staring at me blankly. Assessing what her next words to me would be, I could practically see the wheels turning in her head.

"Okay, let me have it."

"That was stupid," Moe said curtly, dead faced.

"Amaia"—Reina's face softened as she moved to sit next to me on the couch and bring my legs into her lap—"we're just concerned, that's all. This isn't the time to talk about it all, I know. But we just want to make sure you're okay? What you just did out there, I know it was hard for you. I know that's not what you wanted to do. You handled yourself well."

"Yeah, well, when's the last time anyone around here has cared what I want to do?"

Reina flinched. "Prescott would be proud." She pushed, deciding it was worth the effort.

"This isn't the time to coddle Reina. She won't even remember this in the morning. Her tears reek of tequila, so much so that I wouldn't doubt I missed the second stash hidden around here somewhere while I rushed to take the first. Her boyfriend is half dead laying in your bed by some recruit she didn't even sign off on, and she just sent him back out there to do it again. Probably to the next settlement he ends up at. We can't say for certain he was telling the entire truth out there. All you felt was his fear. You can't tell the difference if it was fear from her or fear of being found out as a liar."

It stung to hear. I knew they were both right, both had valid points. Reina was like the angel on my shoulder, while Tomoe always gave me the harsh truth I needed to hear. One to make me a better person, the other to keep me honest.

Still, I wasn't yet ready to have this conversation, and their incessant pushing had given me a headache. I stood, pushing myself out of Reina's lap, and gave Harley a good rub behind the ears as she sat at my feet.

Looking them both in the eye, I let my frustration flow.

"The closest settlement is two days away. He has no food, no water, no weapons. Just the clothes on his back and a compass. He can't fight, which is why he didn't pass my test. He possesses one element, fire. It can only get him so far. Let's see if he passes the test of life without the crew he showed up here with. He's The Pansies problem now. You really think Niklas would take him up in San Jose?" I chuckled at the genuine concern on both my friends' faces. Surely, they must think I've cracked.

"Besides, Riley's already sent out two scouts to ensure he doesn't find his way back here again. And his compass is a piece of junk from Prescott's tinkering collection that he hasn't worked on in months. Who even knows if it will work, survival of the fittest, right? Well let's see how well the unfit survive." I tilted my head and gave my friends a quick squeeze of their hands, and strode off towards Jax.

Deep down, I honestly wasn't sure if I hoped he'd make it or not. He clearly had no other information. Was a pawn in somebody else's game. He did what he needed to protect the ones he loved. But it didn't excuse him from the consequences of his actions.

And now, I had to focus on finding the traitor who I suspected lay at our feet.

CHAPTER
FIVE

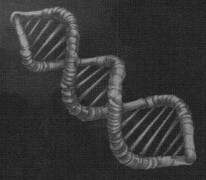

REINA

I released a breath I hadn't even realized I was holding and shifted on the couch to face Moe as she took a seat at the edge of Amaia and Jax's bed. "How are you feeling?" I asked.

Amaia had been worked up, though she tried to hide it. Which, to my dismay, meant that she'd forgotten that Jax had been a brother to Moe. I needed to check in and make sure at least one of my friends would be okay while the other entered self-destruct mode.

Before she could answer, a knock came from the door. "I'll get it," she said quietly, always quick to avoid emotions.

She glided across the room and turned the metal lock. Seth slid through the heavy wooden door and pulled Moe into a tight embrace. They exchanged no words, but for the first time in hours,

I saw my friend's posture relax. Though they never admitted to it or acted on it to anyone's knowledge, their chemistry was undeniable. The Ice King and Queen. Although my brother pushed me away years ago when we arrived at camp, I could tell they both brought each other a sense of peace and warmth.

My brother faced me and glanced away as I met his eye. "Are you okay?" I inquired, considering the fight he started moments before. If it could even be called that.

"Just fantastic, little sister. Though I appreciate the concern, some of us are distressed over more pressing matters than how people are feeling or whatever the latest apocalypse trend is." He gestured towards my pleated work pants that were rolled at the ankle stylishly. They showed off the closest thing I'd put on to combat boots, Doc Martens, and a lacy tank top.

He'd never appreciated the transition I'd made from farm girl clothes to apocalypse-chic. A middle-class suburb with couture clothing that still had the tags on surrounded us. I worked in a lab most days. What was the point of living through an apocalypse if I couldn't enjoy the smaller thing's life never offered me before?

He continued, "Like an almost slain friend laying not even a full block away. Has anyone even been to talk to him? Asked him what he saw? Will he live?" He scanned over my body, eyes as icy and full of storms as ever.

We had never sat down to discuss what had changed between us since we got here. I was too nervous to hear the truth. I had always suspected settling here and seeing ourselves prosper while our family never made it out of Montana drove him insane. Though I would never have the spirit to say those words aloud. It would open Pandora's box.

We were never super close during The Before. I'd spent my childhood admiring him, seeking out his attention, but it had never been well received. He'd always been closer to our oldest brother James and his twin Hunter, and while him and James could pass for twins, Hunter and him were fraternal. Which left a lot of room for Hunter and I to favor each other as our dark features made us family outliers aside from our deep blue eyes. I understood, but it still hurt every time I was on the receiving end of his harsh gaze.

For a while on the road, I thought there was hope for us in this new and scary world. He'd taught me to fend for myself. We spent days at a time riding our horses, once pets turned transportation and weapon, searching for a safe place to go. He'd saved my life more than once, and I his. He'd reminded me of funny childhood stories while we crossed through Yellowstone. Distracting me from the human-like but not quite screams that rang out around us at night, always gave me the extra bite of food or the last drop of water before I'd learned to control my gifts. Then we arrived here and things changed.

"I'm concerned too, Seth. We all are. But there isn't anything we can do but wait. He hasn't woken up yet, so no one's been able to question him and he was in too much pain to ask anything before. When I took the pain away, he passed out. His vitals are stable for now, but his body is trying to heal. Moe got what she could from a vision, but as you know, memories are only told from one perspective."

I forced my brother to face me, eyes wide and chest forward, begging him to see me as his little sister from the farm.

Moe cleared her throat. When the tension imploded between Seth and I, she typically tried her best to stay out of it. Occasionally, like now, she'd step in as a distraction to save me from the discomfort of the situation. "I think Amaia just went to check on him. We should give them some privacy in case he's awake. Come on, let's clean off and see what's left to grab for dinner. I heard they scored big on the fish this morning. If we're lucky, they'll be some stew left."

I forced my mind to focus on the excitement of fish stew. Since the bombs went off, our oceans had suffered. With less light coming through, marine algae had died off from the drop in oceanic temperature. It wasn't as devastating as scientists had predicted, but the effects on marine life were bad enough that a good batch of fish was a luxury.

Moe walked me back through the Scholar Building to her quarters, opting to wear something of hers in order to let Jax and Maia have their space. We passed through a long well-lit hallway and by the Public Library. A place of gathering for those who enjoyed reading and the monthly historian accounts to gather news from the other compounds around the territory, and entered Moe's private study. As the most powerful Scholar in the territory, her abundance of knowledge graced her with working right under the Head Scholar. Working under him purely because of her disgust with having authority and being responsible for others, she enjoyed having freedom over her research and time. *There are other qualifications besides power that make a great leader* is how she weaseled her way out of that one.

As soon as the door opened, I was greeted by the earthy aroma , and a hint of dust and Oolong tea in the air. Her desk in the corner next to one of the reinforced windows was covered in piles of books as usual. The shelves had books turned every which way, caked in dust with the only proof they had been used recently being a break in the soft white, leaving drag marks towards the edge. The leather couch had been angled as if she recently needed a boost to reach the top shelf, and a half-filled teacup sat on the edge of the arm.

"You know, I'm a sucker for an organizing Sunday, Moe," I offered for the millionth time, and she ignored me for the millionth time.

She kicked open her sleeping quarters, handing me a pair of ripped black jeans and a black hoodie with a grin on her face. "Oh, Moe, ever the most fashionable."

42

Encouraging the friendly banter, she fluttered her lashes and put on her best impression of my booming voice. "Only the best for the best of friends, Reina."

Maybe Seth and Maia's chaos had rubbed off on us, but after the intensity of the day we released our tension in laughter. Sighing, I fell onto her bed, sprawled out imitating a snow angel.

"I need you to do something for me, Moe."

Her head tilted slightly to the left, accentuating the sharp angles of her cheeks. "You want me to ask Seth what he saw, don't you?"

I nodded, rolling onto my stomach, and threw my head onto the stiff mattress. "Ow, this thing is like a brick, Moe. But yes, I don't know why he hates me, but he does. I'm just concerned what happened today may bring back what happened to Hunter."

She pursed her lips together and moved them side to side, considering the repercussions this could have. Even she couldn't predict Seth's temper.

"I'm sorry, I can't exactly go to Mattress Firm and ask them for their most expensive Tempurpedic." Moving to go sit near her antique vanity, she picked up her brush, moving the wet blue-black hair from her eyes. "And your brother doesn't hate you, Reina, he's more concerned about you than he lets on."

Her way of telling me she would ask.

Moe braided her hair back and out of her face, and I walked towards her bathroom. Studying myself in the mirror as I washed my face at the sink, I willed my water magic to keep it running from the aqueducts that ran in between the walls, thanks to the Tinkerers. The pale skin on my face was still red from the night chill, heavy raindrops, and the overall intensity of the day. The reflection in the mirror stared back pathetically sorrowful. If only I could pull the sadness from myself that my magic let me pull from others. I watched as I forced myself to pull the soft smile that typically rested on my face and tried to bring some light back into my eyes.

"Ready to go?" Moe said, coming up behind me.

"Ready if you are my bestest of friend."

CHAPTER
SIX

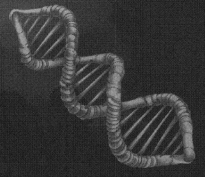

AMAIA

Clearing my head was a necessity before going to check on Jax. Call it escapism. I'd be no good going to him in my current state. When people needed healing, they also needed comfort, and I couldn't provide that with all the thoughts buzzing in my mind.

I needed a moment to think through everything that had happened today, so I went for a walk through The Compound. It covered around twelve miles, mostly lined in palace sized buildings that were intricately carved from stone thanks to the artsy earth magic residents. Those who developed earth magic typically worked in the community as builders, when they also doubled as Scholars, the *real* magic of their skills was astounding. You could tell who took up art as a hobby in The Before, as they took an extra amount of pride in their work. The mix of Gothic, Victorian and medieval complimenting each other in an ironic yet visually pleasing way.

Prescott's idea for this place was for us to develop some semblance of normalcy to keep civilization within grasp. *Good for the mind and the soul Amaia, we didn't get this far without it.* He reminded me that every chance he got, part of the way we bonded was through our love for history.

Prescott found me out on the road two months after it all happened. I was making my way down to LA from Seattle. There was chatter amongst travelers that the rumors of the government survivor camps set up around the city were true.

It only took a few weeks for the smoke to clear. And once the smoke cleared, people had assumed it would be safe enough to leave wherever they were bunkered down and take their chances on the road. Hoping for a better chance at life elsewhere.

At first it was cold, felt like a winter day up north when it was August in the Pacific Northwest. The hole in the ozone layer and the UV rays it allowed to seep through were part of the running theory of what happened to humanity in the aftermath. A large part of the Tinkerer community felt that it wasn't radiation alone that changed our DNA at the base.

After weeks on the road alone, I had learned to fend for myself. Tried to remember everything my dad had taught me. I always thought he was dramatic. His military experience always had our family prepared, no matter the situation.

Go bag by the door, non-perishables in the cabinets. You dress practically not cute, keep the colors neutral and your bag light. Necessities only; enough food to last you a minimum of three days, food to last your dog a week, water purifying tablets, a canteen, *and* a LifeStraw. First aid kit that satisfies basic injuries plus some of the more critical. Heat reflecting poncho that also keeps you dry, emergency blankets, sleeping bags, and a basic tent to provide just enough shelter. Batteries, flashlights and a weather radio. The entire pack weighed maybe twenty pounds at its fullest, definitely light enough to maneuver when needed and not gas you out.

Always pack two of everything in case one gets damaged or you travel with someone who may need it. A basic tool-kit, a compass and a map of your general area. And, of course, hiking boots and thermal socks.

I followed every rule but the 'practical, not cute' similar to Reina I felt you could be both. Of course, there was a line to be drawn when cute became dangerous, but crop tops are cute, especially under an all-cargo outfit. Plus, it gets hot when you're constantly moving.

Prescott found me fighting off three Pansies right outside of Salem, Oregon. Half drunk, of course, without a care in the world. In my defense, I'd finally entered the grieving stage of losing my fiancé Xavier, my parents, and my best friend Sammy. Turns out until death do us part started before the vows and not after. He had possessed the Pansie gene. I did not.

When everything happened, we'd been sitting on the couch on a Friday night eating terrible sushi and scrolling through Pinterest for wedding ideas. Our phones went off just as I'd made my argument to chance the rain and do something outdoors. The Russian government had launched an R12 from a nuclear submarine at New York. Before we even had a chance to peer up from our phones, Atlanta and Chicago were hit. Los Angeles. Then San Francisco fell, and finally DC.

The U.K. was gone before they even notified us of our own attacks in the US. Denmark and Berlin were next. Russia had taken its chances and was tired of the war in Ukraine. What was supposed to be a quick invasion had turned into two years of embarrassment. And it wasn't on the Ukrainian end.

Once one button is pressed, everyone else pressed their own. The one thing scientists got right was the radioactive fallout. It changed us. Scientists had theorized radioactive particles could stay in the air anywhere from seconds to a few months. No one really knew how long it stuck around, but if I had to make a guess, I'd say months. There were people who didn't go Pansie until about eight months in, were just walking around, normal.

Around month four people suspected who would turn by who didn't develop any magic. Elementals showed signs of power almost immediately, often triggered by intense emotions. And considering all the death and Pansies going around, emotions charged the air.

Around six months, people formed large community-based groups. Hunters and gatherers, if you will. *Nothing new under the sun,* Prescott would say, *just different players.* A year in, larger groups settled, forming trade networks in their immediate areas. Small trade routes collided nearly two years after The Before and thus, the four territories were clearly defined.

When people gathered in groups, naturally innovation followed. Those with skill-based magic dominated, and when people started talking, similarities shone through. Scholars that had visions could solidify, no it was not, in fact, mental illness forming from intense trauma.

The *Umbra Mortis* individuals soon realized that it wasn't simply just good luck on our side, and the Supra could sleep peacefully knowing the radioactive air wasn't only changing them, but others too.

Perhaps that's why civilization could be formed so soon after it all fell apart. We had a clear advantage of rapid adaptive evolution.

For Xavier, he only lasted minutes. Pretty much every settlement within our network had a few Tinkerers trying to figure out how the mutations turned to magic, and why some people turned Pansie faster than others. To our knowledge, today's leading Tinkerers had discovered no farther than a difference in DNA.

Some people possessed genetic mutations like the Aqua gene, others had the Ignis, Terra, Aer, Umbra, Scholar, Physicus, Supra, and, of course, Mortuus Est. No sign of the why, and certainly no reason for the delay in some and lack of delay in others.

Xavier's deep brown skin turned ashen, and he dry heaved, gasping for air. He stumbled into the bathroom and brought every piece of tonight's sushi back up to the surface. After hanging over the toilet for what felt to be half an hour, he came back out, a more grayish color, his eyes bloodshot.

"Amaia, I love you," he said, and then he collapsed.

Harley went into a frenzy—barking, growling, and lunging at him as I pushed her back, hanging over his fallen body, trying to give CPR with my one free hand.

His fingers intertwined in my curly hair and pulled hard. A deep, inhuman growl left his throat as I tried to pull myself away.

"Hey General, another stormy night, I suppose. Read anything good lately?" Ms. Schuller, one of the older residents here, asked as she carted vegetables from The Gardens towards The Kitchens, startling me from my thoughts.

I blinked, realizing I was now in the center of The Compound. "No ma'am, but I'll keep you posted the next time I do."

Giving her a small smile, I continued on my way. Letting my legs do all the work, I surrendered myself back to my thoughts. Willing myself to remember those last moments with Xavier.

I lost that battle and allowed my mind to pick up where it wanted, where it felt safe.

I locked up the apartment, banging and screeching coming from inside, grabbed Harley, and ran. Sprinting towards my best friend's apartment down the street, I practically yanked her out the front door, and drove her car over to the grocery store. Tears ran down her terrified face. Her chestnut hair tangled as if she'd pulled against her roots amid a panic attack.

My dad had trained me for this, waters and essentials first, canned goods, nuts, jerky, anything worth any kind of protein gets grabbed. Grab what you can for first aid, but our go bags had always stayed stocked and ready. We grabbed every battery we could find and headed to the gas station. Took what we could and left what we couldn't, then hid at her place for a week.

Silently, I cursed Xavier, then cursed myself for cursing him so soon after what had just transpired. He wasn't comfortable with me having a weapon in the house, and I obliged him, opting to leave my Glock 43, Glock 19, and beautiful Ruger Precision at a storage facility.

I didn't grow up in a gun happy family by any means. In fact, both my parents advocated for better laws and regulations surrounding guns. My family was willing to give them up if it meant true change. But we were also a military family, and that meant we spent family days learning to protect ourselves and others until that change could be made. *Better to be over prepared and alive than under prepared and dead Amaia.* My dad's words of advice rang in my head loudly, as if he was there next to me.

So instead of getting rid of them, I stored them. Halfway across the city like a dumbass. I'd worry about that another time.

A week later, Sammy and I were reading in our respective corners, nearly sick of being locked up with no answers from any government officials and not seeing any sign of the military. And then, the universe played some sick joke. The cell towers popped back on for just a moment.

Text messages from her family came through, showing proof of life. The last texts I had were from my mom, telling me she loved me and my father had turned. It was from that very first day. None of the messages I tried to return went through. I frantically dialed her number over and over, and nothing happened. Not a ring, not even voicemail.

They'd recently sold everything and headed abroad, ready to live out their retirement dreams. Before it all happened, they'd been spamming my phone with pictures from Spain, Italy, and were supposed to be heading to Berlin. I shuffled through them briefly, while Sammy enthusiastically spoke to her mom on the phone. Planning. There was no happy ending for my family and I. I could only hope and pray we'd find one with hers.

I could tell Sammy was eager to hit the road and take her chances to reunite with her family. They were just over the border in Vancouver and if we kept our heads down; we had assumed we'd be fine.

She never made it out of the building.

We packed all that we could and exited her apartment, looking around one last time at the place that had handled many drunken nights out and hangovers the day after. Survived crappy boyfriends and provided a haven for tears and girls' nights in. It cost us.

Harley, who was still a puppy, let off a bark as ferocious as possible. By the time I turned around, Sammy was being dragged halfway down the hallway by two Pansies. The elderly couple who had lived across the hall. Her eyes were wide as she said nothing, her vocal cords caught by surprise.

When Prescott came across me, the only thing keeping me alive was the tequila in my stomach and the need to make sure the last living thing I was responsible for would survive.

Harley.

I'd sliced through those Pansies with glee after they tried to grab her tail and pull her back into their slimy, rotting mouths when we stopped for lunch. After the last one was down, I simply told Harley I loved her, gave her a pat and tossed her a canned anchovy, singing a song from my favorite historical Broadway production like a maniac. Prescott grabbed me from an alley as I skipped by, telling me to hush up before I blew his cover.

He was on the run from a group of psychopaths he'd run into right off an interstate. He'd joined them for the convenience and the fact that it was safer to travel in groups. Not to mention easier to acquire food when you could be sure someone had your six as you rummaged through abandoned houses and stores.

He figured he could suck up their antics for a few weeks, planning to tag along down to LA until they came across another group telling them it was up in flames overrun by Pansies. So he split, hoping he'd come across another group that had better intentions, possibly settle somewhere safe. Well, the psychos were exactly that, and didn't appreciate his haste departure.

We spent a few months on the road together before finding Jax in the Redwoods. Prescott telling me bedtime stories on everything the history books left out from his memory alone. He respected my passion for it and, as an ex-marine turned politician, he reveled in finding the truths in-between the lies of history himself.

I stumbled over a gap in the stone path and looked up. Should've known this is where my thoughts would lead me once I'd hit the center of town. I raised my arm and tapped three times on our leader's door.

It opened as if he was waiting on the other side. "Come here."

"Prescott, I can't do this anymore," I said, dropping my head and stepped inside.

CHAPTER

SEVEN

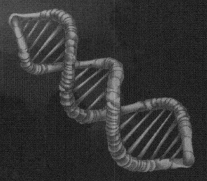

AMAIA

Prescott pulled me close and wrapped me in his solid arms. The comfort caused my tears to unleash over his tan tattooed skin. His essence smelled of cigars and homemade shaving cream. Saying nothing, he let me break for a few minutes before pulling me back by my shoulders and bringing me down to reality.

"You have an obligation to your people to continue, my sweet girl."

I blinked away my tears, heat rising in my face. Anger took over. "I don't want to. I don't want this responsibility. I don't want to have obligations. I didn't sign up for this, to send people out to their certain deaths. To be responsible for the lives of others. Making sure every time I send someone beyond these walls, I don't have to knock on their family's door and tell them their worst fears have come true. I didn't sign up to lose another life partner. I didn't ask for any of this."

My chest shook, and I opted to take a seat on the leather love-seat in the sitting area near the door.

"None of us asked for this, Amaia. The best leaders in history rarely ask for the responsibility that falls upon their shoulders, but that's what makes them great. You inspire people, you show them that there is a way to be powerful and have boundaries with regard to others. Your compassion and will to survive is the reason many of these people are even here."

He pulled my chin up as he hovered over me, searching my eyes for the right words to say. Prescott had no kids in The Before. I was the closest thing he'd ever had to a daughter, and probably ever would. Similar to any parent, it took him a few mistakes on gauging how to best comfort me and guide me through troubled times. He didn't always get it quite right, but I appreciated the effort.

"There are over thirty-thousand people here, and I am willing to bet you know the name of more than half of them. You walk through The Compound and speak to each like they're your closest friend, yet you demand respect and authority when the situation calls for it. There aren't many people in this world left with that kind of skill-set." He paused, thinking over his next words, striding over to the fireplace. "You're General because there isn't a person here who wouldn't trust you to make the right call in keeping them safe. I trust you with my life, as do many others. You may have fooled them all out there tonight, even yourself. But I know you let Caleb walk out these gates to give him another shot at life. You see good in everyone, even in the worst, and that my sweet girl, is why you have the responsibility that you do."

I rolled my eyes, blushing at the words that I knew deep down were true.

"What if Jax doesn't make it?"

"He will."

"But what if he doesn't? What if I lose him?" He handed me a ceramic mug and picked up the coffee kettle that hung over the fireplace behind me. Stopping to grab three cubes of brown sugar, he dropped them into my mug, and poured me a cup of my comfort drink.

"Then we'll get through it together. We had a vision for this place, all three of us. We'll continue on for him, with his piece of *our* vision in mind. Everything he wanted, we'll accomplish. But for now, we'll sip this coffee and he'll be pissed we had it without him."

I chuckled at that. Every evening the three of us sat in Prescott's study, sipping on coffee and whatever effort of dessert The Kitchens made. Using the time to recount the day we had before diving into the needs of The Compound. Jax, who was chronically late, always got pissed if we started without him.

There was coffee readily available in The Kitchens at breakfast and dinner for the overnight crew, but occasionally on patrol trips Jax or I would find some name brand coffee container, stashed away or tossed in rubble. We'd stock it in Prescott's study to enjoy for ourselves later on. It was no slight to the earth elementals who grew our coffee in The Gardens. Just sometimes it was nice to have a taste from The Before.

We had a council of citizens that also had a say in the happenings around here, but the three of us had started this place. It was our baby. Every decision we made was always fair, always taking the Council's votes into account, but our votes counted twice theirs. Mostly, we followed the majority, but there'd been a few instances where we had to step in for fear of the stability of The Compound. Even if it wasn't an option we wanted to follow through with ourselves.

Each Council member held their seat as respective to their powers, representing those who possessed similar gifts. But simply possessing magic didn't make them knowledgeable when it came to the safety of The Compound, and that's why *our* votes mattered the most. Our role was to put Compound first, our wants second.

Prescott sat at my side, a feeling of comfort washed over me as we sat in silence, allowing the minutes to pass us by until he left to meet with the Council on today's incident. My absence would be excused, for now.

BY THE TIME I LEFT, THE RAIN HAD STOPPED. SLOSHING THROUGH THE puddles, I made my way back to Reina's quarters, stopping only once to pick up a surprise from The Library.

I hadn't noticed the blood on the white hides she used as decor on the floor before. Reina was adamant that every part of the animals be used if we were going to raise livestock. I'd always assumed that's what her parents did back on the ranch.

Pulling the wooden chair from the table under the window and I brought it over to the light oak poster bed, Jax lay in, his breath still shallow.

"Hey, Jaxy," I blubbered, putting his large hand into mine as I sat down. His light brown eyes shuttered open slightly, and I swore a smile tried to pull across his thin pale pink lips on his heavily freckled face. The tips of his fingers tapped faintly against my own.

"I brought Lord of the Flies. Your favorite."

This time I was certain he smiled as he huffed a quipped laugh, followed by a groan at the pain it caused. "That's your favorite, you goon."

I shifted over, allowing him to face me, his now cleaned auburn hair fell towards his face. Reina must have ordered someone to clean him off a bit while we were at The Pit.

"I know, but now you can't run from it, or cover your ears." Smiling back at him, I cracked open the book.

It had always been a favorite, and Jax had always teased me for having an *old white man's taste in books*. I'd first read it my freshman year and was fascinated. Always felt it embodied humanity perfectly. Id, Ego, and Superego. It represented civilization and its fight against savagery, how certain conditions could result in the loss of innocence, even in society's purest population. Children. To me, it had always been a timeless read, one that would be relevant no matter the era humanity tumbled into.

Holding his hand, I read to him for hours and he listened. Watching me intently, studying my every feature. He'd always had a way of making me feel truly heard, I rambled for hours about anything and everything. Jax would hang on to every word, asking questions when appropriate, and staying silent as I processed my next thought.

"I love you, Amaia." I stopped reading.

Each syllable left his lips with emotionally charged intent. Trying to express everything he felt and wanted to say, plus more. We didn't say those words. I'd hated them after Xavier. Never wanted to hear them again. Jax had lost his fiancé in an accident months before bombs were dropped. This was something to which we'd always been on the same page.

Our union was more for the benefit of The Compound than it was for ourselves. A representation of strength and hope for the future. Neither he nor I protested it because we understood that in this new world, love and romantic soulmates were a luxury many couldn't afford to nourish.

We were life partners and occasional lovers, but more than anything, we were family. Soulmates in a way that romantic love couldn't touch. His inner fire only fueled my flames. He nourished my soul, and I his.

So even if those words meant to me what they meant to others, they weren't words that we'd throw around the way he was now. They represented nothing but death and loss to us. I *felt* love, sure. I would show it to everyone I cared for always, but I refused to say them because I refused to say goodbye.

"Stop Jax." I glared at him. "Whatever you're about to say, stop. I don't want to hear them because this isn't goodbye. Next week you'll be walking around on the mend, laughing over a cup of coffee and crappy pie with me and Prescott. Just like we did without you tonight."

"You prick, I knew it. Guess you could say I felt it in my gut." He smiled, as if he had a sudden burst of energy. Leave it to him to find a way to throw in a morbid joke, one I would typically build on, but not today. Not in his condition.

"Yup, I'm an asshole. Prescott's an asshole. Now channel that anger and get better because I need you. *We* need you."

Squeezing my hand once more, a tear fell from his eye and he moved his finger to tip the back of the book. "Finish reading your shitty book."

Sticking my tongue out in tease, I continued on as he fell into a deep sleep, reading until dawn, when I too fell asleep. Squeezed up into the bed next to him, I tried my best to be light as a feather, taking extra care to not hurt him with any of my movements.

I awoke to Tomoe's sniffles and Reina's soft voice. My eyes squinted open at the bright warm light coming through the floor to ceiling arched window. I shifted in the bed against something cold and froze. My friends went quiet in recognition that I was now awake.

"Amaia," Reina whispered.

"No. No. No," I mumbled. Turning over and shaking Jax's lifeless, hard body. His arms swayed with every shake that I gave, body heavy. Tears streamed down my face with no intention of slowing anytime soon.

"No, no, no no no! No!" I wailed. My fists started banging on his chest, as if the pound of my flesh against his would pump life into a body that was long past the point of return. Reina approached, attempting to pull me away.

My body flayed wildly in defense, falling out of the bed and shoving her off like a rabid mother bear whose cub was under threat. Harley must have found her way in as I slept, opting to always settle for the night near me. She crept low to the ground, neck hanging and tail tucked, growling at Reina in warning of separating her beloved owners.

I kissed all over his face, frozen forever in a peaceful smile. One he often gave me after reassuring me on my toughest of days. A way of letting me know in his last moments he hadn't suffered, but took comfort in the warmth my body had provided.

Wailing in a way I didn't know was possible, I fell to my knees, leaving myself completely vulnerable to what remained of the family I had found and valued more than anything this life had to offer. *Another loss*, another loss where I was completely useless and unable to prevent the worst from happening.

I should have been there; I should have sucked up my exhaustion and gone out with him and Seth. Usually I did. But I'd worked twenty days straight with no rest and Jax assured me I needed at least twenty-four hours to myself to be an effective leader without clouded judgment. *Always my voice of reason*, always recognizing my limits often before I did.

Tomoe and Reina approached me slowly, bringing me to my feet and guiding me towards my own quarters, my hands intertwined with theirs. The short walk back left me exposed to the onslaught of stares and gaped mouths.

Let them look. Let them talk and news spread. I didn't want to be the one to announce it myself. My role required it. Made me make others aware of those who have passed on to the other side when they were amongst my ranks or a casualty of the world outside these walls. Not today. Today I would let my emotions convey what my words could not.

Compound first, except this one time.

In the haze of my thoughts, I hadn't realized Tomoe had stripped me from my shoes and clothes while Reina had drawn water for the wooden tub. The stone walls chilled the air of my bathing room. I let the water burn my skin as I dropped in, staring straight ahead.

Submerging myself under the scalding water, I let my lungs burn, forcing myself to stay under for as long as I could hold. The shadows of my friends faded away, leaving me for some privacy. I was willing to bet they hadn't gone farther than my room, worried about what I would do next.

Using my fire magic, I willed the fireplace in the middle of the center wall to light, further heating the water and the room. I wanted to feel every bit of the heat, to distract myself from the pain of everything else.

An hour later, I emerged from the bath and walked out of the bathing room into my sleeping quarters, allowing the water to drip off my naked body. I didn't care about drying off, nor did I care about covering up for the sake of others. I just wanted to be in my bed, needing to be comforted in the smell of Jax on his side of the thick, red oak poster bed.

My friends parted, letting me pass through, immediately soaking the light blue cotton sheets. They positioned themselves on either side of me, Reina pulling Jax's favorite hoodie over my head, pulling my arms into it. Then pulling the sheets up to cover the rest of my body. I allowed them to embrace me as my heart fell into two.

Morning faded into the afternoon, and soon the bright sky turned to black through the window. Reina and Tomoe left to attend Council meetings and make arrangements for Jax around midday. They returned around dinner time, trying to get me to eat as they pretended to sip the vegetable soup in their own bowls, offering me their corn bread as a lackluster way to cheer me up in whatever way they could.

They attempted making small conversation, filling me in on the details of the day. Jax's funeral would be Wednesday, as was the tradition in The Compound. It signified the end of a rough start of a week and the start of a more promising beginning. Jax had ironically been the one to start the concept of it. When it felt like the weight of the world was crashing in on me, he'd always tell me to give myself until Wednesday to pout, and then put on a new face and attack the resolution of my problems.

A promise that after Wednesday, things could only get better. Seventy-two hours to wail, cry, scream, laugh, get it all out. Something in me told me that wouldn't work, not this time.

I laid in bed for days without sleeping. Every time I closed my eyes, Jax's cold, lifeless body stared back at me. A body without a soul attached, empty.

Hot. The days had become scorching. After the initial cooling period and all the smoke had cleared, the hole in the ozone only allowed Earth to warm faster than anyone could anticipate. The days were blistering hot and the nights cold. Weather was a funny thing now, doing as it pleased and dancing in The Before scientists' faces.

Wednesday came around, and Moe was the first to enter my quarters. Dressed in a long black dress with bulky straps, a slit going up to her mid-thigh, and chunky black heels to complement her slender tawny legs.

"Hi," she whispered.

"Hi," I said back, shifting upright in the bed. "How are you?"

"I should ask you the same thing," she huffed in a breathy voice laced with laughter.

Knot in my chest, I looked at my dear friend, here to comfort me in her own way.

"I brought you something." Her face turned sinister, "Promise not to tell Reina. She'll have my head with Wrath itself."

My eyebrows lifted, deciding to engage in whatever she had to offer.

"She'd have to be fast enough to get Wrath from your grasp first," I teased, not missing the katana strapped to her back for a second. She went nowhere without it, and it'd take her dead body for anyone besides her to get their hands on it.

Satisfied with my response, she motioned for me to scoot over in the bed as she shifted the katana to hang from her side, pulling out a small bottle of sake.

"You little demon on my shoulder." I grinned at my friend as I took a long swig. Once it was down, my suspicions took over, noticing the way my forthcoming friend opted to not meet my eye.

"Spit it out, Moe. Just get it over with." Sighing, I laid back all the way. Savoring the taste of the sake on my tongue, Tomoe always made hers with a hint of honey for flavor.

"You need to appoint a second today. It's time."

"Let Prescott handle it. I trust his judgment. I'm not ready—"

"No one's saying you need to get back to work. Take your time to heal. I promise we all want a mentally coherent General. But you need to appoint someone. *Today*. At the funeral. A show of strength and Compound first. If not from you, then who Amaia? Riley and Seth have been handling what they can, but their power only goes so far. The explosion led a herd this way, and they handled it well enough, but without the authority to send more companies out, they're forced to redirect what was already out patrolling. That leaves our borders exposed, Amaia." She took a breath, more words than I'd been accustomed to my friend saying at once. "I'm here for you, and I love you, but we need you today. Pull it together, just for a few hours."

I observed my friend, hurt in her eyes. Not just from Jax's passing, but from the strength she's had to put on for me the last few days, without my concern for her own emotions. I was a shit friend, but right now I didn't have the capacity to think of that. I would sift through that later. It was more than not being ready to return to my position. My thoughts had been all over the place in the days that passed, chewing over every detail Moe had offered up. I felt … unstable. And now I needed to put my people first.

"The Compound must survive at all costs. Compound first," I said, chugging the rest of her bottle.

That didn't mean anyone would be happy with my decision.

I FORCED MYSELF TO GET OUT OF THE BED, OPTING TO SLIDE OUT ON the side that didn't require me to climb over the accountability partner, helicopter parenting to my left.

My bathing room was left untouched from the last time I had used it days before. My clothes and boots that had been stripped from me were still tossed on the floor. Rolling my eyes, I scooped them up and put them in the hamper that was nearby. Leave it to Tomoe to be visually blind to anything representing some semblance of organization.

Man, I truly stunk, *gross*. I yanked off Jax's hoodie and snatched the scrunchie that was currently containing my black curls. Not caring to be careful enough to not pull any strands that had inevitably wrapped around due to lack of maintenance.

A single thought in the back of my mind sent a signal to the fireplace, the dim light casting shadows across the circular room. While the rest of my window ridden room allowed heat to enter naturally, the all-stone bathing room was nothing but cool air.

Stepping into the wooden tub, I pulled the lever and released the water from the aqueducts above. The cool water cascaded down my skin and I sent out small waves of my fire to warm the settled water to my desire.

Scrubbing my skin raw with the loofah grown in The Gardens and homemade soap, I ducked myself under to let the soapy water cleanse my hair as much as possible. Lack of motivation preventing me from cleaning it properly.

When I finished in the tub, I walked over to the wooden armoire at the edge of the room. Pulling out Jax's favorite black dress of mine. We had just started the official establishment of The Compound and were out goofing off in the surrounding suburbs that had taken us months to completely clear. Everyone that was the new 'normal' was invited to reside within our walls. Pansies were cleared house by house.

We had gone for one of our walks that usually ended up with us taking things from those who were long gone. In an apocalypse, what was once theirs is now everyone's. Everything is fair game when it was evident a space was uninhabited for an extended period.

Most of our walks at that point had been spent wandering through abandoned or deserted homes, making up stories about the people who populated all the photos. Our initial sweeps were to check for persons or Pansies, the second and anything after were for supplies.

We had entered this massive home. More bedrooms that they had space for and found one very lucky woman's closet. It was less of a closet and more like an entire wardrobe room. Beautiful dresses hung from the wall of stacked racks and Levi's folded over hangers, tags still on them. Athleisure galore. My own personal heaven. It appeared me and the homeowner had similar taste. My lucky day. While I shot over to her lovely shoe collection that had every color of Doc Martens and Vans one could think of, Jax had pulled this dress.

Told me that the second the first restaurant of the apocalypse popped up, we'd be there opening night, and I would be wearing this.

"The prettiest girl in the next world," he'd said, taunting me, daring me to give him a sassy retort back.

I obliged, "It'll go perfectly with your lumberjack attire. What a couple."

Things had slowly turned flirtatious between us once we were settled and felt safe. Emotions that we hadn't felt in well over a year had started to pour into our friendship, catching us both by surprise. We hadn't discussed it, just silently agreed to let things naturally flow and see where they ended up.

I pulled the black cami slip dress over my head. It hit mid-thigh, falling less than an inch longer than the black spandex I wore underneath. My drop leg holster was next as I grabbed my Glock 43 from my weapon shelf in the armoire. Once it was holstered, I walked over to the mirror, examining the dark circles that now framed my prominent, deep brown eyes. My brown skin appeared ashen. *Nothing you can do about that now.*

Flipping my head over, I grabbed my thick hair and tossed it into a messy bun. *Who cares what you look like? Jax is gone. Gone. Gone. Gone.* I caught the tear that burned my left cheek before it could fall to the ground.

Sniffling, I reached down for my platform black Doc Martens and slid them on, tucking my throwing knife into the sock near my ankle. As dressed up as I cared to be. I took a deep breath and opened the door, finding both of my friends now waiting on my bed, Seth and Riley at the door.

Refusing to meet the eyes of those who remained to be taken from me, I entered the room under their watchful gaze.

"Thank you," I said, and pushed out the room, each of them falling into line. Riley a step behind to my left, Seth taking suit to my right. Tomoe and Reina at my six.

The heat from the afternoon sun was blistering. The Pit was empty as everyone had already headed towards The Arena in The Entertainment Square of The Compound.

We kept pace through the streets and arrived half an hour later to a buzzing arena. I knew this untimely death had caused a sense of uncertainty and there were bound to be rumors now about a potential coup at play. While I hadn't yet prepared my speech, a sudden realization hit me as Tomoe's words echoed through my head. I needed to provide my people with the feeling of safety and peace, and to do that, I needed to lead by example. And since I wasn't in the current headspace to do so, I it was time to appoint someone to take charge until I was ready. Someone who instilled enough fear to keep things in order. Someone who was capable of preventing any escalation of a possible coup d'état.

I took Riley's hand and squeezed it. Understanding filled his eyes, and he gave me a small smile.

CHAPTER
EIGHT

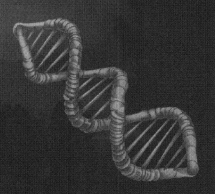

AMAIA

The Arena was a massive Roman inspired building; the inside was filled with large columns and archways that coined elaborate designs engraved into them and the ceiling above. Beautiful paintings complimenting the shimmering limestone and flooring.

Once we hit the bottom stage before the long steps leading to the center stage, I stopped. Riley and Seth lined up shoulder to shoulder with me. Unity. Tomoe and Reina took their seats at the front. A soldier brought Harley out and placed her on the side of Reina, dropping her leash with a clank on the hard floors.

I took my time looking around, not caring that I was leaving a now hushed crowd waiting. The large room was framed in towering archways that allowed both sun and candlelight to highlight the pinkish tone of the limestone.

The earth elementals had taken their time in this building, allowing their magic and creativity to guide the way. Civilization needed the arts to ground themselves in humanity. Theater and music paralleled the need for bars. Always needed to allow people to find a way to shed pent-up emotions, cry and laugh in the same space as their peers, and bond through the shared experience.

Every inch of The Arena was thoughtfully made to complement each elaborate detail. The pinkish marble and burgundy pattern on the floor was polished so perfectly that I could see my blurry reflection off the rebound of the gaslights that light up the columns under the archways. They were encased in vintage inspired bronze fixtures, the welder opting to remind himself of the architecture in his hometown fifty miles east.

Chairs had been laid out in wedding fashion. Curving around to fit the bottom stage, though we were here to celebrate the end of a life, and not the beginning of a new chapter. I turned my back to the crowd and ascended the long staircase, leaving Seth and Riley behind.

One. Two. Three. Four. I counted my way up all thirty-eight steps and took another deep breath before facing the crowd again.

My soldiers rose, standing to face me at attention. Their moving bodies left an echo through The Arena. I glanced up, taking comfort in the well-crafted designs that were engraved across the ceiling.

"At ease."

They dropped their arms and took their seats once more.

My eyes wandered around the room, finally landing on Prescott who sat with the rest of the Council to the left of the stage. He gave me a reassuring nod, eyes encouraging me to go on.

"Lieutenant Brennan represented the best qualities of us all. He showed kindness on his worst days and showered all with love and patience at his best. His ability to understand each of us when we could not understand our own desires made him not only a great lieutenant and natural leader, but also a great friend. A great partner."

Taking a moment to collect myself, I cleared my throat. A ball seemingly caught in the middle of it, making each swallow hurt more than the one before.

"He challenged us to be better every day. Showed us there is no glory in battle and war, only immense pride in a place to call home and a fierce desire to protect those that we love. But what happens when we lose the one who showed us that going off the deep end isn't always a path to darkness but rather a chance to ground oneself and find the light in a new beginning? A place to grow rather than drown."

Wide eyes, some filled with tears, met mine as I took a chance to glance around the room once more.

"Every one of you here before me today is proof that Jax's vision of this place is possible. That new beginnings and faith in every soul, no matter their past, are worth having a place to go. A place to grow into someone new. Someone who makes their own mark on the world. He saw something in each one of you and granted you a second chance. That is something that-" I stuttered, deciding to change course. "I'll be honest with you. There isn't another Jax. He is irreplaceable. There will never be another."

Gasps crept from a few and shushes flew from those next to them, hanging on to the edge of every last word.

"And that's okay. Because he would never want that to happen to begin with. There can't be another Lieutenant Brennan, but there can be the promise that the future will be bright and his legacy will be upheld, even in a new light. I have full faith that Seth Moore will fulfill the role of my second with the fire and intensity needed to help us recover from such a loss as a family. One unit, one compound. Lieutenant Brennan would be honored to be succeeded by a man he called a brother."

Seth's shoulders pulled back slightly, and his head angled high as the soldiers muttered, *One unit, one compound*, back at me. He appeared proud, even on a day as sad as this one. His temper could cause us trouble. I was taking a chance on him with this one, but I knew it was the good faith and toss of opportunity for a friend I had known to be as solid as could come, that Jax would expect me to take. To always give someone a chance to show who they really are, what they are capable of once given a chance.

Riley's face showed no indication that he'd heard the news that now shook the room, but I know he did. He understood where I needed him the most, without me having to communicate it to him. We would have our chance to discuss things later, but for now, he would not embarrass me by looking taken aback. No, he would show his general nothing but respect.

I could feel the intensity of Reina's glare, now solely focused on me. Her sense of betrayal and confusion seeped up all thirty-eight steps as if she was pushing them out with her magic, though I knew she wasn't.

"Riley Sullivan will continue on with his current duties and responsibilities for controlling the gates and the safety of the community. He'll also be working closely with Lieutenant Moore and I on selective missions. He will begin putting together a trusted team this week. I expect you all to be operating at standards Lieutenant Brennan would find nothing but exceptional. The safety of The Compound depends on it. I want you all to hear me loud and clear when I say I will allow no further threat to our safety. I promise you, even if it means I have to take out each potential threat with my bare hands."

Which themselves, if nothing else, were weapons. They all knew that. My hand-to-hand combat skills alone were enough to have me qualify as General if Prescott wasn't intent on having a general that checked *every* box, and not just the physical ones. But this promise was aimed at whoever the traitor out there, probably in this very crowd, was. A promise that although I could use anything in this world to take them out, I would rather use my hands to feel the life escaping them, for the life they allowed to escape from my partner.

With that threat hanging in the air, four soldiers entered the room carrying Jax's casket. Blacker than death itself, with a red cursive J painted down the center and a golden snake to intercept in the middle. Per his request, I made a mental note to thank Reina for being delicately precise with the arrangements. Despite how angry she may be with me at the moment, she was a phenomenal friend. One I was lucky enough to also call a sister. I would make sure I lost no one else. Her safety and the others meant everything to me. Even if I had to risk others in The Compound to secure it.

If that made me a crappy General I didn't care. Everyone had a weakness, and losing another family member was mine.

They placed his casket in front of Seth and Riley, a slight thud ringing out as it hit the ground. Now was the time for me to say my goodbyes in front of everyone.

As I descended the stairs that felt like I had ascended not too long before, I focused on keeping my knees steady and eyes ahead. Willing myself not to tumble down and appear confident with each step.

A white butterfly appeared from nowhere, landing on the top. A gift from Riley, a silent offer of comfort in a time where he knew innately that I needed strength.

Dropping to my knees, I allowed a moment of vulnerability to show from leadership, letting all the titles and optics fade into the background as I said my final goodbyes to my friend. My life partner.

"Jaxy, you will always be the flame that fuels my soul. There won't be a day that I walk this ugly fucked up Earth that I won't live out your dreams and visions in your honor. I promise to take you with me with every step that I take, every decision that I make. I will channel your heart. Every beautiful thing I see, I will think of how to describe it to you in the next life, because I will find you there. I promise to. I promise you that as long as I breathe, I will be fine. You don't have to worry about me anymore. I live for you, so you can live through me."

Harley let out a long, mournful howl. Sniffles and coughs circled The Arena.

Standing up, I glanced around the room one final time, making eye contact with as many of our citizens as possible. Flicking my fingers, I surrounded his coffin with silver flames. Flames of eternity.

They would burn for the rest of the night, and in the morning, he would be entered to the cemetery that lay just outside the walls.

As I exited The Arena, my new second and my trusted friend fell back in my wings, my sisters close behind. I didn't need Reina's powers to feel the anger and surprise coming from two of the four.

"Happy now? I've done what's been asked."

Riley sucked in a breath. "Oh boy," he said quietly enough for only Seth and I to hear.

Reina chuckled, face red, eyes bulging. She was doing what she did best, trying to keep the majority of her emotions contained, always keeping up the optics.

"What's the matter, sister? Can't you be happy for your brother?" Seth taunted.

Harley pranced over to my side as Reina dropped her leash in order to close in on her brother. Things had always been rocky between the two and the situation must have deteriorated even more in the days that followed, as it wasn't often Reina stepped in to challenge anyone, let alone her own brother.

"I'm sorry. I don't want to have your temper get good men killed, or even us behind these very walls. Did you think about that, Amaia? Or how about how he won't talk to anyone about the accident? Not even Moe. Imagine that, a lieutenant that is too shaken up to give a solid report back to their general."

Seth's sea storm eyes shot over to Tomoe, whose eyes had darted to Reina full of fury over some unspoken secret between the two. *Whatever that's about.* The crowd poured out of The Arena, now taking in the scene that was unfolding before them.

"Perhaps we should do this in a more private setting, General?" Riley said through his teeth, filling his face in the fakest of smiles in a tone only he could take with me.

"Perhaps you all could fuck off," I stated with an even faker grin, turning on my heels and walking towards my office on the other side of The Compound. Without a doubt they'd all be quick on my heels, following to resume the debate I wasn't in the mood to have.

CHAPTER
NINE

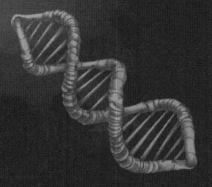

RILEY

The walk back to Amaia's quarters was quiet, which was great for me. I preferred things this way. Typically, Tomoe would have been savoring it with me, but not today. One glance back at her and I could pretty much read the words that were on the tip of her tongue.

Reina was pissed too, more than I'd ever seen herself allow to show before. She was pretty much all smiles, and though we didn't interact much on our own; I knew everyone had their limit.

Something was exceptionally weird between the Moore kids. Everyone here tried not to acknowledge the rift they felt between the two. Mostly for the sake of not having to be in the uncomfortable position of being near them interacting, but it had always intrigued me. I'd been there that very first day; I'd seen how things had changed the second she hopped off her horse.

No one knew the true reason for their distaste for each other and I guess that was their business, and theirs alone. But here in The Compound, what's private business *is* my business. Not a peeping Tom, but in the post 9/11 George Bush Patriot Act sort of way. My insects never had anything to report from the rare moments they shared in private, either.

Probably didn't help that Seth and Reina are aware of my gifts, any fly, ant, or spider they automatically assumed belonged to me. *I freaking wish.* So far, I'd only been able to control a couple hundred at a time. And I didn't waste my time on pointless information. Not when there were 30,019 more important people to worry about, keep an eye on, 30,015 if you counted out Tomoe, Prescott, Amaia and myself. There was something odd about the two of them, secrets they kept for sure.

We all had secrets. But it was my job to make sure those secrets didn't get people killed.

Once the wooden doors to Amaia's office were thrust open, the peaceful silence was over. Amaia threw herself down onto her black tufted leather couch and glared up at the ceiling.

Tomoe and Reina hovered over her, Reina rambling off as if she'd prepared a list of reasons *not* to appoint Seth for this moment, while Tomoe offered quips of support. That was an odd thing to see, considering they were one tragedy away from ending up in each other's bed.

Seth leaned against the dark wooden desk, arms folded across his black shirt, with a smug grin on his face. *What a dickhead.*

I stood back leaned up against the door, always sure to place myself between Amaia and the point of entry to any room. I would give my life for her. She'd already saved mine years before. The Compound had only been around for a few months, in the early stages and about a thousand citizens.

She'd found me hunkered down in a cave near the cliff side, surrounded by insects, to her true horror. I grinned to myself, reflecting on the fact that as much as my tiny friends helped her out, she would never stop gagging if a few made an appearance in her presence.

After my sister passed a few months prior, I had deigned to spend the rest of the days I had left to myself. My survival at the mercy of any fish that I could catch at dawn, which wasn't much. Malnourished, I survived off what edible plants the ants I controlled could bring back to me. My weakened state was why, when I'd gone out to try to fish one early morning, Amaia was able to follow me back to my cave without me knowing. She spent hours right outside watching me from a distance, determining whether I was worth bringing in.

No, not determining my worth, determining whether my soul was good enough to bring back to a second chance at civilization. Right before the sun started to set for the day, she announced her presence. Told me there was a camp not too far off from here. If I wanted to, I could come back and join them, but she needed to make some arrangements first and she'd be back. She took off before I could even give her my answer.

Little did I know it was a test, the first of many. One based on trustworthiness. To see if I would follow her back to The Compound, or worse, try to catch her off guard and take advantage of her. The After was no place for women to travel alone, but I knew from the moment I saw her I could trust her. So I waited for her to return.

In the morning I awoke to her and Jax standing over me, my bags packed and a container *for my little friends,* she had said, winking at me. Doing her best to welcome what mattered to me, what I had left, despite how odd it must have appeared at first glance.

She wasn't General yet. Just a soldier out enjoying the sun that many had been afraid would never return only months ago, searching for new recruits, for new soldiers to protect the home she had started to establish.

But she was smart. Even then, I could see the intelligence that ran deep in her through and through. She let me forge my own path at The Compound. Not once did she try to persuade or pressure me to fulfill a certain role. It was my own offer that got me to where I was now. Amaia hadn't been surprised when I brought it to her. Had long ago thought of it herself, but she wanted *me* to be the one to speak it into existence. Told me that how I lived here at The Compound would be my own destiny to fulfill. Back when hope filled her eyes. Not the way they were now, not as burdened and now lost.

I was a foster kid who fought tooth and nail for my sister's future after our parents passed, one that didn't exist anymore. Never did I think I'd have the opportunity to build my own. Not in The Before. If I wasn't already sure of it, I was now. Her sincerity not only in her words, but through her actions from the months prior sealed the fate to my future. From that moment on, my gifts and talents were at her disposal and hers only. I answered Amaia and no one else, not even Prescott. It was understood and never challenged.

I preferred things this way, a life in the shadows. Playing good soldier but always being something just a bit more. No one knew of my specialty aside from the people in this room and Prescott, and it would stay this way until Amaia said otherwise, though I know she'd never expose me without my say. As far as we knew, there weren't any others with the same ability. At least not in this territory, though I suspected somewhere out there in this big world of ours, there had to be another, maybe even a lot. There was good reason to keep my talents hush-hush.

Reina's loud voice snapped me back into focus on what was happening around me. Shame on me for letting my awareness slip with Amaia around.

The red undertone had seeped from her sepia skin, curls now coming loose with every shaking stroke she took through her hair, absentmindedly forgetting the scrunchie that reined each spiraling curl in.

I could see it in her face. She was drained and had nothing left to offer, not at this moment, at least. I wouldn't question her decision to make Seth lieutenant, not now and not ever. I trusted her with every fiber in my body and I owed her my life and the life I now lived for my sister, who couldn't.

Whatever her wishes were, I would follow them. Enforce them. Protect her in any way that I could, for my now fallen brother and for her.

The others argued with her for hours, patience growing thin and the desire to see their pain from a place of understanding drained away under her own immense grief. This was enough.

I cleared my throat, a bit scratchy from the time that had passed without use. "General, if I may."

"You may not, actually." Tomoe took a step towards me, one of the few women here that would step to me in challenge, even amongst the soldiers. We stared each other down, both unrelenting and unwilling to look away first. Neither willing to submit.

Only in this room would it be allowed. Out there beyond these doors, I outranked her. But I knew what she meant to Amaia, so I allowed what she allowed. And behind closed doors, we were a family. Ranking went out the window and all were encouraged to speak freely. She preferred it that way. A true leader who valued all voices and felt every opinion mattered, was worth speaking on.

"Oh, Jesus, Joseph and Mary, could you two *please* stop whatever weird eye challenge thing you're doing and focus on the facts? Seth literally lost his mind in front of *every* last one of your soldiers less than a week ago. That's not just showing insubordination, but could also be perceived as a show of power and strength that you yourself could not present," Reina said exasperatedly.

"Or a show of power and strength that only *strengthens* my claim for the position," Seth chimed in, now leaned back in Amaia's chair. *Please Lord, don't let him put his feet on the desk, just this once.*

"To *some*, it could be perceived as weak leadership under a *female* General, one that's incapable of controlling *men beneath* her position. It's a catch-22 and you know it."

"And to others it showed support, undying loyalty, if you will." His boots thudded under the hollow wooden desk.

Fuck. Within a blink of an eye, Reina unleashed a stream of water towards Seth's face, nearly knocking him out of his seat. Seth's face went from red fueled by anger to red of sadness as tears poured from his face. Before that emotion had a chance to fully take hold, his mouth formed into an O, a guttural scream unleashed from his mouth and his brows shot up in true horror. Reina's face intensified and Amaia stared off into the distance, bored, allowing her friends to have a few moments of sibling debauchery.

"Feet off the desk, Seth."

Reina's powers pulled from Seth as she turned back to face her friend, who had spoken her first words in hours. Seth gasped for breath, veins popping in his face and neck from either embarrassment or anger. Likely both. It had to suck knowing even as a Lieutenant, his sister could kick his ass without even lifting a finger.

"I chose your brother, Reina, because it's exactly what Jax would have wanted had he been given the opportunity to appoint a replacement himself."

I tried not to wince at Amaia's words, though it was hard to pretend as if they didn't sting a bit. While Amaia had become my newfound sister, Jax had become the brother I never had but always wanted.

"But more than anything, I chose Seth because it is *my* decision. *I* believe he deserves this opportunity to exhibit signs of leadership while helping *my* troops maintain the level of intensity and fearlessness that's going to be needed to keep this place safe.

It'll give us time to figure out what the hell is going on. I'm *hoping* that having Seth as my second will mitigate any immediate threat to The Compound. At this point, I feel like it's only a plus that he is unpredictable to most, because the very threat of catching Seth on the wrong day may be the *only* thing standing between us and a full-on coup." The defensiveness left her voice as her face softened, remembering that here she was not the General, but a sister to those who were hurting.

"And to be honest with you all, having Seth as my second may fill in any gaps that my leadership may be missing. Maybe we need a little good cop, bad cop around here to keep people in check. Maybe good cop, good cop is what lets us miss things the first time around."

On that note, the girls relented. Not wanting to say anything at all, as no one could be sure it wasn't true, as much as it would suck to admit. And we didn't lie to one another in this room. That wasn't how things worked.

Reina and Tomoe, now visibly exhausted as well, spent a few minutes cuddling up next to Amaia. Nestled in like cats apologizing for scratching their already wounded owner. Once they left, Seth gave her a pat on the back. As sincere as the guy could get for a friend in need, I guess, better than how he treated his own sister, that's for sure.

Once it was the two of us left, one look in her eyes told me she wasn't yet ready for me to go. Mind racing, I made my way over to the couch, ready to comfort my sister in her time of need.

CHAPTER

TEN

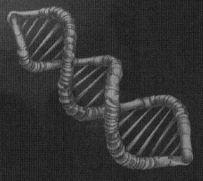

AMAIA

R iley left my office a few minutes after the others. *God, why can't everyone be as agreeable as him?* I never had to worry about Riley challenging or questioning my orders. Sometimes I wished the others possessed similar qualities, but I knew it was a better decision to have so many personalities around. Their questioning was good. Old me from The Before would have praised my friends for having minds of their own. Questioning all authority and not taking answers and decisions from officials like a blind sheep.

My conversation with Riley had been quick. They usually were. I gave my orders, and he asked what was relevant, allowing me to disclose anything further should I wish. I usually offered everything I had, and had always felt that it's important for people to know and understand the *why* behind their work and orders.

I didn't need history or military experience to understand that. That was a lesson I had learned living a regular civilian life in The Before.

Mentally exhausted, I stared at the ceiling and wondered what to do next. It was odd. Now that I had time to process things, the tears I spent all day holding back didn't seem to want to come to the surface anymore.

There were many things I could have done immediately to help me distract my mind. But I opted to do something that had always helped me feel better, even as a little girl.

Read.

I walked over to the dark wooden shelves on the left of my desk, a perfect match thanks to Riley. He spent much of his time dealing with work, but when he made time for what was probably his *only* hobby, the results of his woodworking belonged in a museum. Every piece of furniture in my quarters except a few had been crafted by him with his earth magic complimenting his raw talent. The result reminded me of the fantasy worlds I'd often read about.

I grabbed a few of my favorites off the shelf. There was some irony in some of my choices. It wasn't too long ago, I'd once wished I could live in a world mirroring the characters of my books. Now it was a reality, and it was not nearly as fun or glamorous as it had appeared. It was scary and life was hard.

But I guess that's what made these such a comfort for me. In The Before, I used books to escape my problems and enter the mind of my favorite character, taking on their problems as my own. Using each outlandish situation or obstacle to navigate my own emotions. I could laugh, I could cry, I could go through the five stages of grief, all through the eyes of someone else, instead of working through my own. And if the situation happened to relate to mine, even better.

After I gathered what I deemed essential for my reading session, I walked through the lengths of my office and entered my sleeping quarters. I tossed the collection of novellas from my favorite series on the bed. It was still early on in the afternoon and I had already had one of the longest days of my life. I had no plans to leave my room for lunch. Dinner was certainly out of the question and honestly, breakfast the next morning probably was too.

But I knew no matter how tired I was, how emotionally drained I felt, I wouldn't be able to rest until I'd at least read a few pages.

My fingers traced the outside of the book. It had a hand painted cover, and was obviously cared for by its previous owner. Jax had found it on one of his sweeps in the neighborhood and brought it back to me, saying he felt it was "some bullshit" I would read. I knew he didn't mean it. It was actually in that moment I knew I'd be all in with him, as much as our hearts would allow, no matter what. Knew it meant he had not only listened to me, but chewed over every word. I'd briefly mentioned the series in passing during the long weeks we'd spent making our way down the coast.

I opened the book, ready to leave this world behind and be captivated by the world I was now entering. The words came alive on the page, a movie in my mind, taking me back to a better place where I would read until the sun came up and it was time for work. It wasn't just a way for me to escape my thoughts, but also a way for me to truly connect to the pieces of me that had long been disconnected from who I had to be while I was here.

"What are you reading?"

The heavy wooden door opened and a whiff of cold air swept past my face. The breeze almost pushing the light pages around as my book lay flat on the bed, spine down against the comforter. I looked up, expecting to see Riley hovering, making sure I wasn't too lost in my grief, only to find Prescott instead.

"Oh, hi … I … um. My …" I had been taking a leap of faith, hoping he'd just trust me and my thought process.

Prescott smiled knowingly as he stepped fully into the room, with his hands full of a fat berry pie and a pot of coffee.

"Figured you needed something sweet," he said as he took a seat at the wooden bistro set near the window. I had a bad habit of wearing my emotions on my face around him. "And a push to eat since you don't plan on leaving here anytime soon." He motioned to the pile of books that lay on the other side of me.

I gave him a vacant smile, trying my best to make my eyes match my round lips. I scooted to the edge of the bed, too lazy to walk a few steps, and opened the pot of coffee. Telling myself for no other reason than to feel the warmth of a home brewed coffee on a crisp morning, even if it was now late in the afternoon. I closed the novel and dug into the pie, enjoying the sweet and tartness of each bite, always savoring the crust, grateful for the momentary distraction it provided.

Prescott watched me eat carefully without a word, undoubtedly loading up for his *Father Figure of the Year* award winning speech. I would've rolled my eyes had it occurred to me, but at the moment I found myself feeling incredibly thankful I had yet another person looking out for me.

Prescott cracked, asking me conversationally, "So what's the consensus? Does our heroine finally find her way?" I peered back up, hesitant to answer the question. I knew he wasn't talking about the book, but knew it wasn't the time for outright questions.

I decided to play into his little game, my chuckle covering how tired I had already grown of this conversation. "And give away the ending? No way. You'll have to see for yourself." I could see a smile slowly form from the corner of my eye, and I knew he was trying to convince himself everything was okay for the both of us.

Prescott finished his coffee and inched a tiny bit closer to me. "You know, it's fine if you just want someone to hang out with in here until you're feeling a bit more up to moving around The Compound on your own."

"I'll be fine, Pres. I just need a few days." I put as much effort as I could into those words, but I knew I had failed at that, too.

I was tired of speaking today. Of thinking. I just wanted to be alone, let my books take control and become the antidote to my problems, to grieve through them and them only. To feel like none of this was real.

He took the hint, realizing he was at the limit of what he could do and offer at this immediate moment. "A few days," he stated as he walked back towards the door, pausing slightly once as if he considered saying more, but left after weighing the possible outcome.

I slumped back on the bed, and for the first time in a long time, I decided to pray. I didn't know to who; didn't really care. I'd had my doubts about religion in the past, not really doubts, but questions. No more than the next person, but ultimately after my college studies and exposure to different cultures, I determined I kind of believed them all. With all the similarities, I felt that no one was wrong, just had their own interpretation.

So I prayed, to whatever higher power was out there, whatever one was right, to all of them and the long forgotten.

Before I knew it, the light had given way to a dark night sky. Time seemed to move slow yet fast at the same time. I felt weightless, numb.

Suddenly, I found my mind going back to Xavier. How I never had a chance to fully process his change, his death. Sammy, Xavier, my parents, everything happened fast and then life moved even faster for months and years after that.

Eventually, as time went on, I just became numb to it. Had learned to keep them to that 'other' part in my mind, the part that lay hidden in the back, laced with trauma and pain. I kept it all back there, so I wouldn't break. It was the only way I could keep going on.

There were nights where Jax and I lay awake the whole night, talking about the good times in the past, how our lives had been. How we probably would have never crossed paths in real life. Each conversation leading us to realize our lives couldn't have been more different. We were different people then, and that had shaped our personalities now. Forcing us to be compatible for the sake of survival. We stopped there most nights, because it only led to thoughts on how odd it was that such a precarious situation could lead to something more.

We rarely spoke of the hard times, the bad times, the times of desperation, the sadness. All the bad from The Before and the time that led up to where we were now. Then, I guess. Past tense.

He's gone, you idiot, and he's not coming back.

I broke at that thought once more. I didn't have time to grieve in the past. So now I would grieve for them all, as if Jax was the final stick holding the dam together.

My fingers started to shake, and my heart fluttered, imitating a hamster running, spinning on a wheel just under the skin of my chest. Every part of me became porous, feeling clammy though a cool draft had begun to enter my room through a window Prescott had cracked open during his stay.

I could no longer think. Felt as if I was sinking into an endless hole and my fingers couldn't quite grasp the edges to pull myself back up. Flames erupted around my bed as I lost control over my magic, only making me panic further. Tears streamed down my face as I begged my mind to find balance. Begging it to focus will myself into a place of neutrality.

I wanted to scream for Prescott to come back. For anyone to hear me. But the words vanished on my lips as I thought of the repercussions of someone running in to calm the damn General. The one person that needed to be calm in the face of uncertainty and loss, the one responsible for the calmness and lives of over a thousand men and women.

My mouth dried as I crumpled into the fetal position on my bed and let the tears roll from my face. A groan of pain rooted deep in my chest escaped and I let myself wail. The wails slowly turned into gasps, which led to excruciating minutes of hyperventilating. Trying to take every bit of air the world and my body would allow me to ingest.

I refused to give up on myself, on my mind. Refused to submit to the sorrow and heartbreak of all those I had lost.

I failed.

My body released all that it had, and I fell into a deep slumber.

CHAPTER
ELEVEN

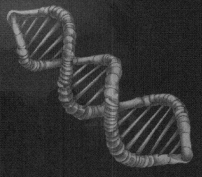

AMAIA

I awoke to my cold and dark sleeping quarters. The tan stone was barely more than a shadow as my eyes adjusted. My limbs felt stiff, unused from not leaving my bed in over a week. Two weeks since Jax's funeral, lost in my mind, drifting in and out of sleep as I made my way through my books. I had only left three times the week before.

The first attempt to convince myself a run would help. The second to actually make it *on* the run, after the first attempt had resulted in me turning around as the second one too many eyes fell on me. And the third, well, I ran until I physically couldn't anymore, and under the cover of darkness Riley carried me back.

Tomoe and Reina had been in and out around dinner time each night, trying to coerce me to eat and engage in light conversation. Reina had even snuck in a few nights to sleep at the edge of the bed, hesitant to take up the side that was Jax's. I'd left it untouched and made aside from his pillow which I often used to settle into my own space, a way to smell him without disturbing his closet that I wasn't yet ready to intrude.

A few times I'd awaken to presumably Prescott or Riley in the chair, pulled next to my bed. Feeling their presence more than anything, I was too lazy, too unmotivated to roll over and see who it was. Both had always been more inclined towards silence, they'd wait until I was ready to speak. Seth peeked his head in every other day, not doing more than giving me a quick glance over, making sure I was breathing before closing the door silently.

My thoughts swirled around, a never-ending cycle of despair and hopelessness. Not remembering the last time I felt anything but numb.

I willed myself to turn over in bed and face the window, the stars bright in the sky through the heavy cloth curtains. I couldn't bring myself to get up, to face those out in The Compound, either working a night shift or taking a stroll before bed. The endless responsibilities that were certainly waiting for me to make motion on. It all felt so … suffocating. Clawing at my throat, I begged my brain to cut me a break, to let me breathe.

Tears burned my cheeks, dripping off my chin as I lay there, once again feeling the heaviness of the lack of weight on the other side of the bed. I'd spent years trying to be strong for my people. And now, I couldn't even find the strength to do a simple task such as getting myself out of this bed. It'd taken Jax's death for me to realize I had reached the limit of my strength.

I suppose it had been building up for a while. Been the reason I'd started drinking again in the wake of the recent attacks and herds that appeared to be targeting The Compound, breaching the borders I'd spent ages ensuring were secured.

There'd been some time when I'd stopped once we'd settled, not completely, but 'socially' as Prescott had put it. Said there was no need for me to drown in my sorrows when there was now hope for the future. At the time, I had been inclined to agree with him.

Spent years determined to see all the positives in life that Prescott and Jax had been intent on seeing. But as I grew into my role at The Compound, and eventually took on my duty as General, I found myself wondering how much longer I could hold on to the hope that had sustained me for so long.

At twenty-seven, it felt like every decision I made weighed heavier on my soul, being responsible for the lives and deaths of many. There were many people I'd admired throughout history that had the weight of the world on their shoulders at my age or much younger, and had handled it with such grace. Persevered through it all and made it appear easy. I never thought I'd be able to relate on an innate level, though I had much doubt I'd ever be a notable part of history at all.

I knew I should reach out for help, reach back out to my family, who'd extended their hand time and time again. But the thought of burdening them with my emotions was too much to bear. Aside from being their friend, their sister, I was also their leader. I couldn't bring myself to let them know such private thoughts, and I hated myself for not allowing my guard to fall with those closest to me.

Even as I felt myself slipping into the darkness, further and further, week after week, a small spark of hope still burned within me. A reminder that Jax's soul had left a permanent, ever-burning ember on mine. I knew there was still a chance for me to find my way out of this darkness, to find the strength to keep fighting.

I sent a flame to the gas lamp next to my bed and rolled to my stomach to start on my next book, beginning my newest journey into another world that wasn't my own. After a few hours, my focus faded, and I allowed my mind to think back to a time when

I'd been happy. The version of me that had been bursting with energy and full of hope. A small part of me knew I could find that happiness again one day if I tried, no matter how far off into the future it was. If only I could bring myself to take that first step.

Maybe tomorrow.

I lied to myself for another two weeks. Every day was another tomorrow. Until one day, two months after Jax's funeral, I dug deep, and I found a spark. The disgust for abandoning my people, my friends, overpowering my despair. This was not the end, it was just another chapter in a sad, miserable little life. Even though my happy ending was not promised, I could still ensure the same fate would not fall upon others. Slowly, I sat up and swung my legs over the edge of the bed.

It was a small victory, but it was a start. Taking a deep breath, I forced myself to stand up, officially determined to face my depression head on. *Just take it day by day Maia, give it a chance to get better. You're way past due your seventy-two hours.*

Harley peeked her head up from her corner of blankets and stretched as she saw me move, ready to follow.

Today, I would begin my journey forward. Mentally, I tried to arrange my thoughts. I had always been a planner, even through the issues I had with my mental health during The Before. When I finally felt that I was in the place to get out of a slump, I needed a plan of action.

So, I would start small. Today, I would go visit Jax's grave and attend dinner with my family. *I can do this.* With a heavy heart, I made a silent vow to keep fighting, no matter how hard it might be, no matter how much longer it may last.

DRAGGING MY FEET AGAINST THE SUN-WARMED WOODEN FLOORS, I made my way to my bathing room. Taking a peek in the mirror, I studied my reflection. My curly hair was a bird's nest on the top of my head, tangled and wrapped around the scrunchie I hadn't removed in weeks. Dark circles haunted my eyes and framed my now gaunt face. I'd never had an appetite when I was upset and that hadn't changed, even though my survival was now based on my strength.

Sleep had never been my friend in The Before either, and that certainly hadn't changed these last few weeks. I looked like shit and smelled even worse. My nose scrunched up, finally taking in the stench that circled my body. *They must love me.* I wasn't sure how my family had been able to tolerate being around me in this state. They were troopers, that's for sure.

My body shivered at the quick change in temperature and my lack of clothing. Promptly, I sent a flame to the fireplace and pulled my oversized t-shirt over my leaned-out body. Entering my tub, I decided to embrace the chill as the water poured from the ceiling. Shivering from the shock, I waited for the tub to fill completely before using my magic to heat the water to my preference.

I reached to my left and grabbed the shampoo bar that was left untouched for longer than I'd care to admit. With thick, coiling curls, this was going to be more than a one day job for it to be back presentable. But baby steps.

My eyes swelled with tears, realizing how much I had let my body, my appearance that I had once been so proud of, deteriorate. I dipped my head back, allowing the warm water to soak my scalp, gently lathering the shampoo in. Slowly, I guided my fingers in small circular motions, remembering how my mom used to wash my hair as a child, taking comfort in the familiarity. I rinsed and repeated twice more and then grabbed for the conditioner bar next.

I let it sit on the ends of my hair as I took my brush and gently untangled my hair, fingers shaking, a whine leaving my trembling lips. Maybe it was vain, but I wanted my first appearance in public again to reflect that I had *some* aspects of my life under control.

There was no hiding the hollowness of my face, nor the leanness of my body. The circles under my eyes were outright terrifying, but maybe I could hide some of it behind my hair.

A quick rinse revealed my initial thoughts had been correct. I still had some more work to do, but I would worry about that another day. *Small steps, Maia, small steps.* I allowed the tub to drain, hating the feeling of shampoo and conditioner on my body. I lathered my body with soap and then stood under the aqueduct that allowed the water to flow freely from the ceiling, pulling the lever down as I rinsed off.

Grabbing my towel, I made my way to my wooden armoire. It was August now. The days were pretty warm from what I could tell each time I looked out the window and saw the attire of those out in The Pit and what my friends wore when they had come to check on me.

Given the fact that I planned to spend part of my day outside the walls, I should've probably rode on the line of practicality when it came to getting dressed. Problem was, I couldn't bring myself to care. I didn't plan on taking a stroll through the woods or going on a patrol route, so I grabbed the first thing that stood out. Something that exuded a sense of confidence.

I walked back over to the tub and took a seat on one of the steps leading up to it. Reina had laid out an array of homemade body butters on the edge, the girl took skincare during an apocalypse oddly serious. My dry skin thanked me as I put it on, pulling on my black cargo shorts next, followed by a matching black crop top. I opted to make up for the loss of practicality in weaponry. Securing two of my personal Glocks, and my throwing knives in my drop leg holsters. My socks and boots were last before I tossed my head over and scooped my curls back into the bun I had removed only an hour before. *Guess everyone will see it all.*

Taking a deep breath, I moved from my bathing room, through my sleeping quarters, and out into my study. Everything that needed my attention was put in three neat stacks, more than likely divided by what was critical, urgent, and what could wait. I felt a tinge of guilt while silently thanking Riley, knowing he'd been the one to sort through them all, saving me a bit of time. I wouldn't put it past him to have known, somehow, someway, that I was slowly coming from a cloud of darkness and out into a new dawn.

Before I could talk myself out of it, I went to the door and opened it without hesitation. Opening for the first time in months, by my own hand. It took my eyes a moment to adjust to the sunlight. Every soldier training in The Pit had now turned my direction, as if the small squeak in my door hinge had been broadcasted over an intercom. Uncomfortable under all the scrutinizing attention, I kept a quick pace with Harley in tow, keeping to the path on the outer edges and crossed onto the courtyard that served both the Scholar Building and The Pit. The sneers and scoffs from some of the soldiers didn't go unnoticed, but I couldn't blame them, although Harley released a few snarls in warning to a few.

I had abandoned them after a major event that had killed many, and left all survivors but a few injured. And for that, I wouldn't fight it if they wanted me replaced entirely. I would merely accept my fate. Do my best to be of use somewhere else, whether it be here at The Compound, or somewhere outside these walls.

The acceptance of my position came after the complete failure of my predecessor. He'd died out there due to his own ignorance and overconfidence, and walked us straight into an ambush. Ultimately attempted to abandon our unit for his own self-preservation. He'd died a coward, and we didn't bother to bring his body back. Not for a traitor.

I'd acted quickly, recalling my father's stories from his tours in Afghanistan and my general understanding of history, and admittedly a little of fantasy war scenes. Every last one of my comrades made it home, even though it had nearly cost me my own life. Well, everyone except for the General.

I didn't see any of my friends as I made my way through. Seth was also nowhere to be found. *Good.* I wasn't yet ready to face them.

It was a bright day, cloudless, which meant the heat was almost unbearable. Every ray of sun that hit my skin almost burned my only thankfulness to the weather, being that we didn't have to suffer the humidity of the south.

As I made my way to the North Gate, I found myself trying to take in the details, wanting to see how the place had held up. Seth had come by a few times, briefing me on a few Pansie attacks a few miles from The Compound near the border. Nothing major, and no deaths, only a few minor injuries. He seemed to have things under control for the most part. There hadn't been any attacks in the last two weeks, which meant his Scholar gene had allowed him to communicate with others and fill in any gaps or make adjustments accordingly. I'd make a point to set up a meeting with him later in the week, but everything I'd seen suggested things were under control.

The massive concrete walls that surrounded The Compound rose twelve feet high and six inches deep, my first initiative after I was appointed General. The previous one supported metal walls. His arrogance left us vulnerable, deciding to ignore my requests for improvement. They were prone to erosion, which meant they would weaken the harsher the elements got. Our weakest point of entry now would be our gates during a shift change or while they were being opened for trade. I had placed watch guards sporadically, at the top of the walls to accommodate for it.

The soldiers eyed me, noses scrunched as I approached, inevitably curious about what I had to say.

"Good to see you, General. Where are you off to today?" Mohammed asked, one of Riley's most trusted.

"I'll be headed out to The Graves for a bit. No need for concern," I replied, trying to appear as confident as possible.

"Will you need an escort, ma'am?" he inquired as the soldier to his right shifted uncomfortably. I didn't know her name, but she looked familiar. *Ah, that's right, Unit A.* She was there during Jax's attack. A recent recruit and, if her presence here meant anything at all, a damn good one. Riley trusted few at North Gate.

"That's not necessary," I stated, wanting privacy, and turned towards the woman. "Happy to see you made a full recovery," I offered as she gave me a tense nod with a half-assed smile.

I wasn't hurt by her display. I deserved it, after all. She had likely lost a lot during the past few months and I hadn't come to check on her. Something in prior times I made a point of doing. Ensuring that every one of my men and women recovered and were in a good enough place to go back in service.

"Open the gates, Private Collins, Sergeant Amin."

I released a breath as Riley saved me from this uncomfortable interaction. I turned to him, trying to meet him eye to eye, though my height rarely allowed me to do so with anyone, male or female. Every emotion poured across his face, but no words left his mouth. I knew in that instant he would be coming with me, if nothing else, but as my shadow.

Tilting my head, I offered him a slight smile. I wanted to simultaneously punch him in the gut for hovering, but also hug him for being a great friend.

The gates opened, and we stepped through, out into the open and on our own, but I would never feel unsafe with him by my side, or at my six.

WE EXITED THE NORTH GATE AND PASSED THE ABANDONED MONTErey Bay Aquarium with Harley a few feet ahead, enjoying the open space to roam. The only sound was the crash of the waves against the rocks and the crunch of the ground beneath our boots. I pretended not to notice the concerned glances Riley threw my direction, still waiting for me to be the first to speak.

I wasn't ready to give in, continuing the half mile to what was once Harbor Seal Lookout, now the place where we lay our fallen to rest. There were delicately carved headstones throughout. Jax had made it where loved ones were able to request earth elementals to craft during arrangements if there weren't any that were close enough to the dead to make themselves.

I paused, suddenly feeling overwhelmed and questioning if I was strong enough to do this. To be here. I didn't even know where to begin my search. There were hundreds of gravestones here. We didn't lose many for the size of The Compound, but every death was certainly felt.

Riley grabbed my hand and gave it a squeeze, guiding me towards where he knew Jax would be. He kissed his hand and touched the snake shaped headstone, matching the tattoo that went up Jax's forearm. I glanced down, giving him a moment of privacy, noticing one of my own tattoos. *Memento mori.*

Remember, you will die.

As the tears burned my cheeks, Riley backed away, giving us some distance for me to do whatever it was the hell I had convinced myself I was here to do. Harley let out a low whine and circled the base of the tombstone a few times before plopping down, whines escaping every few breaths.

I didn't know what I was doing here, what I was looking for, what I hoped I would gain or feel from visiting. I just knew I had to come. I had lost people before, a friend lost to an accident, another an innocent bystander, wrong place, wrong time. Grandparents, a cousin. Xavier. Sammy. My father. I wouldn't let myself think about my mother. While the latter didn't have a grave to visit, the first few did, and I went as often as I could in their memory. But this felt different somehow.

Visiting a gravesite or a memorial of a loved one to pay your respects was such a common thing in The Before. A way to remember their life and find comfort in their memory. I found no comfort here, only despair. And rage.

What should have been a meaningful or therapeutic experience only fueled the fire under my ass. I wanted vengeance. I wanted to make whoever did this to him suffer. And I hated myself for letting it take this long for me to reach this point, and hated myself for not being there to protect him in the first place.

I knew there wasn't a wrong or right way to grieve. Everyone did so in their own way, but with the rage I felt built up in my chest, I prayed I wouldn't let it consume me when the time came for justice. I wanted to be levelheaded, sane when I found out the truth. I wanted to make a logical decision that would prevent whatever anarchy was forming from spreading.

But with a long, spiraling road of healing ahead and no way to release all of my anger, I just felt lost. In the process of trying to rein in my rage, I felt another emotion take back over. Sadness, and suddenly I realized navigating this deep sea of grief was going to be a longer journey than I was ready to accept.

I felt my fire power boiling under my skin, ready for me to release it, when I felt a tight squeeze on my shoulder. I knew who it was without turning around, and my power disappeared as quickly as it arrived, not wanting to hurt an extension of myself. Instead, I released my feelings the way most would before magic. I cried. Riley came down to his knees and brought me into his lap, wrapping his arms around my waist and pulling me closer.

"It's okay, Amaia," he said softly. "I'm here for you. Whatever you need, my sister, I'll do my best to help."

I sniffled, leaning into his body, feeling the warmth and comfort he was offering up, knowing this level of vulnerability was hard for him and appreciating it that much more. "I don't know what to do, Riley," I said, breath shaky. "I feel so lost."

"I know," he replied, rubbing my back soothingly. "But you don't have to figure it out on your own. We'll face this together, all of us. No matter what happens, I'll always be here. Till death comes for us, together we'll go down."

I took a meditating breath and slowly let it out, feeling some of the tension in my body start to release. A sense of ease came over my body, knowing he was right, that I wasn't in this alone. I just needed to accept help from the ones that loved me most, to find the strength to get through whatever challenges lay ahead.

As if the word challenge had been a request from whatever higher power lived above, Harley stood posture forward, tail twitching high. A low throaty groan sounded from our rear, then another, and another. We shot to our feet, shocked to be faced with three Pansies not yet aware of our presence. Harley looked at me, awaiting direction as I signaled for her to lie down and remain silent. She obeyed.

We crouched down, attempting to stay hidden, another shape amongst the headstones, scouting out the area further to see how many we'd have to face. The stench of rotted fruit mixed with rotted meat overtook our nostrils, even from a distance. My nose scrunched up as I faced Riley, ready to make a snarky comment.

"Look," he mouthed, directing my attention back towards the enemy. My jaw dropped as the rotting creatures faced each other, engaged in conversation.

Communicating. *Impossible.* Pansies did not communicate. It was believed that they traveled in mindless herds. While I had always held the belief that there may be people deep down still in there, I'd never expected communication as being a possibility. This was new. *Had they been playing us? Pretending to be simple-minded in our presence as some larger scheme? Impossible.*

We watched for a few more minutes as the three male figures continued interacting. As my shitty luck had it, two deer crossed into our path, unaware of the danger a few feet away as they moved freely, hooves crunching against the ground. Perfect timing in synchrony with the wind just as it changed directions and picked up, I froze. The Pansie facing our direction nostrils pulled up as much as his grayish purple rotted face would allow, picking up on all of our scents . His eyes locked on us. An ear-piercing screech rang from his throat, and the two at his side swiveled around at an inhuman level of speed.

I was on my feet within half a second. Riley at my back and Harley at my side ready to attack, as the rest of The Pansies' eyes landed on our bodies like we were their next meal ticket. Riley grabbed my arm and shoved me behind him, ready to place himself between me and death.

"I got this," I commanded in a cold, detached voice. The voice of a general.

My soldier stood down without question and I signaled for Harley to stay put.

Three hundred yards. Two hundred fifty. Two hundred. One hundred fifty.

I raised my left arm, willing to play a bit with death, knowing damn well I was right-handed and this was not proper form. None of that mattered. The sound of thunder rang out, and two of them fell in a matter of seconds, bodies hitting the ground with a thud.

As quickly as I drew my gun, it was back in my holster and my throwing knife was now within my grasp. I flipped it in my hand and let out a guttural yell as the remaining Pansie closed in on his final fifty yards. My knife flew, hitting him in the middle of his forehead. *Bingo.*

I pranced over and pulled it out as a wet, slushy sound graced the knife's exit. "Man, that felt good," I voiced, suddenly feeling a lot better than when I arrived, as if Jax had sent me a gift for relief himself.

I glanced back at Riley, who hadn't yet moved, his face even more concerned than when we'd arrived. He knew I was good; I was *Umbra Mortis* after all. Riley also knew I was taking a dance with death by allowing them to get close. A chance I would have never taken if Jax was still around, holding me accountable. You could be good, but Pansies were unpredictable, and even the best had to meet their maker at some point. But Jax was no longer here, he'd been taken from me.

"Race you back," I called over my shoulder as I took off, Harley racing against me and the wind, smirk now on my face and knife still in hand. Daring something else to come for me.

As expected, Riley was exactly where he would always be, at my side.

By the time we arrived back at The Compound, it was time for the first dinner wave. If things hadn't changed too much in my absence, my friends would just now be sitting down for dinner before any final meetings or training we had to attend for the day. Often keeping our nights open for leisure or making up personal things we couldn't tend to during the workday.

Collins and Mohammed were completing side work, preparing for shift change in a few. As we passed them, I stopped to give Harley a pat behind her ears and told her to go home. She pranced off towards my quarter, Riley and I working our way towards The Kitchens, moving through The Pits, the Scholar Building and the General Living Quarters. Tigers on the hunt.

The Kitchens themselves were part literal kitchen, part cafeteria style seating. It was the size of a small mall, quartered out to make space for residents as they filtered through on varying work schedules. With nothing but time on our hands during the settlement period, the earth elementals had outdone themselves by putting together yet another beautiful building. It was exceptional.

One of my favorite things about The Compound was how each building had its own unique charm and character, leaving behind a touch of its creators. Though there were a mix of style buildings in such a few square miles, each building complimented its neighbor. Most would say that each section of the compound had its own vibe and neighborhood charm.

Since it was connected to The Gardens, The Kitchens had been made both beautiful and functional. Most of the building was crafted by strong glass that allowed it to be temperature controlled and operated as a greenhouse. Even when there was no cooking happening on the other side of the divider, the place smelled like the herbs that littered the glass ceiling. The huge building had different rooms that presented as if they were different restaurants. Another one of Jax's brilliant ideas.

He'd proudly worked with Prescott on setting up the Customs & Culture committee. Understood the importance of building a community, of returning to a collective society and not an individualistic one.

The room off to the left was the only part that had a solid roof that was of a near black wood. It was casually decorated with woven furniture that littered the oak floor. It was still early enough that only a few lay sprawled on couch-like booths, awaiting dinner companions.

Straight ahead was a tea room styled corner, floor to ceiling glass with an apple tree allowed to grow from the outside in. White bistro styled furniture across the pink-tiled flooring and banana leaf trees throughout.

The center was my favorite place when I dined alone, the black-and-white checkered tile flooring reminding me of my favorite brunch spot back home. There were bamboo-colored tables and chairs throughout and longer tables to accommodate larger parties in an elevated area near the large window.

Riley and I passed the now silent room to the darker room on the left. Crossing through the entrance area, headed towards room on the right where we knew our friends would be. Soldiers turned away under Riley's harsh gaze as he walked behind me.

We entered a more intimate area that resembled a Hawaiian bar, lanterns hanging down from the ceiling providing ambience lighting for the now darkening sky. It was reserved for Council members and those who had a certain security clearance within The Compound. Providing us a more secure place to discuss Compound matters away from many ears while having a meal.

Reina stopped talking and Tomoe turned around to see what she was gaping at. She offered me a soft smile and then elbowed Seth, who jumped to attention in my presence.

"Seth," I muttered, begging him to sit down, knowing full well at mealtimes we were all equals. Merely a family dining together and catching up on one's days. As we sat, the table remained quiet, no one really knowing what to say. I glanced behind Reina's shoulder to see Prescott who offered me a reassuring thumbs up as I rolled my eyes and looked away. Taunting him by not allowing him to see the humor that threatened to populate my eyes.

"Let me get you a plate," Reina offered, breaking the silence with her echoing chipper voice.

"No, it's okay. I'm not that hungry. I just came to see you guys, see how you were doing."

I smiled lamely, wanting everyone to know that was all I wanted, to spend time with them. As if on cue, Prescott walked over with a piece of pie and coffee. "Three sugar cubes and a splash of oat milk." He winked, walking back over with a cocky pep in his step. I wouldn't put it past him to have had one of his eyes in the city relay back to him that I had left my quarters. Probably been waiting a few hours for my inevitable arrival.

My friends focused on their plates, eating the chili noodles and vegetable stir-fry that was one of tonight's meal options and we continued the evening in mostly silence. Every now and then someone would toss out a joke and we'd all pretend to laugh. Them for my benefit and me for theirs.

Without it being said, I knew that things were changing. I could feel it in the air, a sense of determination, and hope. The unity of being back around the people that I loved dearly, transforming the room to a place I wanted to be, both metaphorically and literally.

Sure. There were plenty of conversations we needed to have about the future of our people, where to go from here and putting the pieces our lives had been crumbled into back together again, as best as we could with a major piece missing.

But for now, we were a family sharing a meal before getting to the hard talk of what was to come.

"Ready to go?" Seth said, tugging at Tomoe's arm.

She wiped her mouth with the cloth napkin and smiled brighter than I'd ever seen before. Her happiness comforted me, my cheeks flushed, and I smiled at her knowingly. As if she could hear the thoughts churning in my mind, she tossed the napkin at my face and choked out a weak excuse. "We're just sparring down at The Pit, don't lose those curious eyes of yours. I've been giving Seth a piece of my Wrath the last few weeks."

"Sure baby, whatever you have to say to make yourself sleep at night," Seth joked and I burst out into the first moment of genuine laughter I'd had in months. My friends joined in, happy to hear what they probably feared they never would again. Seth and Tomoe took their exit, and I turned back to Reina, grabbing her hand.

"I missed you," I said.

"I missed you too, love bug."

CHAPTER
TWELVE

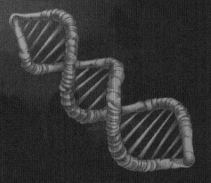

TOMOE

My cheeks hurt from forcing a smile through dinner. These past few months have been hell on Earth, part two. Time had moved so fast, yet so slow. Hours felt like days, and days, minutes. For a while, we weren't sure if Amaia would make it through, pull herself out and nothing we did helped. If she even noticed who exactly was in her presence, I wasn't entirely sure.

Out of everyone in our makeshift family, she'd probably been through the most, and Jax had been her comfort through it all. But lost in her grief, a sick sense of bitterness had taken root in my heart. She had abandoned us as if Jax had only meant everything to her and nothing to us. And now she was back, acting as if nothing had happened. Couldn't speak for anyone else, but I sure as

As soon as those thoughts surfaced, I pushed them away, knowing she grieved much more than just Jax. While we had all grieved for the ones we lost when we arrived, finally feeling safe enough to do so, Amaia and Jax had been the ones to help everyone through it. Offering their spare time to offer a shoulder to cry on to anyone who needed it. Never letting themselves truly process their own grief and trauma. From what Reina had told me, based on what she pressured out of Riley, it'd been that way from day one.

Amaia had always been strong for everyone. While Reina radiated positivity, Amaia existed in a consistent state of realism, making sure people saw there *was* a light at the end of the very real, very dark tunnel. I admired and respected her for it, maybe even took it for granted for years, not knowing what to do when it was her turn to fall apart.

Reina and I tried to be there for her every day. Showed up when we could, trying to get her to engage in conversation, a puzzle, or even just share what she had read. Some days she'd try to put on a happy face for us, but we could see right through every empty reply or the spaciness behind her doe eyes.

I'd spent most nights grieving not only the loss of a brother, but now worrying about losing my sister as well. When I first arrived at The Compound a little over two years ago, Amaia had just been promoted to General. From all the stories I've heard, it was a well-deserved promotion, and I could see why she had gotten it every day she acted in her duties since. Until Jax died.

From our first conversation, I knew this girl would be a pain in my ass, and my sister. The thing most people didn't understand about Amaia is the girl never *wanted* to be General, just accepted her duties because she felt responsible for others' safety. Didn't want to let anybody down. Namely Prescott and Jax. They'd always held her to a high standard. I knew the feeling. Jax had that effect on people.

My first night here, I wandered into the Entertainment Square, ending up at a little tavern. It was jam-packed with people for a Thursday night and I'd spent the last two years only surrounded by family, and then out on my own. I wasn't used to crowds anymore. Had felt the sensory overload taking its grip on my mental.

Not quite ready to leave all the excitement and the buzz of the crowd, I stepped outside for a breath of air. A familiar earthy, sweet scent smacked me in the face. I turned my head and saw a girl with big curly hair observing me to the left of the steps, grinning widely as she extended her packed herbs to me.

"You look like you could use a pick me up," she offered.

As she leaned forward, I studied her appearance, trying to place who I was speaking to before I accepted such an offer. Her blue jean shorts, crop top, and combat boots offered me no answers, though the muscles gleaning in her legs showed that whatever she did on the daily kept her active.

I'd assume she just arrived here as well, but her leanness didn't scream starvation the way mine did. No, there was a functional, intentional strength that lingered within her movements.

"Where did you even get that from?" I asked, skeptical of this random girl already trying to fuck up my stay.

At that moment, a man stepped out of the tavern, jovial as ever, as a laugh rang out from deep in his belly. I took in his tall stature, ivory skin, and reddened freckled cheeks. If Ireland was a person, it would be embodied by him.

"Corrupting the new girl already," he stated, more than questioned, "Typical Mai. Imagine, a general promoting drug use amongst a potential soldier, the scandal this would bring in The Before."

"The Before?" For a moment, I wish I had just stayed inside, suddenly more overwhelmed out here with them than I was surrounded by a dense crowd.

Mai giggled, clearly amused that the new girl knew nothing of this little dystopia. "Yeah, that's what we call all the good times *before* all hell broke loose. And to answer your first question, what fun is having earth magic if they can't grow the good stuff, too?"

I took in how she said *they* and not *me*, curious about what gifts she had gotten in the fallout.

Taking the spliff, I inhaled deeply and said, "I'm not a soldier."

As if he took it as a challenge, the man inched closer to Mai, grabbing her by the waist and pulling her in. There was nearly a foot difference in height between their shoulders, "You could be, if you wanted to be." Though he was smiling, I knew it was a serious offer.

When I first arrived, I was told I'd be given a week to adjust to life here and see what The Compound had to offer. Then I could choose an open job after my skills had been assessed. I was sure that parodying what they called The Before, soldier was an everlasting opening and I hadn't considered it for a second.

In fact, I hadn't considered anything at all. I was talented with my katana, passed down through generations. I'd renamed mine after my family died, Wrath. But living the rest of my life in a job that had me in the very environment that I had just spent the last few months trying to get away from wasn't an enticing offer.

Then there were the visions. I hadn't met anyone like me yet. My family had each possessed the gift of fire. I didn't. For a while, we thought I would be the unlucky one and turn, but then I had my first vision and we remained hopeful on a different outcome.

I didn't mind my powers, but there were times where I wish I had been gifted with something different. The visions made my mind feel spaced out, never able to focus on one thought, often wandering to the next thing. I realized I was having a moment as I came back to focus and saw the girl studying me, in a way that almost felt invasive before a smile pushed back through, teeth shimmering under the moonlight.

"Okay, not a soldier," she offered tenderly, "but everyone here trains now, for safety purposes," she added, "so you'll have to find an open group to train with once a week. I didn't catch your name, by the way. I'm Amaia, and this is Jax." She extended her hand, offering me a sincere introduction.

"General Bennett," Jax threw in, giving the wild girl before me a stern, pointed glare.

"General Amaia. You'll have to excuse *my Lieutenant*," she mocked, before extending her hand to me once more.

Taking her hand, I saw something in her eyes. A defiant spark that let me know she's exactly the kind of friend I'd get along with in my old life. *The Before.*

"Tomoe Sato. Is there a way I could train in a … less public way?" I asked, something about the softness in her tone made me think I could trust her. "I'm just not ready to be back around a big crowd. I think I need a more, well to be honest, I've never liked crowds. And training like I didn't just spend the last few months on my own outside these walls fighting for my fucking life isn't the most enticing offer one could receive right now."

No use in pretending to be anything other than myself now that I was here. They both looked at me, before glancing at each other as if they were exchanging silent words that only they could hear before bursting into a fit of laughter.

"At least she's honest," the General said from the ground, hunched over hand on belly.

Jax tried to compose himself, but he was nearly a lost cause, too.

"How bout a morning spar and then we'll see what arrangements can be made?" he offered. I nodded quickly and got the details for the next day before scurrying off, ready to retire to my new quarters and seclude to my own thoughts.

The next morning we met at the asscrack of dawn before he was expected to tend to his duties. Most would have complained, but I preferred the early hours. They were quiet and peaceful, and for a moment, if you really tried, you could forget the chaos of the world we lived in.

I think that's what I learned to love the most about sparring with him. We moved as a symphony, lost in a language only we could understand. It was our therapy. Most mornings, the only sound would be the clink of our weapons or the slams of our fists against skin. The grunts and oomphs of pain. Then there were the mornings where we talked, where we let everything out, even our deepest, darkest thoughts. Thoughts we trusted with only each other, thoughts we were too afraid to share with the others close to us.

After our first spar, Jax panted that he had never been so easily matched in swordplay. It was a lost art in a world where automatic weapons and magic made the most sense. But for us, the more un-hinged ones, the ones that had vengeance to pay, deaths to avenge, we appreciated the more personal touch.

One morning led to the next morning, into the next morning, and then the next. It was such a natural thing that the only day we didn't show up was Sunday. A day he thought we all deserved to rest. We showed up every morning, a routine we had never verbal-ly decided on yet dedicated to each other no matter what, every morning, including his last.

I missed my brother, but I missed my sister even more, and I needed her. I was happy she made it tonight, but a part of me wanted to scream and shout. Shake her and ask *what about the rest of us?*

"What's on your mind?" Seth asked, squeezing my hand and bringing me back into focus. "You're doing it again," he added ten-derly, obviously confused at my state of confusion at his question.

I was more shook by the change of location that had passed by without me realizing. We were back at The Ring in The Pit, minutes lost from the walk from The Kitchens to here.

Seth had offered to spar with me every evening after dinner when he had walked in on me, shredding into one of the punching bags. Without my spar partner, I didn't have a release for all of my pent-up emotions, but I'd been too hurt to step foot here on my own for days, anyway.

"I'm fine," I replied, colder than I had intended.

Seth had become someone I'd rather depended on these days, growing closer every day. I'd never say it out loud, but I waited for the day he may see me other than just a flirt or friend. Spending time with him had become the highlight of my day.

My eyes blurred a bit as I felt a vision coming on, stumbling as Seth reached to steady me, knowing what to do when my visions took over. *Pansies. Sunset. Carnage.* My eyesight found its way back to reality as quickly as it had disappeared.

I scanned the sky, taking note of the sun's position as it began to set. Reassured by the fact that I heard nothing but silence, *surely it wasn't today*. An attack of that magnitude would take ramping up and we would hear it coming.

Besides, the sun was merely a minute or two from taking the same position in the sky as what my vision relayed. Which meant reporting to Amaia what I had seen could wait, no need to bombard her the second she assumed her duties again, anyway.

Seth's eyes narrowed, head tilting, waiting for me to speak and explain what I had seen. "Nothing, it's fine. Nothing that can't wait for tomorrow."

With that, I set Wrath down a few feet from the edge of The Ring, and grabbed one of the practice knives off the weapon wall. He studied me once more, trying to decipher exactly what it was I had seen without pushing me further. For a moment I wondered if he would try to push my boundaries.

He gave up and pointed to the knife in my hand. "Knife play, eh?" he jested, as he tilted his head and winked.

"Quit messing with me before I trade this baby in for something that can do some real damage," I playfully added as I made my way to the center of The Ring, assuming my fighting position.

I placed my left knee down, centimeters off the ground. Right knee up with my left arm holding the knife pointed towards Seth and kept my right arm bent and steady, ready to block his advances.

"Maybe I'm ready for a little pain. Maybe I like it," he added, circling me in an attempt to throw me off with his flirtatious banter before assuming a wrestler's position. A lingering feeling of danger seeped from him, his movements reflecting a viper trying to find the perfect place to strike.

I poked my chest out slightly, daring to distract him with the cut of my sports bra, and succeeded. Happy with my effort, I threw my left arm out ready to strike his chest and leaned back slightly to dodge whatever blow he likely had coming my way.

He put his right arm out and grabbed my left wrist taking me off balance for only a moment before I flung my back towards the ground. I used the momentum to pull myself along the floor and twisted back on my feet, flipping my knife back towards an outward position ready to strike him once more.

Before either of us could make our next move, screams rang out near North Gate, followed by the terrified cries of civilians who now ran our way. I glanced at Seth before reaching for Wrath near The Rings borders. He pulled me back in alarm.

"Stay here," he commanded through his teeth.

Taken aback at his sudden urge to helicopter parent, I shook his arm off in bewilderment. He knew I could fight, hold my own.

"I'll be damned. I can fight Seth. Those people need help." Picking up Wrath and slinging my baby back over my back, I took off towards the gate before he could stop me.

I felt a presence nearing me and glanced over my shoulder, expecting to see Seth following behind but instead was faced with Riley. He only offered me an encouraging smile before racing ahead, giving out commands to the soldiers who stood around awaiting orders like dumbasses. Precious moments wasted that never would have happened had Amaia been around.

Since I was *not* a soldier, I decided that I didn't need orders and continued sprinting in the direction of the gate. Soon stopping in my tracks and taking in the group of Pansies that had made their way inside. Riley's friend Mohammed and another female soldier in the mouths of two of those disgusting creatures, the formers face in an O shape, as if forever frozen in a scream.

The Pansies skin was pale and pasty. Their eyes sunken into their heads and staring blankly into the abyss as if they were doing nothing but grabbing a few half-priced beers after a long week of work.

My heart pounded in my chest as some of the undead continued their approach, their moans getting louder, frenzied and more frequent at the promise of food. I pulled Wrath out from the harness at my back and took a step back to put some distance between myself and the enemy as possible. I forced myself to focus, losing track of who was who as people continued to run past on both sides.

Suddenly to my right, a Pansie lunged towards me, reaching out with its blood-stained hands. While Amaia at least tried to pretend there was still a person in there, I didn't believe any of that shit. Man, woman, old lady, I never stopped long enough to see, simply because it didn't matter to me.

These assholes had taken everything I ever loved. My whole family had lucked out only to meet their demise under the jaw of what was once another human being. I swung my katana with all my might, connecting with its head at the cusp of its neck, and sending it crashing towards the ground.

I looked up, taking in my surroundings. There were so many of them; I knew if I stood still any longer I'd be doomed, succumbing to their fierce bites. I scanned to find Seth, wanting to fight at his side where I could know without a doubt he was safe, but he was nowhere to be found. Likely providing orders to his troops and escorting those who could not fight to a safer location. A familiar yell came from somewhere not too far ahead on the path. My feet were moving before I even had to will them to.

My eyes widened at the gruesome scene before me. Two small children were tucked under a large man, creatures gnawing at his back and his shoulders. He screamed out again in pain as the one closest to me pulled back, removing a piece of his flesh.

I swung Wrath through the air, moving akin to wind in a relentless storm. One head, two heads, then the third. Pulling the two children from under my friend, I ordered them to run towards the center of The Compound, and not to stop until they were in their homes. Not for anyone or any sound. Kneeling on the ground, I moved Riley's arm over my shoulder, bearing most of his weight as he commanded me to be his eyes as he removed his pistol and fired as I called out Pansies locations that remained in our way.

We'd almost made it to the safety of one of the entrances to The Pit when I felt cold fingers amongst my scalp. It gripped my hair tight enough to lunge me back, Riley's head found a wrong angle on an uplifted stone on the path, rendering him useless as he lay knocked out cold and his weapon right out of my reach. Wrath unusable, pinned underneath the weight of both me and the undead.

The Pansie lowered closer towards me, mouth snapping and blood dripping from its mouth on my face. My eyesight went blurry again, daring to bring me into another vision, inevitably my final vision if I let it take hold at this very moment. Grunting, I braced myself. Pushing and shoving it away. Channeling every ounce of otherworldly magic I had in my body and putting it towards the tremendous effort of keeping what it was supposed to do away.

I fought hard, but I couldn't fight forever and everything faded away. *A beautiful blonde-haired woman, her face kind. Wolves, running wolves. Reina crying, Amaia struggling, exerting her energy, but struggling. Handcuffs.*

My body shook. I heard a dog barking in the distance. "Moe, Moe, get up. Come on we have to move, get up!"

I came to and saw Amaia and Harley standing over me, Riley slumped against her as she tried to keep her balance in her weakened state. The guilt of having to add to it had me attempt to get to my feet. It would be a strain on my sister knowing taking on someone Riley's size had been a struggle for me, let alone someone of her stature.

"Can you walk? They're all dead, but the gates have been breached. We need to move." She offered me her hand, and I took it, using it to leverage my body to a standing position.

I took in my surroundings. The Pansie, who'd been about to end my life, lay sprawled on the cobblestone path, a piece of the cobblestone missing, and found in the middle of its head, courtesy of Amaia's powers. The girl could make anything into a weapon, and probably didn't even get her nails dirty doing so.

Pain radiated down my left side, and I glanced down, taking in the large bite on my thigh. It'd heal easily enough, but it would be a pain in the ass to get through my day with it messed up.

Amaia's eyes scanned my body, taking in my current state as they moved up and down. Ultimately, she decided we weren't going far. She took on both Riley and my body weight, forcing me to loop around her other shoulder, ignoring every effort of a fight I put up. Adrenaline pumping, she practically dragged us both to her quarters not far from where we stood.

She'd pulled the couch in from her study to her bedroom, placing me on its cool surface while Riley, who was larger, took up her side of the bed. I caught her stealing glances in between stitching towards Jax's side, double checking Riley hadn't moved a bit too far to the right.

Riley's head was cleaned first before she placed a tourniquet on his shoulder as it bled profusely. She took a double take of the salt she kept near the side of the bed and sprinkled some into his wound, then focused on the hole to my leg next. I had always teased her about her need to always add extra salt to things, but I guess it had come in handy.

"Why the fuck do you know this?" I screamed out in pain.

"Chopped off a small chunk of my finger cutting an onion once. Xavier dumped some to stop the bleeding. Never been a fan of the ER," she recalled as she continued to work on us both in order of urgency for our injuries. I wasn't even sure if she had noted the bruises of her own that she sported.

A bruise peeked out from under her crop top, making me almost positive she hid bruised ribs a few inches up as well. Her knee was gashed in, indicating she'd had an altercation or two before she reached me.

"Maia, we're fine. Go clean yourself up," I whispered. She ignored me once more, moving throughout her quarters in a robotic manner.

My eyelids felt heavy, and I dozed off. Waking to Seth and Reina entering, Seth hovered over me, placing a light kiss to my forehead. Though my eyes were still too heavy to open, I savored the feeling of the warmth it provided. Straining my ears, I listened to the report Seth gave as Reina's footsteps moved away from Riley and towards me to see what she could heal.

I felt some of the pain lift away from my body, feeling as if feathers gently scraped against my skin and were being pulled by a delicate string, away and into the ether.

"How bad is it?" Amaia asked, this time taking on the role of a General, any remnants of family in her voice gone and distant.

My chest hurt, knowing my friend was surely going to blame herself, and only herself, in the wake of Seth's report.

"Ten dead. Six soldiers, four civilians. Three adults, one child."

The room grew still, daring someone to exhale.

"Which of my soldiers have fallen, Lieutenant?"

Seth's voice hallowed, any hint of emotion removed as if he were distancing himself at the thought of losing yet another soldier, another friend.

"Private Collins and Sergeant Amin were the first casualties." I heard Amaia's breath catch as Seth continued on.

Mohammed Amin was one of the few people aside from Amaia that *truly* got close to Riley. "They perished in defense of the North Gate as they prepared Private Smith and Sergeant Greene on the details of their shift. Private Smith also succumbed to his injuries as medics worked to stabilize him for transpo at the gate. Sergeant Greene is in Unit A, critical condition. Officer Sullivan, Officer McCormack, and Private Washington went down while transporting the daycare children and their teacher on their evening walk out of the area. They managed to save all but one teacher and one of twelve students. The other two civilian casualties were from those who deserve to be honored. They heard the commotion and gave their lives to ensure every other civilian in the immediate area made it away."

All I could hear was my family around me, breathing near hyperventilation at such losses, each awaiting the next to speak. Yet Amaia said nothing. The next thing I heard was the screech of a wooden chair against the floor, and Reina offering it to Amaia. Had my friend gone into shock? I fought hard again, willing my eyes to open, but they refused to listen.

"How many?" she finally inquired.

"How many—"

"How many Pansies breached the wall?" Amaia interrupted Seth before he could ask for clarification.

"Fifty-one."

Reina gasped. Impossible. The sons of bitches couldn't be quiet if they *wanted* to.

"Fifty-one." Amaia mumbled, "Fifty-one, Seth and not a single person saw nor heard them coming? That doesn't make any sense." She pushed, half-baiting him towards a fight she could win. A win she probably needed to stay motivated to come back to her job after such a loss. A loss I knew she blamed herself for.

My eyes finally gave in to my fight as I squinted them open and watched the scene at hand unfold. For once, instead of giving in, Seth took us all by surprise, as he simply moved forward and extended his arms, offering her a hug. My sister looked towards him, skeptical and confused at his display of affection, one he didn't offer too many and even not often to those that he did. After a few tense seconds, she took it.

Reina, not one to miss the opportunity to hug the two people she cared for who were typically affection-retardant, joined in.

"We'll make it through this, guys. I know we can." And for a few sweet and peaceful moments, my family united.

A loud thud a room away had my eyes shooting wide open on defense as my family jumped apart. Amaia's gaze fixated fiercely on the door, listening before she told Seth and Reina to stand down. Seth with his hand on his holster, ready to draw, and Reina with her elemental magic swelling in her hands.

"Stay here," she said, game face on and full of command as she headed out her room with both fear and determination in her eyes.

CHAPTER
THIRTEEN

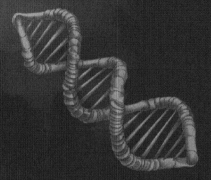

AMAIA

"Oh, good, you're here. Glad I was able to catch you at a good time," Prescott bit off angrily, noticing me slipping from my bedroom as he stopped to pat Harley on the head in greeting.

His dark gray shirt pressed tightly against his body under the weight of his sweat. I took in his drop leg holster as well as the weapon holstered at the waist of his pants. He must have been outside the walls.

"I've already been briefed. I don't need an accompanying lecture."

He frowned sarcastically and clasped his hands, making me jump at the noise before he spit out, "Don't need a lecture? Hmm, okay. How about some facts? Someone this close to our territory, right after an attack and we didn't know about it because my *General* has been wasting away, just as dead as her dead boyfriend. Can't focus on Compound first. Ten dead, Amaia! Ten!"

As soon as the words left his lips, an expression of shock took over his usually kind features. I chose not to acknowledge it, knowing the words hurt him more to say than they did hearing them. I stepped closer towards him, wanting to comfort him and knowing we had a lot to catch up on from the last few months. I had hurt the people around me in more ways than I could imagine, but now wasn't the time. Stopping short, I looked at him, confused. No lurker had been in Seth's brief, but I refused to let myself appear caught off guard.

"And who would that be?" I questioned.

I tried to read Prescott's face, but it showed nothing as it morphed its way back towards nothing but disappointment. He didn't answer as he turned his back to me to stare out the window. His sleek, peppered hair sat perfectly against his tan cheeks and perfectly cut facial hair.

"Caleb?" I gulped, regretting not putting in an execution order.

He chose to see past the potential fight at the mention of his name, and pushed forward with the immediate threat.

"There should have been an immediate sweep of the area following the attack to secure both the border and the wall. Troops should have been deployed, and then maybe I wouldn't have stumbled upon someone peeking between the trees trying to peer into The Compound while doing my *own* rounds."

If this had been a different situation, I would have laughed. Leave it to Prescott to notice a face in the trees that stood over three hundred yards away. I knew he had taken up bird watching as a pre-retirement hobby in The Before, but something about taking in that small of a detail made a shiver go up my spine. Nothing truly went unnoticed around here. There was always someone watching whether you knew it or not.

"I'm-I'm sorry. Seth and I hadn't yet spoken about me transferring back my duties yet. Riley and Moe are hurt, and I was tending to their wounds. By the time he debriefed me, I guess I just assumed he had done his due diligence on that end, too."

I tried to explain myself, though saying it out loud sounded ten times more irresponsible than it did in my mind. Hating that I felt like I was becoming the man I was brought in to replace.

"Assumptions get people killed," he stated simply.

I grimaced, knowing he was right. As my eyes wandered across the room, Prescott added, "It's time to move on, my sweet girl. Time to push forward. There is no luxury in dwelling on the past, trust me. Every day is a gift, even during a time of grief and loss. It's bigger than you now. You have the responsibility to live for not just you, but them too."

My eyes landed on a few of my books, thrown about where I had last left them months ago. I'd opted not to finish the series once more when things got too familiar, too close to home. I knew he was right. It was time to lift the fog. It had been weeks and weeks ago.

"The heroine hasn't found her way. She doesn't until the last book. It takes her a few fuck ups, a few mistakes, and some really, *really* good friends, but she wins and her family survives in the end." Prescott followed my eyes, realizing the hidden meaning behind my words. Remembering the question he had asked me just two months before.

"And what book are you on right now?"

"Honestly?" I chuckled. "Book three. Out of eight. But I'm ready, I'm ready to be at the end. I'm ready to read that last page."

"Good," he said, as he walked towards the door, "Because you're on prisoner duty. Welcome back, captain."

He disappeared from my doorway, and I called out jokingly, "That's General to you!"

As I pondered what he meant, realizing his play on words and questioning if maybe he *had* picked it up all those months ago, as a towering figure walked in. Harley let out a growl and crawled towards the strange man at the door. I let her, knowing she wouldn't attack unless he posed an immediate threat, or I commanded it. He glanced down at my beast of a girl nervously, then wiped the expression off his face as quickly as it appeared.

The man's beige skin was covered in tattoos from his neck down to his fingertips as they peeked out from his dirt dusted white beater tank. His brown hair was neatly cropped on the side and gelled back at the top. A series of silver and bronze rings littered his tattooed fingers.

My gaze trailed back up to take in the rest of his features, as his small lips curved, smirking. There was nothing kind behind the smile, instead he held my stare. The darkness in his dead eyes unsettled me, a shiver going down my spine.

"You must be said prisoner," I barked.

"Ouch," he said, hand flying to his chest as if I had shot him in the heart. "And you must be the drunk General. And her dog," he said, putting distance between him and what were now gleaning teeth a few inches away. A trace of an accent stressing his R's.

"Well, don't you just catch on fast? What are you doing lingering outside my walls, anyway?" I scooted towards the door and grabbed one of my hoodies as I covertly pushed him back out onto the path.

A discrete attempt to put some distance between those I loved and whoever the hell this annoying person standing before me was. I motioned for Harley to stay as I pulled the door shut.

"I was running from a small herd and was able to pull myself into a tree," he offered simply, as if it were no big deal, "Some took a turn down the cliff side, fell I guess, and the rest kept moving past me and then I heard all the commotion. Figured I'd get a closer look since I heard a few kids, climbed up another tree, ya know, higher ground and all, and saw your little set up. I'd heard about The Compound, just didn't know I'd end up this far in its territory."

Maybe having earth magic grow extra trees around our walls wasn't a great security measure after all. I'd never considered the alternative repercussions of it.

I studied him. His loaded sentences offered me a glimpse of the possible information he could have on quite a few topics and deemed him a worthy prisoner to keep around.

"Do you treat all your prisoners with such distaste?"

Do you ever stop talking?

"Just the ones that come on the heels of attacks. The rest are offered more peaceful options, like the guillotine." I grinned at him, making an effort to be convincing, though nothing I had just said was true.

Execution was rare. Most were exiled or sent off to another compound in the network depending on the problem, but honestly, there wasn't much trouble that popped up. People were tired and busy. Trouble came from boredom, and there was plenty to keep busy with around here.

It landed, and he stiffened up a bit, trying to figure me out, no doubt. He tried again. "I figured this was the kind of place I could come help out in exchange for a place to stay. Given the current state of things, it's easy for one to come to the conclusion that you could use a hand."

Selfishness, of course. "Because God forbid you help out, out of the kindness of your heart."

"In this economy?" he rebutted.

Growing tired of his back and forth, I started walking, making motion for him to follow.

"You're going to be exhausting, aren't you?"

"Well, you aren't exactly a ball of sunshine, pretty lady."

Though he could not see for himself, my lips upturned in disgust at the thought of being under another man's gaze. I walked off, leaving a tight ring of fire at his feet, preventing him from being too far from me in case he proved to be of danger.

CHAPTER
FOURTEEN

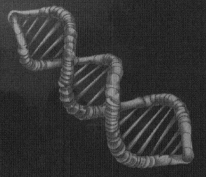

ALEXIARES

I tried to maintain my positive facade, but this girl was getting on my nerves. She upped her pace every time I attempted to walk in step with her and tightened the ring of fire in silent protest.

Following her through the perfectly laid cobble paths of The Compound, I took in my surroundings. We passed under an arch that connected two of the massive buildings near the gate I had originally entered through. The top of the archway had metal finishings on the windows that gleamed against the lamps that now lit the pathway from the dark night sky.

Though the path was empty, I tried to envision it lined with people. I hadn't been around another group in months. My fists clenched together, trying to rein in any signs of anger. Hoping that with a decent enough attitude, I'd be welcomed to stay.

"Where are you taking me?" I asked, finally managing to match my steps to hers.

Her frame was frail in a way that suggested she hadn't eaten in months, clothes just a bit too baggy against the sway of her hips. Her curls sat in a lopsided bun at the top of her head and her eyes were red rimmed, as if she hadn't slept in days. *Some version of a General.* I thought, questioning just how my stay here would go. Her eyes narrowed as if she had read the statement on my face.

"I'm taking you somewhere, called some place, that exists in some part of The Compound, that you may or may not be allowed to stay in," she retorted as she picked up her pace once more, the leash of fire urging me to stay close.

A few minutes later we entered another narrow pathway that had large stone steps with different plants hanging amongst the side of the building walls. Gas lamps littered every few feet to light the small gaps of night sky that peeked through the arched walkways between buildings. It dawned on me that the plants and lamp posts were not just functional, but also decoration, a more personalized area than the one I had just left. Realization set in; I could tell this place was going to be different from what I had imagined when I started my journey here months ago.

The dark archways let up and I marveled at the large Victorian style building at the end of the clearing. The ground beneath me changed to a darker stone and there were patches of meticulously maintained grass with benches along the side. *What is this place?*

It was sure as hell different from where I'd come from. Different environments brought out different people I supposed.

"Compound Hall."

I nearly crashed into her back as she suddenly came to a stop and motioned towards the haunting building. I didn't bother with a response as I sarcastically offered her my arm, indicating for her to lead the way. Her thick brows furrowed, nose scrunching as she looked it up and down. Ultimately deciding against it, and instead releasing her fire magic, offering me a bit of grace with my movements as she led the way once more.

As we entered the building, I noticed the sudden change of architecture, the inside sporting black-and-white tiled floor and tan hallways lined with photos. Some from before the bombs went off, some from around The Compound. I saw the General in a few, or what used to be this ghost of a girl. She smiled in one in the middle of two girls in what appeared to be the green space outside the building.

One dressed questionably considering the times, arms raised and mouth open as if she were having the time of her life. The other with tattoos covering both her arms, smiling meekly, not matching her grungy attire or the intensity behind her dark brown eyes.

The General laughed at someone to the left of the shot, her brown cheeks vibrant with color and thick curls falling down the sides of her pointed face. Her black jeans were filled out and her arms lean with muscle. Resembling nothing of the shell of a girl standing impatiently beside me today.

A door to my left flew open, and she cleared her throat, diverting my attention back towards her. I peered at the inscription at the top of the wooden door frame, INTAKE ROOM, and made my way inside.

Yet again, I found myself taken aback by surprise at the change of decor within. I'd say it was nauseating if I wasn't seriously impressed by these people's desire to pretend life was okay. That life was normal.

A floor to ceiling archway window took up most of the space on the adjacent wall with heavy curtains on the sides. Two large chairs sat with their backs to the windows. A circular leather ottoman lay in the middle with a tray that had a teapot and a few teacups on top.

I realized that there was no variation between the materials of the bookcase and walls, as I took in the wooden vaulted ceilings as well. To the immediate left of the door was a solid wooden desk that had paperwork covering each side.

"Have a seat," she commanded, expecting me to cooperate like one of her soldiers.

"Aren't you going to offer me something to drink? Some tea?" I retorted, as I took a seat in the surprisingly comfortable chair to the right. I could see why the design choice for this room had been made, to make people comfortable, to envision this place as home. Because that's what this reminded me of: a father's home office.

"No," she said, deadpanning me, "But I am going to ask you some questions, then we'll decide if you can or cannot have some of said tea."

"Okay then, as you wish, princess." If she had every intention of remaining unpleasant, then there was no need to keep up the nice guy charade. It would do me no favors with her.

"*General*," she emphasized.

"General … ?" I asked, trying to pry more information out of her, seeing where she would and wouldn't budge.

"General Bennett. But I'm the one asking the questions here." She arranged paperwork on the desk before glancing back up at me at her leisure. "And you are?"

"Alexiares," I offered, "But most call me Alexi."

"Okay Alexiares, last name?"

"Does that really matter in this world anymore? It's not like you can run a background check or anything." I knew I was getting snippy, but shit as dumb as surnames was a stupid thing to ask when they no longer held any weight.

People came and went all the time. People that were smiling in your face one moment, were dead the next. Formalities and that level of personalization and recognition were nonsensical, as far as I was concerned.

"It matters here. While you may see what we have here, and think it's silly or irrelevant or downright dumb, here at The Compound we believe that civilization will win in the end. And the cost of civilization and order being maintained is that we have to *act* like civilized beings. So yes, we keep up with traditions. It's often the little things that keep people grounded in morality. Now I'll ask you one more time, Alexiares. What's your last name?"

I wasn't going to go back and forth with her on this. She'd made fair points, but I wasn't sure how long I was staying and I was damn sure not buying everything the morality police of this place had to sell.

How well were things *really* going for them with this mindset, anyway? Their General looked as though she'd been through five world wars, their gate had been breached in the blink of an eye, and I'd slipped through the gaps in their patrol with a welcome mat laid at my feet. Maybe they should focus on the realities of their situation before focusing on what she referred to as *the little things*.

"What kind of questions?" I asked, holding firm in my decision to not offer up any information I didn't feel necessary. She studied me, her lopsided hair bouncing as she shook her head in disbelief.

"Questions about your family and your background. Where you came from and how you just happened to end up here on the eve we were attacked. About your past and your hopes and dreams for the future. Nothing too invasive," she snarled, "just enough to sate any security concerns. After that we'll do a magic and physical assessment. From there, if invited to stay, you'll be provided a list of opening jobs around The Compound. You'll have a week to get acquainted with your new home and to gather your thoughts. I'll set up another meeting with Prescott, Me or Lieutenant Moore where we'll discuss your level of comfort and job placement details. Any other questions, Alexiares?" She blinked slowly, right eye twitching as she tried to hold on to what semblance of her sanity remained.

"Ask," I said, and for the first time since we met, I allowed her to do her job with ease. It'd been days since I'd slept. Hadn't been off my feet in weeks. At the moment all I wanted was to be offered a bed and a place to put my feet up, maybe a good meal.

"Good, now let's start with your name, your full name." She smirked.

CHAPTER
FIFTEEN

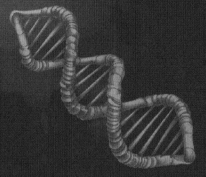

AMAIA

H e was resistant to the question of his name, though I couldn't understand why. After my third time asking, I understood I needed to back off and give up for the moment. Sometimes in this world there were things people wanted to hold close to them, to reveal when they were ready.

Having done intake on nearly half the residents here, either myself or with the help of Jax or Prescott, I'd learned that early on. Eventually, if you stopped pushing and started just listening, they'd tell you on their own at some point.

Something like a last name wasn't truly a safety concern, but merely for paperwork and record for our historian accounts.

If there was someone in our territory that we needed to be wary of, we would learn through the network, and those almost always came with pictures or drawings of the person in question. I didn't recognize his face from any and I had studied them often. Prescott knew them better than me and if he walked him up to my front door, then he'd already deciphered Alexiares was not on any of our lists. Though questionable in terms of his involvement today, he may very well end up on a list soon enough.

"Moving on then," I offered him a chance at another simple question, "tell me about your magic."

His brows furrowed together, noting that this time I had commanded an answer rather than asked him a question. "Water and Fire."

Wanting to take advantage of his newfound willingness to co-operate, I switched gears and moved on to the harder questions that needed answering. "Well, not to get all Rick Grimes on you or anything but I've got three main questions for you, given you're not really open to much else at this point." I tried to throw some humor at him, hoping maybe that would get him to open up, but by his disgruntled demeanor, I could tell it was no dice.

I gave him a few moments, a small gesture to allow him to prepare for another round of questioning. Right as I opened my mouth to continue, he glared into my eyes and answered, "I don't know how many of the dead I've killed. It's been a long journey and oh, I don't know about five damn years. I also don't know how many people I've killed. I haven't really gotten into the habit of keeping count. I'm not a serial killer. I don't keep some sick log of names."

"Odd comparison to make for someone who's trying to get an invitation to stay, but I'll look past that," I mumbled.

"And why? Why do we all do it? To survive," he finished, his honey brown eyes hardening under his intense stare.

"You said it was a journey. Journey often insinuates a long distance, mind telling me where you came from and why you left?" It was an odd feeling, slipping back into my role. The questions came out naturally, mechanically as they had many times before.

"The Expanse. I was tired of the cold, so I wandered west. Heard it was warmer out here."

I was growing impatient with his short, vague responses. The vaguer he was, the more drawn out this entire process was going to be, never mind the fact that he still had to do his other assessments.

Seth and I hadn't even yet had the opportunity to sit down and discuss how things would go now that I was back. How we could work in tandem and utilize each other's strengths and weaknesses. We needed to develop a schedule. Then there were the rounds we needed to make to the loved ones of those we'd lost today and help with funeral arrangements. Basically, a lot of shit to do and one asshole hogging up my time.

I huffed in irritation. "Ya know what, bud? I don't have time for this." Dropping his paperwork with a thud onto the desk, I scooted the chair back and walked to stand directly in front of him, over him. "You don't want to answer my basic questions, fine. You want to be vague, even better. Quite frankly, if I had been the one to find you out there today, you'd not have made it past these gates. But Prescott found you, not me. Consider this your lucky day."

He rose to his feet, purposely positioning himself to tower over me, not appreciating the tone of which I was speaking. A man like him probably didn't let women feel comfortable enough to speak to him in this manner, *ever*.

"We can drag this out as long as you'd wish. It won't matter. Not until you finish answering the questions, *I* deem important enough to be answered. And until any of that happens, until you've been assessed and can be placed, you'll be stuck next to *me*." My eyes narrowed, daring him to push back.

I could have sworn a growl left his throat in challenge at the thought, but I chose not to acknowledge it. It didn't matter what intimidation tactics he attempted to use or how he went about irritating me. At the end of the day, I was the one with power. He'd either have to fall to it or leave. Simple as that.

He must have been on the same mental track as he put in a bit more effort of pleasantry as he mumbled his next words, "And when can I expect this assessment to take place?"

"Tomorrow morning. Or night. Who knows. I have a few meetings I need to set up and some training to oversee. Of course, there are also the funerals to assist with, and I need to check in with my family. I'm extending a courtesy by saying I can either squeeze you in at dawn or late tomorrow night. Had you not wasted the last hour of our time, I may have been in the mood to get all of this over with. But now I'm hungry, I'm tired, and I really, really don't want to hear much more of your voice today. Or I might actually lose my shit. And if I lose my shit … well, you're not going to like the outcome of that."

He didn't need nor deserve any of the details; I was over sharing; I knew that. But I found myself not caring to put in any more effort in formalities tonight. I was damn tired of mourning, but evidently, mourning wasn't yet tired of me.

"Sleeping accommodations?" he asked, clearly just as worn and tired as I was. My eyes shot to his stomach as I heard it growl from my side of our little stand-off.

"There's a holding room in The Pit. It has a cot and a toilet, the essentials." Deciding to be somewhat courteous, I added, "We can grab some food on the way back. I'll have your things brought to your quarters once I've had time to check your bag."

"Check my bag? For what exactly?" His voice went low, not in a threatening way but challenging enough to make you second think your next words.

I understood people could be touchy about it during the intake process. Most of the things they carried with them were the last remnants of their life in The Before.

They were personal items. At times I felt guilty for invading their space, but when it came to uncooperative assholes, it was always better to be safe than sorry. Who knew what he could be carrying on him. I wasn't going to be the one who slipped up for the second time in one day. I couldn't fail my people again.

I wouldn't.

I held his gaze steady, letting him know this wasn't one of the things I was willing to budge on, even tonight. "Yes, it's my duty to my people to make sure that everyone who enters this wall isn't a threat to our security. You'll hear this a lot, but here it's *Compound first.* So I'll be checking your bag for any weapons, and depending on if you'll be allowed to stay or not, you'll be allowed to keep *some.* The amount will depend on your position. The rest you can check out of one of the weapon offices near one of the gates once you leave these walls, or if you prefer to practice with a certain weapon during your training. Everything else is yours to keep. We won't touch it again after the initial inspection."

"Compound first, sounds embarrassingly dystopian," he retorted, a bit of humor coming back to his voice.

"Hey, no one said you had to stay, bud. There are several gates you can take your leave through," I half joked, but my stomach turned.

Something told me I needed to watch him a bit more carefully. He was hiding something, but I couldn't tell what. And I certainly hadn't been able to clear him from involvement in today's events, though I doubted I'd ever know for certain. I'd have to get Reina in here for the next time I questioned him, see if she could sense anything behind his words.

Turning on my heels I made my way through the door, placing my leash of fire around him once more, keeping him close as we made our way through The Compound towards The Kitchens. The moist huff on his breath hit the back of my neck, hard to accomplish from the difference in our height, and I tried to contain my rising anger. I had no desire to satisfy his efforts to irritate me.

I wanted to send him on his way back through North Gate. Wanted to tell him to get lost, but there was something in my gut telling me to keep him around. That he would play an important role in whatever lay ahead.

The streets of The Compound were still pretty empty, and I assumed everyone who didn't need to be out for work would be tucked away in their homes until morning. Reasonable fear taking root in a place that they had once felt tremendously safe in. I nodded at the few people we did pass as we approached the end of the General Living Quarters and moved towards the center of our little town.

The second the aroma of cornbread and soup hit my nostrils, our stomachs growled in unison. Had I been next to one of my friends, I probably would have laughed at the idea of our bodies being in sync, but not with him. I hoped to never be in sync with a man that had probably never said anything genuine or positive in his life.

I stopped and allowed him to stand at my side, calling my fire back into my body as I turned to him, assessing his current mood. "We go in, we get our food to *go*. You stay next to me and you look at me, and only me. Not a glance at a single one of these people. They've been through more than enough today. They don't need to withhold the scrutinizing glare of the scary-looking stranger that showed up at their front door in the midst of an attack."

He cracked his knuckles, his smirk telling me he was enjoying some sick joke inside his head. No words left his lips, and I think that pissed me off more than whatever he could have said. Uncomfortable from his pressing stare, I started walking towards the doors.

We entered the large glass building, and I heard his breath catch, his reaction filling an empty space in my heart with pride.

"Beautiful, isn't it?" I asked, moving us towards the to-go counter that stood in the center of the room, also doubling as the coffee counter. My mouth watered at the thought of a sweet yet bitter cup warming my tongue.

"I don't know. Seems like a waste of energy to me. Somewhere out there, there's a tome full of more important things to do in the middle of an apocalypse than play interior decorator." I wasn't thrown off by his tone this time. I knew how hard life was out in The Expanse.

I'd been out that way once for an emissary trip to one of our larger ally communities in Duluth, Minnesota. They pretty much utilized the downtown area and its existing structures and built a wall around mirroring ours, designed to keep those who were unwanted out. But their way of living was different from ours. Harder living, that was for sure.

The weather extremes were harsher up north. A place where winters were already pretty long, turning into an entire territory of perma-winter, their warmer days imitating the end of fall at best. Sure, their citizens with air magic could temperature regulate the city, but that would mean a consistent, and significant, drain on power, and drained power means vulnerability in face of an attack. Three and a half years ago, when territories were being established and borders were being drawn, the idea of an attack was much more likely as groups sought to display their dominance or expand their area.

As time went on, attacks from other groups were less likely, and since humans took more time, effort, and magic than the dead, more magic was able to be spared as the attacks diminished. Even still, their time was geared more towards survival, and while they did indulge in some luxuries, decor and infrastructure were definitely not one of them.

Infrastructure was kept up to code for safety and warmth up there, not beauty. Only thing harder than that would be living out in Covert Province, it was hard enough trying to survive, couldn't imagine it being under some sort of dictatorship.

"When you have a community this large, we found that once the more important things were established, people were best fit working in professions they love. Something they have passion and pride behind. It's something I wished there was emphasis on in The Before, and Prescott saw the value in it enough to bring it here. The possibilities of what you can provide to this community are endless, Alexiares." One glance this way and the look on his face made me pity him for a moment. His visage resembling every bit of a lost dog.

"It takes some getting used to, that's for sure. But who's saying beauty can't also be purposeful?" I added, pointing out the herbs and other medicinal flora hanging from the walls and ceiling.

As we approached the counter, I forced a smile at the teenager behind the counter, careful to present a calm demeanor when tensions ran high. "Hey Elie, how's it going?" I asked.

"A little shaken up, but I'm okay, for the most part. Mom and Rex were already off their shifts from the Stables and at home. Dad's still out on the fishing trip, but he asked about you before he left. Wanted to know how *you* were doing after everything? I hope you don't mind me askin'. I told him you were strong, you could get through anything, but he *insisted* I ask. You know how he is." The small girl rambled on, hair resembling mine, though her brown skin was a deeper tone.

I kept my smile pretty, knowing how much she admired me. She wanted to be a soldier one day, though both her parents and I tried to sway her from this life. Representation was important, but I didn't want to be responsible for such a pure heart taking such a dark turn by facing the realities of life outside these walls.

Surrounded by death, the dying, and the dead.

A few times a week if I missed lunch, she'd stop by after her shift with a warm coffee and any remaining scraps before The

Kitchens started prepping for dinner. She'd sip on her own coffee, watching me interact with my soldiers and mimicking their fighting stances.

It wasn't that I didn't care or appreciate her family, but Jax's death was the last thing I wanted to talk about moving forward. I knew that they cared about me too, but I was ready to try to let go of the hurt and focus on figuring out what was going on around here. *That* would do more good than my tears.

Alexiares sighed next to me, clearly growing impatient with the one-sided conversation taking place. I waited for a natural pause before I interrupted, "Hey Elie? We're on a bit of a time crunch, can you please bring us two coffees to-go, two orders of cornbread, vegetable soup for me and turkey & veggie soup for him."

She smiled and nodded her head in acknowledgment before heading towards the back where the actual kitchen was. Alexiares and I turned towards each other at the same time before awkwardly turning away as I let him survey the rest of the rooms.

"So, you're not just informal with me. Good to know," he muttered low, testing my patience and seeing if I would react.

I moved my neck side to side, letting his words roll off me as if they didn't matter. I didn't understand why he was rash and testy with me, someone who was responsible for whether he could stay or go, but chalked it up to just being his personality. Shit, maybe he was this insufferable in The Before too.

"Why would I require a regular citizen to treat me as if I were their superior?" I deadpanned.

The idea of that made no sense to me. I wanted their respect, sure. But respect was earned, not given. And at the end of the day, I was here to serve them and their safety, not the other way around.

"From what I've seen so far, maybe a traditional approach to things would do some good around here." His eyes lingered on my chest and my shorts as the words slipped off his mouth and my eyes squinted in disgust.

I turned towards the counter, fully intending on being the one to go quiet this time, but biting my tongue had never been a strength of mine. "You've been here for what? Less than five hours? How would you know? Besides, traditional is an ironic word choice coming from the likes of *you*." My eyes lingered on his chest and waistline this time, giving him the same energy in return, making my distaste for him clear.

I knew it was a low blow. Watched it slap him in the face, an apology formed on my lips as he replied, "Turkey soup for me, but not you. Why?"

Shocked at the sudden turn in conversation and his sudden interest in my eating preferences, but thankful for the change in conversation, I hesitated before replying, "I'm a pescatarian, but most days I prefer no meat at all."

"Hm." My eyes squinted at his non-answer. I found myself pleading with Elie to stop chatting up whoever was able to corner back there so this entire interaction could come to an end.

"Hm," I mimicked.

"I was going to suggest some extra protein may help your ... condition,"—he gestured to my body, clearly meaning my frail state—"your strength. But I see now that you wouldn't take advice from *the likes of* me."

His dig at my appearance stung. My exhaustion and hunger turned to anger at his audacity and the way he felt comfortable to comment on my body and judge my decisions, but it faded as his point hit home. I'd just done the same to him.

My lips pursed at the guilt. "I'm informal with the citizens because I want them to know that they can trust me, feel safe with me. Not only that, I *want* to know about them, I care about them and, more importantly, I'm responsible for them. I know that I'm

General, but I don't and never have claimed to know it all. I do my best, Alexiares, it's all I can do. The rest I just learn along the way."

He said nothing as we both faced the counter once more, just in time to spot Elie headed our way. *Finally.*

I thanked Elie and grabbed my portion of the food. Alexiares' eyes slid towards my cornbread container, noting the difference in size between my pan and his small plate wrapped in foil.

"The extra carbs should help with *my condition*," I teased, suddenly energized by the thought of one of my favorite foods. Stomach excited at the little pieces of sweet corn that littered throughout the perfectly fluffy yet squishy bread.

He chuckled at the desire in my eyes and walked off as if he knew where he was going. I found my footing and led our way back through the parts of The Compound we had already walked, not yet ready to expose every side street, tunnel, and alley to him.

When we arrived at The Pit, I surveyed the damage remaining. From what was visible to my eye, not much was left aside from a small bit of debris. Water and fire magic helped speed the clean-up process along drastically. I sighed with relief at the one less to-do item on my list, still daunted by the long night that lay ahead. It was around eight p.m. and I'd likely be up working until the early morning hours, only to be up again to resume my duties not too long after my head hit my pillows.

I walked towards the lounging room at the center of The Pit to see who was hanging around, wanting to keep their hands busy or take on an extra shift. There'd be a few antsy soldiers desperate to find some way to spend their time as their nerves were fed by the pulsating air from the attack. Though I doubted watching a prisoner who wasn't technically a prisoner was on their list of ways they wanted to spend their night.

A few soldiers eyed me upon entering, blinking slowly, trying to process if it was actually me standing before them. I knew chatter had probably been going around about me being out of my quarters today. Followed by more chatter on my small role in defending our home, but they probably assumed it was just that, chatter.

After a few awkward breaths, every soldier in the room snapped up at attention.

"Soldiers," I said, acknowledging the gesture and placing them at ease. I pushed my shoulders forward, head high. "I need two guards outside Cell C for an overnight shift."

I didn't bother making it as a question; they understood that me posing it as a volunteer opportunity was a privilege in itself. A series of "Ma'ams," flew around the room as each one offered up their services, though most didn't sincerely desire to be selected. Glancing around the room, I settled on two whose faces shone from genuine interest, bringing them out towards the courtyard to brief them as Alexiares lingered behind. The distaste for his situation obvious in his scrunched up face.

"If you keep on scowling like that, you'll need rounds of Botox that we don't have," I called over the soldiers' shoulders as they chuckled in response.

His brows furrowed even further as he bit down on his lip, resisting the urge to respond. A few moments later, when the soldiers were up to speed, they turned towards Alexiares, ready to guide him towards his cell. They stopped, giving me a moment to speak to him before they departed.

"Your belongings will be to you before morning once I have time to settle in and review. After you eat, the guards will take you to the bathing area to wash up, or before if you wish. I suggest you get some sleep. Tomorrow will be long."

"What time should I be ready?" he asked.

"When I can get to you," I said, leaving it at that as I went to find the next available soldier to send a message to Seth about setting up a meeting for tomorrow.

CHAPTER

SIXTEEN

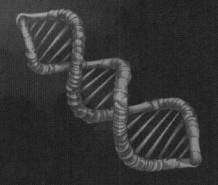

AMAIA

After leaving the new town psycho in the guards' hands, I made my way back to the lounge. Opting to recruit a few more soldiers to do my bidding in order to cut down on my action items for the evening. I sent one soldier to arrange a morning meeting with Seth in my study to discuss the transfer of power and the second to go gather Alexiares' belongings from the gate and to bring them to my study.

On the walk back to my quarters, I mentally prepared my schedule for the day ahead. I'd oversee some training to assess the condition of my soldiers before and after my meetings. Then I'd have lunch with my family, make sure everyone was okay and on the mend after today's events.

There was a hole in my heart from their absence in my daily routine, and I longed to have that piece of my life back. But I also knew it would take a lot of work for us to get back to how things were before. *If* things could ever go back to how they were when we were all missing such a large piece.

Given that the day had already been long and traumatic enough for everyone, I pushed meeting the families and helping with funeral arrangements to the next afternoon. Coming to the conclusion that it was best to at least give loved ones a night in private grief. It hadn't been too long ago that I'd appreciated the privacy everyone had given me, allowing me to grieve in my own space, on my own time.

I'd deal with Alexiares' assessment in the morning if I felt up to it, otherwise he could wait as long as I cared. There was no desire to start my day with such negativity, though, I found it to be more refreshing than a morning coffee to start my day with a good fight. Maybe I'd hop in there myself. I could use the practice. I'd been banking on muscle memory, and it'd be good to step in with training, offer guidance or provide a demonstration without revealing myself to be an uncoordinated idiot. Not to mention it'd probably feel good to smack the smug grin off his face as well.

I entered my study, slumping onto one of the chairs as Harley greeted me with licks to the hand, my skin cold against the touch of the soft leather. I closed my eyes for a moment, one hell of a day, and it wasn't even my first official one back. I was exhausted, but more than exhausted, I was *hungry*. Realizing the containers of food that now sat in my lap, I took a long sip of my now warm coffee and savored the bitter yet sweet taste. The thought of that excited me, suddenly realizing what had taken her so long.

Opening my tray of cornbread, I grinned, taking in the slightly undercooked center of the pan. Elie had gone back to request a fresh pan be taken from the oven, just to appease me. Give me something tailored to my liking. To make my day even after hers had likely been terrifying as she awaited news of her loved one's being okay on the other side of the attack. A tear slid down my face and I made a mental note to thank her later as I dug in.

Halfway through the pan, I remembered the soup I'd set down on the table nearby, using it to wash down the thick bread. My stomach hadn't been this full in ages, and I couldn't help but admit that it felt good. Sipping the remaining broth, a knock came to my door, startling me as I wiped my lips and made my way towards the door. Harley stood alert, ready to defend me if need be.

A soldier stood there holding a large backpack, the sizing of his gear odd for someone who'd been traveling for the time the journey to the coast would have taken. I took the bag, thanking them and closing the door, sitting it down across the room near my desk.

Swiftly, I cleared it from all the backlogged paperwork I had to catch up on. His heavy book bag thudded against my desk as I dropped it down. I cursed, remembering my friends seeking rest in the next room. *This thing is heavier than it looks.*

The first zipper contained the typical items I'd stumble across when opening every pack: a compass and a few maps. There weren't any markings on the maps worth noting, nor were there any words along the sides showing where he came from and where he was trying to end up. Either he was truly just putting his life in fate's hands and seeing where the wind took him, or he was smart enough to never mark his comings or goings. Which would make sense if he were another territory's spy.

Especially one from The Expanse. They were not gentle or innately kind people, everything there was about survival, and their soldiers were highly trained to ensure that they would. Or their secrets would die with them.

While most occupations up north were friendly with us, if not allies or within our trade network, everyone had their own secrets. Riley was living proof of that. Not a single soul outside these walls knew of his gifts, and I had to imagine there were more like him out there. There were probably a million other gifts or research discoveries out that we'd never know of, unless an ally felt the need to disclose it, for reasons of their own.

I moved on to the next zipper in the middle, yet again finding nothing to be surprised at. A few throwing knives sheathed in their respective covers, an extra holster, some ammo. An emergency tent, rolled up cargo pants, some extra socks, a balled-up camo jacket, and a bunch of individually packaged dried meats and fruits. The only thing nagging me in the back of my mind was that there were no clothes in here that would sustain him in a colder climate, especially the one he claimed to hail from.

My skin warmed as anger burrowed into my chest at the thought of being lied to. *The Expanse my ass.* I tugged at the final zipper; toilet paper, soap, a canteen, two guns, gas mask, a small blanket and, at the bottom lay a notebook. *Gotcha.* I took a seat in my chair, ready to get comfortable as I read through it, but found myself irritated instead. Not a single word was written in English.

They were dated, and I thought back to my undergraduate European Archaeology course, *Greek. The son of the bitch speaks Greek, perfect.* I thought, both impressed that the asshole was bilingual, but annoyed at the extra legwork it would take to decipher this. That explained the accent. No one I knew spoke Greek. Though there was bound to be someone, it would take a while to get the message out and have it read through. Would probably take just as long for Tomoe to divert her own research, and spend time using books to translate it. I could just ask him, but it would be naïve to take a stranger by their word, especially one that had been this cagey.

Slamming the book shut I let out a deep sigh, throwing my head back on the chair's headrest. Closing my eyes, I tried to drive out my frustrations and center myself in the now. It'd been a long day, and I was drained. My head felt lightheaded and my heart palpitated every few minutes under the weight of all the stress.

It was time to call it a night. Glancing at the clock on the edge of the desk, I noted the time. *Eleven p.m.* I groaned, realizing I would be up in less than six hours. Before heading to my bathing room, I opened the main door, letting Harley out to relieve herself while I took care of my own needs in the tub. As I brushed my teeth, the loud, dramatic howl of my girl came from outside my door, begging to be let in for bed.

"You're so dramatic," I said as I rushed to open the door. She pranced in, oblivious to the fact that she just woke up half The Compound. "As if I would ever leave you out there all night. Please." My final words were muffled as my mouth filled with saliva and toothpaste.

Minutes later, I slid into bed between Riley and Jax's untouched side of the bed, letting out a quiet huff. Riley's breathing was back to normal, and I heard Moe's snores from across the room.

"Night, Jaxy," I mumbled pathetically to his side of the bed, before turning towards Riley and letting myself surrender to sleep.

BIRDS CHIRPED OUTSIDE MY WINDOW AND MY EYES SHOT OPEN. IT wasn't unusual, I'd always been a light sleeper. In fact, I banked on them being present in the mornings as a natural alarm. Even when it was too cold or rainy for the birds, my internal clock shook my body awake.

The sky was a beautiful mix of pink and purple, letting me know it was time to start my first official day back. My stomach turned at the thought of being under all the pressure once more, but my duties were my duties. I surveyed Harley as my feet hit the floor. In typical fashion, she didn't budge. I smiled. No matter how well I trained the girl, early hours would never be instilled in her stubborn mind. What *was* unusual was the fact that Riley had managed to sneak out during the early morning hours without my detection. Hs feet often moved as quiet as the creatures he commanded.

The floor of my bathroom chilled my toes as I sent fire to my feet to keep them warm, knowing my magic wouldn't dare betray me and turn me into its victim. Definitively deciding I would take advantage of the opportunity to train myself this morning, I slid on some leggings, a sports bra, and a black tank top before putting on the rest of my gear and sneakers. Not bothering to check whatever horrid version of me reflected back in the mirror, I pulled my hair up into its typical bun and headed out the door.

Still pissed from my revelation of his lie, starting my morning with a bit of chaos sounded like the best course forward. The guards I'd posted outside the door took one glimpse at the sinister smile on my face and the bucket of water in my hands, and moved aside before I opened my mouth.

Moving faster than even I expected, I swung the door open and tossed the water directly onto him and his cot in one quick movement. In the next motion, his bag followed, swinging from my shoulder and onto the floor on the other side of the room.

His eyes blazed with fury and surprise as he let out a feral scream shooting up from his bed and onto his feet.

"Up and at 'em. Time for your assessment," I said, tossing some training clothes towards him. Turning on my heels to leave, I passed on the chance to give him a moment to process what had happened or a chance to respond.

His heavy footsteps sounded as he made an angry beeline towards me as I sat on a nearby bench minutes later, picking at my nails.

"What the fuck is your deal? Huh?" he spat, not afraid to enter my personal space or paying mind to the soldiers that were once guarding his door now closing in, ready to intervene on my behalf.

I moved my hand up, gesturing to them to let me deal with it myself. Rising to my feet, I took a step closer towards him, closing what little gap was left, making my breath nearly his.

"I don't appreciate being lied to," I said frankly, not interested in holding back.

"Lied to about what," he challenged.

A command, not a question. I didn't appreciate the alpha sense of authority he felt that he posed. I wouldn't back down, and I damn sure wouldn't submit.

I was ready to tell him that he would no longer be treated as an impending resident, and that he was now officially a prisoner when Seth rounded the corner.

"What's going on here?" he said as I looked towards him, eyes already storming, waiting and ready for a fight.

"Nothing," Alexiares replied with familiarity, as if he had already spoken with Seth before. His eyes were still trained on mine.

Seth removed the usual cowboy hat he sported when he was out in the Stables with the livestock and his horses. Given the time, that was probably where he was headed now that I took in his jeans and riding boots.

"I was just about to tell this *prisoner*, it was time to go back to his cell until he can get escorted out," I said, turning to face Seth completely, thinking he would support my decision.

Seth took in my features, recognizing my current state, and extended a hand to pull me aside for more privacy.

"I'm sorry," he said, catching me off guard, "I didn't mean to put you in this situation. I meant to tell you last night, but there was a lot to discuss and Tomoe was doing bad. I just—" His voice cracked as his thin lips pulled into a sad, exhausted smile.

I saved him the awkwardness of having to bare his emotions to me. We were family, but that boundary of emotional intimacy had never been breached in this relationship. "I understand that, and appreciate the apology. But he lied to me. I think. There're just things that aren't adding up around here and I feel like he has something to do with it."

Something changed in his freckled face. He was calculating. "Then let him stick around," he decided. "Keep him close and see what comes of it. Have Riley put a detail on him and wait it out. Keep your enemies close and all that. Do you have anything concrete?"

I glimpsed over my shoulder to find Alexiares watching us intently, studying my lips, reading our conversation. Taking a step closer to Seth, I lowered my voice, not knowing the full extent of Alexiares' powers.

There'd been so much time between now and the last time I'd seen my friend that'd I'd forgotten the extent of his stature. I assumed he'd been reasonably tall and athletic in The Before, but his *Supra* gene had only accentuated those details. At nearly seven feet tall, each graceful step he took was powered by pure functional strength and muscle.

If an outsider were to observe the two of us speaking, they'd likely wrongly assume who was in charge here. Not knowing that the ones who were the biggest threat often lay in plain sight. Overlooked.

"Just a few hunches," I replied after some thought. Opting to keep some things to myself until we were able to meet in private later on.

"Then continue on with the assessment," he said simply, "the rest we'll deal with as we're presented with information. I'm not sure throwing out someone who could be our enemy is the best course of action. And unless you have a plan to convince Prescott of execution without a fair trial ..."

I rolled my eyes. *Fair points.* I started to turn away before he grabbed my hand, wheeling me back. "Welcome back." Grinning, he pulled me into a hug and turned away himself.

Restraining the desire to send shards of gravel through his skull, I brushed past Alexiares and his smirking face. It was my turn to smile.

"Let's go," I ordered. "The first part of your assessment starts now."

"And the lie I supposedly told?" He clearly wasn't ready to drop the subject.

I could see the defiance in his eyes. The way my call out personally affected his ego made my stomach churn.

"We'll get to that. After the assessment," I leveled, not wanting to speak any more than I had to.

His dark eyes scanned the area, waiting for someone else to show up. "Against who?"

"Usually recruits, but I could go for a punch or two at the moment, so ... me."

He blinked at me, clearly thinking I was joking. "No offense, but you don't exactly appear to be in the position to throw or take *any* type of slap at the moment, let alone a punch from a grown ass man." Gesturing towards my body, not focusing on one weakness, but rather referring to the entirety of me as being one. I sent a jab to his ribs to prove a point, and he bent over, gasping for air.

My lips turned down as my nose crinkled, face mocking him and his current state. "Nah, I feel just fine, actually. And just because you say 'no offense' doesn't mean someone won't take offense. Now"—I nodded a few feet away where The Ring was as I removed my weapons strapped intermittently on my body—"go on in. First, we'll assess hand-to-hand, then we'll move into weaponry. Everyone is assessed by the standard three; bow & arrow, guns, and metal. Though if you have a weapon of preference outside of those, I'd be happy to add in an *extra* portion of the assessment."

"You don't find it a bit silly to focus on weaponry when you have magic literally in your hands. Ain't that a bit of a risk? Hell, why waste time training and making materials—"

Before he could finish asking yet another stupid question, I decided to save him the breath, ready to get this over with and move on with my day. "Magic fails. Magic has different levels of power. People lose control in tough situations and in the face of danger. When one thing is no longer an option, it's always good to have a few things in your back pocket. Besides," I added, "some of our magic *is* the gift of weaponry."

His eyes sparked with realization as he glanced over me, finally seeing the danger that lay within me. I smirked at him, happy that for the first time in a long time, someone looked at me for the dangerous person I once was. *Still* was. Not some fragile damsel mourning the loss of her prince. It felt good to feel a bit like myself, and I knew only one thing would make me feel even better at this moment.

I grabbed onto his arm while throwing a strategically placed kick on his shin, and pulled, tossing him onto the ground as if he were nothing but a rag doll.

"Now. Get your *grown ass* into The Ring," I said as I hopped in, turning my back towards him, refusing to recognize him as a threat.

CHAPTER
SEVENTEEN

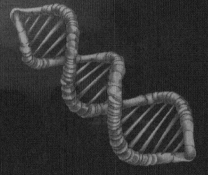

AMAIA

The second he entered The Ring, he made his move, taking a quick step towards me as I threw a punch, not giving him a chance to get his bearings. His left arm reached for my left side in an attempt to distract me as he threw a strong right. I quickly fell into my rhythm, the thrill of a fight invigorating me. A dancer hitting the stage for the first time after a torn Achilles.

I was ready for him. Dropping my left shoulder and I grabbed his right wrist once more, catching his eye for a moment as I smirked in my accomplishment before I dropped him to his knees with the same move I had only used a few minutes prior.

It was his turn to be ready for me. He didn't quite come down to his knees, but I took advantage of his stagger. Jumping a few inches and throwing a kick towards the upper portion of his to so. He caught it. Just barely, using the momentum to pull himself back to his feet, ready to throw another punch. *Impressive, but not that impressive.* I thought to myself as I continued to dodge his every move, always just slightly out of reach.

A small crowd of soldiers had gathered near the edge of The Ring, enthralled with watching their leader back in action. I fed off their energy, allowing the rage of the past few months to surface and fuel my next move.

Reaching for his right side, I hooked my hand near the cusp of the bend in his arm and pulled down using his weight and the momentum of my movement to hoist myself airborne and twisted. Wrapping my legs around his neck, I forced him to carry me.

Taking a deep breath, I threw the weight of my body down, making gravity bend to my will as I brought him to the ground, flipping him onto his back. A whoosh came from his lungs as he gasped for air and cheers from the small group that had gathered rang out.

His cheeks turned bright red as he glared at me with embarrassment, gasping for air, teeth chattering, and I smirked at him, not caring to spare his feelings. I knew what I'd done wasn't right. Making a public display out of someone who, to be fair, had fighting skills enough to qualify for a soldier, depending how the rest of his assessment turned out. I shook off the thought, knowing there were still secrets he held that made the rest a moot point.

If his ego was fragile enough that he allowed himself to be embarrassed by that, then oh well. That was a him problem. But I knew that the truth was, he *was* really good. Even I could admit that he fought with precision, speed and skill that reflected a well trained soldier, which did no favors for my current suspicions. He'd surprisingly winded me a bit, though I had no intention of letting that be known. I wasn't in the best of conditions, but he was quick and forced me to fight at a higher skill level. One that only

Jax and Seth had forced me to match, well them and a terribly intoxicated and pissed off Tomoe.

I stood up and offered him my hand. He glared at me in return, opting to stand on his own, leaving me hanging.

"Mad you got your ass kicked by a girl?" I teased.

"What's next?" His voice was harsh. He was pissed off. Eyes darting to the side at the soldiers still watching from the sidelines.

Humbling myself, I forced myself to act as a proper leader and put the personal issues I had with him aside. Raising my voice just loud enough for the onlookers to hear, but still quiet enough to sound natural, I offered him an honest out, "I'm impressed. It's been a while since I've felt challenged in a fight."

"I don't need your pity," he said quietly, brown eyes staring into the depths of my own, making a chill trickle down my spine.

"Whatever," I said as I watched the soldiers disperse under my intense gaze. "Take it to heart if you want. I'm *Umbra Mortis*. My entire existence is a weapon. Our shooting range is through here. Helps keep away The Pansies."

Nodding my head in the direction of my home away from home, I grabbed my weapons from the side of The Ring. Not bothering to check and see if he followed in my wake.

The shooting range stored most of our troops' weapons that were general knowledge. We also had the weapon offices around The Compound. They held the rest plus what the civilians had brought in with them available to check out, and then there were the *better* weapons. The advanced ones that required research, the ones that were known to few. Only on a need-to-know basis.

Aside from helping with sound proofing efforts, the location was rather difficult to get to. It was well-guarded due not only to what it contained, but also an emergency bunker for those vulnerable in the community as a last-ditch effort. Though everyone was expected to fight if things went to shit and the walls were ever seriously breached, everyone under sixteen, pregnant women, and those who were gravely injured, would hole up down here. It would remain the last place standing for The Compound.

I held the first door open for him as he approached on my heels before stopping near the next door. The soldiers stationed outside nodded as they knocked twice, the soldiers behind the door unlocked it from the inside. It was another measure I'd made changes to when taking over.

It was important that the knock pattern used was changed up every so often. It would only make it that much harder to breach should someone who wasn't wanted attempt to enter. Once the door opened, we entered a dark corridor. I lit the lamps with my magic as we approached each torch, and I felt the unease in his tense body as he kept close.

"Why the hell is it in some dingy dungeon?" he blurted out, sounding more nervous than he probably intended.

"It's soundproof." I smirked. "Amongst its other purposes." The idea of furthering his discomfort warmed my heart.

His shoulders sagged slightly once we approached the end of the long corridor. Gunfire erupted from the furthest door.

"We're forty feet underground." I answered his next question before he could utter it, knowing he'd probably felt the extreme change in temperature from the morning heat above.

"A bomb shelter," he stated simply.

"Yes."

I swung open the door and pointed towards the racks on the left filled with different types of guns, knives, swords, and various style bow and arrows. He walked over without me having to extend a verbal invite, grinning as he slid his fingers along the side of an EK 44. *Because that's not concerning.*

They were made for stabbing, not slashing, six inches long with a tip sharp enough to cause a sea of blood with one prick. It was a lethal weapon, meant for fighting and not as a tool. Sharp and efficient, they weren't for anyone who didn't know their way around some knife work.

He eyed me excitedly. "Which one do we start with?"

"Well, the range is just around the corner there," I said, gesturing towards the other side of the room. "Metal combat can be done in our indoor combat room, which is in the room next to us, so …"

He dropped the knife he was holding and moved towards the guns. I watched him closely, trying to gauge his thought process as I said nothing, allowing him to select weapons of his own. This was part of the assessment I never voiced to prospective citizens.

I wanted to know what they felt drawn to, what they felt comfortable with. One's choice of weapon says a lot about them. It gave you an idea of their level of confidence, and where their head is at. Observation reveals a hell of a lot, especially when people are distracted and don't think you're watching.

His hands stopped over the KAC SR15, and he grinned, pulling it down, moving on to select a pistol. "Helluva lotta options," he mumbled, curiosity lacing his voice.

"Trade networks help, but you'd be surprised how gun crazy even the most liberal of states can be. Rich assholes that wanna play tough guys were all over the nearby neighborhoods. An empty house makes the belongings fair game." I shrugged.

This time he inspected a KelTec CP33, and my blood froze as I took in his final selections. Once again, taking note of the level of skill each took to operate sufficiently and my suspicions heightened. He turned to me, awaiting my next steps, moving side to side like a kid waiting to open gifts on Christmas morning.

"Interesting choices," I offered.

"Yeah, well, I'm used to an optic on a KelTec, but the range and accuracy are pretty damn reliable. Have some extra mags and a suppressor, and it's damn near the perfect weapon. Not the best baby in the world when you're on the run, but that's what this guy's for," he said, lifting the SR15 towards the ceiling, hand away from the trigger. "And this, this beauty, well they don't call 'em America's Rifle for nothing."

My jaw dropped slightly, off guard by his analysis. "What city did you say you came from again?" I was testing him. He hadn't specified the day before, and I'd been too irritated to keep pushing.

"I didn't." He stiffened up, ready to protest at my clear intrusion but decided otherwise. "Right outside of Minneapolis."

I titled my head to the side, "And your position?" I pressed, hoping he was in the mood to be a bit more forthcoming with information today.

"A little bit of everything, worked with the troops at times, community relations at others. Pretty hands on for the most part. Jack-of-all-trades, if you will," he replied vaguely before adding some reassurance, "honest."

I chuckled, as if his swearing meant a damn thing but taking what I could get. "Won't," I replied as I started walking again, turning the corner and grabbing the ear protection on the wall before opening the final glass door.

It was his turn to go jaw slack. "You bunch don't do anything simple, do you?" he asked. My eyes narrowed. It wasn't the first time I'd noticed it, the slight bit of an accent. Regional, and hard to place, but there.

Guiding him to one of the empty rows, I pulled the string that returned the target and gave the dense object a hard shove. The momentum and track attachments made it go two hundred yards out.

"If you can hit two hundred yards, you can be trained for anything that goes out further," I said, completing the ammo set up and backing away for him to take position. "A hundred fifty yards out, you and anyone that ignorantly puts their faith in you make it out alive. A hundred yards out and your chances are already fifty-fifty. If you can't hit a damn thing past fifty yards, then, well, we have more … domestic positions available. Because at that point you're considered a safety hazard and liability more than anything else."

Grinning, I motioned for him to begin and his nose crinkled in disdain before picking up the KelTec, and showing me everything he had.

He hit the mark each time. No matter the distance, as I had a soldier with air magic, move it back and forth, simulating a moving target. His face was hard and unyielding with each pull of the trigger. He placed it down range and turned to me at the last bullet.

"Next," he said, glaring into my soul.

"Lights out," I yelled as one of the air elementals in the room suffocated them from the room at my command.

I sent my fire magic out to the firewall set up in the back of the room, making the targets nothing more than a silhouette in the distance. The soldiers around me continued as shots rang out, circling the room.

Picking up the SR15 he placed it upon his shoulder keeping eye contact as he reloaded five bullets. Placing his support hand near the barrel of the gun, he turned back towards the target, firing off a few shots before relying solely on his strong hand to fire, cheek weld off and using pure muscle memory to land each shot.

I swept my eyes up and down his body, noting every detail, taking in the way he fashioned the training clothing I provided. The black cargo pants tucked into his combat boots; he'd used the black belt he sported from his clothing yesterday to keep the size too big pants at his waist. The black shirt was tucked into his waistband and the sleeves were rolled once, showcasing the dark-haired woman integrated within the intricate design on his left arm.

I hadn't noticed he'd kept his rings on during our little spar earlier and it wasn't lost on me. He had no care if they would cause extra damage if they connected with my flesh or not. A silver necklace shimmered against the floral tattoo design on his neck.

The touch of personalization or choice in accessories wasn't what intrigued me. No. But the *way* he put his clothes on would indicate someone who had once been in a position that required a uniform or to present a certain kind of appearance. There was also something familiar about him. I couldn't shake the feeling that I'd seen him before, though I couldn't place it.

Shrugging off the thought, I waited for him to finish showing off before offering words of approval. "Can't say I'm not impressed, for someone that does a 'little bit of everything,'" I mimicked.

"Consider me honored," he fired back, "coming from an *Umbra Mortis* and all."

I could tell he was mocking me, but I didn't have the energy to care. I didn't know how long we'd been down here and the rest of the day loomed over me, stomach tight at the thought of everything that lay ahead.

"Let's go. We need to wrap this up. Get your shit," I said, tossing some magic towards the walls to illuminate the room for the soldiers that remained once more.

There were a few that now lingered in front of the weapon racks, getting ready to start morning training in their respective areas. They bellowed their good mornings as we passed through, placing our ear protection in the bin for whoever had that side duty for the day to clean for the next group. We moved to the table against the wall to disarm his weapons and place the pieces in their bins to await cleaning as well. I waited as he grabbed the EK 44 with a grin and we headed out the door.

He was just as quick on his feet with the knife as he was in hand-to-hand, forcing me to move quickly to avoid a nick of the skin. I wasn't in the mood to chance if he would stop just short of the connection of blade to skin in the spirit of sparring. It didn't take long for me to scope out his skills to see he had clearly been well trained. The ability to get up close and personal with a knife was an art form for him.

A craft he took seriously and well-practiced, and I wondered why there hadn't been any impressive weapons on him when I searched his bag. He clearly had an acquired taste when it came to what he wielded, and there was nothing in his belongings that reflected so. *Unless he left on the run and this was all he could grab.*

His archery skills could use some work, but they weren't totally shameful. Few were great at it anyway unless they had used them in The Before. They were pretty useless on the run unless you held higher ground. Reina used it as her weapon of choice out of familiarity from hunting with her family. But if things were happening fast or in tight quarters, she'd be able to rely on her magic, rarely choosing to use a gun or knife, no matter how much her brother or I insisted.

She claimed she wasn't comfortable with them, but who knew the true reason? There were secrets that she kept close to her heart, even from those who were closest to her.

He stopped to catch his breath and I stared him down. It bothered me that I couldn't figure him out, but what bothered me more is that although my gut warned against making him leave, it didn't warn me of danger. He was cagey, sure. But frankly, he hadn't been any cagier than half the people who arrived here in the years this place was established. The longer you lived outside these walls, or the walls of another settlement, the harder your soul became and the harder it was to trust people you came across. Even if you wanted to let your guard down.

I guess the same could be said for inside these walls too; I thought. Knowing that even inside, we lacked trust in those who came fresh from the outside. Wanting to see the good but always wary of those that could be bad. We occasionally got them, but mostly just a disruptive few, or people who couldn't cope with the constraints of morality and set on lawlessness after having to be a fucked up individual for so long. There hadn't been a *real* threat to us in years, not until recently. *Making your wariness justified.*

We moved back through the long corridor quickly, blinded by the sunlight that entered as the soldiers opened the door. It hadn't taken him long to finish up weaponry and we could speed through elemental assessment, as well as it was pretty straightforward. You either had a lot of power or you didn't. You had a cool trick, or you didn't. Might as well be a yes or no question. We could train you into using it as a true weapon, no matter the amount of power. How much you held was only measured in order to structure our lines. Knowing who would run out first and who possessed the strength to take a hit before running on fumes, could make all the difference on the battlefield.

CHAPTER
EIGHTEEN

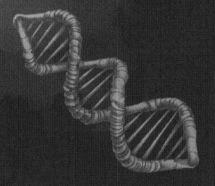

AMAIA

W e stood in the blank Element Room nearly identical to the walls of an asylum, but it was much more than that. Tomoe, Reina and a group of Tinkerers worked for a year straight developing it. Moe used her visions to see glimpses of the future, trying to *see* what they had accomplished years from now. Stealing peeks at the geniuses of the past and the inventions they were on the brink of creating until everything in their lives changed. Using it to direct their research and inventions to ensure they were on the right track, and Reina using science, studying DNA structure and using her own body to test out theories. It was all put together with random equations that would make sense to none but the mad scientists assigned to build it.

"How does this even work?" he said, confusion contorting his usually smug face.

"After a prick to the finger, the machine in the center of the room will be able to determine and confirm magic capabilities. Once I give you the go ahead, you'll just blast everything you've got towards the wall." *I really should tell them to set up a recording feature here*, I thought to myself as I jumped into my usual script. "It lets us get a look at how much magic a person holds, measured one through a hundred."

I gave him a second to process before continuing, "Most people range between forty and seventy on the scale."

There were a few one offs that hit right around seventy-five, people similar to Riley and Seth. Reina was at a strong eighty-eight, and Tomoe just slightly outranking her at ninety. Jax hadn't been super powerful. He ranked out at sixty-one, but it was his passion for life and determination that got him placed high up in the hierarchy.

Let people trust him with their lives and the fact that he literally helped build this place. According to the machine, I outranked them all. Ninety-eight it said, no one ever reached one hundred. At least not here. I'd been proud of the results. I loved my power. It was an infinite well, but that didn't mean I didn't fear it. Everything came at a cost and there were times I'd felt the magic inside me swell up. Causing me to scream out in pain. My skin feeling as if acid ran over it, begging me to be released.

It scared the shit out of me at first, figuring it all out on my own, not knowing if my body was fighting off turning into the dead or not. Eventually, I realized the ecstasy and relief I felt was tied to me, expelling my magic. In the beginning I'd thought the flaming fueled temper tantrums and Pansie killing sprees were purely therapeutic. Feeding the chaos, sadness … loneliness in my soul. Then I met Prescott, and like the good adoptive father figure, he taught me. Showed me how to use my magic in ways that would ease the pressure before it overtook me, teaching me to control it rather than let it control me.

So I used it casually throughout the day, even when unnecessary. Most of the lights in The Pit channeled my magic either by my own will or via some Tinkerer device I didn't understand other than it held a kernel of my magic. The kernel allowed even those without the power of flame to ignite, letting my magic be satisfied by a constant state of simmering.

Most people could use their magic here and there throughout the day. Many of my soldiers had enough to last them a day or two if they used their training properly. But the average person needed downtime, time to rest and recover. It didn't take long, but they all needed it or they'd face the consequences of being depleted. Empty. And even though most of the population had been born on this Earth without magic, we could now die if we went too long without any at all.

"And you?" he pried, grinning with confidence once more.

"Does it matter?" I shot back, knowing there was a level of raw curiosity lacing the question.

Only a few larger communities within our territory had similar machines, and none were out beyond our borders. Though I was sure that we had breached the grape vine as soon as it was shared with the 'trusted' few. We never made a point to brag about our discoveries, what got out got out, but for the most part, we were pretty ethno-focused. Caring about what would be for the benefit of our people and The Compound, what would keep us safe and protected, rather than making a name for ourselves or establishing dominance the way other communities itched to do.

The Expanse having something of the sorts would be cause for concern, more for leaked information than what they would do with it. I couldn't imagine anyone residing inside Transient Nation caring, but if the Covert Province got their hands on this ... well it'd likely be used to persecute rather than the benefit of the greater good. *I guess that is their greater good.*

Since the wall was only able to get a read on elemental magic. Scholars and Tinkerers were hooked up to a brain scan, and the machine did the rest. It was one of the few 'high-tech' areas in The Compound. But that's what happens when you put the best of the best on a high-level task. They achieve the impossible.

As far as *Umbras* went, our skills were pretty obvious in other portions of the assessment, and anything can be taught to be used as a weapon. There was no way to measure that. You either got the shot every time or you didn't.

Other skills that came naturally in life decided the outcome. You could either think quick enough on your feet to use the closest thing to you to your advantage or someone died, and hopefully not you. You were either fast enough or you were dinner to someone else. You either panicked, or you didn't. There weren't many of us, and that alone made us powerful. An invaluable asset to have around.

"For someone that was so keen on using magic to fight, you sure seem uncomfortable using it," I taunted from the side, noticing the uneasiness in his face and posture as he stood staring at the wall.

"Not everything is for show, General," he snapped.

"Right," I muttered, focusing on the read of his DNA, annoyed yet again with his vague answers. "Whenever you're ready then, fire first, we'll finish with water."

He took a deep breath and blew out before slowly raising his hand towards the wall. Unlike my own flames, there was no comfort or security to be found in the light and heat in the glory of his flames. The heat was immense, painful, but the flames were beautiful.

I was mesmerized by the blue and white light that battered the wall, forcing the invention to bend to its will and absorb his power, challenging its capacity to do its job. His shoulders were slack and his eyes flickered, lip curling into a snarl as his left knee fought to keep his weight. *He has no control.* I registered suddenly, struck by the realization that I needed to interfere before one of us got hurt.

"Water!" I yelled out, "Water! Water!"

His fire roared loudly and I could barely hear my own voice. I coated myself in my own flames, knowing they wouldn't dare hurt me and preparing myself to rein them back in once I tackled him. But his fire soon turned to water so blue no photo or art could do it justice. My magic fizzled back beneath the surface.

I thought his flames had been loud, but his water echoed a freight train, hitting the wall with ear shattering thuds. He let out a feral yell before falling to his knees, panting.

My body went still as I glanced down at the results from the machine. "Who are you?" I demanded.

Ninety-seven Ignis, Ninety-eight Aqua.

"Get up," I said. "Impossible. Get the fuck up." I moved to pull him to his feet, and he shoved me off him. Disgust and shock on his face as he took in his results. He had surprised even himself.

I tried again. "You." It wasn't a question, not an interrogation. This was just me pissed off at him, the world. "Where did you *really* come from?" I captured his face, forcing him to look me in the eye. I couldn't keep holding onto my anger. I could feel it fueling my fire, threatening to bring it back to the surface of my skin.

He shook his jaw from my finger. "I *already* told you that. Outside of Minneapolis. That not good enough for you?"

"I don't believe you." I glared.

"The hell does this have to do with anything?" he said, tossing his hands in the air in frustration.

"It has *everything* to do with it all. You show up here—"

"In the middle of an attack." Mocking me, he turned his back towards me and moved to the other side of the room, taking a seat against the wall.

"Yes. In the middle of an attack, swear your innocence and claim to be from 'The Expanse,' yet nothing in your pack indicates that any of that is true. Your maps are unmarked. You have nothing substantive that could have supported you for the miles you claim to have traveled. You don't even have a proper winter coat," I countered.

He tilted his head as he scoffed in disbelief. "My pack? The 'little lie' is about my pack?"

My only answer was to hold his stare, feeling like I was about to be made a fool of. *You know what they say about assumptions.*

"Just curious." He said, getting up, "have you ever thought about taking your head out of your own ass for a change and consider that *maybe* someone new and not exactly welcomed with open arms might not feel comfortable enough to come in here, secrets exposed?"

I scoffed, still having nothing to say to him, not wanting to apologize or trust what he had to say. Not only did I not believe a damn thing he said. I didn't have to. All I had to do was keep the people I cared about safe, and the only way to do that is to keep my eyes on him.

His power made him a liability. While executing him on the spot certainly wasn't off the table for me, Prescott wouldn't ever agree to it. There wasn't anything I could do *but* watch him closely. If I were to order his release, even drugged up and ditched in the middle of the night, there was no telling he wouldn't come straight back here with an army in tow.

It was becoming clearer each day that the attacks were orchestrated with the help of someone within, and we had not a damn clue of where to start looking. The least I could do is start with the most obvious culprit, watch him, see who he chose to interact with, where he spends his time. The answers would follow.

Uncomfortable under the weight of my silence and obvious display of disbelief, he added, "I have the rest of my belongings nearby. Despite what your fragile little mind thinks, I'm not dumb. I know better than to bring the things I care about into unknown territory."

A glimmer of hope filled me at the opportunity. "We'll go get it tomorrow then."

"I don't want it here," he said firmly. He stepped close to me, once again leaving nothing but a small breath of air between our bodies.

I wouldn't let him intimidate me. "I don't care what you want. You want to be cagey, you don't want to share information willingly, therefore it's *my* job to protect the people here until you can be trusted. If that means going through your shit, then so be it. You see this here"—I pointed back down to the results—"take a good fuckin look, bud. All you showed me is that you have *precisely* the amount of power to pull off stunts like yesterday. Like what killed Jax."

My voice trembled as I forced myself to maintain my composure, holding my head high, wishing I could be eye to eye. "I'll be damned if I let it happen a third time."

He brought a hand to his face, gripping at his skin absentmindedly. "And I have no other options?"

I shook my head.

"You're insufferable," he leveled.

"Hell yeah, I am."

He started pacing, flustered and red in the face, just as a knock came to the door before it cracked open.

"General," a soldier said, clearing her throat, "Lieutenant Moore sent me. He's waiting in your study."

"What time is it?" I asked, caught off guard.

"Eight forty-five," she replied, biting her lip before adding with uncertainty, "He said to 'Move your ass and stop wasting his time.', um ma'am."

"Shit," I cursed under my breath, moving towards the door. "Take him back to Cell C after he gets some food in him. Don't let him convince you to make any detours or stops. He's not to be trusted. He doesn't leave this compound, and he speaks to *no one*, not even you."

We glared at each other as I inched out the door, remembering there was another person now falling victim to his miserable presence. "Take Daniels with you. And, thank you," I added, though it wasn't necessary. I wanted her to know I felt *something* about the way I was about to ruin her day.

CHAPTER
NINETEEN

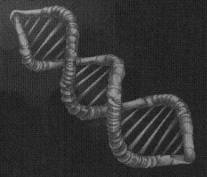

AMAIA

I was greeted by Seth leaned back in my chair. His large feet were kicked up on my desk as Harley's foot tapped the ground, and she let out a throaty grunt, pleased by the head rub services Seth was providing. His face was hollow, countenance just as exhausted as I was now that I was able to see him in the light of day. With Seth taking over my duties, he'd also remained in his old ones as he awaited his new orders as lieutenant and an official transition of power took place.

"Thanks for stopping by!" He grinned, clearly amused at my tardiness and the person that caused it.

"No problem," I replied, trying to keep the annoyance out of my voice. "Looks like you and Harley have been keeping each other company just fine."

Seth chuckled and scratched behind Harley's ears. "Yeah, she's been keeping me company while you've been … occupied." He laced the last word with hesitancy, trying to gauge where I was mentally.

I rolled my eyes and walked over to my desk, trying to push my emotions away as I pushed his feet off the desk and waited for him to move. "So, how's everything been going? Any updates on the transition of power?"

His expression grew serious as he stood up and moved to the chair on the other side of the desk. "Been a bit of a mess. I thought we were on the path of finally getting things sorted, but then, well, you know? Yesterday."

He winced at the last word. "I'm meeting with Ford after this to discuss him taking over as head weapons officer. Ramona's pretty much been groomed to replace me as Stable Master should my untimely death occur so"—he sniggered before seeing my face and realizing his dark humor wasn't hitting home—"sorry. Anyway, it shouldn't be too rough of a transition on that front. I'll keep training the cavalry, but everything else she'll be okay taking on."

I nodded, relieved that at least one thing would be settled pretty easily. But now was time for the harder questions. He knew it too as he shifted in his seat, waiting for me to take the lead.

"Seth," I said begrudgingly, "we have to discuss yesterday."

He nodded in agreement. "I know. It won't happen again. I just got caught up in everything that happened. I meant to tell you everything as soon as it happened, but then I saw Riley. Moe."

In the wake of Jax's death, I'd seen Seth show more emotion than he had in the years I'd come to know him. It was unfamiliar territory, and I wasn't sure how to navigate it. He'd become something of a brother to me the last few years. The type who comes to your room and sits on the bed in silence, just happy to be in your presence. Agony etched over his rough, angled features. Yesterday too and as I laid in bed last night, I couldn't help but find myself questioning if I'd made the right call.

This place deserved people in charge who could keep them safe. I had failed them, and Seth had failed them too. And as much as I wanted to, I couldn't comfort my friend right now. In this meeting, I was a general, and I would act as such.

"Not only were we attacked, Lieutenant, you failed to follow protocol and send out a patrol to secure the area." His pale face reddened as I continued, "Once it was secured, an intruder was located, a possible *suspect*, yet you failed to inform your superior, soldier."

I peeled my eyes from his as I fixated on his fingers, now bone white from clutching the edges of his chair before the tension released. The neutral expression returned to his face once more.

"Like there was a superior to report to," he mumbled under his breath, knowing I'd hear him but wanting to speak his truth. I'd take it, but that didn't negate him from his own blame.

"I was out there fighting, Lieutenant. Where were you?" I wanted to stop there, but the stress of the last twenty-four hours tore at me and my anger reached its breaking point. "Matter fact, that's *twice* now that you've failed to give a proper report. Maybe Reina was right." It was a low blow, bringing his sister into it.

My words hit home as he broke my gaze. Before Jax had died, I'd never once questioned his leadership before, but then again, he'd never questioned mine. I'd questioned his temper sure. But to question his capability to fulfill his role, his duty, that was new territory for me and if I was honest, part of me blamed him for Jax's untimely demise.

Riley had explained that Seth had been out with the group that day on one of the horses he was trying to train, which meant he'd been pretty far ahead, especially with Jax hanging back to turn those soldiers around. It baffled me that even with his gifts, he'd heard nothing, seen nothing. The thought of blaming someone I loved and cared about, blaming them for the death of someone *they* cared about, made my stomach churn. It only led down a further road of destruction.

If I wanted to, and thought too hard, I could blame Tomoe too. It wouldn't be fair to her, as I knew she made a point not to try to channel visions around our deaths.

There was still the unknown about trying to change things that had not yet happened, the repercussions. We were only one entity in the grand scheme of things. The only time we used visions to our advantage was when it came to serving the greater good.

There were things like the Element Room where we could take a peek at the future, consequence free because it was something we knew we wouldn't stop until we got right. We *knew* we'd invent it and thus, there was no harm in giving us the slight advantage of confirming our formulas were right and we weren't creating the downfall of the innocent people who resided within our walls.

We hadn't yet crossed that line of using them to be a weapon of war. Not that I wouldn't have tried if it meant the people here at the Compound would be safe. But Moe hadn't been here when borders were drawn and cities were finalized and none of the other Scholars here were powerful enough to channel visions both consistently and accurately the way she was.

Sure, she couldn't control the random visions the universe forced upon her, but she *could* control seeking out answers that weren't meant for prying eyes. For now, it was safer if we tread her particular gift carefully, the butterfly effect and all.

A trail of ants squeezed through the crack of the door, announcing Riley's arrival. I stood to move towards the door. "Poor leadership gets people killed, Lieutenant, and I don't know about you, but I'm tired of losing people. *Our* people, good people. I'd prefer the number of deaths I'm responsible for being limited to those who deserve it."

"Agreed. Am I dismissed?" he hissed.

Riley entered the now open door, taking in the scene and tension that filled the room, and opted to stay outside. "Still have a lot to discuss, but for now. Yes." I stepped out of the way as he brushed past me, saying nothing to Riley.

"I hope he proves me wrong," I whispered.

"He will," Riley offered as he entered my study and closed the world out behind him.

THE ANTS MOVED UP HIS ARM AND CIRCLED HIS WRIST IN FASHION OF a bracelet. I grimaced at the sight; I would never get used to it. "So? Anything?"

Shaking his head and he leaned against the door, wincing at the pain in his shoulders. "I gotta be honest with you. I don't even know what I should be looking for."

Fair enough, I didn't know the answer to that either. I just knew I needed something to go on. Something that would help me piece this all together and figure out where things went wrong. How our vulnerabilities were being exposed when there was nothing concrete to tie it all back to.

"Thank you, by the way," I said, "for holding the fort down all these months. And when it literally fell too. I'm glad to see you standing on your own. Didn't think I'd see you up and moving so soon." His eyes danced at the recognition, but there was something else lingering there, too.

"Well, you summoned," he teased me.

"I didn't."

"No, but you were going to." He offered me a small smile, knowing there was no denying that.

He quickly debriefed me on his version of the events yesterday. Similar to Seth's version, the attack was over in a matter of moments. He'd learned that the watchtower had seen some of them come from over the cliff side and the rest from the trees, and had rung the alarm bell. *They were just too damn fast*, he'd relayed.

The soldiers remaining in the barracks had stumbled into action as they'd been trained to do, racing their way towards the gate. Most soldiers had been in The Kitchens enjoying their dinner or were out in different parts of The Compound. Although the barracks were close to North Gate, they weren't close *enough*.

Seth had ordered the ones standing around focusing on getting people to safety first, fight second. Only a small portion of them had been ordered to stay and fight. And they had, without hesitation. It may not have been the way *I* would have chosen to direct my soldiers, but Seth wasn't me. *Who was to say there wouldn't have been more deaths under my command?*

The fight had pretty much been over by the time the soldiers from the barracks had arrived. That much I'd seen myself; Reina and I having been making our way back from dinner. The rest of the events had occurred once Riley and Moe were in my presence.

"How are you?" I asked, wanting to move closer to comfort him, but wanting to give him his space all the same.

Medicine and magic worked funny in this new world. I knew his wounds were likely healed by now. They were deep, but they were still flesh wounds, meaning they could be tended to by herbs and medicinal blends. Add a healer with water magic and you'd likely just feel a bit of muscle fatigue the next day. But he had lost another friend yesterday. My heart broke for my brother, not wanting him to see any more pain when the universe had already given him enough.

He shrugged. "I'm better when I'm working."

I nodded, understanding everyone had their coping methods, and that once had been one of my own. I wouldn't push, but I sure as hell would keep an eye on him. He wasn't in this alone. Not anymore.

"Can you tell me about the breaches from the last few months, then? I need all the information I can get."

He obliged. Our borders had been attacked primarily on the border of the land between us and the San Jose Compound borders, about fifteen miles from East Gate. An emissary had come down from San Jose a few weeks ago. Making a case on joint efforts to continue to secure the area without having to pull more men from other areas and conserve our resources.

Our troops were a mighty force here alone. I'd restructured them during my time and done the math over and over, opting to stack them duplicating the US in WW2. One US soldier for every forty Germans during their period of occupation. If my math was correct, which often kept me up at night, with our current population we'd only need seven-hundred and fifty men and women. I'd ensured we'd had over a thousand. One thousand and fifty-one by head count on my last shift before everything happened.

If everything went to shit and we were faced with the worst-case scenario, I'd have an unheard of ratio in these times. One soldier to every twenty-eight citizens. That on top of the fact that all adult citizens now received training twice a week and kids once, we were a force to be reckoned with. Which was the only thing keeping this place from going under or we'd had been crippled by the assaults months ago.

Though our forces were stacked, San Jose had a decent army too, and they were well trained. Our relationship with their city was as close as two allies could be. We traded, shared inventions and discoveries, and from time to time combined our troops' efforts to ensure we *all* were safe. A threat to their borders was a threat to ours, and vice versa.

The Salem Territory consisted of nineteen cities, seven of which were in California. Though we referred to them as compounds or settlements because of the walls that bordered our well-populated areas, there were still people who chose to live outside them, that weren't exactly citizens but were allowed in for a visitor trade. Each city had borders far past their walls, ending at the territory lines of the closet city.

Of course, those who lived outside the city walls weren't allowed to just cruise in and out unannounced the way those who lived within did, but it was an amicable relationship.

They didn't act as a threat. We embraced them to an extent. They vowed to fight for our side if things went south. Either way, it was a win-win situation, depending on how you viewed it. They were able to keep an eye on the miles in-between our walls and borders, be our eyes and ears when we could not. Fill in the gaps.

Land was still land, always worth something, and as San Diego and other larger settlements re-established themselves, they started to build *outside* of the walls, too. Expanding.

There had been a few skirmishes near South Gate as well, but it appeared unconnected to the others in Seth's eyes. Riley requested to send some of his people out, people akin to him that did well in the shadows, people he trusted.

People like Mohammed.

But Seth had overruled him, opting to keep more people closer to base in case the threats closed in. Not deeming the effort a wise move when the people Riley recommended for the job could be better used keeping an eye on things around here. Making sure there wasn't tangible evidence pointing towards an inside threat. I guess in the end both had been correct.

Ultimately, now that I was back, I had a final say in the matter. The only option in my mind was to do what felt right. What my gut said needed to be done.

I gave Riley permission to send out his men. He straightened, hiding his emotions behind a sniffle. Though he had been the one to make this request, we both knew he was now faced with the possibility of sending another friend to their death.

Taking a seat on the edge of my desk, I looked him over. "After you debrief your team, you need to take the day off."

"What? No." He rarely protested anything I asked of him.

But I wasn't asking, I was telling. Seeing the state my friends were in was wearing on me. Nothing about them showed that they were okay, and while I had let the world crumble around me, they had carried my weight. He could take one day to focus on himself and the losses he had faced. I wouldn't interfere after that.

"Yes. I'm … I'm sorry Ri. I'm sorry I wasn't there for you after Jax, and I'm sorry I wasn't here to stop this from happening. I'm sorry I let you down. I'm … I'm sorry you lost someone else. If you won't do this for yourself, then please, do this for me. Take some time." I hated myself for a moment, guilt tripping him. But I knew that would be the only way he'd listen, if he thought it was helping me. I wished he would want to help himself for once. So desperately I wanted my friend to feel that he rightfully owned a place in this world. He wasn't disposable. Not to me, not to anyone here.

"Okay," he agreed.

"I'll come with you to talk to his girlfriend about the funeral and headstone."

"No. It's fine," he insisted. "I don't think she'd be open to any other *guests*."

We both knew he meant me. That she blamed my absence. The way he said guests was clear enough, a kind way to tell me I shouldn't stop by anytime soon either.

I blinked back my emotions and offered my friend a reassuring smile. "And I bet you're on headstone duty?"

Knowing though he didn't go around displaying his earth magic arts and crafts, he was quite talented. His carvings and sculptures outlining his room in the General Living Quarter.

"I am." His head held high as he walked towards me to squeeze my arm. "I'm glad you're back. I'll see you later."

"Yeah, hopefully not till tomorrow," I shouted at his back as he left, moving across the floor without a sound.

I glanced at the clock on the bookshelf to my right and threw my head back. *How is the day flying by yet dragging on at the same time?* 10 a.m. I had a few minutes to spare before the next sparring sessions took place in The Ring and decided to take a peek into my sleeping quarters, not sure if Tomoe had awoken yet. She was usually up before the sky, but her injuries from the day before had taken a toll.

The couch in my room was empty, littered with whatever breakfast Reina had probably brought her. I reminded myself to pinch her when I next saw her for the mess. My stomach growled, remembering I hadn't yet eaten breakfast.

That was going to have to wait until after I checked in on the training, which meant basically lunch. *Urgh.* The rest of my morning went as expected. I watched my soldiers spar for a couple of hours and made corrections where I saw fit.

For the most part, their form was still immaculate and their endurance hadn't faded. Their morning runs had been a contention point between Seth and I in the past. He and his crew had seen how easy it was for Pansies to keep up with their horses if they were freshly fed. It was a fair point, but they'd never learn to out maneuver the undead if they just took a jog through The Compound. It was a harsh reality, but I expected my soldiers to be able to hold their own outside these gates, otherwise who was to say they were capable of defending what lay within them?

Once enough time had passed without a single newborn born of the zombie gene most of what was left of the human race felt we would stand a chance. That eventually they'd all die or be killed off and we can truly start over, but that simply hadn't been the case. Either a *shit ton* of people died in the first few months or there were a lot more of those assholes out there than we initially estimated.

There was no real way to determine how many people turned. Without an accurate census, there never would be. Hell, we didn't even have a clue what was going on outside the territories on the continental US.

No one had heard a word from overseas since the last time cell phone reception flickered back on all those years ago. Through the San Diego Compound, we knew they had been in communication with people over the border, so life went on there. I knew from the call Sammy had with her parents that some of Canada had survived the initial blasts, but the Seattle and Spokane Compounds had also made contact with a few stragglers from the other side of the border as well.

As for Alaska, Hawaii, overseas and beyond, no one here knew. At least no one in our allied territories did either, but I assume that a lot of humanity is still trying to get it together out there. I remain hopeful about that.

We were lucky here, to have good enough leadership at different settlements during the last civil war. A small kernel of humanity had remained in this country that prevented more chaos and allowed us to regroup. Even so, many didn't live the way we did here at the Monterey Compound. This was a place built by dreamers, people that wanted to rebuild better than things were before, and not fall back into the same.

But life was still hard, and dangerous, even with magic. We didn't have the luxury to pretend hell hadn't happened and stained our souls. Like we all didn't do terrible things we never thought we'd have to do to get to this point, but future generations could if we set them up right. And that's what this place was, a new tomorrow. A better tomorrow.

I tried to remember that as I made my rounds touching base with the families of the lost, though my words probably seemed empty to them, I meant every word. I was sorry that this had happened, but their deaths wouldn't go unavenged. I promised to figure out how this had happened, *why* this had happened. To end whoever made this happen.

CHAPTER
TWENTY

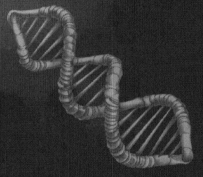

AMAIA

I sat at our usual lunch table alone, wondering when my friends would arrive, letting myself get lost in my thoughts and running through the checklist of what I had left to do with my day. Each task felt as if it had dragged on for hours, just for me to check the time and see only thirty minutes had passed.

Pushing the food on my plate side to side, I poked at my large plate of green bean casserole. I wasn't starving, but was forcing myself to eat. Getting my strength back as quickly as possible was now essential if I wanted to be an effective leader in whatever came next.

Just as I'd given up hope, Reina walked in, her dark red lips pulled into a smile and delight filled her eyes. Despite the events of yesterday, she looked well rested and put together. Her long brown hair fell down her back, wispy strands hung in her face. She wore tight fitting black cargo pants tucked into her Doc Martens and a tan tank top that displayed a good portion of her stomach.

"Maia!" she exclaimed. "Urgh, I've literally missed you so much. I wasn't sure you'd come back so soon after last night. Boy, last night was *awful*. Well, I guess not as awful as your night. Riley and Moe slumbered in your room and all. For quiet people, they both snore like bears. Anyway, Jessa conned her way into sleeping over, said she was 'scared. Guess I kinda like her, but still, a girl has boundaries,'" I let my friend ramble off about her latest woman of the month, taking comfort in the normality of it all. Thankful I had at least one friend that could pick up where we left off months ago.

She grabbed for my attention again, snapping her fingers in my line of sight, "Ya know … I know what will get you feeling like yourself again."

"And what is that?" I smiled at her.

"Coffee! *Good* coffee. Let's take a trip outside." She grinned at me sinisterly, eyebrows wiggling.

My jaw dropped before I slapped her arm and cackled. "I didn't know Jax had told you about that."

"Please, if it wasn't top secret, there wasn't a thing I couldn't pry from that man's mouth." This time we both laughed, knowing Jax was the *worst* person to trust with a secret that didn't exist to keep you safe.

Seth walked in as I scooped the last bit of food in my mouth, a still limping Moe following close behind. Her wound was severe, deep to where she came within a few centimeters of magic and herbs, no longer being sufficient, where surgery would be required. Her muscles would likely still be pretty sore for a few days.

"Those two have been spending *a lot* of time together lately." She tsked, a schoolgirl giggle leaving her lips as she shifted in her seat. Seth met Reina's eyes and gave her a warm smile I hadn't seen the siblings exchange before, ever. His blue eyes turned to ice as they met my own, turning to offer Tomoe a goodbye before taking his tray and sitting down with Ramona.

Tomoe's gaze locked on mine as she made a beeline for our table. "I need to talk to you," she said.

"What's wrong? Is everything okay? I came to look for you—"

"I saw it," she interrupted. "I saw it right before it happened. It's been years since it happened this close to … not without me channeling it."

My friend was rattled, guilt now displaying over her face. "Saw what, Moe? Slow down, start from the beginning," I asked. Grabbing her hand, I offered a bit of support as Reina did the same, using her magic to offer a sense of peace to our sister.

She explained it all, the brief vision of The Pansies inside the wall, the placement of the sun. How it had lasted merely half a second before she was pulled back into reality. She hadn't run to tell me because it was the first time in four years that one had come to fruition this quickly. That she had noted the sky and assumed we had another day, that she had time to practice and relieve stress before she would come find me to explain. That she wanted me to have a few more minutes of peace before chaos. Trying to reassure her, I told her it wouldn't have made a difference, that she would have likely made it to me as it unfolded, anyway. The outcome would have remained the same.

Inevitable.

Her posture lightened as she took in my words. She recalled the vision she had when I'd found them. I'd been terrified that would be the end as I rounded the corner, sprinting for them and Harley coming to meet my steps. My braid spun, trying to recall the beautiful blonde woman she described, not having recognized her description and the rest of the trauma that followed. Moe fell slack. She'd actively spent time learning to avoid seeing our deaths and lately her visions had been consumed with our eventual trauma.

Fed up with our supposed fate, I vowed to change the outcome, ensuring this wouldn't be another inevitable future in our life. There was a lot to take in, but nothing that could be solved sitting there at the table. One thing was for sure, our troubles were far from being over. No, they had merely just begun.

UNFORTUNATELY FOR REINA, SHE WASN'T INCLUDED IN MY PLANS TO go outside the walls today. I threw open the door to Alexiares' cell, and he jumped to his feet from the bed. I took in his appearance. He'd clearly bathed from this morning, his dark hair slicked back away from his face though he wore the same clothes from earlier.

He glared at me. "What now?"

"We're leaving," I said as I turned my back to him and urged him to follow. I let out a whistle and Harley came from God knows where and pranced at my side, growling low at Alexiares as he walked on my heels.

"To where?" he snarled, boots heavy against the ground, his anger shedding into his every move.

"You know where, don't ask me another stupid question. Or I'll ensure you'll lose the ability to speak at all," I leveled, not really in the mood to be in his piss poor presence again today.

He muttered a few choice words under his breath, my fists clenching a few times to avoid hitting him in response.

We passed through North Gate, still not wanting to expose him to the other three gate locations. If we hadn't been there ourselves, we wouldn't even be able to tell something had happened there as recently as yesterday. The only sign was the solemn faces of the soldiers tending to their duties.

He took the lead naturally, being the only person knowing where we were headed I let him, Harley staying nearby. We walked along the coastline for a few miles and I took in the sea green water and misty blue sky above. I would have loved to have lived here in The Before. Heard so many great things about Monterey but had never had the chance to visit. Always tied up in some school or work commitment. Saving my travel funds for international experiences, never thinking I'd actually get the chance to settle down here after all.

A little over half an hour later we approached an old house. It was small and had probably been quite beautiful in its heyday. Now its gray-blue paint was chipping along the sidings and the windows in the front had both been burst out. The once immaculate landscaping was now overgrown and the stench of death clogged my nostrils. I withdrew my gun and his eyes narrowed.

"It's not a trap," he scoffed, as if he were insulted by the idea.

I signaled for him to continue leading the way, as if I would walk into a house *in front* of some weirdo and get sandwiched into a less than favorable situation. Harley whined as we ascended the destroyed brick steps, clearly not happy about the situation I was dragging her into.

He leaned his head against the door as if he were listening for something and I scowled at him.

"What the hell are you doing?" I asked, moving my gun up and pointing it at him.

"Relax, Black Widow," he murmured, ushering me to lower my weapon.

I took a step forward and pushed the gun into the back of his head. "Excuse me? Want to repeat that?"

He whirled on me, grabbing the pistol in one swift motion and pointing it towards the triangular archway above the door.

"Not really." We glared at each other, my chest pressed against his, daring the other to move before I forced myself free and took a step back, nodding towards the door.

"After you."

CHAPTER
TWENTY-ONE

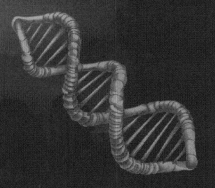

ALEXIARES

I pushed open the dark blue door and entered the small house I'd bunkered down in, in the days prior to heading to The Compound. It was okay, nothing fancy, but was one of the homes in better condition for the area.

After some scouting, I'd specifically chosen this neighborhood. The conditions of it were too poor to have people living in it, to be discovered before I was ready, but also nice enough to feel relatively comfortable resting your head for a moment. Not much of my time had been spent here sleeping though, rather spent most hours along the inner borders and casing The Compound walls. I'd slit my own throat before telling her, but for an absent General, her patrol teams were pretty tight.

I'd had to cover my tracks multiple times, spending hours hiding in bushes and trees as they overlapped. But it was a good place for Suckerpunch to recover while I gathered myself and my plans. The air inside was stale and smelled of mold and decay from the few pests I'd seen littered throughout the house.

Suckerpunch rounded the corner from the kitchen and ran to place his giant paws on my shoulders, licking my face and letting out a deep whine. He noticed Amaia behind me, pounding over to greet her when Harley came from her heels and rammed into his side, latching onto his neck and forcing him into submission. Her eyes moved towards Amaia, waiting for her command.

"What—"

"Harley, no! Release!" she demanded, her eyes wide but tone in control. Harley released Suckerpunch, prancing back over to her monstrous owner.

I moved towards my son, kneeling down at his side I rubbed his neck for injuries and kissed his head as he melted into my arms. "What the fuck is wrong with you and your sick ass dog?" I yelled.

There was no broken skin. Not a single puncture wound, which meant Harley was well trained. But if a well trained dog did *that* off instinct, then what the hell were they training it to do on a daily basis?

Amaia moved closer to me, each step slow, she raised her right hand up, commanding Harley to wait. Suckerpunch receded at first, skeptical of this unbalanced woman before ultimately deciding that she was alright, licking her frail hand in acceptance of her sorry ass apology.

"I'm sorry. Harley thought I was being threatened. I have to say, unfortunately, that's not the first situation I've had where she witnessed a creature or two lunging at me." She tried to make light of the situation but it only made me question what type of situations her leadership placed her in.

She kept prodding. "What's her name? His name?" Her voice trailed off as she peered around to find the answer.

Suckerpunch towered over her, the difference in size laughable. It was hard to imagine the woman before me was responsible for so many deaths. A lone wolf waiting to be provoked.

I rose to my feet and gave the two of them some space. "He, and Suckerpunch." Her nose scrunched up and her head tilted in question, but she giggled and kept whatever questions she had to herself.

Her tone shifted to a baby voice as she said, "And what happened to you, Mr. Sucker?" while grabbing his face and moving it around as he lapped at all the attention.

Her fingers now tracing the outline of the bandage on his midsection. Harley whimpered from the other side of the room, jealousy taking on the fight against her training.

"Mountain lion." I grinned, proud of my son, then frowned that the fight hadn't left him unscathed. Her round lips turned down and her eyes went sad. For some reason, I felt the need to reassure her, "You should see the other guy, though he's probably started to rot by now. You know how it is. Don't see them until it's too late."

She nodded, knowing very well, and I wondered if it was because a mountain lion had been one of the creatures Harley too had to put in its place. Harley was large, even for a Doberman, pure muscle. And though she had taken on a surprised and injured Suckerpunch, she was no match for a healthy version of my Cane Corso. His head alone was bigger than my own, one hundred-fifteen pounds of muscle.

It was *never* going to be in that mountain lion's favor. Suckerpunch had only been injured from lack of focus, too concerned about my safety. He'd frozen in his steps a few feet ahead of me, sensing the danger but unable to determine where it had come from.

Only a few seconds later did I see a swift movement from the side of my eye. My reflexes were the only difference between a flesh wound swipe to my chest and my insides pouring out. The shout of pain I released had distracted him for only a moment, turning his head to ensure there was no other threat, but it had cost him. The mountain lion had grown desperate, doing all it could to twist and turn off its back and had swiped his side as well. His wound was deeper than mine, but still not fatal. Mine had healed pretty well, my packed herbal blends from a healer back home working almost as well as magic itself.

Suckerpunch hadn't been as lucky. Slower to heal as his wounds were deep, just shy of surgical, and although I had water running through my veins, I possessed no healing component.

"That's okay," she said, attention still on him, "we have a great little doggy doctor. You'll be good as new." Her voice turned lethal, "You were just going to leave him here?"

"Obviously not"—I rolled my eyes and crossed my arms—"but I'm not going to bring my precious boy around people I don't know, especially when he can't defend himself."

It was her turn to roll her eyes. "We're not monsters."

"Said the tyrant that ordered me to take her to my belongings to raid and judge at her leisure. Then had her mutt"—I threw a finger Harley's way, and she growled—"*attack* him like some rabid animal."

She made a mocking face and inspected the living room behind my shoulder. "I'm sorry I didn't know you'd be so overprotective of a raggedy ass teddy bear," she said, picking up Evander's bear that I had zip tied to the outside of my bag. *My baby brother*, I fought off tears at the thought of him. He was only sixteen. It wasn't fair. I was tired of life not being fair.

I snatched my bag from her boney fingers. "Give me that," I snapped, our moment of peace clearly over.

"Sheesh, touchyy,"

"Am I? Or am I just sick of the bullshit? Just tell me if I need to get my shit and hit the road or not. Simple as fucking that. I'm done with the games." I had come here for a purpose, but enough was enough.

Nothing was worth dealing with her, having to talk to *her*. Having to be around *her*. I'd make sure Suckerpunch was fully healed, found a good home, and that would be that.

"You're a bitch," I growled, shaking my head in distaste.

I'd spent a better part of my life condemning my father for speaking to women without respect, yet here I was. But it wasn't just some stupid teddy bear, and I was tired of her talking down to me. Insinuating that I'm the villain. The one that gets people killed, though I supposed I was that too, in another life.

"No, I'm a general." Her voice had turned hard, cold. My words had pulled her back into her responsibilities and the reason we had come here to begin with.

"You think I give a shit about your little title? You can barely take care of yourself, let alone keep thousands of people from dying."

Her stone face didn't break. "Yeah, okay. Don't even bother coming back. Let's see how safe you are then."

"Made it here, didn't I?"

"Barely. From the looks of it, bout two of your people didn't though." Her hand gripped the woven bracelet around one of the straps.

My fingers closed in on her throat, Suckerpunch injured but circling in on Harley to keep her from coming to her owner's aid as I slammed her into the wall. The back of her head bounced off, though no flicker of pain crossed in her eyes. As expected, her flames encased her body, ready to defend itself but I'd already let go, expecting her to resort to magic upon the familiar feeling of helplessness.

"Let me ask you something, *General.*" I ground out, "Does everyone that walks through these gates go through a ten-day thirty-night hazing affair where their privacy is invaded? Or their belongings scoured through? Or is it just me? Hmm? How about you? Does anyone go through your shit? Make sure you're playing by the rules? Playing fair?" I wanted to grab her, shake her, wanted to force her to let me keep this last piece of privacy.

Her hand reached out to grab my pack back from me and I grasped onto her hands, ready to incinerate them in my defense.

She beat me to it. Fire made its way down her body from her hair moving like a snake down to the hand I was currently holding, "You have two seconds to take your hands off me, before you're left with no hands at all."

I released her hands as she added, "Besides, nobody smart plays fair, Alexiares. Any survivor could tell you that."

Her words stung, but she was right. My rhythm calmed, my vision going from red to clear. Suddenly realizing that maybe she was just doing her job. I thought she was terrible at it. That she *looked* to be in a terrible state too, though there was more color coming back to her face than there was yesterday. She'd made her way into this position for a reason. The people here clearly trusted her. And if I were to do what I came here to do, then I'd have to let her do what she needed to as well.

Tossing my bag at her feet, I said, "Here. Take all the looking around you want, go crazy. Just let me know if I need to pack my shit or not. I'm not going to beg for a place to lay my ass."

Her face softened a bit as she picked up my belongings and ruffled through. Outside of Evander's bear and Tiago's bracelet that his daughter had made him, there was nothing in my pack that required true privacy. Not anything she could translate. It had a bit more food, Suckerpunch's food in case he had a hard time coming across something to hunt out, and some extra layers for traveling through the cold. I had ditched my large coat over a hundred miles back.

I wouldn't need it after this.

When she was done playing Inspector Gadget, she tossed my pack back, gave Suckerpunch a pat on the head, and walked towards Harley.

"You can stay," she said, both of them disappearing through the door we'd entered minutes before. Some shuffling and a thud sounded from the front yard.

Quick on my feet, I sprinted outside. One of the dead lay sprawled across the overgrown grass, a knife through its skull. Amaia and Harley lounged off to the side, taking in the rays of sun, feigning a normal day in the park.

Her face rested on the palm of her hand, black coils framed her innocent face, knocked loose from our altercation inside.

"We're waiting," she said impatiently.

I stared at her for a moment, questioning my sanity for coming here. There wasn't a solid plan in place, so much of my focus had been on arriving alive. I hadn't put much thought into what came in the immediate after. She was unstable, if luck had it, I wouldn't have to do much at all.

Pivoting sharply, I gathered my belongings. Hugging Suckerpunch, I pulled his head back, rubbing gently behind his ears.

"Here goes nothing."

CHAPTER
TWENTY-TWO

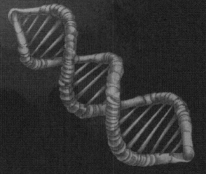

AMAIA

The walk back to The Compound was fast and silent. I felt bad for prying, *sort of*. There genuinely wasn't anything in there that he'd been hiding. Nothing overtly obvious at least. I allowed him to walk freely, uncontained by my fire or without the weight of my stare, but that didn't mean I wasn't aware of his or Suckerpunch's movements as they walked to my side. Neither of us wanted to let the other walk behind us. To be caught unaware and off guard. *Don't see that changing anytime soon.*

It was mid-afternoon now and the inside of The Compound was busy as people ended their work days. Picking up their children from school, and made their way to their homes or to dinner. My mouth watered as I remembered my favorite restaurant in the Entertainment Square. The owner made the best vegan chili and smoothies. It was an odd pair to some, but I was never one to allow a weird combination stop me from enjoying the robust flavors.

The food at The Kitchens was free to all and rationed accordingly, but there were a few approved restaurants in the midst of the theaters and taverns that took our local coin. After a year of being established, we figured with the steady flow of resources, some businesses should be allowed to form and some type of currency should start being exchanged. Bring some sorts of civilization back into our lives slowly.

Everyone was paid a fair wage according to their duties. The more strenuous or less sought after roles offered the most pay, but no one was 'rich' in the way people could be in The Before. There weren't any *bad* housing options, some just were a bit more elaborately designed, or had more space, but everything was far from uninhabitable. Of course housing was assigned strategically by Prescott.

I didn't know all the semantics of it but there was a certain amount of housing, that had a certain amount of space, for a certain amount of people, that cost a certain amount of coin every month. Then that money did some cyclical economic shit that I *also* didn't understand. Point was, it worked and for the most part everyone was happy.

You couldn't please everyone, but you could please most when you actively worked to make their life easier, better.

Any clothes outside of the basics we provided from the shops. Some were handmade by people using earth magic to create elaborate designs or fabrics. Others were restored or taken from surrounding neighborhoods in good condition.

It was the same thing for furniture, nothing around here was truly fancy, but I couldn't deny that it reminded me of a cute, quaint small town overseas somewhere. Where community was abundant and everyone did their own thing without getting a side-eye, where money didn't matter. Another dimension from the US.

Then I remember we're all trauma bonded and holding ourselves together just barely, one stone away from shattering our little glass house, and I have a good laugh.

A few kids ran in our path as we approached Compound Hall, by their age probably coming back from school. Everyone under sixteen went to school while sixteen was seen as being an adult in this new world. We considered it old enough to put in their fair share of work and support The Compound however they could. Just not as one of my soldiers.

For that, I preferred they waited until they were eighteen, though that didn't stop some of the young and eager from trying. People like Elie. I couldn't blame them. Five formative years of their life had been consumed by gore and violence. Of course, they wanted to do something that put them in the midst of danger every day.

The joke was on them. Unless they had some crazy skill that couldn't be found in someone older, more mature, I never placed anyone near the age of eighteen out near the front lines. If I could preserve even a drop of their innocence, I would.

I wouldn't let them see the things I had to see or do the things I had to do as a soldier. As a leader. Hell as a fresh out of college kid that had to figure out a lot of shit on her own. My throat bobbed at my loss of innocence, the option I was never given because I never had someone to advocate for me. The truth was, I stopped being me so long ago that I couldn't even remember who that person was. It'd been years since I felt my true self. Turned into this new person.

The new Amaia.

If I could stop that from happening to any of them, I would.

BACK AT THE INTAKE ROOM, ALEXIARES SAT ON THE OTHER END OF the desk from me. We stared at each other, saying nothing. Both aware that whoever spoke first lost whatever bullshit game we'd been playing since last night.

I cocked my head and squinted my eyes, trying to will to words out of his mouth. His face remained blank, blinking every few seconds, trying to reflect a face of calmness. Suckerpunch and Harley had decided somewhere along the walk here that they were going to be best friends. Harley licked at the wound on his side, nestled into each other in the corner of the room.

"What's this?" he asked, finally breaking at the intrigue as I slid a packet of information across the desk.

"A lottery ticket." I smiled brightly at him.

He looked up, unimpressed. "I'm trying to maintain the peace here, if you would just cooperate, General I'd appreciate it." Distaste floated off his tongue when he said the word *General*.

"If you don't want a sarcastic answer, then my recommendation to you would be to stop asking stupid questions, *Alexi*." I tossed the insult behind a simple word back at him.

His lips parted, but he said nothing as he awaited my honest answer. "It's a survival guide for The Compound." I realized how sarcastic that could sound before adding, "It's just the basic layout of the area. For *civilian* eyes, though honestly, what's on paper probably doesn't make much sense until you see it for yourself. Then there's a list of jobs and their pay. You have a week to decide which one suits whatever sick desires you surely have."

I remembered the peace we were supposed to be keeping, though admittedly I found it incredibly hard to make it through an entire sentence without insulting him. "There's also a list of open housing we have in comparison to jobs you qualify for. But you won't need that," I said, flipping the packet back closed. "There's an open room with a friend. You'll be staying there."

"Why list out open housing if people don't get to choose where they wash their ass?" he inquired as he snatched the packet back, flipping through the pages one of the Scholars had typed out, over and over again on our typewriters. Bless their heart, couldn't be me.

"Well, it's listed there because most people *do* get to choose where they lay their heads at night. As for washing your ass, there's communal bathing houses for that. Though there is a drain in your toilet area where you can use your water magic to rinse off."

He made a face at that before deciding it wasn't worth the fight and probably nothing he could do about the situation, but a question lingered behind his chestnut eyes. "Uh, and why don't people have their own bathrooms?"

"Did you have your own bathroom where you came from?" I tossed back at him.

"Uh, no."

"Then why expect one here?"

He tossed his hands towards the windows as if it were obvious. "Considering the elaborateness of the place, I figured basic plumbing wasn't considered a luxury."

Fair point, I thought as I considered my response. Shrugging, I offered him some of our history. "When we built the initial structures of this place, we didn't have an aqueduct system in place yet. Then our population boomed quickly after lines were drawn. Adding in a full bathing suite in every home didn't seem realistic when you just wanted to get a roof over people's heads. I don't cover city planning, so I don't really know, but some of the newer houses have them, leadership has them for obvious reasons. Chain of command must be kept in *some* aspects. But no one's ever complained about them. They're free to add them once they move in, but I think people enjoy the community aspect of it all."

He pondered that, and I allowed him to browse through the packet some more, waiting to see if he had any questions.

When he said nothing, I figured that was the end of it, but he looked at me, words as cold as ice. "I assume it's you that has my notebook then?"

Had he been holding onto this the whole time? A chill went down my spine as I realized just how capable he was of concealing his emotions. His motives. He'd tried to maintain the peace between us the better part of the day for this exact moment, aside from our small scuffle. He'd allowed me to do my job and appear as amiable as possible in order to make his inquiry seem small. An innocent accusation. He'd likely confirmed it when he grabbed his stuff earlier at the house, assuming he had misplaced it in his other bag when his first bag was brought to his cell this morning.

"Yes," I answered confidently, "but since I can't read Greek, it's being translated. Hope you understand." And he should understand. Any reasonable person would have to understand the need to translate cryptic text. *Dated* text when your home had been under constant threat for months, and no other real suspect had presented themself.

His body tensed up, and he shifted in his seat, fiddling with his fingers as he refused to meet my eye.

I took note, tossing an extra piece of information at him to see where his head was at. "It shouldn't be long, though. Nothing of concern, right?"

He shook his head, still refusing to meet my eye. "Right. Okay. Well, glad we came to an understanding."

The next few minutes consisted of me explaining our training expectations for everyone here and that he'd meet his roommate once we headed to dinner. He appeared zoned out, but I was clean out of energy today to care. Just glad I'd made it through my first official day back, but was ready for it to be over.

There was one stop I wanted to make before we hit The Kitchens as we wandered next door to Prescott and the Council's Quarters. Knocking on the door, I wondered if he still waited for me every day for our coffee chat, hoping that one day I'd snap out of it and be back. The door opened before my third knock finished and a pretty older woman with light brown skin and silky black hair opened the door.

"Amaia!" Her face lightened as she pulled me into an embrace.

"Luna." I hugged her back. It'd been months since I'd seen her. She was one of our older emissaries, always on the road. But always in Prescott's quarters when she wasn't. I admired her, one of the few women left in this world that traveled alone and held her own. If the biggest threat to her safety wasn't some sack of creepy shit, I'd *almost* feel bad for them.

"Prescott! She's here! Sweet Girl is here! Come on in, he was just going over some paperwork for the new trade agreement." She ushered me inside, before her deceivingly kind face took in Alexiares sulking figure behind me.

I nodded my head in indication that it was okay. Harley barreled in from behind me, Suckerpunch in tow as she headed to her designated corner Prescott had set up with her toys.

Luna and I used *Sweet Girl* as my nickname mockingly. Poking fun at Prescott's lack of imagination when it came to the touchy subject of referring to me as his daughter. Though daughter was the best and easiest way to describe our relationship, I didn't want to disrespect the real dad I had known and loved my entire life, and Prescott never wanted to take that away from me. Often joking he'd never take ownership of raising such a headache. *Sweet Girl* it was.

Prescott came from the room around the corner and offered me a sincere smile.

"Glad to have you back," he said, his apology from yesterday lacing the words as my hug sent a signal of my acceptance.

Luna, if nothing else, could always read the room, saying nothing to Alexiares. She offered me one last hug, kissed Prescott's head and walked out the door. I took a seat in my usual spot as Prescott brought over three cups of coffee, handing Alexiares one before making mine just the way I favored and placing it down in front of me.

We snacked on some pan dulce Luna had brought from her last trip while playing mancala, chatting about unimportant things and enjoying each other's company. Pretending that the last few months weren't real. Alexiares said nothing as he sipped his coffee, observing us.

Every few minutes I'd peer up to see Prescott studying my face, my condition. The worry reflected clear across his face, lost in convoluting some plan to help that he hadn't noticed my own gaze. His eyes were sad too. He'd aged from a few months ago, the wrinkles crested on the corners of his eyes heavier. The worry lines on his forehead creased even when his face went relaxed. My absence had cost him too, probably in more ways than I could ever atone.

After two painfully long games of mancala, Prescott led us towards the door. Saying goodbye as we went our separate ways and he left for a meeting down at The Docks.

"So you guys are … oddly close," he said, not posing it as a question on our walk towards The Kitchens.

"Do you have a point?" I deadpanned.

He pursed his lips, shaking his head no in response. "Just an observation," he mumbled.

I stopped in my tracks before deciding to shake it off. It wasn't as much of an observation as it was an insinuation of more being there.

"Whatever, dude." Shaking my head, I went back to the happy silence we had walked in earlier.

Harley took off running. The reason became evident moments later as she rubbed her nose against one of the livestock vets. There were quite a few dogs and cats here. Some were brought in as companions people refused to let go of, then we had a few strays who wandered in on their own in hopes of food. Over the years, a few individuals who had thrived as veterinarians in The Before had come to settle. Now spending most of their time catering to the Stables and livestock, but also handling domestic vet work when needed.

The man laughed. He was a tiny ghost of a man, and I assumed he used ghost-like tactics to survive long enough to make it here. You could always tell who was haunted from their time out beyond these walls and who had escaped fairly lucky, rarely having to interact with the undead or worse, people who thrived in a world of anarchy.

"Hey there, Harley"—he grinned patting her head—"General," nodding in my direction as he took in Alexiares and Suckerpunch. His frown exaggerated as he took in his injuries as Suckerpunch hung back uncertainly, like he could smell the vet on him.

"And what happened here, big guy? Come here, buddy," he clicked his tongue, crouching low.

"Funny to find you out this way. We were headed to the Stables after dinner," I explained.

Alexiares described how he'd attempted to treat Suckerpunch's wounds and how the events had unfolded. I admired the dog from the side. A mountain lion was no small feat. Alexiares must have responded pretty promptly with some knowledge of what he was doing in order for Suckerpunch to still be here with us and not riddled with infection. Personally, I would've been a screaming mess. People were one thing. My baby Harley was another.

The vet assessed his wounds some more, wrapping the bandage back around his stomach and said he would take care of this and keep him overnight for monitoring. I surveyed Alexiares' face, noticing his initial anxious features turn to a more tangible visage of concern. It was beyond me considering he'd left the dog in an abandoned house overnight. Unsupervised. But I understood the fear of leaving your dog in the arms of an unknown stranger. Sympathizing with him, I commanded Harley to go with them, knowing she'd make her way back to our rooms before the night was done.

His face softened, but his anxiety lingered.

MY APPETITE WASN'T QUITE BACK YET, BUT MY BODY WAS FIGHTING TO win its war of hunger. Tonight was Shepherd's Pie, and the vegetarian version was decent enough to cause my stomach to grumble as Alexiares picked over his plate.

"Should I get a plate to pack it up for Suckerpunch? I have a feeling he would appreciate the food you're ready to discard."

His head rose as he looked me in the eye for the first time in hours. He said nothing, but the coldness in his eyes was clear. He wasn't in the mood. To shut me up, he shoveled the food down his throat, parroting a barbarian as Riley walked in and took in the view.

Confusion stretched over his classic features, brown eyes dancing in amusement at the disgust stretched across my face.

Chuckling, he asked, "Hey, uh, what's going on?"

He offered his hand. "Riley."

Alexiares glanced at it for a few moments before taking it, eyes focused on Riley. Completely missing the ants that left Riley's wrist and made their way up his arm and down his shirt.

I tossed my head towards Alexiares. "Riley, asshole. Asshole, Riley. Your new roomie."

The boys' eyes tore from my face and back to each other. Taking each other in and reading the situation. I knew Riley would say nothing and ask questions later, but I didn't expect Alexiares to be so docile.

One by one the others started to pile in, Tomoe first. Who, to her credit, said nothing, though I could feel the questions swirling her mind as she practically threw them at me with the daggers of her glare. She'd never been a fan of surprises, but in my defense when I'd seen her earlier, I had no intention of letting him stay. Let alone bring him to dinner.

Then came Reina, everyone's saving grace, as she introduced herself to him, slicing the silence of the table with her chatter and excitement. Filling us in on the last few hours of her life as if we hadn't seen her earlier in the day. Proceeding to dive into excruciating detail of every item of clothing she'd bought from one of the shops in Entertainment Square on her way back from a house call earlier. Alexiares watched her, both bewildered and annoyed at her ability to talk without stopping for air.

Seth strode into the room last as everyone else nearly finished, fists balled at his sides as he made a point to keep his gaze directly over my head. He sat towards the end of the table, saying nothing as he fixated on the space between me and Alexiares. There was a strong chance he'd have an attitude with me for days, but I was used to playing the waiting game with him. He'd get over it soon enough.

We both had consequences to pay when our leadership had failed. I was ready to accept mine. The least he could do is own up to his.

CHAPTER
TWENTY-THREE

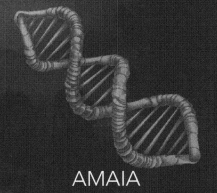

AMAIA

The few hours I had to myself after dinner were eerie. It was the first time I had truly been lucid in the last few months and had gone about my day as normal. It was a surreal feeling coming back to my room and not finding Jax there. Expecting to see him sneaking in a nap on the bed. Or running around my study causing chaos with Harley, tossing one of the many shoes Reina would drop off after talking it up with a vendor in Entertainment Square, introducing it to Harley as her 'new toy from Auntie Reina. I hated it. I moved around from my couch, to my desk and eventually to the floor leaned up against his side of the bed. Zoned out and exhausted from the day, I craved the taste of alcohol on my tongue.

One of the nights I'd attempted to run right after his death, I'd picked up some of my favorites in the darkness of the night.

Knowing my friends wouldn't be back for a few more hours to check on me. I'd taken advantage of the opportunity, filled a duffle bag with bottles of liquor and wines, and had plundered in it as I read away my reality.

I knew my pores reeked of it. Knew Reina could smell it on my breath, saw the disappointment in Tomoe's eyes when she'd take the empty bottles from my bedside and tucked it away before Reina could return. I'd heard Prescott demand Riley to have me cut off around The Compound and Riley remind Prescott what it would look like to the public if he did so.

If they openly addressed my drinking.

I dug my nails into my flesh, using the distraction of the pain to ignore the urge to pour a drink. My mind raced with Jax's words, echoed by Reina's wisdom ringing true. It was a hard pill to swallow. Admitting that the bottle was a crutch, not a requirement for survival. The alcohol was my escape, a way to dull the pain and forget the memories that haunted me. It was a choice, but one that I refused to let dictate the rest of my life. I'd decided nearly two days ago that my new beginning would be just that, another new Amaia.

The Amaia that existed without Jax. The Amaia that could stand on her own, take care of herself.

So I spent the rest of my evening distracting myself with the positive. I ran throughout The Compound with Harley, making sure to take a route that passed in front of Riley and now Alexiares home in the General Living Quarters. The lights were out in all the rooms. Whether that was a good or bad sign, I guess I'd learn in the morning.

Grabbing a coffee, I walked back to my quarters, taking a deep breathful of the salt from the ocean air. For once, it felt nice—in another life, I'd call the night peaceful. But I knew better than that. Was wise enough to never say *at least it didn't rain*, in the middle of a cloudy hike.

214

As I turned the corner, I halted in my steps, Harley bumping into the heels of my foot, caught off guard. Alexiares was in front of one of the apartments near the edge of the GLQ, talking to a man with honey colored skin and dark wavy hair. He was a bit shorter than Alexiares, but muscularly built. The man constantly checked over Alexiares' shoulder, an indication of the intensity of the conversation taking place.

I stepped back, catching my breath and cursing myself for being careless. *Interesting.* Too far to hear what they were saying, my only hope was that Riley's ants had hung in there and Alexiares wasn't sensitive enough to feel them creeping along his skin and clothes.

After a few seconds, I peered back around the corner, catching them in an embrace, neither of them ready to pull away. I hadn't figured him capable of having a genuine, empathetic bone in his body, and he'd never mentioned knowing someone in the community. Granted, I hadn't asked, but this only added to the extensive list of questions and suspicions I had surrounding him.

Alexiares headed down the alley to the right as I took a step back into the shadows. Wisely opting to give myself some space to casually walk past the man he'd been speaking to, now headed my way.

He gave me a sincere smile as he passed by, greeting me with a, "Good evening, General," and I took in the red rimming the bottom of his hazel eyes.

I recognized him but couldn't remember his name. He'd come here within those first few months, but had always kept to himself. It was a group of them, him, a few other guys, and a woman. None of them seeming *too off* for today's standards, but that was the extent of my memory. A girl could only retain so much information.

Quickening my pace to catch where he was headed, I stopped short, noticing the emptiness of the alleyway as I stared at his inked back. *Damnit.* No go. He'd whirl around the second we'd enter the alley.

Continuing back towards the way I had originally been headed, I let my thoughts wander, trying to unpack what I had seen. Every second replay in my mind like photos. Trying to pick out anything that stood out as being overly suspicious, what I could gather from their interaction and how it played into everything that was happening. I came up empty.

That night I fell asleep reading, eyes glazing over the text as my mind focused on the world around me.

"Fuckin' hell," Prescott uttered, leaning back into his chair. I'd made my way here at first light, determined to act on this as quickly as possible. Tossing and turning in my sleep, I woke before the sun rose, deciding to get started on the *critical* pile Riley had arranged on my desk.

If we were going to send people out, we needed to tell them as early as possible. Give them a chance at making good time or at the least have enough light to make decent progress today. There was no telling how bad things had gotten in between requests, and I'd sat on this for long enough already.

Before my leave of absence, Monterey had been the only settlement in the area under pressure. There were one off attacks along the other borders, but none that could hardly be deemed as out of the normal.

Luna was in full emissary mode. "All seven of us?" she mumbled. Running through all the information I had just presented them with. All seven of the settlements left in California had been facing similar attacks, but some of their forces weren't as strong as ours, and some simply just weren't as large. They needed help, they needed physical resources.

"Reno too, but I know that's a stretch." I was leaned up against the door, not wanting to sit down as I worked through my thoughts.

Selfishly, I wasn't sure how many soldiers I could spare already being on thin ice here ourselves, but I knew I couldn't leave them hanging without repercussions. That would take a few hours of discussion alone, and I wanted Luna's recommendations on who I should send. The emissaries wouldn't be able to head out a few days ahead in groups per our usual process.

"Absolutely not." It wasn't a command.

Luna would never command me to do anything, but she knew I trusted her opinion when it came to sending out emissaries. She was out there just as much as my troops. Instead of relying on the brothers and sisters around her, she had to rely on herself and herself alone.

I wasn't going to push her. "Okay. But my guess is if they've reached out to us, then they've reached out to Sacramento, San Jose, Fresno, Elko, and Vegas, too. We won't have confirmation unless we send someone out. I'd bet my best soldiers that Boise and Bend are on their short list if we reject them."

"So let them call for 'em," she pushed, waving her hand in the air with dismissal. "Sending someone out there alone through Yosemite is a death wish."

"What about Tahoe National?" I countered, it would take longer, but it was another option.

Her voice was grave as she stared into my eyes. "If The Pansies don't get them, the wildlife will. Those woods are dangerous, Amaia."

My attention shot towards Prescott, trying to see where his head was at. His fingers tapped against the arm of his chair and the fire cracked to the right of him. The room was tense as we both awaited his reply. I could take information that was provided to me as General to Prescott, but ultimately he made the final call.

The day-to-day calls were up to me; staffing the troops and sending out routine patrols and such, but sending out aid to others was a big decision. Some things required checks and balances. Same as in The Before. It wasn't so much a political situation as it was a safety one. We needed people here to keep *our* people safe first and foremost.

Compound first, always.

"So they won't go out in advance. They'll go out with our reinforcements. What's our headcount?" He examined me, and I wanted to find a hole to hide in.

I was tired of people looking at me with wary eyes, trying to see if I was in the right frame of mind and within all my senses. I knew he was just doing his job, but it bothered me most when it came to him. From someone who was supposed to have my back, no matter what.

"One thousand forty-five." I cleared my throat. "Two hundred are out on patrol right now. Our conditions are … less than desirable at the moment."

They looked at each other before I added, "But that doesn't mean we shouldn't help. I can make it work. I know my troops. They can help."

Prescott's hand ran through his beard, his blue eyes scanning me over once more and I held firm under his scrutinizing gaze, ultimately deciding to trust my work, at least in the moment. His eyes lingered a moment in warning, this was a trial run.

"Okay, I'll sign off on it." He sighed and shook his head, fighting with the logic of the situation versus doing what was right. "It still has to go through the Council and they're going to want answers that we don't have, Amaia. You may want to help, but we can't afford to send anyone to Reno, no matter if an emissary went ahead of your soldiers or not. Let's just hope they can come back with some useful information. There has to be a reason for an uptick in attacks. It doesn't make any sense, the numbers in Pansies should be *dwindling*, not—"

"About that." I gulped, remembering what I had seen out there with Riley. "I think they can talk to each other, Prescott. Or communicate in some kind of way." Concern covered their faces but they allowed me to continue.

"Two days ago, I went out to Jax's grave. There were three of them there, standing in a circle. They've developed some sort of language, I guess? Nothing but a series of grunts and moans, but it was *weird*. Then the attack later that day, all of them showing up at once, not moving like a normal herd, targeting the gate ironically during a shift change. Of all times of the day to attack and *no one* saw or heard them coming? Come on now, you can't think that's just a coincidence."

"Amaia," he said, brushing me off. His hand fell to his temple. "We've been over this, and I'm not interested in returning to the conversation. When resources are solidified, I want a full briefing."

A dismissal. We'd been down this road many times before. From the moment I met him, I told him I believed there were people still in there, that a cure was possible. They were just sick. He'd quickly corrected that thought, bringing a Pansie to me and making an example of them, telling me that silly line of thinking would get me killed.

It'd changed nothing for me in that moment, I knew what'd I'd seen in that apartment with Xavier. His eyes when he'd thought I'd burned him. But when you're told things long enough, you start to believe there may be some truth there. I couldn't say I still believed it in totality, but a small part of me couldn't comprehend that a human soul was there at one point. And now it was just gone.

It wasn't like someone that had died and left their body behind, departed this world and went to whatever was next. No, this body was still animated, it still moved, it still ate, still had needs. A person with rabies is still a person.

But that's not what this was about. This was about something that I'd seen with my own eyes, that someone else had witnessed. I left the topic alone, only because there was no point in pushing it without Riley here to back me up. Even then, Prescott would simply claim his bias, besides the fact that it was one situation alone. That was no case study, only a small sample group.

Luna took a deep breath, her kind features filled with worry. "I hope you know what you're doing," she said, as she took a seat on the arm of Prescott's chair.

Her words weren't malicious. They came from a place of genuine hope and trust in my abilities. Hoping I was sane enough to effectively do my job and not get her friends killed.

We spent the next few minutes running through a list of emissary's Luna felt capable of executing our needs and holding their own in the current climate of things. There was no 'Head of Emissaries,' just people that were trusted to handle various aspects of Compound business.

Some were great for trade, others were great for simply maintaining relationships that kept the lines of communication open, others were used during times of establishing borders and handling feuds. Very few people had the competence and confidence to do what Luna did. Were capable of handling all the above.

Seven emissaries would be sent out, though they would only be going to six settlements. Two would go to San Diego since they'd have to pass the chaos of Los Angeles on the way. There was a chance they could be there two days ahead of schedule if they booked it after passing the city.

Each emissary would go to discuss coordinating further efforts in the immediate future. Reinforcements would then be sent to help stabilize the borders and allow for more coordinated offense initiatives. Although I knew how many soldiers I planned on sending out, I needed to check with Seth first and confirm he was okay with this course of action. My biggest challenge would be seeing if he was feeling gracious enough to lend some of his calvary.

MY MEETING WITH SETH WAS LESS THAN PLEASANT. HE STILL HAD AN attitude about yesterday, but I could tell it was slowly fading. He agreed to send out men and had no qualms about the numbers I intended to deploy.

Sending out a hundred men would be a push, but sixteen men and an emissary were better than nothing. It would show good faith on our end if nothing else. Two *Ignis* soldiers, two *Aqua,* two *Terra,* two *Aer.* Two *Ignis* and *Terra,* one *Aqua* and *Terra,* and one *Aer* and *Terra.* Four *Supra* as they practically counted as eight soldiers and one from Seth's calvary would be sent in addition in order to escort the emissaries safely. They'd all make a last-ditch sprint on the final day of travel.

No cavalry would be sent to support the mission to San Jose since it was so close. Our troops already heavily populated the area, thus making two of Seth's men available to join the trek to San Diego instead. I debated sending out some medics, uncomfortable with the idea of sending men out there without proper resources, but our resources here were already thin. Without the ability to wait for the next patrol troop to return, a tough call had to be made. We'd have to hope the *Aqua* soldiers with minor healing gifts would be enough to tend to any minor wounds. Herbs would have to do the rest, if anything could be done for them at all without surgery.

We split the missions into a list and each planned three routes to get there. One that was the most efficient, a Plan B, and a failsafe that would take twice the amount of time, but would ensure they all made it there. It was up to the mission lead to determine which was their best option once they assessed the conditions when they departed. Seth would check in with them every day at a set time per squad.

I left my meeting with Seth feeling accomplished in handling one item on a stack of critical, but uneasy for what I was sending a hundred men and women out to do. No matter how successful each mission went, a handful of them wouldn't be returning.

CHAPTER
TWENTY-FOUR

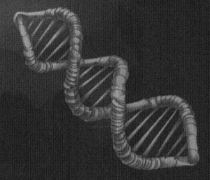

AMAIA

T he rest of my morning went as planned. The Council had met
for an emergency meeting and one of my soldiers returned
with notice that my plans had been approved. I'd taken a trip
to the Infirmary to check on the injured from a few days prior,
taking a moment to sit and talk with them each individually.

It was important to show face as a leader, but the time I spent
with them went beyond that. I genuinely cared about their recovery and the idea of my failure causing their pain consumed me in
a way I never knew guilt could. It clawed at my soul and whispered
in my ears vile things every time the room went silent.

I wanted to personally avenge them all, but I also wanted
to be there for them through this in any capacity that I could. It
wouldn't take them much longer to heal. Magic speeding up the

process, but I'd be sure to honor each one of them when this was all over.

Even though it made me uneasy to have Alexiares free to roam about The Compound, part of me was glad at the peace his absence provided. I hadn't seen him since last night. Before lunch, I ventured throughout the entirety of The Compound for the first time in months. Sure to take note of the status of our infrastructure, seeing what maintenance was needed, and envisioning what improvements could be made.

Each one of the four gates received extra scrutiny as I took in each detail from the spikes, to the barbed wire, blasting my fire at the metal and testing its durability. As I took my leave, I informed the soldiers on duty that there would be drills run once a week regarding gate protocol for the foreseeable future.

We wouldn't be caught off guard again.

I saw off the soldiers' deployment from the South Gate after lunch. Although they were headed in different directions, it would make us too vulnerable to have all gates open at once. It was equally irresponsible to delay their departure by stacking the timing.

From there, they'd break off into a small group until each of them reached a necessary split off point. It wouldn't make a huge difference as most would have to split after the first day, but an extra night of protection would always be a plus.

The gate sealed shut, and a presence crept up behind me. Tomoe wore her hair clipped up to escape the scorching sun, while her ebony tank top matched the hilt of her katana and harness. Her fingers clutched a familiar well-worn notebook.

"It's done?" I asked, reaching to take it from her.

She moved me into the shadows near the gate, replying in a hushed tone. I'd asked her to spend time translating Alexiares's notebook, intending to keep the contents inside close to home. Deciding to err on a side of caution in case there was pertinent information. Of course there was a chance something could be lost in translation by not having a native speaker do the translation. But I'd decided that Tomoe would get the first look, and if what she discovered appeared to have any holes in it or anything dire, we'd explore our other options.

"Here, you were right. It's Greek. But"—she handed it to me and I realized her smile wasn't full of worry, but rather sadness—"we have nothing to worry about."

It was evident she had no intention of divulging more details. "You okay? What's wrong? He's a serial killer in his past life? Fuckin knew it."

"Honestly, Amaia, it's none of your, my, or anyone else's business. It's a journal, he's grieving. Why are you hyper fixated on him?" Her voice was harsher than most would appreciate, but I knew my friend was just trying to understand where I was coming from.

The familiar feeling of guilt racked over my body. *A journal? Grieving?* Another feeling I knew all too well.

We'd been two grieving people, using our words as weapons to mask the pain. But that still didn't excuse his resistance to answer simple questions, and it certainly didn't explain his sense of timing with his arrival. Matter of fact, he hadn't arrived at all. He was *hiding* and was found. There was a difference.

I squared my shoulders, deciding that I should still proceed with caution with him ... but that didn't mean I couldn't have a little bit more compassion.

"There's something off," I said, shaking my head. "I don't know what it is, Moe, but he's hiding something."

"Maybe it's not for us to find out."

I gave my friend a grim smile, wanting to dive deeper but also trusting her position on this. If anyone understood grief, it was her. She wasn't the same as the rest of us. She'd been lucky when it all happened. Her whole family had made it out alive, just to be torn apart later on. Literally.

"Moe ..." I decided to try pushing *just* a bit more.

I didn't want to pull the General card, but there were things I needed to know to do my job properly. Vengeance was still fresh on my mind and I knew grief could make people do crazy things.

She obliged, knowing where I was headed and sparing me having to pull the power card. "His little brother. All he does is talk about his little brother. He's using it to work through his grief. Some are poems, some are letters. But like I said, it's not meant for anyone's eyes but his. It's invasive."

There was distaste in her voice, they'd said nothing since I'd gotten back. At least nothing to my face. Wanting to keep what fragile peace existed within the group. But I saw the whispers under their breaths. The side eyes that were thrown my way about my skepticism towards Alexiares. Riley double checked my math on each route, and Seth had made me read my list of materials for the soldiers' packs out loud before signing off.

They were questioning my judgment; I was sure of it.

"I skimmed it for the most part, but it's some real heavy shit in there, Maia," Moe concluded.

I frowned, deciding to back off for now. I didn't have any siblings. I couldn't possibly understand that level of loss.

Finding myself stuck with more questions now than ever, I changed the subject. Opting to give her a different reason to feel uncomfortable, "So ... tell me about you and Seth, miss ma'am. Apparently, I missed a lot."

Moe's face reddened as she turned her head to the left, trying to hide the wide smile that replaced her sad one. We walked back towards our study's, ready to wrap up the rest of our work for the day. Chatting, two normal girls out for a gossip walk in the park. It felt good to feel like this again, to feel weightless and carefree even if it were just for a few fleeting moments.

Seth and Moe had spent the last few nights together, Seth pushing to stay close in case things went wrong in the middle of the night. Moe pretending that she was insulted by his insistence on playing protector, but the tenderness in her face betrayed the words on her lips, looking every bit like a woman in love. I was happy for her, for them, truly, I wanted to support my friend, but they were fire and ice. And part of me feared that one day the intensity of their connection might consume them both.

A FEW DAYS PASSED. SETH HAD HEARD FROM ALL GROUPS BUT ONE. San Diego had last reported near Riverside and had gone silent since. He'd tried each soldier multiple times and had received nothing but brain static.

I wasn't naïve enough to be hopeful any of them were alive. It wasn't just that they had chosen *not* to answer Seth. He'd attempted to feel around in their minds, poking and prodding, but there was nothing.

I'd had to bring Reina in, her power claiming him, bringing Seth to a sedative state. No matter how death had become a standard in our daily lives, it would always be a lot to handle. To insert yourself into the mind of another person was an intimate, personal thing.

You felt the essence of that person as you spoke to them. He could only enter a willing mind, but with effort he could take what he needed if no magic was there blocking him out. On the off chance that there was, he'd be able to feel it, pushing defensively against his magic as he searched for an in.

There was none. No magic telling him he was forbidden to enter. If someone died with Seth having access to their minds, he would be able to take on their entire being, or what was left of them if entered in time. He'd done it enough for me to know that the feeling of death on someone who was very much alive, was, well, a feeling worse than death itself. Because although you were alive, you now knew exactly what it felt like to die. Knew exactly what the immediate after felt like too.

I was torn about my next course of action. Sending someone out after them was to send someone else on a death mission. It could prove futile. Pointless. But I also couldn't just leave them out there. Those were *my* people. I was responsible for them.

And I'd sealed their fates the moment they walked out those gates.

It was Riley who offered a solid solution, to redirect some of the men he'd sent out in that direction days ago. They were men of shadows, who evaded both the living and the dead assuming their life depended on it. They *did* depend on it. I was reluctant, not wanting to damn what was left of Riley's family, but knowing we needed answers.

Moe's visions were only able to provide so much, it had drained her magic completely, channeling that many people, but their deaths had been savage and quick. We'd received the answers we needed. It'd been Pansies, and no, we wouldn't be able to send people out to retrieve them even if we wanted to. There were too many of them.

Riverside was overrun.

It hadn't been an active city, but that didn't mean there weren't people who had been living there, in between settlements. San Diego was on their own until the rest of us had time to regroup, and by then, who knew what would be left?

"And Alexiares?" I asked, bringing him up for the first time since he'd left my watch.

I knew if there was anything crucial, anything suspicious worth reporting, Riley wouldn't hesitate to make me aware, but I couldn't help myself from trying to pry information from him.

I'd given him Alexiares' journal to hand back the day I'd received it from Moe. Opting to deliver it indirectly for no other reason than to avoid further conflict. With him vulnerable and my mortification for invading his privacy, an accusation he'd tossed, now true, we were sure to argue, if not come to blows.

"There's not much to tell. He spends most of his time wandering around The Compound. He asks a few questions, but nothing he shouldn't. Just trying to figure out how he can navigate life around here for the most part. A bit of culture shock." He paused, trying to gauge my reaction. "He's not a bad guy, you know. A bit grumpy, sure, but who the hell isn't around here? Look around." *Look in the mirror,* his eyes said.

I nodded my head. "Have you noticed him hanging around anyone consistently? Any friends yet?"

Riley's locs fell forward as he sighed. "No, not anyone besides me. He heads out to breakfast with me, but other than that, he pretty much keeps to himself. Back at the house when I get there, usually smelling like that chili from that place you like. Though not sure where he got the money from to buy it."

Everyone besides me was pretty content with the answers Alexiares provided to their questions. He didn't dine with us at dinner but had come across them individually throughout The Compound over the last few days, and none had found him to be remotely suspicious.

It wasn't that I didn't trust my friend's judgment of character, just maybe they weren't asking the *right* questions. They'd known death and grief, sure, but none of them possessed a vengeful spirit the way I did. None of them knew the things death could make you want to do.

I saw it in Seth sometimes, that twinkle in his eye when he was upset, but it disappeared in quick bouts of violence. It didn't linger. I saw it in Moe at times too, the way she fiercely brought her katana down upon each Pansies head she'd come across. Slicing through them, the ease suggesting that they were nothing but the thick Monterey morning foggy air with a smile on her face. But her smile faded into sadness when she was done, remembering the reason she was so pleased to put an end to the undead.

I doubted they lay awake at night the way I do, envisioning the death of the monster who was behind this all. Picturing in my mind the way I would take my time destroying them, piece by piece, limb by limb. Pulling their organs out one at a time, making sure they were awake as I removed a lung, a kidney, maybe even their spleen. Leaving the vital organs for last, making them watch the pull that ended it all.

Not just for Jax but for each person this place had lost, wanting each of their deaths to represent an hour of pain, slowly bringing them to their demise. I wanted to be the one to do it. No weapons, no magic, just my bare hands.

I didn't see that in my friend's eyes, but I saw it in mine. In Alexiares. And maybe he didn't have an agenda coming here. Maybe he just wanted to heal. Maybe I had him entirely wrong.

But maybe I didn't.

"ABSOLUTELY NOT," I EXCLAIMED.

Alexiares sat in the chair on the other side of my desk, smirking, his honey eyes dancing with amusement.

I looked from him to Riley, who was currently avoiding eye contact, sheepishly inspecting his dirty ass boots. This was a first for him, for as many times as I'd caught him off guard, he'd never once returned the favor. Never once pushed back.

"What would help this go down a bit easier? You want an apology. Would that help feed your ego?"

The pencil in my hand snapped under pressure as I choked down words sharper than knives, deciding that him down on his knees, groveling for my forgiveness would please me after all. "Hm, actually yes. An apology would be a fantastic start considering you just waltzed into my office to ruin my morning." I gave him a fake grin.

"Yeah, well, I don't apologize to malevolent little girls so un-fuck you or whatever. Can we move on like adults now? Or am I missing a please and thank you?"

Riley cleared his throat and took a seat against the door. "You're not helping your case here man, just tell her what you told me." Alexiares didn't turn to him, but his face softened at his words.

I rolled my eyes at him, annoyed at his continued defense. "Yeah well to be honest Riley, I'm waiting on your apology next. I'd implore you to stop talking too. Just a thought."

His tongue rolled over his teeth, but he said nothing as he leaned his head back, thudding on the door.

"Look, I've been out there for the last few months. I've got a good idea on the situation out there and can help—"

"Help?" I let out a small laugh. "And why would you want to help? You've done nothing but made it clear I've displayed poor leadership, that I get people killed, right after you shoved me against the wall. The hell would I let you under my leadership for? To cause chaos?"

He leaned into the arm of the chair and smirked. "That was actually *before* I shoved you into the wall. But I understand it was a hard hit. Would it get me bonus points if I at least pretended to respect you?"

"Okay, this is going to go nowhere," Riley said, pushing to his feet and walking towards us as Alexiares fingered at his rings. "Amaia, you haven't been here the last few months. Things *aren't* normal. Something's going on and you're nowhere close to getting to the bottom of it. Seth and I don't even know where to start. We were barely holding on while you were away. I love you, but he's right. He's been out there in the midst of it all. His power levels match none but yours. He can fight. I heard about your spar.

They say they haven't seen *anyone* match you like that. *Ever.* Shit, he kicked *my* ass a few times at this point."

My eyes shot to Alexiares, who met my stare blankly.

Riley continued, "What I'm saying is, we could use his help. If nothing else, he's another soldier we've got on our side. If you don't want him out fraternizing with the others, put him under my command."

"Are you?" I asked.

Alexiares blinked. "Am I what?"

"On our side?" It was a simple question. If he truly was, there wouldn't be any hesitation, a need to second guess his mission here.

"Yes." He didn't hesitate. His eyes didn't flicker from my own, no longer fidgeting with his fingers.

He displayed no signs of discomfort, or dishonesty. "But just because I want to fight on your side doesn't mean I have to blindly support leadership without question. It doesn't mean I have to like you, or respect you." The latter came out in a snarl.

As much as I hated how much his bitter words pitted themselves deep in my soul, I knew he was right. He didn't have to do any of those things, he just had to listen to my command. In fact, if those words had come from anyone else's mouth, I'd respect them for it. Only a sheep would follow blindly, and the last thing I wanted in my troops was a bunch of sheep.

No, I wanted lions. I wanted wolves; I wanted savages. I wanted people who fought tooth and nail and gave their very last for the greater good. And while I had no question that he would give his life for a greater cause, I wasn't sure it was mine.

Each day that passed was another day I came up empty for evidence on his role in the larger part of what was going on. Shit. If I had any clues or evidence that something larger was going on, I still hadn't completely ruled out that this wasn't the collective result of shitty leadership from every settlement in the state. There was no reason but my own gut to keep Alexiares from working under Riley.

It was the next best option for Alexiares, anyway. He wouldn't be an official part of my troops. Wouldn't have the luxury of knowing our operation plans, take note of our resources, know of our contingency plans or anything else important.

While Riley's men could be soldiers, they weren't always. And the men he was responsible for deploying out into the world or living in the shadows of The Compound, they operated on a need-to-know basis only. They worked off information that was essential to getting the job done, and that alone was enough to get me to agree to this stipulation. That and he would remain relatively monitored while he reported his daily movements to Riley in their mandatory debriefs.

"Fine," I ground out, making sure Riley took note of every minuscule displeased movement of my face, "if you're willing to risk everything you've worked hard for on this degenerate, then as you wish. Now get out of my office."

Alexiares offered a smug grin as I rose from my seat and moved into my bedroom, pulling on the running clothes that I'd dropped onto my floor late last night. I needed to run. It was the only thing keeping me from spiraling.

CHAPTER
TWENTY-FIVE

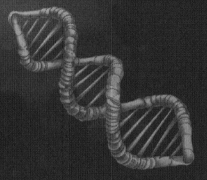

AMAIA

T hings were tense with Riley in the days that followed. We'd
never had a falling out of sorts before and it was new territory
for us both. The time we spent together didn't change. He was
still there throughout my days. Showing up when I needed him the
most and for any planned meetings, unfortunately accompanied
by the nuisance named Alexiares anytime there was no confiden-
tial information being discussed. In the moments where Alexiares
wasn't around, the air between Riley and I was still heavy.

Our usual easy, comfortable relationship felt weighted, an-
chored in my anger and his silence. He apologized. Insisted it
didn't mean he supported me any less, apologized on behalf of
him and Alexiares for the words Alexiares had spoken and described the near squabble they'd had after they'd left.

Riley was disgusted with the change he'd seen in Alexiares behavior, seeing the side of him I'd complained about for the first time. Had felt guilty for bringing him into my space and cornering me. He also emphasized he remained firm in believing having Alexiares on our side was acting for the good of us all. Trying to give us any advantage possible.

Not once did he apologize for questioning my judgment. The words were on the tip of his tongue, I could see him fighting with the words. Ultimately, deciding not to say them at all. He'd never be sorry for that. For me. For the others that were left of the family he'd found. Riley would never apologize for questioning what would keep us safe.

I didn't fault him for any of it. Still, the first rift in our relationship had every interaction feeling forced and unnatural. The effortless flow in our conversations that were once as if we were connected in the mind now stumbled and stuttered. Neither of us wanted to address that either, hoping time would heal all.

He fell into stride with me as I ran throughout The Compound late Wednesday night. We'd laid the final soldier to rest from the attack, the officialness of all the loss overwhelming. I'd only lasted a few minutes alone with my thoughts that evening before prying up the floorboard under my bed and downing half a bottle of tequila. It'd come back up in my toilet moments after. I wouldn't let it win.

The reflection in the mirror scared me the most, the emptiness in my eyes that replaced the hope that had once gleamed in them.

Every night I ran through a list of ways to up our surveillance and patrols. Drafting up new questions to ask when debriefing returning patrol units, creating new training plans to prepare the new units that would be sent out in a relief effort. Double and triple checking all communication transcripts that sometimes came through over the radio. Making sure I didn't miss any records of emissaries that had been in and out of our gates the last few months. Reviewing Tomoe's vision transcripts from the witnesses she channeled after each attack. I'd read through Jax's final vision transcription more times than I could count, each time hurting just as much as the first.

After that, I'd move on to reviewing any patterns we could place on the attacks, but if I was honest with myself, there weren't many. They never happened at the same time of day, nor did they present a favored day of the week. The weather conditions were never consistent either, rain or shine. Fog or mist, it didn't matter.

Each of the attacks aside from Jax's had involved Pansies, leading my only solid conclusion to be that that was an assassination, an execution. Not an attack. Had they been lucky, had Jax not told me to take my first day off in weeks, I'd likely be six feet under right next to him. If I was a gambling woman, I'd put everything I love on the fact that the second explosion was meant to be the one to take me out.

The motivations were all over the place. Trade caravans, others were patrol units, Jax's assassination and our gate being breached, then there was our San Diego squad, though we'd never be sure if Riverside was simply overrun by a herd or if they were ambushed. We wouldn't know the extent of the situations at other settlements until the emissaries were able to give a full debrief to Seth in a few more days. From an educated guess, I had to assume their situations were the same, if not more dire due to lack of numbers and solid infrastructure.

When my brain was mush and I could no longer take it, I ran. I ran until I couldn't breathe anymore. Until my legs burned and the only thing I had any energy left to do was lay in my bed and fall asleep.

So Riley ran with me.

Two weeks. That was all we'd gotten. Two weeks of peace and quiet, free from any attacks. Fom funerals. Fom death. All the other groups had made it to their final destinations aside from San Diego.

San Jose, Fresno, and Bakersfield were now under control. Sacramento was stable for the moment, but calling on our closest neighbors in Vegas for help. Reno was out of the question for aid considering their recent pleas for help, and Portland had agreed to send a few soldiers down but would take longer to get there. Redding was also stable. We all knew it would only remain that way for as long as Sacramento and Reno could hold on.

The reports from all had been the same, borders had been under constant strain, and if the General didn't fall, the Lieutenant had. Sacramento had lost both. Niklas, Prescott's closest ally in San Jose, had been slain. He'd been attacked visiting his old home right outside their walls on the anniversary of his late wife's death.

It wasn't hard for me to figure out these had all been targeted hits. An attempt to cause chaos by taking out crucial leaders in the community in the midst of instability. Two questions remained: who, and why?

Reina and I had been cuddled into the little couch. Moe, sitting on the floor, leaned up against us in her study. Moe and I were reading while Reina pretended to. She hummed as she thumbed through the pages of her book and Moe elbowed her every so often, telling her to shut up.

I smiled to myself. Happy things had finally started to feel a bit normal around The Compound, as I'd found a steady new rhythm of life. Most of my free time I still spent hyper fixated on figuring out what was going on. But, I'd made little efforts here and there to focus on the way forward, and not all that I had lost. I'd even changed the sheets for the first time since Jax's passing.

Reina insisted that burning them in a fit of rage while dumping every bottle of alcohol in my room on top didn't count, but we all grieve in different ways.

A cup of chamomile tea warmed the top of my lip when the door to Moe's study flew open and bounced off the wall.

"Shit," I yelped, surprised by the splash of hot liquid that now covered my shirt, "Reina, what the hell." I glared at her, her jumpiness causing me to now be covered in chamomile and honey.

"Oh hush, don't blame me, blame this asshole," she said, sitting up, gesturing to her brother glowering in the door frame. She turned to look at me. "Darn. You're all sticky now. Here I'll help!"

I was up in an instant as she chased me around the room playfully, trying to pull my shirt over my head. Eagerly offering me one off the floor from Moe's messy space.

"Seth, what the hell?" I heard Moe exclaim as she rose to her feet, her inked arms crossed over her chest, pulling her long silky hair taut over her head.

I couldn't hear his response outside of *attack* as Seth's voice muffled in my head as Reina trapped my arms against my ears with my shirt.

"Urgh, Reina, get off—"

"Got it! Here!" she cheerily said, handing me a black tank top.

I snatched it from her, turning back towards Seth. "What's going on?"

His eyes remained on mine, not bothering to take notice of my now exposed bra. We'd been out beyond these walls together many times, it wasn't anything he hadn't seen before. He'd had my back as I washed up in rivers and streams, and I his. Privacy didn't exist when you were focused on remaining as safe as possible.

As his lips parted in response, Riley came from behind him, his brows furrowed and his jaw was tight. His gaze was heavy with sorrow, and my heart dropped into my stomach. Things were bad again.

Seth turned as he felt Riley approaching his rear. Two beady, dead chestnut eyes met mine, followed by a slow look up and down my body with a smirk as I pulled my shirt down into place. The feeling of his gaze lingering against my skin.

"Oh gross," Reina blurted, taking in the interaction and taking a step forward to obstruct Alexiares' view. Squeezing her hand, I gave her a quick thanks as I put my new shirt on for the sake of having a serious conversation.

I cleared my throat. "Well somebody speak up. What's going on? It's ten p.m."

"One of my men. They showed up with one of Seth's. It's bad."

As much as I wanted to press forward, I gave him a minute to collect himself and his thoughts. Alexiares guided Riley through the door and closed it, then gave him a comforting pat on the back, urging him to continue. Tears of guilt swelled in Riley's, brimming the bottom lines of his dark eyes.

I shook my head, rolling my eyes, not bothering to hide my annoyance at his assumption of being important enough to take up space in this room. Let alone have the audacity to offer an ounce of comfort to anyone inside of it.

Seth took over, realizing it was his turn to step in to debrief, as Riley had taken on for him many times before. Always having his back, despite the natural distance that existed between the two. "One of my calvary practically rammed his horse through East Gate with Riley's guy barely strapped and hangin' on to the back. It's fuckin' bad y'all. Bites everywhere. My guy found him as he hauled ass back towards us from Reno. Trade line's been compromised."

Moe took a seat in my peripheral. *I knew we should've sent people that way. I knew it.*

"No. You don't get to do that. You don't get to blame yourself and leave us dealing with the pieces again," Moe said quietly from her seat.

My fingers curled and my gaze shot back up, realizing they were all watching me. "Yeah, this ain't your fault. No one could have predicted this," Reina added.

Seth and Riley were still, soldiers awaiting their orders, each of them looking exhausted. No longer from a lack of sleep since the last few weeks had slowed down, but from never knowing what was coming our way. Always wondering which friend would be next.

"I *should* have sent people that way. There's no denying that, and that's my mistake to own. But there's nothing I can do about it now," my eyes wandered to Alexiares, who was now leaning up against the door next to Riley, studying my every move, "I guess—I guess we're going to Reno."

"Us?" Riley questioned tentatively.

"No. Not us, but someone else that's qualified. We have too much to lose if we send one of us right now, knowing the risk for Seth, Riley, or me. I wouldn't send just one without sending us all. And where things stand, I'm not seeing Reno as being the source of all our problems, but merely another victim. It'd be a waste of risk. We're staying here."

Seth and Riley nodded in agreement.

"Is he awake and talking?" Moe asked, cracking her knuckles, ready to play her role.

The men nodded again and Moe was back on her feet headed towards the door. Riley and Alexiares moved to either side of it, she paused, turning back towards me for further instructions.

"I need to know what they saw, so spend a decent amount of time on them both, but don't exhaust yourself. You can always finish in the morning. I need to know whether it was a full-scale attack or an ambush. The more details you can pick up, the better. Anything like noticeable strengths or weaknesses is key."

Their eyes shot in my direction skeptically, questioning why any of this would matter when it came to Pansies. As far as everyone else in this side of the world was concerned, Pansies were aimless, uncoordinated, unstructured creatures who acted on impulse. Everyone I knew held on to that belief. Pretended it was the last piece of science from The Before that made sense. I'd never fully bought that. Had seen with my own eyes reason to believe otherwise.

And now so had Riley.

He nodded at me to continue on. "If ... see if you can pick up on any communication patterns as well."

She gave me a concerned smile, the question they all wanted to ask lingering in her eyes. "Yeah, you got it, Gen," Moe said, giving me a mocking salute before she headed out the door.

"I'll go see what information I can get from their injuries," Reina chirped, a bit too excited for the subject matter. I knew it was only the love of the job. The ability to heal and learn fed her soul, and I loved that for her.

"So now what?" Seth asked, pacing a bit in his immediate space, ready for me to give him something to do.

It was just the four of us left. Alexiares and Riley were still on either side of the door, and Seth now leaned up against the arm of the couch. I moved next to Riley, my head resting on his shoulder, offering him a small token of comfort as the next words left my mouth.

They were bitter and tart, leaving my lips, but they were necessary. "Now we send out a team to gather what Moe can't from her visions."

Seth's eyes turned violent. "A suicide mission, then? Fuckin' fantastic." A sharp laugh left his throat.

"He's right, Maia. What sense does that make? There's a reason Luna said no. We already knew that was a dangerous trade route." Riley's voice was toneless. He'd had to distance himself from the conversation, set his personal relationships to the side. "They knew the risks."

The shock of his second deferment in my judgment rattled me to my core as I moved a step away, studying his face. It was a gut blow. The feeling that we were no longer connected the way we had been, knowing my absence had caused that, no matter the weeks I'd spent trying to make up for it.

"Well, what else would you all like me to do? Hmm?" I paced the room and tossed my hands in the air. "Twiddle my thumbs some more, perhaps? Something's got to give and playing it safe isn't going to cut it anymore. We're sitting fucking ducks."

Their eyes followed me. Alexiares toyed with the silver rings he always wore no matter what he did during the day. I'd only seen him remove them once, during his assessment. He hadn't so much as blinked since Moe and Reina had left the room.

"I'm not asking for guidance or permission for this. I've made my mind up. We're never going to learn anything if we keep relying on old information to come in from emissaries and whatever scraps Moe can pull from a vision. Seth, can you *feel* anything?" I looked at him, not missing the confusion on Alexiares face.

He hesitated, taking a second to threaten Alexiares with his storm filled eyes before glaring at me and answering, "Yeah. But it's weak and nothin' strong enough to latch onto and figure out what's happening out there."

My nose scrunched. A weak connection meant they were dying. Whoever we sent out next wouldn't make it in time, but it did mean there was something left for us to go back to. We didn't have that confirmation for the San Diego mission. We could have lost them anywhere from Riverside to their next check in location.

With Seth's man being a witness, we not only had a live account for what happened, we also had a scene to go back to for clues.

"Well then, sounds like we've got a reason to go."

My words echoed in the now silent room. Minutes passed before Riley nodded in agreement.

Seth threw his head back, sloshing onto the couch. "Then *you* figure out who we're about to send to their death."

"I'll go."

Our bodies rustled, slicing through the air to listen to Alexiares, speaking his first words since he walked into the room.

"Yeah buddy, I don't think so." I scoffed, turning to Seth and Riley to finish our conversation.

"I'm serious, let me go—"

"I don't even know why you're here, let alone speaking."

Seth leaned forward and motioned for me to be quiet. "No, let him speak. I wanna hear what the kids gotta to say."

Of course you do.

"By all means." I motioned for him to continue.

He strode towards the center of the room before clearing some of the mess from the coffee table and taking a seat. "Think about it. I just came through the area a few weeks ago. Suckerpunch and I holed up during a stormy week. I can eliminate some risk because unless a helluva lot has changed since then. I know the general layout, and any traps that need to be evaded along the way. I take it y'all won't be taking your usual route"—He looked at me—"or your Plan B. Thus leaving it up to chance. *Unless*," the words sang from his lips, "you follow the steps I took to get here myself. Leaving only the last few miles a real risk."

"Ironic, isn't it?" I accused, "You just happened to pass through a now tumultuous piece of land that was once stable enough to cross through at mild risk. And now you're here, a walking tornado if you will."

Riley cleared his throat and rubbed the back of my shoulder, trying to talk me down, but I shrugged him off.

"He's not wrong, but neither are you," Seth decided, eyeing him from the corner of his eyes as they all faced me, awaiting my decision.

"Fine. You can go. But only because that means there's a strong chance you won't come back." I threw him a fake grin, teeth shining, before flipping Riley and Seth off in response to ganging up on me.

I succumbed to the silence of the room as Seth met my eye. We were thinking the same thing. We needed a way to approach this mission without Alexiares knowing of Seth's abilities.

He couldn't get inside his head without him knowing Seth was there, and that was a secret we both weren't yet ready to expose. Which made Alexiares a liability. Meant whoever else we sent out needed to be people we trusted completely, to study Alexiares and ensure he could be trusted. But we also had to make sure they were capable of doing a thorough job of investigating what was left of the site.

Seth groaned. "Ahh, fuck it. I'm in," he said a tad too enthusiastically, like brother like sister. "I could use a bit of action right now. It's been too calm around here, anyway."

There was fear dancing in his eyes, but also excitement at the idea of violence. My stomach turned. I hoped I'd made the right decision for once.

CHAPTER
TWENTY-SIX

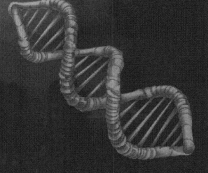

ALEXIARES

"We go on foot from here." I hopped off one of Seth's horses outside of a few stables in Lake Tahoe.

I'd taken them on the longest route here, hanging wide to avoid the friction near Sacramento. That and they hadn't bothered clearing any of the interstate this way. Most travel was that way now. The fastest way being the longest simply because the shortest way was the one everyone took when flocking out to wherever.

His horses and his men were well trained, covering about fifty miles a day, clearly bred for both speed and endurance. It was impressive. The horse he'd provided me with moved with preternatural grace and power. Each one of her strides hitting the ground with precision, never tiring. Her soft neighs and huffs indicating she was almost irritated when we stopped each night.

We'd pushed them hard over the last four days, riding as long as the sun would allow us to. There'd be plenty of days to rest once we'd made it here. Luck was on our side, each late August storm passing over us. Though the static in the sky suggested our luck had run out. Most of the ride had been easy going. We were able to outride most of the undead we'd come across, and Seth and his men easily blew through the more stubborn ones who stood in our way. Our pace was quick enough that sound wasn't much of a concern. We'd be long gone once anything made its way to where we previously had pranced.

The sun had been relentless, beating down on us all day, but as we approached the lake near sunset, the air took a frigid turn. Seth's red hair plastered to his head as he removed his cowboy hat and hopped off his horse. The word 'idiot' resonated with me when I looked at him. All of them. Sporting a long sleeve cotton shirt tucked into his slim fitting jeans, his riding boots made an impression against the bottom cuffs. Insisting the material not only protected him from the sun during the day, but also the cold air in the night.

He removed his riding gloves next, taking in our surroundings. "What's the plan? Looks like it's 'bout to rain."

The other men gathered their packs from the back of their horses. There were six of us. They'd decided that the smaller the party, the less attention that would be drawn. Large party or not, if someone wanted us gone, they'd figure out a way. Hell, the size of a party never stopped me from getting the job done.

"There's an old campground not too far ahead. We can hole up there for the night. I found a tent with a … not so happy ending inside that had some canned goods, expired but edible. We can save what we got." One of Seth's men searched my eyes, lip pulling in disgust.

I shrugged it off, used to the judgment and disappointment and walked towards the trail. Most of the trip was ridden in silence. Seth didn't talk nearly as much as his sister. Where Reina had been welcoming and forthcoming answering any questions, whether I asked them or not, Seth had been relatively standoffish. I noticed he did that a lot, stayed in the background. Him and Riley both did though the two of them didn't interact much.

Seth rode next to me most of the way here, studying me. An unyielding gaze as he bore a hole into the side of my damn head. That was fine by me. I was watching him too. From what I knew, he'd only recently entered his current position, and despite the tension between them, he and Amaia appeared to be relatively close. Their tempers evenly matched, cut from the same cloth. He hadn't fought in the last war as a lieutenant. But who was to say he was completely absolved from the sins of the past?

We reached the campsite just as night took over the sky. The storm had passed over us, stars now lighting some of our way. The orange and gray tent was only a few feet away from the convenience store near the main road. It was pretty clear what you would find if you entered the tent, which is why I'd assumed no one had ever done so in the first place.

"Ah, that reeks," one of Seth's guys said as he ran towards the road to throw up.

The smell of death smacked the air as I quickly opened the tent, reaching my arm in and grabbing a few cans without so much of a gander inside. There was no need to take a peek around. I'd seen all I needed for the first time. Someone who couldn't take it anymore, and what remained of them was left splattered against the tent, their body dusted into a slump.

"Didn't know you brought children with us," I said, smirking at Seth as I zipped the tent back up.

Something about the way he watched me made me uncomfortable. Both him and his little girlfriend. While most conversations I'd had with her had felt unfocused, her eyes looking through me, the weight of his gaze was like ice, heavy and cold. As if he were looking right at me, seeing the core of who I was.

He opted not to entertain my comment. "Where are we sleeping?"

Man of few words indeed. "Yep, this way," I said, leading them down the dirt path towards the lakeside.

SETH PULLED OUT A MAP FROM HIS BAG AND SPREAD IT OVER THE TAble inside while one of his men held a small ball of fire in the palm of his hand to light the space. The remaining four spread out inside and outside the cabin to secure the area. It was darker here now that the tall pine trees covered most of the night sky.

"We're here"—I pointed to a spot on the map—"Camp Richardson."

He nodded his head. "We should stick towards the water. It'll give us easy access to a food source for a good leg of the rest of the way, not to mention give us a nice barrier. Less to worry 'bout."

"Or it traps us. Only way out is through the water," I countered.

No wonder they were easy to compromise, their thought process was one-dimensional. Simple, easy to predict.

"Hardly wanna face a bear or cougar surrounded by the woods either," he challenged, voice strong and I knew he was pulling rank.

"Your death wish, not mine." It'd be tough to talk my way out of, but I didn't have plans to stick around Salem Territory if things went south anyway. "We pull back out to hit Spooner Summit Trailhead then. There's a small community of about a hundred fifty right outside Glenbrook and they're less than pleasant to encounter."

His gaze found mine, clearly wanting me to elaborate. "Gated community, pretty well off before the mess. Feel like they got shit to defend."

"Don't we all." A loaded statement.

His men had finished surveying the space and were now closing in around the table, awaiting the game plan. I watched him instruct his men, confidently relaying the information I'd just fed to him. Occasionally stopping, the silence heavy as if he were awaiting any corrections.

The full moon shone on the steps as I ate my food outside, volunteering to keep watch at our only exit, but really just wanting my own space. Not giving a rat's ass about their resistance to accept me into their little brotherhood. Shit, I didn't even *want* it. But there was something to be said about feeling like an outsider. Always feeling watched and out of place. Every word I say overanalyzed, my actions under a microscope. I needed a moment to breathe.

A breeze whisked through the night air, welcomed by my blistered skin. I chuckled to myself. Maybe the cowboy had been right. These weren't problems I'd had to deal with before. The Expanse air was cool at best, but never hot. While the UV rays had been able to pierce our skin from the hole in the ozone layer, my skin had grown accustomed to feeling more chapped than burned.

Even my life before this hadn't prepared me for these conditions. I'd spent most of my time in Chicago. My father always dragging us back to Mykonos for the summers. Dealing with whatever shady business deal he'd weaseled his way into under the table. Doing the Valentzas family's bidding. My later years consisted of mornings shuttered indoors with the curtains and blinds drawn. Asking the house staff to make me something greasy and disgusting just to spend the nights throwing it up over a toilet in some random club in the corners of the city.

I pulled out my journal for the first time in months, savoring the privacy and moment to spend with my brother, and I realized I wanted a moment with Tiago too.

August 28, 2029

Tiago,

Been awhile. Feels like I've been lost for so long. These days anger and bitterness control just about every thought. This world took so much from me, took you from me, my closest friend, my only friend. My only remaining family.

There was a time where I wandered aimlessly, trying to find solace in the chaos that had somehow consumed my life, even after somehow surviving the fall of everything we once knew. A few weeks in, I knew where I was headed. Knew to go to the one place that made sense. The place that took everything from us. Where I could pay homage to you, make you proud.

I spent a lot of time trying to imagine what you'd do, retracing our steps through the memories we shared. But I get it now. Why you brought me here. Always one step ahead, adapting. Resilient. In the midst of the very place that took you from me, the place that brought me so much pain and sorrow, I finally get it.

So I'll make this one last promise to you, my friend, my brother. I swear to you to answer this final request. No matter what it takes. Our bond is unbreakable, forged through the battlefields and tribulations. And even though you're gone, you live on forever through us.

Πάει καιρός που χαθήκαμε. Αυτές τις μέρες ο θυμός και η πίκρα ελέγχουν σχεδόν την κάθε μου σκέψη. Αυτός ο κόσμος μου πήρε τόσο πολλά, σε πήρε από μένα, τον πιο στενό μου φίλο, τον μοναδικό μου φίλο, το τελευταίο μέλος της οικογένειάς μου.

Υπήρχε μια στιγμή που περιπλανιόμουν άσκοπα, προσπαθώντας να βρω παρηγοριά στο χάος που με κάποιο τρόπο είχε καταβροχθίσει τη ζωή μου, ακόμα κι αφού κατά κάποιο τρόπο επιβίωσα από την διάλυση όλων όσων γνωρίζαμε κάποτε. Μετά από μερικές εβδομάδες, ήξερα πού πήγαινα. Ήξερα να πάω στο ένα μέρος που είχε νόημα. Το μέρος που μας πήρε τα πάντα. Όπου θα μπορούσα να σου αποτίσω φόρο τιμής, να σε κάνω περήφανο.

Πέρασα πολύ καιρό προσπαθώντας να φανταστώ τι θα έκανες, επαναλαμβάνοντας τα βήματά μας μέσα από τις αναμνήσεις που μοιραστήκαμε. Αλλά το καταλαβαίνω τώρα. Γιατί με έφερες εδώ. Πάντα ένα βήμα μπροστά, προσαρμοζόμενη. Επίμονη. Μέσα στο ίδιο το μέρος που σε πήρε από κοντά μου, στο μέρος που μου έφερε τόσο πόνο και θλίψη, επιτέλους το καταλαβαίνω.

Θα σου δώσω λοιπόν αυτή την τελευταία υπόσχεση, φίλε μου, αδερφέ μου. Σου ορκίζομαι ότι θα απαντήσω σε αυτό το τελευταίο αίτημα. Δεν έχει σημασία τι χρειάζεται. Ο δεσμός μας είναι μαχών και τις θλίψεις. Και παρόλο που λείπεις σωματικά, ζεις για πάντα διαμέσου εμάς. άθραυστος, σφυρηλατημένος μέσα από τα πεδία των

Evander,

I hate everything now. The world is back to being dark, gritty, and cold. That hope you saw? The possibility of love, and hope that there was still good in the world? You and Tiago were that for me and now you're gone. But I'll be damned if I let you both down.

So this is me writing you assholes, letting you know I'm taking a stand, making this right. A vow to do right by you both. To carry your spirits and keep them alive, so when I look up at the sky, and take my last breath, I can smile knowing we died together, in spirit and then in life.

Μισώ τα πάντα τώρα. Ο κόσμος έχει ξαναγίνει σκοτεινός, αμμώδης και ψυχρός. Αυτή την ελπίδα που είδατε; Η πιθανότητα της αγάπης και η ελπίδα ότι υπήρχε ακόμα καλό στον κόσμο; Εσύ και ο Τιάγκο ήσουν αυτό για μένα και τώρα έφυγες. Αλλά θα είμαι καταραμένος αν σας απογοητεύσω και τους δύο.

Λοιπόν, σας γράφω μαλάκες, σας ενημερώνω ότι παίρνω θέση, διορθώνοντας αυτό. Ένας όρκος να κάνουμε σωστά και οι δύο. Για να κουβαλάω τα πνεύματά σας και να τα κρατάω ζωντανά, οπότε όταν κοιτάζω ψηλά στον ουρανό και πάρω την τελευταία μου πνοή, μπορώ να χαμογελάσω γνωρίζοντας ότι πεθάναμε μαζί, στο πνεύμα και μετά στη ζωή.

SETH RELIEVED ME FROM WATCH HALFWAY THROUGH THE NIGHT, OPT-ing to take the brunt of the shift in order for the rest of us to be well rested for the hike tomorrow. His magic went further than having predator-like limbs and speed. Beyond the larger pointed ears with enhanced hearing, he was better equipped to survive overall. Which meant he could go without sleep and still have a bit of an advantage over the rest of us.

If we made good time, we'd hit Spooner Summit Trailhead by four p.m. Leaving the rest of the night to figure out where to shelter up and check the rest of our route. The morning started out fine.

It was a clear day, and the weather was tolerable. About eighty degrees a few hours after sunrise, not too far outside the weather in the area before the bombs. The lush trees helped provide relief from the sun, making it easier to keep a sustainable pace.

The woods were quiet. I'd taken the liberty of clearing a few stragglers in our path. My hands were itching to kill something, *do* something to shed the emotions that still weighed on me from last night. The EK 44 still felt nice and comfortable in my hands. It wasn't as graceful as the one my father had gifted me as a child, what I had grown up using, wasn't nearly as beautiful a weapon, but it got the job done. It got the thrill out.

A mile from the trail entrance, Seth and one of his men stopped to relieve themselves, another to re-wrap his ankle he'd twisted a few days back. There'd been no healers to spare on this trip, though Reina had made every effort to join once she'd found out her brother was going.

From what I'd seen the two couldn't be in the same space for more than a few seconds without tossing an insult towards each other. Why she wanted to come, I couldn't guess. Just knew I was sure as hell glad I didn't have to suffer through their bickering.

I listened for any signs of life near the edge of the trail and woods, noticing the remaining men doing the same. A sense of uneasiness had fallen over the group. No one had spoken up, but I knew we all felt that creep up our spine under the pressure of being watched. Quiet woods were always a bad sign, no matter the situation. Still, we saw nothing and heard even less. Soon finding ourselves back on the trail headed towards our final stopping point for the day.

Cautiously, weapons at ready, we made our way down the narrow trail, no longer waiting to fall victim to whatever was causing the eerie feeling on the back of our necks. The years had taken a toll on the once-beautiful path, nature claiming back what rightfully belonged. Brush and branches now made the comfortable stroll a series of ducks, crawls, and climbs. We moved as a unit, when one man was down and crawling, two more guarded their six and their twelve. Instincts making it clear we needed to stay vigilant. Alert.

A figure blurred past my peripheral as I covered for the man at my rear. If I was untrained, unaware, or anything alike Amaia, I'd likely think I was seeing shit. But I wasn't any of those things, and neither was the man at my side. His brown hair whipped to the side, head following the movement.

"Move, move, move!" he urged, dragging the man on the ground to his feet and encouraging those ahead of us to take off down the trail.

On my left, savage growls echoed, prompting me to sheathe my knife and brandish my pistol, a more fitting choice for the chaos that surrounded us.

"Seth, there's going to be a small breakaway on your right a few feet ahead. If we can get towards it, there's a parking lot. At the very back, there's a red pickup truck behind a tree. Can't miss it. It's loud as hell. It'll draw unwanted attention, but it'll get us out of here."

I felt his eyes on my back, inevitably questioning why I knew that.

He was hesitating, questioning if he could trust my words. "Go!" one of the men screamed.

The urgency in his voice pulled my attention in his direction. Five more undead came at us, freshly fed and coming at a pace we couldn't outrun. We were surrounded, and they were closing in fast. We'd have to fight our way out first.

Quickly forming a circle back-to-back, we readied to defend ourselves. A man at the forefront clearing as much space as possible, giving us enough space to move about. His movements were quick and efficient. He was like Seth. I hadn't noticed at first. He was tall, sure, but I hadn't had a chance to take in his features. His hat had stayed on his head, only moving it slightly forward to cover his face when he slept.

A couple of the men harnessed their weapons, one with water swirling in the palms of his hands. Pieces of earth floated up towards the hands of another. The other two kept their weapons drawn, while one without other gifts, possessing nothing elemental, I saw the flames burning behind the eyes of the other. *Fire.* I was willing to bet he didn't want to cause an even larger problem with his flames, surrounded by dry August air.

Good choice, one I'd be making as well.

Seth stepped forward, firing his shotgun at the closest rotting creatures near us. The rest of us followed suit, shooting, and slicing our way through the throng of flesh. The more we slaughtered, the more that came. We held our ground. Branches flying through the air and pinning creatures to the stumps of trees as others used the might of their water to pressure the heads of the undead, popping them open and chunks of gray brain matter splattered through the air.

As the assault waned, I slipped on a fallen branch and icy, clammy fingers tore into my flesh, ripping skin as a shrill cry erupted from my lips

I met the eyes of what was once a woman. For a moment, the cloudiness in her eyes cleared, and she looked at me. I blinked; her eyes clouded back over. The dainty facial features now drooped, undisciplined across her face, jaw loose in uncontrolled snaps with caked dried blood in the corners of her mouth. She snarled savagely, hungrily as I kicked at her chest with the full weight of my body going through my boots. It gave us some distance, made my limbs safe from her snapping jaws, but not enough for her to stop her attack. A shot rang out behind my ear and I flinched, waiting for the blistering pain of a bullet to flare up somewhere in my body.

I waited, welcomed it secretly, but no pain came. The undead fell. My ears rang and everything around me slowed down. Three more rotting shits headed straight for me then stopped in their tracks, eyeing something behind me in the distance. They faced each other and one snarled, yelling. *Their eyes*, something about their eyes was off, different, but I couldn't place it.

A scream pierced the air, and time resumed its flow. Seth's man bled profusely as a zombie clamped down on his wrist. I locked eyes with Seth briefly holding his intense gaze, before he tilted his head, trying to read something off me before springing into action. Another of the undead emerged from the woods just as Seth moved out the way. I plunged my knife into its foot, securing it into the ground before pointing my gun at it and firing.

Another shot rang out and the creature who'd bitten Seth's man fell to the ground, the rest fleeing back into the woods. With incredible speed, they bolted from our line of sight, leaving us behind in a hail of dust and debris. We stood firm, determined to hold our position to the bitter end. Only when the last of them had vanished from view, did we dare to let our guard down, hurtling towards the parking lot at first chance.

The truck is where I said it'd be. Seth's guys hopping in the back, dragging the now passed out soldier into the bed. Wrapping a tourniquet around his wrist to slow the blood loss.

"How do I start this shit?" Seth growled in a frenzy.

I edged him out of the way, urging him to scoot to the passenger side. "Move." I reached down, flicking the switch near the ignition.

"What the—"

"Solar powered. Tinkerers," I answered, knowing the next question, addressing that preemptively too. "Stole it. How do you think I know about the pissy community down the road?"

He gaped at me, and I threw the car into reverse. Not knowing where else to go, I headed back the way we'd come.

"FUCK! FUCK! FUCK!" SETH YELLED, SLAPPING HIS HAND AGAINST THE dash, hopping back in the truck.

His men peered in from the rear window, concern clear over their faces as they removed items from their pack to keep their friend comfortable on the bumpy road.

We'd been driving for thirty minutes, but the road was blocked by a fallen tree. Seth attempted to move it, to no avail. Too old, too heavy. With the only other man strong enough to help out severely injured, we'd have to try the rest of the way on foot from here. Which meant carrying a grown man who was now dead weight, despite the last bit of life he clung onto.

"You can't tell Amaia what you saw," he said simply, checking what remained of his pack before we got out of the car to descend on the remaining trek back to the cabin.

I looked at him. "Why would I waste my time telling that girl anything?"

"Good," he said, "I don't need her getting distracted from the facts. We've been down this path before. It doesn't lead anywhere good. She's finally getting better."

"Didn't realize you two were so close," I grumbled under my breath, baiting him for more information.

"We aren't."

My eyes narrowed, shocked at the definiteness in his answer.

He read me, adding, "But we're family. You don't have to be close to act in their best interest."

I nodded my head. None of my business whatever fucked up family shit they had going on back there. There was clearly a lot of that going around.

"Fair enough, but my best interest is staying alive. So whatever needs to be said to ensure I stay that way, let's make sure that's what comes out when we get back." I hopped out, slamming the door behind me and hustling over to help the rest of the crew waiting for us to keep going.

We made it about a quarter of a mile before realizing that carrying him would be impossible, especially making it before nightfall. Bunkering down near the truck for the night would have to do.

With the stench of blood and flesh in the air, we couldn't risk keeping him out in the open exposed to whatever predator lurked in the woods. We agreed he'd take the cabin of the truck and the rest of us would stack up in the bed. At first light, the earth elemental and I would run back to the horses. Hopefully making it back to them in time to hit the cabin later that night to rally and decide what to do next. I hadn't bothered learning any of their names this far, and I didn't plan on learning them now.

I didn't need another name to write to. There was no comradery in war. Things were easier that way, better.

The bed of the truck was slick with his blood as we tossed some dried straw and leaves to soak up most of it. He'd bled a lot, the undead nicking his ulnar artery, the herbs we placed on them, and the tourniquet being the only thing slowing the bleeding. His face had gone pale and his skin clammy. His words disoriented as he faded in and out of consciousness, but he made it through the night. We all did.

I was up just as the sun crested over the trees, ready to move from out in the open. I'd give it to the guy. He held my pace the entire way. His endurance was not only admirable on horseback, but on his own two feet as well. We covered a little over twenty miles in about two hours, and I wondered what kind of training Seth and Amaia had placed these men through. For men in the calvary and not foot soldiers, they were well equipped to adapt to any situation thrown our way.

They spent most of their time on the backs of another animal, yet their combat skills and physical abilities were commendable. If this was what they could do with low morale, I found myself fear-ing their capabilities a few months before they'd lost a leader. Both leaders, really though Amaia was still very much alive.

Fear in my world didn't make you weak, it made you alive, kept it that way. And I'd be lying if I didn't fear the situation I'd put myself into. I'd spent my entire life running, for fun, from the cops, from my father. But as we sprinted through the rugged terrain, I found this run for life terrifying. Those fuckers had been fast, come out of nowhere and disappeared even faster, not like any of the undead I'd faced in the past.

Then there was the fact that Amaia had been right. She appeared out of it most days, focused on other things, but if nothing else, she was observant. I found myself under her watchful gaze enough to know she noticed every detail, even the ones left unsaid.

As we stopped to sip from our water, I came to understand two things; I'd stumbled into a situation I was no longer in control of, and there were now only two of us versus however many were out there. But I'd rather be out here, then waiting back at the truck. Nothing fun about being a sitting duck. Best I at least make them work for their next meal.

It was a good thing we were able to cover as much ground as we did in just a few hours. The way back was harder than we'd anticipated and took us twice as long. The horses were bigger than some parts of the overgrown trail, forcing us to hop off and guide them between trees at some parts. By the time we made it back to the truck, six hours had passed and we couldn't afford any hiccups if we were to hit the cabin before nightfall.

He was still in and out of consciousness, which didn't mean much of anything once I strapped him to the back. His hands were tied to the straps around the horse to prevent him from falling off and I made sure to knot his feet to the satchel for extra security. Seth led on the horse in front to keep the other horse on track while I guided the way, the remaining men flanking when possible on constant defense.

Night encapsulated the sky as we tied the horses to the front of the cabin. It was ill practice. Any passerby would know someone occupied the inside, but we'd agreed to worry about that after checking on the now leaking, rotting wound.

"Dude, that looks bad," one of the men stated the obvious, nose pulling upward in revulsion. The skin around the bite was red and swollen, puss crusting around the edges.

His skin was warm, and tender as he groaned under my touch.

"We have to chop it," I suggested, hardly bothered by the gore.

"Holy shit, we can't just *chop up* Logan," another exclaimed, throwing a mortified glare in my direction.

Wouldn't want to be responsible for it anymore anyway, I thought, cursing the fact that I now knew another name.

"No," Seth leveled, weighing our options. "We can't chop it. He'll bleed out."

"Well, I'm fresh outta ideas. So if anyone else has a better one, speak now before he forever holds his peace," I muttered, more to Seth than anyone else. Where I came from, this wouldn't even be a discussion.

We wouldn't waste time in the field like this. Chop, sew, or in this case burn, and be done with it, then adjust. My father had taught me that the first time someone had shown up on our doorstep. They'd been green in the face and kilting over from an infected bullet wound to the leg.

"Let me think."

As if on cue, Logan woke up for the first time in hours, screaming out in pain. The rest of the room went silent, everyone looking to Seth for direction as the man passed back out.

"Herbs, we can use more herbs until we make it back. Keep him comfortable," he decided.

I scoffed. "Herbs? That's your solution? Where was all the playing it safe a few years ago—"

Seth had me pinned against the cabin door before I could finish my thought. "What about a few years ago, huh? Go head, tell us why you're really here. Been waiting for this one to come out."

I shoved him off me and spat at his feet. "There it is. I see why she has you where she does, *Lieutenant*." I let my tongue grace over my teeth, hanging on to that last syllable.

"Yeah." Seth nodded. "You wanna see huh, boy?"

He charged me, but I was fast, dodging his initial punches and weaving around each elbow he threw. Where I was fast, Seth was agile and smart, adapting to my fighting style and landing a blow to my right cheek.

Blood filled my mouth, and I grinned, embracing the pain and bitter, copper taste of my blood.

"That's fair." I chuckled.

Our bodies slammed into each other, both trying to gain the upper hand, one of his men yelling out to us in the background. Fire glowed in my peripheral, causing both of us to stop mid-fight.

"Logan! Logan oh shit, dude! Wake up!" I could hear the man more clearly now.

The other two circled the table, the one with water magic actively using his power to battle the flames and keep it from engulfing the cabin.

Seth and I untangled arms, his hostile eyes meeting mine.

"Uh, something tells me he couldn't do that before. Could he?" I asked.

"No. No, he could not."

CHAPTER
TWENTY-SEVEN

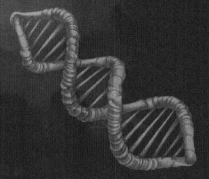

TOMOE

My fingers fiddled with the sheets on the side of the bed I'd grown accustomed to Seth sleeping on these last few weeks. I sighed, my head was pounding from all the channeling I'd done the last few days. While I hadn't come up empty, there wasn't anything I'd come across that was particularly helpful, either.

It'd been almost a week since Seth had left to investigate the scene near Reno. Before his group left, I could confirm Alexiares was correct in thinking our other routes were out of the question. I'd bounced around head-to-head, following our traders, our people, on their journey, and ultimately I'd been there with them all through their last breaths.

I couldn't be sure if it was the manipulation of time in my visions or if The Pansies were in fact moving faster than I'd seen before. It wasn't necessarily helpful when it came to ensuring a safe route. Nor did it lead us any closer to figuring out all the weird shit and influx of attacks that'd been happening. Amaia had only agreed that since they were going on horseback, speed made no difference and not to stress myself out about what I'd seen too much.

Seth made sure to page into Amaia's head every day and give her status updates. He'd conveniently decided to use this time to stay out of my head and let me know he was okay. Said he wanted us to both be able to focus on our jobs, not what the other was feeling, that my job was to keep my head clear and free for my visions to take hold easily.

Compound first, personal feelings second.

We hadn't told Amaia about what happened the night after the gate was breached. Honestly, I wasn't sure if she could handle another shock to the system. In a moment of vulnerability, he'd confessed to me what went through his mind as the attack ensued and he'd lost sight of me. Told me everything he'd felt seeing me slumped over on her couch, when he'd thought I'd been about to die. In the moment I'd sworn he'd been about to tell me he loved me, his hand gently gripping the base of my neck, eyes locked on one another. His pupils dilated, mouth parted and then ... my head snapped back. My eyes glossed over, and I lost myself.

I *was* Seth; I didn't need him to tell me how he'd felt because I'd felt it. I'd seen pieces of his mind, his memories. I was Seth as a five-year-old boy learning how to ride a horse. I was him graduating from high school taking a picture on Reina's phone with a boy who looked just like Reina; I was him in the future, his eyes worn and sad. He'd peeled away from our embrace, pushing me off his lap, fear and anger written on his face.

In twenty-eight years, I'd learned a thing or two about men. His reaction wasn't directed at me, but rather the confusion and unnaturalness of the situation. If he had felt anything like I did, it was a suffocating, overwhelming, all-consuming feeling that made you want to peel back your skin to release the pressure. The tension.

He never fully opened up to me about what he went through during that moment. Instead he'd claimed that instead of having a visitor pass to my mind, to speak with me, that he was able to claim residency. My thoughts were his thoughts. Soon after that, he'd insisted we go to sleep, to forget that it happened. Keep it to ourselves, not wanting to distract from the real issues and that this could wait to be figured out.

There were moments when I wanted to share with my friends, especially Reina, given the abilities and gifts she possessed. I knew she'd get it. But Maia had finally gotten her focus on The Compound, and now with our current situation, Reina was too. Bringing up that moment of vulnerability, what was likely just a magical glitch, would pique Maia's interest and consume Reina's mind until they could fully understand what had transpired.

It would be a disservice to The Compound. A disservice to the friend I'd just gotten back. He refused to sleep without me after that, reassuring he wanted to be near me in case things went south. To protect me. Still, he refused to speak about what happened. Adamant that we should make an effort to stay out of each other's heads, and he hadn't let us get that close again. Even during those toe-curling moments, there was a wall up now, like he was actively making an effort to block me out.

Tossing around some of the clean clothes I'd thrown from the bed to the floor, I snatched on my go-to black pants, a black crop and laced up my Converse. Striding over to my open window, I took a deep inhale of the cool sea air before slamming it shut not wanting to let the scorching heat of the day take over.

It was still early morning, but the temperature was already near seventy degrees, a clear indication that the brutal summer heat had yet to be done in the Monterey area. When I was a kid, my mother and father would bring my sisters and I here to watch the sea otters coming to shore. Had always made a point to take a few weekends a year out this way during their more active times a year. If we were lucky, we'd catch a whale breaching the ocean from an overlook on a cliff. Coming here had made perfect sense though I didn't know what to expect when I arrived. I'd hoped to find answers, but instead I found a new family. One I was damn determined to never let down.

A note on top of the dozens of books stacked on the table in my study grabbed my attention on my way out the door. Amaia's handwriting, she'd heard from Seth in the middle of the night and to meet her at her study before heading to breakfast.

I inflated my cheeks, slowly releasing the air, ready to get troubling news but realizing if it was Seth she'd heard from, he'd have to be okay. *Unless it was his last words. No*, I reassured myself, Reina and Amaia would certainly wake me if that were the case.

Strapping Wrath to my back, I grabbed my leather tote containing my notes and transcripts inside, and headed out the door, ready to give them to her in case she needed them. It'd save myself a trip back here for my work day if not.

The hallways to the courtyard were still empty. Most people were still asleep and the ones that were awake weren't exactly rushing to get to the Public Library right next to my quarters. As the morning fog lifted and the sun crested over the walls of The Compound, the courtyard started to bristle with soldiers preparing for their morning training. Methodically going through their checklists for the day.

None paid me any mind. They were used to seeing me here spar with Jax, or bothering Amaia during the most inconvenient moments, attempting to add some spice into her day. The sister in me enjoyed the annoyance in her voice when she told me to leave her be. I missed those times.

Everything had become complicated. There was a time when I first got here, when I'd found my friends, that I thought I could pretend this was normal, and always had been. The way a long lost friend had told me I would.

Jax's death was just a reminder of how delusional I had been. The attacks in his wake had been a constant reminder to never let myself feel that comfortable with my surroundings or my situation ever again. Everytime I let myself feel safe, people were taken from me.

I didn't bother knocking. It was technically during the hours she was required to be available to her soldiers. Most had grown accustomed to her not showing face until much later in the day. Nevertheless, if she was awake, the door would be unlocked. And only two people in this place would just stride on in, ignoring the fact that her body alone was a weapon.

Reina's grave face greeted me as the door opened. She was on the couch with her knees to her chest, biting her nails. Her brown hair was heavy in a loose bun, an oversized hoodie nearly covering the plaid pajama shorts. Red marks from her constant nervous rubbing blemished her pale long legs. Harley and Suckerpunch were laying on the floor beneath her feet asleep, hoping their presence would be enough to soothe her. My heart sank to my ass.

"What happened?" I demanded, not wanting to hear a cookie cutter explanation.

Amaia knew better than to drag it out. "They were ambushed. Logan was bitten. From what Seth told me, they didn't think he was going to make it."

Something about her face told me there was more. "But?" I asked.

"He pulled through, *but* there were complications. His magic's changed. Seth wasn't too clear. I don't even think he understands. Logan's still not conscious. Lost a lot of blood, so they can't ask him any questions."

A chill went down my spine. "We don't know that it's like Michael."

"We don't know if it is or isn't, there's nothin' concrete indicating that it's not. Won't know till they make it back," Reina added, quieter than usual from the couch.

I could see the wheels spinning behind her eyes. The worry for her brother but also the endless possibilities of the scientific explanations that had been troubling her since one of Seth's guys had ridden in with Michael strapped to the back of his horse.

He'd been rushed to the Infirmary where Reina treated his wounds and tended to him in the aftermath. It'd been days before he'd realized he now possessed an additional element. In the midst of a PTSD induced nightmare, his roommate had woken him up, their apartment flooded with water, the energy behind it creating a small current underneath his bed.

Luckily, Reina had thought to do a biopsy around the skin of his bite, "Never leave a stone unturned," she'd said.

Her and a few other Scholars that specialized in biology and anatomy had been focused on it the last two days, nothing concrete had formulated. Nothing we hadn't seen before.

In the first few days I'd arrived years ago, Reina had been chatting my ear off. Filling the gaps of what I deemed pleasant silence with all the things she'd learned or discovered since her and her brother had arrived. She'd spent most of her time tending to soldiers injured in conflict. Sometimes using her time to help soldiers amongst other citizens with recent trauma rehabilitate into new roles and learn how to function with missing limbs. Even going as far as helping them process things with her magic.

But on the side, she'd been working with a team across the Salem Territory and in conjunction with other scientists in parts of Transient Nation. Even found a way to cooperate with the friendlier allies of The Expanse, trying to understand the root of the changes within the human race.

Biological warfare, they'd determined. Something released into the atmosphere in the wake of the bombs had changed human DNA. They'd been able to identify each gene, *Ignis*, *Supra*, *Umbra Mortis* and so on. But science had yet to be able to definitively conclude why an individual developed a specific gene mutation.

"It's like with the children," Reina continued, voice shaky. "It's a waiting game, and even though his power has awoken, he hasn't. We can't be sure until we test him, if they can make it back."

The current hypothesis was that from now on, magic would be determined through passed down genes, recessive versus dominant. The parents' genes duking it out. All the children here had been tested. Their DNA logged in our records for reference in the future. None of their powers had been awoken yet. It lay dormant beneath their skin and only time would tell when it would come to the surface. If it did at all. For all we knew, the genes may need an agitator to present themselves. We could see what we believed to be *Aer* or *Terra* in their DNA, but without confirming in practice, we couldn't rely on just a working theory.

It was plausible the same thing was occurring with the bites. Until recently, the survivors of attacks were mauled at worst, or if you were bitten, it was a failed attempt to be eaten. Similar to the bites during the last attack at The Compound. The intent behind Riley's wounds were clear: a meal. But Michaels wounds resembled a carefully actioned bite, a singular bite, not the usual nibbled skin exhibited in the past. And if that were true, we were looking at far worse issues than we were prepared for, and the possibility of Amaia being correct in her long-standing theory.

I was brought back to the word *if.* "If ... they make it back?"

Reina nodded. "They can't calm his flames, only keep 'em contained with Alexiares and Eddie's water magic. Guess it caused some attention too. Seth and the rest of 'em have been fending off staggering Pansies all night."

"They're in need of a clear path to the horses, but they need Logan to relax before they can attempt it," Amaia finished.

"So knock him the hell out." As far as I was concerned, that was a simple solution, and I wasn't sure why nobody else had considered it at this point.

"Well, duh, ya don't think that was my brother's first call to action?"

"Or Alexiares," Amaia muttered under her breath.

That didn't address why it wasn't possible.

"And?" I asked once more.

"And it only made things worse."

Reina nodded in agreement and as I took a seat next to her, "So It's just a waiting game then?" I concluded.

"Just a waiting game then," Amaia concluded, coming around to sit next to us both.

REINA AND I SPENT THE NEXT FEW DAYS KEEPING EACH OTHER IN HER idea of uplifted spirits, staying occupied in either her study or mine. Distracting our minds by thumbing through the accounts of the survivors, running analysis on the biopsy she'd done on Michael, and going down a list of possibilities, cross-analyzing with the archives and historical records the other historical Scholars and I kept in the Public Library.

By the time we'd come across a conclusion and were ready to present to other Scholars, three things had become definitive; of all attacks in the last six months, every single soldier that'd been bitten on duty or in the field, had been healed within minutes of their bite thanks to Amaia's careful resourcing in each company. Of the bites prior to six months ago, 98 percent of them had been healed within minutes. 2 percent within a few hours of being bitten, and the last 1 percent had been two people who ended up separated from their group and had trekked their own way back to The Compound for aid. We brought them into the Elemental Room for testing to confirm, but as we suspected, no new magic had manifested in their veins, nor in their DNA when Reina cross-checked.

We knew that Michael had been found and returned to The Compound within three days of being bit, but infection had settled. This had led to Reina's hypothesis that infection was key to Michael's unique situation and was turned into a hardened theory once Seth confirmed with Amaia that Logan too, had developed an infection before displaying a new power.

And by the time Seth, Alexiares, Logan, and the others returned five days after their initial distress call, the third thing had become crystal clear. We were in for some shit.

I waited outside South Gate, Amaia, Reina and Riley at my sides, Suckerpunch and Harley at Amaia's feet, guards at our backs. Seth had paged Amaia that they were fifteen minutes away and coming in hot, Pansies fresh on their trail. It'd taken us half that to get there from The Kitchens. We'd stopped only for Reina and Riley to pick up their weapons and Amaia to add on to the ones she usually sported with every outfit.

It wasn't long before the ground shook with the sound of the galloping horses. Amaia's face hardened. Flames burned bright in the palms of her hands, an artillery lined every inch of her body, from the thigh holsters containing her guns of choice and extra magazines, to the multiple knives tucked into the holster outlining the shape of her chest. Her eyes were fierce, determined and focused on the six horses now speeding our way, dust kicking up on the trees lining the border of The Compound. At least ten Pansies flanked at their sides, two bodies flopping on the backs of their respective horses uncontrolled. *Unconscious,* I realized, praying Seth wasn't one of them. Suckerpunch and Harley rose to their feet, heads low and gums snarling.

Riley tossed the wooden handle of his ax back and forth between his hands, his long legs itching, pacing in place, ready for a fight. The sharp metal pierced through the air as he swung it with deadly precision, loosening up his shoulders.

Reina raised her bow and arrow, the string taut between her slender fingers. Her eyes fixated on whichever target she'd decided on first, her breathing slowing down to make pace with the calmness of her heart. She leaned into the correct posture, aiming and awaiting Amaia's command to fire.

I unsheathed Wrath from my back and gripped her tightly, angling my feet and rooting them in place, ready to guard my home with my life. There were only ten. Seth had warned Amaia who promptly decided, albeit with a little urging from me, to handle this ourselves, not wanting to further raise the alarms and disturb the perceived peace inside the walls.

Reina hadn't protested, and I could feel the emotions leaking from her as she focused on harnessing them back in. She craved violence as much as Amaia and I did at the moment. Needed to feel this fight. Wanted to be the one defending her brother.

I prayed for the person who'd underestimate my sister. Underneath the makeup, and the wildly inappropriate lace-based apocalypse-chic outfits, she was tough as nails. I'd never known her to shy away from a chance to get her hands dirty.

Riley was a given. Where Amaia went, he followed. If it came down to it, without a doubt, he'd lay down his life for her as well.

We were a force to be reckoned with, united in our mission to protect Seth, to protect The Compound and everyone inside that we had learned to love. As the horses neared, Amaia let out a war cry, and we sprang into action. Her flames blazed flying into the air. Riley sprinted forward, meeting a Pansie head on, cutting it off in its path towards Amaia, distracted from the horses now sprinting past. His ax swung and Reina's arrow flew as The Pansies descended. The guards opened the gates for Seth and his men to flee to safety, keeping the area secure and clear of any innocent bystanders.

I dodged the lumbering attack of the sack of rotten meat in front of me. Wrath struck my target decisively, splitting its head in two as its eyes focused in on me, meeting my gaze. My vision went blurry and time slowed as I felt my eyesight starting to fade.

Determined to stay focused, I screamed at myself out loud, demanding my mind stay in the present and continuing on in the fight, noticing two more coming from behind the trees. Clicking noises came from their throats as they fixated on the dense landscape. Arrows flew past me from a high angle, the watchtower. I threw a few fingers in the air behind me, thanking them for having my back.

As I charged towards the tree line, I took in the scene around me quickly. For only a handful of people, we'd ensured a lot of ground was covered. Each fulfilling our roles, moving as a unit. It was enough to encourage me to branch off and secure another piece of our land. I stumbled, vision going blurry again, and I found my mind distracted.

Where was Seth? I turned my back, noting the distance between me and the nearest Pansies. There was time, they were nearly two hundred yards away. *There he was*, fighting next to his sister atop his horse. The rest of the men must have entered the gate already. *Good, I'll just wrap this up.*

I was met face to face with snapping jaws, too close for me to use Wrath. In the moment I was faced with death, my mind drifted to the visions I'd channeled over the last two weeks. The Pansies were getting faster, and I would die without knowing why or how. A sharp, crunching noise filled the air, and it went stiff, hitting the ground with a wet thud.

Alexiares stood over me, a savage grin taking up his face. The blood's dark coloring was nearly black, covering the tattoos on his forearms and smearing on the corners of his mouth as he wiped his face, offering me a blood covered hand. I took in the large knife that populated the hand near his face, Amaia hadn't been exaggerating. There was a level of insanity that had to exist in a person for them to choose what would be most people's 'last-ditch weapon' as their main way to fight.

I hadn't seen him near me when I'd stopped to scan the scene. *Quick and insane*, I think I'd quite like having him around. Harley and Suckerpunch tore into the second Pansie a few feet away. Suckerpunch glancing up at his owner for approval, letting out a satisfactory howl.

Before I was fully back on my feet, three more Pansies came from the woods and the dogs turned on guard.

"Shit," Alexiares mumbled, moving to position us side to side, dogs in tow.

"You go right, I go left?"

"I'm left-handed."

"Fine, have it your way," I teased, and we dove back into action.

Another five minutes and all Pansies were down. Reina had already made her way back to the Infirmary to take care of the injured in Unit A when Alexiares and I arrived at the gate to huddle with the others.

Seth met my eye and I threw myself into him, slowly backing down, embarrassed at my outburst of affection, especially given the circumstances. There was no denying my happiness with him being alive and making it back in one piece.

Alexiares and Amaia grumbled half-assed hellos to each other. Riley approached, giving Alexiares a genuine hug, glad to see him back. Awkwardly Alexiares accepted the embrace, not knowing how to receive such a genuine reaction from a friend.

Seth pulled me from our hug, putting some distance between us to take me in. Excitement shone in the eyes I'd happily get lost in for the rest of my life, making me feel a sick warm and fuzzy feeling. His mouth moved, but I heard nothing, no longer able to feel my legs. I felt the ground underneath my back. Seth and Amaia were now over me. Alexiares mouth was moving, but I couldn't hear him either. If I had to guess, his lips seemed to ask what was happening.

My vision took over.

I was surrounded by state-of-the-art equipment, nothing like anything I'd seen in The After. The walls in the lab were lined with rows of test tubes and beakers of various sizes, filled with different colored chemicals and substances. Some were flat, some bubbling, some appearing carbonated. I turn my head. Near the center of the room is a large, high-tech workstation with multiple computer screens surrounding it, connected to a storage area that appears to be refrigerated. Biological specimens were labeled on the outside.

The lab was organized, well maintained, and the room was cold. A tall red-haired man with olive-colored skin walked in, yelling at a woman. Her hair is dark brown with beach-like waves. A scientist who just appeared at the workstation, but I couldn't hear what they were saying either and their faces were blurred.

I look down. My hands are brown, darker than Amaia's, but with a more yellow undertone. I'm typing, there's a screen in front of me. I'm looking at DNA sequences, they're labeled Test Subject 383, Test Subject 384, and Test Subject 385.

The man with red hair is in my face now, gesturing angrily at the screen. My hands are shaking. I don't want to be here.

"Shh, it's okay, Moe. You're okay."

I was back in my own mind, my own body. My head rested in Amaia's lap, Seth's hand squeezing the blood flow from my own. The last thing I wanted to see when coming out of some intense shit was the contortion of confusion still smeared across Alexiares tan face.

"Never seen someone have a vision before?" I snapped.

He was quick, ready to toss words back at me. "Have I ever seen someone fall into a vision like they're seizing up after an intense trip on shrooms? I'm afraid I haven't had the pleasure yet, nah."

"Oddly specific." I smirked at him, taking his hand for the second time that day to help myself up.

I dusted myself off, facing my friends' expectant faces, Seth now glaring at Alexiares hands, daring him to touch me again.

Clearing my throat to break the tension, I mumbled a quiet joke, "Well, that was intense."

"Yeah, no shit," Amaia said.

"It's gotten worse?" Seth pestered, grabbing hold of my wrist, pulling me closer to him.

Amaia looked at me accusingly. "What's getting worse?"

"Nothing," I said, pulling my wrist free. "My visions have just been a bit more … vivid, lately. More personal, felt like I was there."

"Your eyes went white," Alexiares added.

I rolled my eyes. "Thanks man, appreciate your observance of the situation."

He smirked and Amaia threw an elbow into his gut, not finding any amusement in the situation.

"I think it's best to sit down somewhere private. Amaia, go get Prescott," I uttered with a sense of gravity.

An hour later, we were gathered in Compound Hall around a large table reserved for Council meetings. Our new reality came crashing down once Reina joined. My visions only confirmed what we already knew; a new kind of Pansie had been released into the world that had the power to change our DNA once more if bitten and not treated within a few hours.

These attacks were intentional, and Amaia had been right, they could now communicate. Seth sent a glare Alexiares' way when he corroborated her claim with his own experience on the road to Reno and detailed the attack. I also didn't miss the shy admiration he and Amaia exchanged as he told it, the flushing in both their cheeks.

In the end, everything changed, but nothing changed all the same. My visions provided no insight into the *who* or the *why*. Just proved we weren't egotistical maniacs that wrongly accused the world of being out to get us just because we've been down on our luck.

The group dispersed after a few hours, Amaia asking me to focus on the *who* and requesting all my research and energy be put towards the task. I accepted my new role reluctantly, not ready to admit that I was beginning to feel overwhelmed by the weight of my own powers. Not ready to accept the toll it was taking on my soul.

Seth, Amaia, Riley, and now Alexiares, put their lives on the line for all of us every time they left these walls. Reina too, when needed. I could do this for them.

I would do this for them, even if it consumed me.

CHAPTER

TWENTY-EIGHT

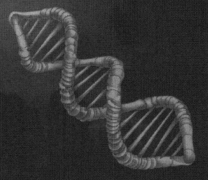

AMAIA

I sighed heavily, watching the dark blue ocean and crashing waves as I sat atop a large rock on the edge of the beach. Sea otters were sprawled out in my peripheral. The day was nice, not too hot as the mid-September weather took over on the bay. In The Before, I'd probably be convincing Sammy to some stupidly intense outdoor workout class or dragging Xavier to get bottomless mimosas on a restaurant patio.

It was beyond stupid for me to be out here alone, unprotected, but I just needed a moment to catch my breath. To pretend that I wasn't responsible for keeping thirty thousand people alive and protected. That it wasn't up to me and the people I loved to figure out what terror was being released out into the world and why we were a target.

Each day was a struggle, putting on a neutral face, not letting any of the emotions I wanted to succumb to show. I refused to let the people I loved down again, but I wasn't young and dumb, maybe reckless at times but certainly no fool. I knew where this was all headed. There would be a cost to shutting down whatever evil Tomoe was focusing on. It had been two weeks since she'd set her sights on figuring out more from her foreboding vision, and nothing had come of it.

Not for a lack of trying. I'd witnessed my friend become a shell-shocked version of her fierce self. Her skin paler than usual, eyes haunted and dark circles claimed the spaces beneath them. The long silky, raven colored hair that usually swung as she walked was matted and unkempt. She hadn't left her room in days, determined to learn more and frustrated that she'd been mentally blocked. Only able to recall the same vision, over and over but was stopped shy of channeling any other information.

Religious and spiritual books stacked on her coffee table. Torn out pages strewn about, marked up. I wasn't quite sure what she was researching, though I recognized some from my own studies. Mythologies, and philosophical teachings. Historical research on ancient cultures and their practices.

It was new territory for us all. Once someone with Moe's gifts had you in their mind or merely seen you once, they'd be able to tie themselves to you, channel you for targeted visions. But with the faces blurred out in her visions, it made things harder. She didn't know who they were, which only added more questions. Questions of *why* their faces appeared blurred in the first place.

It's okay, I'd told her, *don't kill yourself over this. It's not worth it.*

If it's not me, then it'll be a dozen more, she'd implied.

The words burned at the etches of my soul to hear, but I knew she was right. And though I was willing to burn down the world to keep my friends safe, I knew they felt the same about me, and I refused to take that opportunity away from her. Even if I felt my life wasn't worth dying for, Reina, Seth, Riley, Prescott, Luna, hell in the last few weeks I'd be willing to bet even Alexiares, were worth it to her. It didn't matter if I cut myself out the equation.

So outside the walls I went. Deciding to savor this moment of sadness and allow myself to feel, but not brave enough to do it in the sanctity of my own room, behind closed doors where I could plunder and become lost in myself for months at a time. And after a few hours of tears, of dry heaving, and shamefully licking the rim of an empty bottle of tequila, I'd be able to put on a brave face once more. Continue to lead my people through this never-ending nightmare.

The feeling of a set of eyes fell upon on my back and I turned around, throwing knife out in one hand, fire simmering in the other.

"You look like shit," Alexiares greeted, hands in the pockets of his khaki-colored cargos, striding towards the rock next to me.

I groaned, tossing my head back and feeling my curls tickle along the nape of my neck and down my shoulders. "Oh come on! My last hiding spot, and even that's been compromised. I'm seriously going to punch Reina."

"She didn't tell me. I tracked you." He tossed his hands up in a sign of peace. "Would've been a bit harder if there wasn't a literal trail of tequila leading up to this sad little corner of the beach."

Not that peaceful, I guess. "I dumped it."

"I know."

He took a seat next to me, our feet dangling at the water's edge, the waves crashing against the shore, I couldn't help but feel the weight of our past and present struggles bearing down on us. The ocean stretched before us, a vast and mysterious expanse that both terrified and enchanted me. It held secrets beyond imagining, depths that had never been fully explored. Yet, despite its dangers, I found comfort in the constant ebb and flow of the waves. A gentle nudge that life was never stagnant and that even in our darkest moments, there was always the possibility of a new beginning.

My mother had always told me that the waves were a symbol of resilience, a sign that life would persist even in the face of great adversity. As we watched them crash against the rocks, I couldn't help but think that they were more than just a force of nature. These waves had existed long before humanity, and would continue long after we were gone. They were a testament to the enduring cycle of life, and the unstoppable power of nature. Despite our attempts to tame and control it, the ocean would always prevail, a reminder of our own fragility in the face of something greater than ourselves.

He interrupted the silence, and I met his pained eyes as he spoke. "Good place to come if you wanna focus on all of your life's problems. Ever think about just jumping in? Save everyone else the pain of having to deal with your chaos. Your destruction."

The words echoed in my mind. He was talking to me, about me, but also about himself at the same time, the barely noticeable accent creeping forth once more, "Yeah, and what problems could you possibly have? Daddy never loved you? Couldn't find anyone else to either? No, let me guess, mom chose the pill bottles over raising you?"

He chuckled, breaking our gaze. "You expecting me to believe that with a shitty attitude like yours, that yours loved you?"

"He's the one that warned me about people like you. To tread carefully."

His warm brown eyes darkened as he rose to his feet, boots sinking in the wet sand. "Ya know, you keep saying that, but you haven't taken a moment to learn a damn thing about me." He moved behind me, forcing me to swivel away from the water though I was sure to keep myself centered in case this turned physical.

"Twice now," he continued, "I've saved your friends. That's two separate occasions that I had the opportunity to let them die, should have let them die if I based anything on *your* actions. If I was as shitty or as callous and calculating as you claim, I would have. But I didn't, yet you still treat me as if I'm the villain."

I remained seated, glaring down my nose at him, refusing to fall to his intimidation. "Didn't realize it was so important for you to have my favor."

"It's not," he deadpanned.

"Yeah, I'm not about to do this here. Not in my last secret spot. Do me a favor and don't let the waves hit your ass on the way out." I ground my jaw before turning back around, trying to settle into my feelings once more.

Still feeling his obnoxious presence, I found him standing behind me pathetically. His lips parting in a way that led me to believe he had some secret he was waiting to spill out.

I tossed my hands off my lap and craned my neck. "Oh my gosh, please go."

"Well, if I leave, then I won't be able to tell you that some locals trapped a bunch of the undead about fifteen miles out. Thirty of 'em in the middle of some trench bullshit they built. Riley and I are heading out with a few guys to check it out."

"And you waited until *now* to tell me this?"

"Well, Riley said it was protocol. Sent me to find you." His expression was one of genuine confusion, not understanding my reaction.

It *was* protocol, but I knew Riley was trying to force this working relationship between Alexiares and I that I'd already made clear I had no desire to make. He wasn't one of us, never would be. He could get as close to Riley and Moe as he wanted, even be cordial with Seth. I wanted no parts, not after all the words we'd exchanged. Not after the remarks about my drinking, my mental health, the validity of my position. I was under no obligation to tolerate his presence any more than required to fulfill my duties.

"You believed him?" I questioned, deciding to double down just to mess with his head.

"How am I supposed to know? You're impossible, and arrogant. Damn sure haven't tried to work with any of his requests to include me in full training to do my job. I learn as I go, and Riley told me to go. And now," he said, a cruel smirk passing over his lip. "I've learned, princess."

He enjoyed the banter in a sick way. I understood his game.

Each time one of his words pierced my heart, he thrived. And I let him. Let his hurtful words bring me down. Let them make me feel like the dirt beneath my boots, because they reminded me of the words that often echoed around my head.

I don't deserve to be happy.

I PUSHED THE DOOR OPEN. IT BOUNCED OFF THE WALL, POPPING BACK and nearly hitting Alexiares in the face as he followed in my wake, just as I had intended. Riley grinned at me as he stood in the corner behind my desk in my study, knowing too well I'd seek him out here first in a blind rage.

"Seriously Riley, g—"

He cut me off, "I'll just go ahead and go fuck myself. Now that that's out the way, he went off with Seth. What's the difference?"

I scoffed. "You're not Seth, and Seth isn't you. Damnit. You keep testing me, Riley! Pushing buttons that don't need pushing. You used to always have my back."

I didn't give a damn that Alexiares had witnessed it all. He'd bore witness to the true war that raged within me, out on the rocks, the true battle that I faced.

His face softened, and he moved to meet me halfway across the room. "I hardly think you wanna do this here. I do have your back, sis. Always will."

Alexiares cleared his throat awkwardly from the corner, making sure we were still aware he was here.

Riley ignored him. "That's why I'm challenging you. You don't treat people this way. You're better than that Maia, this whole place was designed under *your* ideas."

"Jax and Prescott's," I corrected.

"Yes them, but it was *you* that was adamant about this being a home for those who didn't belong anywhere else. A place that welcomed all."

"I still want that." My body softened under his reassuring touch.

"So then, what's the difference between him and them? Him and me?"

It didn't take long for Alexiares to give him the answer to that. He ate his words when I walked past my study the next day. I'd been following up with one of the Scholars on amplifications to some of the security measures I had planned for outside the wall. Promptly excusing myself due to incessant gagging noises beyond the door.

Only one person could slip through my locks with such ease.

"Man, what the hell." Riley heaved between each word, jumping to the sound of The Pit now buzzing into the room.

I looked down on my desk, unpleasantly surprised to find 2x2 pieces of gray, cracked flesh touching the beautiful, dark wood desk I had grown to love. My jaw dropped, eyes darting to find the only savage soul I could think of that would think setting up a display of rotted flesh on someone's personal property was okay.

Alexiares' eyes flashed with mischievous intent as he grinned at me innocently. "Tah, duh."

Closing the door to any onlooking eyes, I glared between Alexiares and Riley both.

"Proud of your judgment skills?" I asked Riley accusingly.

"Not necessarily." He moved away from the desk and opened the door to my bedroom as if trying to create an extra sense of space between him and the flesh.

I shook my head, turning to Alexiares to question him instead. "Where did you even store that?"

He shrugged. "My pocket."

"Your pocket? Dude." Riley's face went green again at the thought.

"It's not like I had fancy field gear or anything. Probably lost in the approval pile stacking up right here on her desk." He grinned, fingering through the papers as I quickly moved to smack his finger away.

I gestured towards him, nearly hitting him in the face with my thumb. "Now, do you see why I want him gone? Who does that?"

Glancing down towards the square pieces of skin, I too wanted to gag, but forced myself to appear unfazed at the gore.

"Well, I suppose I could have drawn a picture, but then I wouldn't get the pleasure of soaking up this moment and watching you squirm."

Before he could blink, my fingers latched onto the back of his neck. I slammed his head down on the desk, making his flesh meet the improper biopsy lab he'd imported into my personal space.

Riley's arms latched around my waist, pulling me off him as I released my grip, satisfied for a moment, until I saw the unwavering grin still on his smug, bloodied face.

"Everyone's upset about *what* I brought, but no one's talking about what it means."

Riley and I glanced at it with an open mind for the first time, and my legs went numb, body cold. Riley met my stare. He recognized the symbol, too.

"Duluth," Alexiares confirmed.

CHAPTER

TWENTY-NINE

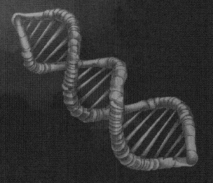

AMAIA

My family stared at me from around the room. Reina's hair pulled into a tight ponytail, her pale skin taut, showcasing the lines of worry across her face.

"Duluth doesn't make any sense. After all this time … they've been nothin' but friendly to us in the past. There's gotta be another reason." Her usual singsong voice was tight in confusion.

Her hands were trembling as if she'd had too much caffeine. The thought of another cross-territory conflict triggering emotions she'd long worked to bury from the war to establish our borders. Surprising us both, Reina jumped at the touch of Seth's hands, rubbing the thumb of his sister in an attempt to help calm her nerves.

Tomoe sat cross-legged from the floor in front of them, fist propping up her head as she answered contemplatively, "They've been friendly out of necessity. Amaia practically held their troops together during the last conflict. Poor leadership makes for a great ass-kisser."

Riley nodded his head in agreement, and I felt Alexiares attention turn towards me. I let myself wonder where he'd been during that time, who he had fought for, if anyone at all.

"Let's all just slow down for a minute and look at this objectively—"

"You, objective?" Riley interrupted Seth from his usual spot against the door, his right eyebrow arched towards the ceiling.

Seth's face remained stone-faced, intent on getting his point across and stepping into his role as my lieutenant. "Yeah Riley, objective. We got nothin' but pieces of skin that one of *our* guys sliced off the back of *their* guys' necks. Can't exactly walk on up to their front door, soldiers in tow and demandin' answers that we don't even know they have."

"He's right," I said, giving him a slight nod of agreement as I met the storm behind his eyes. "What if they accuse us of doing this? I've been up to Duluth, seen what they have to offer, and high-tech is the last thing on their minds, let alone lab experiments."

Alexiares mumbled in agreement. I made note to add that to the list of things that's taken me by surprise in this room during the past hour.

I continued, "I think it's bigger than that, beyond experiments. We have to think holistically, like why run experiments at all? What's the end goal, and—"

"Why they've turned on you to begin with? This isn't something they're doing alone, she's right. They wouldn't waste time focusing on this, they've got much bigger shit to deal with."

The room turned to Alexiares now, absorbing his first words since they'd all joined us in my study.

290

"And you know this because ..." I asked, accusation electrifying my words.

He glanced at me, answering carefully, "I did work up there, for my old community. Stayed for some time."

There was something in his eyes that kept me from pressing on. *Is that ... regret? No,* I told myself, *it's shame.* A feeling that came naturally in our line of work. Despite the continued banter, a shift had occurred in our dynamic since our conversation by the rocks.

He'd become more transparent, more vulnerable. Our words had been harsh, meant to sting each other, but there was also the unspoken understanding of each other's pain that had somehow surfaced. I didn't know where his pain came from, and he only knew fragments of mine. But, the fact remained that there was only one thing rooting us to remaining in this bleak world. Each having our own reason, but understanding that neither was driven by our own will.

"So then, what do we do? Keep sitting here waiting to get our asses handed to us until it all crumbles around us?" Moe burst through the silence, never one to sugarcoat anything.

"No. Just because we can't pull up soldiers at ready doesn't mean we can't do some recon followed by a little emissary visit. An innocent one of course."

Seth leaned forward, my mischievous tone piquing his interest, and I wasn't sure if I should be worried, or excited at his eagerness to head out on this mission.

"You *just* said you'd have to be dumb as hell to send us all at once not more than a few weeks ago," Riley noted.

I made a face at him, recognizing his slight embellishment at my words.

"Um, didn't say dumb as hell. But maybe I was wrong." I huffed, plopping back down into my seat after adding to the anxiety of the room with my pacing.

"I'll be honest with you guys. This is the only thing I can think of. Like Moe said, we can't just sit here and wait for everything to crumble around us." I gestured towards her. "Everything I've done so far has been reactionary. On defense. Maybe it's time to play offense for once. Besides, it won't be all of us, just three."

They looked at each other as if trying to decide who would go. It wasn't fear for themselves, but for the ones who would inevitably go. We couldn't afford to lose anyone else; the weight of our previous losses still hung heavy. The truth was clear, the odds of survival were slim. Whether it was the perilous journey or the unknown terrors that awaited us, we were certain to face more loss. Someone wouldn't return. Perhaps none of us would.

Reina faced me, a cheery smile creeping onto an exceptionally determined face, "Well I'm sure as hell ain't gonna let my bestest friend go out there alone."

"I thought I was your best friend," Moe said, the corner of her mouth twitching.

"Well, duh, y'all all are! I just lumped ya all together since I know you're coming too."

"And you assume that because?"

Reina grinned at her knowingly as Moe turned to her and slapped her knee.

"Reina, stay away from my emotions!"

Of course, they'd all volunteer. I expected some pushback from them. Had prepared for it. The boys still had their attention directed to me, awaiting further information. Soldiers listening for the details of their mission.

And, of course, they all assumed they were included in the mission trio. "I *meant* Seth and Alexiares."

Riley stood at attention. His body rigid as he awaited me to continue. I knew my words were hard to swallow, and hoped at this moment he wouldn't find them targeted due to the recent tension in our relationship. That wasn't why I wanted him to stay.

I *needed* him to stay, because out of everyone here, I trusted him the most. He'd proven to me time and time again that he would *always* act in the best interest of both me and The Compound. His behavior of late only proved that. His coffee brown eyes showed no emotion beyond a single blink. A soldier accepting their duty without question.

He nodded at me. "Understood, General Bennett," he said, his gravelly voice steady and strong.

"No," Tomoe countered strongly, "that's bullshit. If you're both targets, why would you *both* serve yourselves up on a silver platter with the *one* person you suspect to be part of it? Why is he even in the room?"

"Ouch, and here I was thinking we got along," Alexiares snarked, hand flying over his heart. "I assume I'm going because I know the area ... and have connections."

I felt my head moving in agreement, though that was the last thing I wanted to do.

"Please, you've been the main one besides Riley telling me to focus on the facts at hand and their relation to him. Like you *both* have made very clear that I have nothing, and as he made very clear the other day, he saved your ass"—I pointed to her and then to Seth—"and your ass. Now you don't have to support my decision, or feel satisfied by my orders Tomoe, but at the end of the day, I'm the one responsible if this goes to shit. What would be reckless for me is to send you both out there if you're not needed."

"Hey! I'm needed," Reina whimpered. "What if someone gets hurt? We literally have several examples of *why* a healer should be with you no matter what."

Solid point, once again.

"Valid. Riley is needed here as third in command to keep everything in order with our troops, the gates, *and* his men. Moe, we need you here where"—I moved towards where she sat and grabbed her hand, slouching down to her level—"I need you to do something for me that I swore I would *never* ask you to do in a million years. But now I have to. I need you to stay here and focus on us. On making sure our path ahead is clear, as seamless as possible, so we *can* make it back here in one piece."

She squeezed my palm. A solemn look on her face that reflected both defeat and acceptance before I added, "Seth can communicate with you both and report back to me, and vice versa. That way, Prescott can stay up-to-date too."

"No!" Seth and Tomoe said in unison, both going red.

What in the hell. Reina met me stare, wondering the same thing and shrugging her shoulders, as clueless as I was.

"I mean," Moe recovered. "I can easily do that from the road. It's not essential I do my job here. Not like Riley."

Riley glared at her.

She offered a fake grin. "If she can go, I go too."

Reina clapped excitedly, pushing the emotion through the room before it simmered under the weight of my intense stare. *Well, hell,* I knew there was no convincing them otherwise.

If I told them no, they'd only trail us in the end anyway. Moe would simply use her power to determine our route. Even if I was sure to change it up and keep all the details at random, Reina's tracking abilities were innate from her time hunting as a child. They'd be right on our ass for days until ultimately, I pretended not to notice someone was hot on our trail and let them join, anyway. We'd been down that path many times in the past for smaller missions, both of them eager to see what Jax and I did. Wanting to leave the congestion of The Compound.

Seth's irritation shone through and he groaned as Moe and Reina beamed at me, knowing they'd won.

"Well, if we don't die this is gonna make one helluva story," Alexiares mumbled low enough where only I could hear, and probably Seth with his hearing.

PRESCOTT'S FACE WAS FUMING ACROSS THE TABLE THOUGH HE KEPT his voice even and calm in front of the Council. Four hours had passed since Alexiares had plopped chunks of flesh down on my desk and we were now standing in front of an emergency Council meeting. Luna squeezed Prescott's knee under the table, urging him to keep his cool and sending me supportive yet disgruntled glances for putting him on the spot. Like adoptive father like daughter.

It wasn't that I wanted to put him on the spot, so much as we didn't have the time to argue with him on this for hours. That would force us to postpone the meeting with the Council until the morning. The hour was already creeping into the later side of night and if we were going to do this; we needed to leave soon in order to beat the winter weather extremes.

We'd already likely have to find refuge through the worst of the weather and make it back here by early Spring at best. Two thousand thirty-five miles, if we remained healthy and well fed, pushed ourselves. We could cover about thirty miles a day, weather permitting of course. If all went well, it'd take us about seventy days to arrive, and who knew how much longer after that would be spent on recon and playing ignorant emissary?

My lips swished side to side as I watched Prescott awaiting his response. The Council was merely here as a courtesy call. I'd hear them out, but ultimately, I wasn't putting any soldiers at risk other than the ones that had volunteered to move at my side. It was a military based mission and as General; I had final jurisdiction, but I'd fully expect pushback on my second in command accompanying me. Taking the best healer and Moe, who they knew was focused on developing more on her visions, would be a tough sell.

None of us had pushed her, but they had. They'd demanded answers and were tired of being scared, of biting their nails every time their loved ones went on patrol or went out to trade. Which I guess is why I wasn't surprised when the Head Council of Trade voiced the first, "Yea," followed by Head of Fire. The rest bellowed in at once.

All 'yeas.'

"Clear the room please," Prescott requested, making it clear he intended on speaking directly to Seth and I and no one else.

Seth tugged at his ear and placed his head down, before remembering to appear unfazed and gazing past Prescott's head as if he were bored.

I took a deep breath, waiting for whatever argument would happen as soon as the door shut. Alexiares was the last one to leave, his eyes trailing over me before he offered a small reassuring smile, and walked out.

The second the door clicked shut Prescott's voice boomed across the walls. "This is ridiculous, the answer is no."

"Pres, I need you to trust me on this," I tried, deciding the innocent daughter approach may get me farther than playing General at this moment.

The expression on his face told me he wasn't going for it. "Oh, don't 'Pres' me. Now I love you Amaia, but trusting you is asking for a hell of a lot as of late."

"Okay, well first, ouch. I deserved that," I agreed, pursing my lips, "But I have the right people coming with me and a solid plan in place. You didn't even let me get that far!"

Seth grumbled in agreement and something about not wanting to get caught with our pants down again.

"I need you to forget about the last six months, and focus on the last few *years* that you've known me. Molded me into who I am today. Right here, right in front of you. You once told me that the strongest soldiers learn from a stronger leader. And that the 'greatest leader is not necessarily the one who does the greatest things, but that—"

"'He is the one that gets the people to do the greatest things. Don't Ronald Reagan me, Amaia."

I grinned, feeling prideful in gaining a foothold in the conversation, "One of the *only* good things to come out the man's mouth might I add."

He sighed; the internal struggle displayed behind his eyes.

Keep pushing. "So let me be the woman you helped mold me into being. Let me do the great thing, *please*. Trust us, trust me to do this. Blindly if you will, but just know that in my heart I'll do anything to keep the people here safe. Compound first. If not for them, then you, and Riley, and Luna, and Elie. For all of you guys that I have to leave behind, even when I know there's a chance I won't come back to enjoy your safety."

Seth cleared his throat. "At least let us explain the plan, man."

"Fine," he gave in, "have at it."

So we explained it all. How long it would take. How one of Riley's men had already been placed there as a sleeper agent shortly after the war, was placed on guard duty and would sneak us into the walls where we would gather as much information as we could from the shadows. They were more unorganized than us and wouldn't recognize individual citizens by the time we arrived.

The weather would be beyond freezing at that point, large coats and scarves, hats and all would be a must unless you were a fire wielder. In the meantime, Riley's sleeper would get to work on his own. Finally able to see if the contacts and relationships he'd established with disgruntled high placed citizens over the years could play in our favor in getting any helpful information they could.

The time spent around the city would allow me to identify their weak points and determine the condition of their troops. After a few weeks, my request, that would actually be sent by Riley, would have arrived announcing my 'diplomatic arrival.' I had a somewhat positive relationship with their leadership after the war.

We still exchanged letters through emissaries and such now and then and their General had played nice enough on the battlefield.

My inquiries would appear innocent, ignorant even, but well aimed for the recon that had already taken place. Things could go either way from there. We'd either realize our accusations were ill placed, or we'd get confirmation that our suspicions were right, and possibly identify who they're working with.

The journey back would be the most dangerous if that were true. It'd be a mad dash to Boise, the closest settlement in our territory. We'd sound the alarms for the other settlements and receive transport back to Monterey to prepare The Compound for the worst that was sure to come.

"Riley has it all under control," I tried to reassure him. "He's been instructed to debrief you should it all go to shit, but I can't risk losing any more of our troops. I won't risk it. We go there guns and magic blazing, and I guarantee you no one's coming back."

He grew increasingly hesitant, worried. "How will he know?"

"He just will." My gaze begged him to leave it at that.

"And Reina? Tomoe? All of you"—he was sad now, a worried father—"to put all of you at risk at once …"

"I won't leave my sister, and my sister won't leave me," Seth said firmly. Prescott's eyes locked on mine, brows scrunched. *Guess I'm not the only one caught off guard.*

I rubbed behind Seth's shoulder. "Of course not, I understand. I should have never mentioned it in the first place." Looking back to Prescott, I added, "Reina was right, with this new development it's better to be out there with a healer, plus Moe. That way we won't have to bop around into Moe's minds for her visions, she can just tell us along the way. No need to play telephone."

"With Alexiares … you trust him?"

The question was directed at me, but Seth answered in my stead, "He saved my ass, and Moe's. Not to mention he's pretty damn good with a knife"—he shuddered—"can do some weird ... sick serial killer shit with 'em. Solid in a hand-to-hand fight too."

"You're the one that dropped him at my doorstep like a stray dog." I tossed my hands up. "He also left The Expanse on his own free will, so he's in good standing."

I recalled what he had told me as he pulled me aside before entering the room. "He's from a settlement not too far from Duluth. They know him and can help take us in should we run into trouble. He knows the land enough to keep us out of any sticky situations, and if we do end up caught, they may be able to be persuaded into believing we're there in good faith."

Seth's eyes burned into the side of my head, wondering why I'd held back that piece of information, but I refused to turn to him, wanting to remain someone united in front of Prescott. Willing him to say yes.

Prescott slumped into his chair, a groan escaping his lips as he glared at us. "Don't. Fucking. Die."

CHAPTER
THIRTY

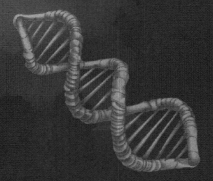

AMAIA

The morning after, the sky was grim, mirroring our spirits at breakfast. I hurried towards The Kitchens, picking up the pace as rain drizzled down, not wanting the maps in my bag to get wet.

Elie's face lit up, a broad smile spreading across her lips as I walked in. Her warm greeting easing my nerves. "Good morning, Amaia! I was just ending my shift and was heading out to ya." She pointed to the items she had set aside in the corner as she removed her apron.

"Morning, Elie, thanks." My heart pounded against my ribcage, threatening to burst through my chest. The realization dawned on me that this might be the last time I see her for a while, maybe ever. "Hey, El?"

Her curls bounced in the scrunchie atop her head. She must've had a few cups of coffee herself for her overnight shift. Energy radiated off her feeding to my own.

"Yeah?" She looked to me hopeful, like this would be the moment I invited her to train with my troops.

"I'll be headed out for a while, secret mission and all." I tried to make it lighter than it was, but her body stiffened in response. *Nothing gets past this kid.* "I know things have probably been a bit ... scary around here lately, and between you and me, they may get a bit scarier."

Her eyes widened, but I continued, "But it'll be okay, because Riley will still be here and if you can trust me, then you know you can trust Riley too. So if Riley tells you to do something, you listen. Okay, you hear me? If Riley says hide, then you take your parents and your brother and you go to that spot I told you about. You remember where that is?"

She nods, yes.

"Good. And what do you do when you get there?"

She stared back at me with the poise of a seasoned warrior, though the tremble in her small voice betrayed her. "Rex is to check the bug out bags for inventory, Mom and Dad check our weapons, make sure they're working and ready to use."

"And you?"

"I stand guard and fight, and if I can't fight, then I give the signal to run."

"Quickly. Run through the checklist."

She was confident in her answer. In a way that told me she recited it each morning as she brushed her teeth. "Assess the situation. Identify a route of escape. If I can't escape, stay behind cover and fortify my position. Find any weakness I can exploit. And use them."

"Yeah, you got it, El." It took everything in me to keep a tear from streaming down my face. I never had a little sister, but I'd always wanted one, and Elie had slowly placed herself in my life to become something quite similar to that for me.

I didn't want her to fight, but she spent enough time around my troops to hold her own. Our lessons would help too, we hadn't had them recently, a now regrettable decision. But she would never be defenseless, I'd taught her better than that. Her brother, Rex had picked up a thing or two from being around Seth's calvary as well.

Within moments, she was around the corner and pulling me into a tight embrace. "Blueberry muffin, warmed of course, and your coffee." My body went tense, caught off guard before relaxing into her hug. The smell of flour and honey meeting my nostrils as her hair tickled the side of my face.

She stepped back, motioning to the private dining space, "They're all in there and Seth is in a *mood*."

"Isn't he always?" I chuckled, grabbing my muffin and coffee before giving her one last glance over, taking in the image of her innocence and joy for life, and walked away.

It was still pretty early in the morning, making us the only ones there. The ambient lighting from the lanterns hanging from the windowless room, and smell of stale coffee fit the moods radiating off my friends who were gathered along our usual table.

Moe looked to be on the mend. She'd only taken one night off focusing on channeling more visions of the lab. Her once dull and lifeless dark hair now appeared silky and vibrant, while her pale tawny skin had regained its healthy glow. She sat beside Seth, just a few inches away, his body language showing he felt far from refreshed. He met my eyes moodily. His tan cowboy hat tipped back, hand bouncing against the crease of his dark jeans, his gun out on the table relieving the pressure of his holster from his side.

Reina wasn't in much better shape, though the red lipstick smeared across her lips and lace rimmed tank top hid it well. The lack of confidence in our mission reflected more through her slouched posture than the outwardly put together appearance. Small giggles rang from her throat as she pushed into her brother's shoulder, ignoring the grumble of his response to knock it off.

Riley turned to face me, causing his short locs to shake and sway with the movement. A small smile played on his lips, apologizing in advance and hoping I'd accept the situation for what it was. Necessary. I assumed he'd taken it upon himself to drag his insufferable roomie to our table since he'd be joining us on our journey north. Better than having to brief him on my own later or rely on secondhand information making its way to him accurately.

My eyes locked onto Alexiares as he tousled with his rings, sliding them up and down his fingers. I lingered over the symbols covering his knuckles, taking note of the letters for the first time.

H E L L

Squinting, I tried to make out the last letters. His fingers straightened, pushing into the table.

H E L L B E N T

Raising my gaze, I met his piercing stare, studying me intently with a ferocity that made me catch my breath. The coldness that usually marked his gaze when he looked at me was gone, replaced by a hint of something else, something softer. For a brief moment, we simply observed each other. A silent conversation passed between us before he caught himself and his eyes hardened once more into his usual glare.

Scoffing, I plopped down into the chair between him and Riley. Propping my coffee and muffin back a bit, I pulled my bag atop the table and reached for the map inside.

"Sour mood, Seth? You gonna share with the crowd or just glare off into the distance in peace?" I opened.

"In peace," he answered curtly.

Reina reached across the table and grabbed my hand. "Don't pay him any mind. He's just pissy. I kept Moe up all night chatting instead of in-between the sheets."

Moe kicked her under the table, face flushed, and flipped her off.

"It's one thing to vent about your woman of the night problems, but it's a whole 'nother when you *refuse* to take any advice. No, you'd rather circle the same damn drain over and over again," Seth fired back.

She groaned dramatically, slamming herself back into her seat. "Oh! To be a woman!"

"Really, Reina, your dating woes are what you want to spend your last bit of time here worried about?" I chuckled, shaking my head. She was the youngest by only two years, her energy and vitality infectious, but the little things that often mattered to her the most never failed to make me chuckle.

She tossed her mousey brown hair over her shoulder and leaned in. "Uh no actually, but I'd be happy to catch you up when we go out tonight. Last hoorah and all."

Alexiares muttered something about the priorities of our group being astounding under his breath and Riley smacked him in the back of the head nonchalantly.

"I think it's a great idea," Riley said, egging her on.

Reina's mouth dropped open as she scanned excitedly around the table for more heads to nod.

"Of course ya do, Ril," I retorted sarcastically, "Can't we just get through our plans first, then worry about going out like filthy irresponsible animals later?"

Her head bobbled in agreement as I used the edges of everyone's mugs to weigh down the ends of the map, showing an enlarged half of the continental United States. I wanted to start planning our route last night but was only able to get so far before needing Alexiares guidance.

"We'll take some of Seth's horses till we reach Montello," I said looking to him and pointing to the edge of Nevada on the map, "from there, we could either go up to Twin Falls, recoup, stay for a night or two. *Or* we can ditch the horses and cross into Utah."

"Why leave the horses?" He rubbed his chin, using the information I provided to map the route in his mind.

"As I'm sure you're well aware, the treaty states we have to have written permission to enter into another territory. At least not without facing skepticism and risking possible execution," all eyes turned to him pointedly and he scratched the back of his head. "Since we won't have that until weeks after we arrive, we'll have to walk the rest of the way to attract the least amount of attention possible. Five horses on the horizon are a lot more noticeable than five silhouettes. And if you aren't leading us to the middle of some trap, I'm sure we'll end up on back roads and trails that were never cleared. Horses will only slow us down."

His head bobbed up and down in a trance-like state, the room silent as we waited for him to speak. "We leave the horses we may not have any to come back to when we're haulin' ass. You okay with that?"

Seth met his eye and shrugged. "Ain't takin my best or my personal, no matter to me. I can break anything we need on the way back. We may need the extra days down the line."

Riley's eyes were trained on Seth, assessing him before he felt the weight of my own stare. I shook my head. *Not now.*

Okay, his face seemed to say before turning back to the map.

"Elko is one of yours, no?" Alexiares asked, breaking my focus on Seth and Riley and back to him.

"Yeah, we'll stop there for a night or two before the final push to Montello. Why?" It was interesting, watching him process and plan.

He'd certainly done it before. There was something familiar, official, about the way he chose to gather information, asking strategic questions before offering direction.

"We'll stop there and decide how to best move from that point. My gut tells me that we should push into Utah."

"But?" I asked, hearing the hesitant pause.

"But logic tells me that preemptively planning our next move without *knowing* the conditions out there would be a waste of time. Might as well receive an up-to-date report from Elko on the state of their borders while we're there. Use that to our advantage."

Smart. It wasn't that I was testing him, but it was reassuring to see he'd approach the situation similarly to myself, given we'd have to put our blind trust in him to guide us there. He may have left their territory in good graces, but something told me he was running from something on his way out. Or someone. And when you're running, you don't exactly take the front door out.

"Makes sense, but hypothetically"—I angled the map towards him like it would help him answer the question—"if we went from Montello to Utah, where would our *first* few stops be?"

It'd be smart to not tie ourselves down to one plan, especially if they had someone with Moe's gifts watching *our* moves. Then there was the fact that we still needed a solid idea on next steps in case we hit trouble or got separated. And perhaps a small part of me resisted blindly following him.

He took a moment before answering. "We have to go around Salt Lake."

"Salt Lake is huge. You might as well hit up Twin Falls and drop the horses off," Riley cut in.

"Nah, instead we loop up to Grouse Creek"—he traced a line down the rough paper—"play it safe along the border. If we keep good pace, we'll dodge Salt Lake and make it out Utah in 'bout uh, six days give or take. Preferably, take."

Moe gaped at him. "That's averaging more than thirty miles a day. You're insane."

"Forty-three for that push from here, to here," Riley added in pointing at a few of the markers Alexiares placed, his head shaking in bewilderment.

"I've seen what his men can do"—Alexiares tossed a thumb towards Seth who only nodded in confirmation what they were capable of—"there's at least three of us that can cover that all day, every day. Without stopping if we really needed to. Something tells me, you two wouldn't be around these other three if you couldn't hold your own."

The table was silent as he went on, "Now, we'll have to walk into the night for the forty-mile push, and take a lot of breaks but the day after that is only about twenty. We can catch our breath and rest then. It's either that or risk getting caught. They've got a heavy patrol in the area and are … less than accommodating to any unwelcome visitors."

"I thought they were supposed to be all holy up there or somethin,'" Reina chimed in, mortified look on her face.

"Great people," he teased, "but a *very* strong will to continue on their legacy. Rightfully so, got a lot to protect. A lotta families survived up there and you don't wanna mess with 'em."

We nibbled on our baked goods and coffee. Each of us studying every inch of the map before going our separate ways, promising to entertain Reina's 'last hoorah' idea and regroup later in the evening.

Everyone had their own things they needed to tie up, goodbyes to say and bags to pack. I decided spending the rest of my day around The Compound was the best use of my time. Making sure to stop by houses of soldiers I'd been meaning to check up on, playing cards with a few of them in the barracks. Took some time wandering around The Docks and the Stables. I finished my day reading on the steps of The Arena, taking in the kids who played their own version of *Cops and Robbers*, Mortals and Zombies, in the streets of Entertainment Square and the familiarity of it all. I'd miss this place, miss the constant noise and feeling of community.

It'd be hard to walk away from it all, but I would give everything I had to keep this place safe. When I looked around, I saw the future of humanity facing me, proof that in the end civilization would find a way to survive.

LIVE ALTERNATIVE MUSIC BLARED FROM THE TAVERN AS MY FRIENDS and I approached, hanging back a second to remember every detail of this moment. Reina skipped ahead, pulling Moe behind her as if she were an extension of her arm.

For such a solemn night, it was nice to see everyone dressed up and acting as if all were okay. They were stunning, all of them including the men, as much as it pained me to say now that Alexiares was included. Happiness was an emotion that suited them well, and maybe it was the shots of liquor we'd taken at Riley and Alexiares house, but it seemed genuine.

Reina had offered me a shot, with the condition that she be the one to provide my drinks for the night to ensure I didn't overdo it. I hadn't planned on it, but obliged, anyway. It was the first time I'd let alcohol pass my lips and enter the depths of my stomach guilt-free in months. It was a slippery slope to walk, but I was intent on living in the moment, wanting to enjoy this time with my family.

All of us here. Safe.

It was a good night to be out. Fridays in Entertainment Square could be lively. The theater space was only used about once a month. That didn't stop the few restaurants and bars from attracting exhausted patrons on the hunt to let loose after a week of work and physical labor.

There were a few bars that were popular, but this tavern had always been my favorite. Our favorite. It was the first in The Compound and never lost that spark for me. The drinks were simple but good, but it was truly the atmosphere and Friday music that made it for me. Popular with my soldiers, I was glad we'd chosen this for the night; it'd been a while since I could let loose around them. And like the way I'd missed my friends the past few months, I also missed the comradery amongst our ranks. No one understood what we went through out there more than each other, which also meant there was no one better to drown the trauma with over a few drinks.

There was no set attire for any of the spaces in The Compound. Entertainment Square was the one silently agreed upon place that everyone went to in order to escape the pressures of our reality. What you would expect someone to wear out for a night on the town in The Before, was similar to what you would find here. Though maybe slightly less dressed unless you were Reina. Her lace bustier propped her girls up high as she jokingly spun Moe in a circle, putting her long legs on display through the slits of her long skirt. Her long brown hair, perfectly placed down her back as she abruptly let go of Moe's hands and took off up the stairs to chase after her girlfriend who'd just entered through the door.

Moe turned back to us, shrugging, her face red from laughter and alcohol, covering her mouth in uncharacteristic giggles as she hiccuped.

"Care to escort me, boys?" she said, grabbing Riley and Seth and looping arms. Her dress hugged her figure. It was short and black, per her usual style, with pieces cut out around the top, allowing Wrath to tuck seamlessly in across her spine. She kept her hair from her face with a simple clip, accentuating the angles of her cheekbones nicely. Her aura radiated similar to a tall goddess, the chunked platform at the bottom of her boots giving her an extra boost on the already inches she towered over me.

Seth followed, his rancher's son outfit the opposite aesthetic from his ladies, but I took notice of the extra starchiness in his simple black tee tucked into the belt at his waist and had myself my own laugh.

Riley swiveled on his heels, noticing that only Alexiares and I would remain if he left us to move inside with Moe and Seth. I nodded at him. It's *okay*. He offered me a smirk, before continuing on. It was nice to see him dressed casually for once, usually in his work cargos and boots. The black pants and casual black jean jacket were a welcomed change, though he still sported some form of combat boots, just less worn.

"What's so funny?" Alexiares asked, closing in on me at the base of the steps, tearing me from my thoughts.

"Nothing really," I answered honestly, "just funny to think back on how far we've all come. It's nice to see them smiling again. I didn't think that I would."

"Scared it won't last?"

"I *know* it won't last. I'm not some delusional little girl, foolish enough to assume we'll all make it back in one piece."

He teased me, "And here I was thinking that just for a moment, you were capable of being anything but depressed."

I pushed his shoulder softly. "I can be fun. Just not around you."

Ain't No Rest for the Wicked poured out of the bar as Reina opened the door, hanging off the pretty blonde woman.

"Maia," she wailed, "come onnn! It's your song girl!"

I tossed my head back, laughing at the scene before ascending up the steps to follow her in. I stopped at the top, looking back at him before following her in. His eyes met mine before the door closed, making me think twice as if I'd heard him correctly.

"Good choice."

The night was nearly perfect. The band played hit songs from The Before, leading to less than respectable karaoke and loads of terrible drunk group singing. Alexiares had grabbed the group a table to keep our drinks on, but most drinks were downed within seconds, leaving only a stack of empty cups. He sat there most of the evening, watching me, watching everyone, his demeanor showing he was rather entertained, if not actually having a moment of fun.

The drunker the crowd got, the louder the music went. Soldiers danced along the edges of the bar, yelling out messed up versions of a chorus or flat out singing the wrong song. I danced with them, without a care in the world, enjoying this moment of respite no matter how fleeting it may be.

Then there was Riley, the tension between us no longer as we danced and talked loudly over the music. He'd always enjoyed dancing. The beats and notes moved through him, allowing him to catch the rhythm no matter the song. It was one of the only times I'd see him let go and not hold back. Seeing the softer, laid-back version of him wasn't something he'd displayed often, which only made it feel like a privilege each time that I did.

Seth and Tomoe moved in sync next to us, eyes focused on each other, tuning out everyone else in the room and stealing kisses in between. His hands moved dangerously low for a public place. I kicked out a foot, nudging the back of her shin and burst out laughing, not wanting to pass up the moment to embarrass them both. The two most stone-faced people I'd ever met, had fallen victim to lust and love, allowing both of their barriers to be dropped.

There'd been a brief moment before he'd left for Reno where I thought the group would have to deal with a different sort of fallout. I was glad to see the distance between them no more, at least for the night. Drunk rage simmered in their gaze in my direction before finding a more private corner in the crowded room.

When my lungs hurt and my feet throbbed, I decided it was time to take a seat at our table, leaving Riley to dance with one of the higher ranked women. As I watched on, he leaned close to her bronze ear and whispered something, causing her face to flush and her eyes to dart towards the ground. She smiled nodding, and her hands slowly moved to the nape of his neck, moving closer to him to hear the rest of what he was saying.

Alexiares cleared his throat. "Does that not bother you?"

"Does *what* not bother me?" I turned, brows furrowed, not liking where this was going already.

He pointed as if it were obvious and I smacked his hand down, not wanting to draw any attention.

"Oh, please. No, gosh no. He's a brother to me." My nose crinkled, disgusted with the insinuation.

"Well, since I got here, if he's not with me, he's with you. Doesn't leave your side much, and ya'll are ..." His gaze fixated on me, shifting in his seat a bit. "A bit, touchy. Handsy. I mean hey, none of my business."

"You're right, it *is* none of your business." I almost left it at that. "I don't I owe you an explanation, but just so we're clear, the answer is no. I don't know what kind of fucked up male-female relations you've encountered in your own life, but not every relationship between sexes has to be sexual. We're very close, nothing more, nothing less."

His chestnut eyes sparkled with excitement. He enjoyed bothering me. Riling me up. I turned my back to him, annoyed that I'd be stuck with him and relying on him in a small group the next few months. We'd have to find a way to work together, or we'd end up getting everyone else killed.

"I'm looking at him like that because I don't want to look away," I offered, hoping that if I offer this piece of vulnerability, he can see what I'm fighting for. What we're fighting for. "If I look away, then the moment is over, the night will end. And in the morning, I'll have to leave my brother behind."

My eyes remained stuck on Riley but I felt Alexiares' attention at my back. He said nothing. Sitting in silence, enjoying the music, I let the moment pass. Giving myself back to the liveliness of the tavern, humming along to the music, I felt Alexiares tapping his foot under the table. The crowd started to diminish and the bartenders hollered for last call, Reina and her girlfriend came into focus.

I hadn't officially met her yet, and she reached out a wavering hand. Her blonde hair plastered against her forehead as Reina leaned on her shoulder, staring at her admirably and moving it behind her ear, "Jessa, nice to meet ya, General."

It was more of a slur of words than introduction. I grabbed her hand, grinning, when Moe clunked down a round of shots onto the table. A varying version of 'yays' and hoots went out around the table as we all reached to grab one.

"To not dying!" Moe morbidly teased.

I shook my head laughing. "To not dying!"

Not a single one of us successfully downed the shot without making a face of pain, when the remaining crowd started jumping sporadically, the band playing the last few of their songs with the remaining energy they had.

I Bet You Look Good on the Dance Floor, filled the air and Reina let out a high-pitched screech, "Oh, this is perfect! Don't you see the irony?".

She yanked me from the seat, somehow grabbing me, Moe, and Jessa at once towards the middle of the room. The four of us dancing in a circle, swaying with the rest of the crowd.

A few songs later and the band began packing up their belongings, moving them towards the back room for the next week. Reina kissed the side of my cheek before promising to meet at first light, leaving hand in hand with Jessa, who could only grin as she leaned into Reina's side. Seth and Moe had disappeared the moment they'd felt unwatched, no one had been surprised about that. I was only grateful my second still had the sense to take what they had almost started out on the dancefloor, back to their bedroom.

I'd waited until most of the patrons had left, wanting to stay behind to help the owner clean a bit and say my goodbye to her as well. Another friend, another reminder at what I was doing this for. Riley and Alexiares almost ended up on the other side of a very drunk fireball, flanking me as I descended the steps.

"Shit! Do you guys wanna die or something?"

"Don't look at me. He's the only one that brought a key. Can't get in the house," Alexiares said defensively.

I glared at him. "I doubt you couldn't find a way inside without him."

Riley chuckled, and we moved through The Compound in silence, enjoying the crisp night air. The rain had stopped earlier in the day, but the wet smell still lingered, mixing with the salt from the ocean air. It had been nearly a year since I'd last woken up to the thick, and heavy inland air. It was an unfamiliar scent in my nose, lost to time, and now I would be months without the refreshing sea breeze that somehow made things more tolerable.

The paths leading from Entertainment Square to the General Living Quarters were still fairly populated with people. Either out for a late-night stroll, chatting in front of the homes of their friends, or laying out and staring up at the partially cloudy night sky in the greenery areas. *What a perfect night.*

Alexiares ignored the key in Riley's hand. Walking to the door, he picked the lock with ease, entering without a glance back or a goodnight. As soon as the door closed, I folded into Riley's open arms, taking in his warm hug.

"You know the asshole asked me if we were a couple tonight?" I fostered, avoiding the more serious conversation that was sure to follow.

Riley made a fake gagging noise, and I punched him in the gut, pulling away.

"Unnecessary," he gasped out.

"Yeah, well, so was the gag."

I made a show of being angry and serious, causing us to both fall to the ground in laughter before leaning against the door.

His locs fell to my shoulder as he rested his head. "I'm gonna miss ya, sis."

"Gonna miss you too, brother."

"You know what you're getting yourself into?" he asked, checking one last time.

"If I did, I don't think I'd be so easy to walk out those gates in the morning."

"Something tells me you'd walk out those gates regardless."

"I'm going to fix this," I said definitively.

Nodding his head, he could only agree. There was hell to pay.

I couldn't linger. Only had a few more hours to gather my things and try to get some rest. An involuntary whine left his throat as we tried to speak at the same time.

"You first," he said.

"I'm proud of you Ril. You've ..." My chest shuddered. "You've been a lot of things for me, a soldier I could trust, a friend, a shoulder to cry on, a human teddy bear, a running partner—"

"This is getting too sad for my taste, not to mention your speech sucks." His eyes were kind as he said it. "C'mon, no good-byes. Remember?"

"Yeah, no goodbyes." I nodded my head. He moved his arm to pull me closer, nudging his fist into the side of my head, rubbing into my curls before kissing the top of them.

"Now get outta here. The faster you leave, the faster you can come back to the shitshow you're inevitably going to leave me with."

I rose to my feet, taking a few steps back to get one last look. "I love you, brother."

"Love you too, sis."

My back had only turned for a moment before I felt a light flutter on my shoulder. It spooked me, my skin crawling off reflex, but curiosity kept my flames at bay.

Riley, I'd assumed. A white moth. *Good luck.*

CHAPTER
THIRTY-ONE

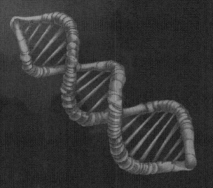

ALEXIARES

T he four of us waited, the horses letting out huffs and inching ahead as Seth pulled the reins on his currently in the lead, keeping the rest at bay. We'd gone back through Entertainment Square, out South Gate once again. The horses had garnered a decent amount of attention from the few shop owners headed to set up for the weekend market.

Their general was leaving, and so was their lieutenant, joined by two of her friends who seemed to have a lot of important shit to do around here. By breakfast, Prescott and Riley would have to make an announcement. They couldn't hide this and if the people here had any sense, they'd start preparing for this place to come down.

A general leaving their post and traveling beyond the walls was nothing to brush off. In the few weeks I'd spent getting to know Riley, the guy appeared to take his job pretty damn seriously, and have a good handle on things. Hell, he did more work behind the scenes than the actual lieutenant, working with Amaia like they were one entity. When she fell short, he filled in without them having to communicate. It was actually pretty impressive. I'd never seen leadership operate as seamlessly as they did.

Despite the circumstances, Amaia had admittedly done pretty well setting her troops up for success, even in her absence. In an ironic churn of events, her absence in the months prior to my arrival had likely primed them for this departure. They could handle it, for some time. The key would be making it back before the rock hit the glass.

Suckerpunch and Harley pounced on each other, full of nervous energy at the sight of the horses and our packs. They'd have to stay behind under Riley's care. Harley might as well have been birthed from Amaia with the way they tended to each other, attached at the hip. If she felt comfortable parting ways under his watchful eye, then I knew I could trust him with my own kin.

That didn't make the sting of leaving him behind any easier. A few months would turn into half a year to keep their pace. Both were extremely fit, but covering more than fifteen miles a day with them would be impossible.

I watched as Prescott pulled Amaia in close, saying something as her body shuddered in response. She nodded her head before pulling back to lean her forehead against his. Her eyes were rimmed with red, I didn't doubt she'd spent the hours apart from everyone else, letting herself fall apart.

He kissed her forehead, mouth moving to form the words *sweet girl*, before she offered a weary smile and made her way towards her horse. She was different from the girl I'd met the day I arrived. Even within the last few weeks, she seemed better. Focused, less reckless. Her mind was sharp and always moving. My original diagnosis of a lackadaisical and irresponsible leader, replaced with an overworked and exhausted one.

Keeping this place safe appeared to consume her every thought. I'd awoken to her and Riley outside my window countless nights, huffing and out of breath. She didn't even stop long enough for him to make it through the door. Riley would come back inside, face grave with worry. Mumbling to himself to take this and that off her plate. Making sure she could get some rest, reminding himself to go through the pile of paperwork on her desk.

Then there was the night I'd found her in the corner of the Public Library. Grander than one would expect for the end of the world, but a pleasant surprise for the casual reader. I couldn't sleep, had wandered in remembering Riley had shown it to me as we went through The Compound during rounds. We'd been the only two there, quiet enough that one squeak from my shoe would have likely ended with a gaping fire singed hole in my body. *Yeah, no plans to be on the other end of that.*

She'd been surrounded by notebooks, crossing things out, talking out loud and trying to find connections. I watched her for a while, careful to keep my breaths even and in line with hers. Exhaustion the only thing keeping her from noticing my presence. I was skilled enough to move undetected through the world, but I found that under my attention, she was fast to respond, seeking out the source of the eyes she felt watching her. She'd fallen asleep there that night, and now she was setting out on an impossible mission that could cost her the people she loved, yet she went willingly. Confidently. Proudly.

Tomoe cleared her throat, moving her horse a bit closer to mine and smirked, offering me her flask, "Sake wa honshin wo arawasu."

I glared. "It's six a.m."

"Six a.m. or last night, doesn't really matter," she shrugged.

321

Intent on ignoring her comment, I pretended to inspect my pack. Amaia had been clear in her instruction on what we could and could not pack. The first few days, we'd be able to travel with more, then once we ditched the horses what didn't fit on our backs would be lost to the area.

My first pack was filled with date bars and other granola the staff at The Kitchens had crafted, some dried meats, bread and cheese. There was a good amount of nuts and other trail mix buried at the bottom underneath some canteens, prefilled with water. We wouldn't need anything to purify extra water with. We had Reina, and myself, if absolutely necessary.

Though I wouldn't put it past Seth or Amaia to have something else with them just in case. A small pack of herbs and some bandages in case we hit trouble. In a separate pouch sat a compass with a smaller version of the map Amaia had brought to breakfast the previous morning. This pack was to stay on me at all times, in case we were separated or had to leave the horses behind.

Two more packs sat on the back of my horse, an extra one for food, and some wipes Reina had soaked in some type of soap and oil. Oddly enough, there was also a toothbrush and mint packed paste. Usually someone with her chipper personality would annoy the hell out of me, but there was something about the way that she carried herself that made me want to accept her kindness and not mistake it for ignorance or weakness. This would be the pack we could ditch if needed.

The final one would come with me if possible. It had extra clothes, some of which we'd change into before crossing into Utah to make up space, and prepare for the weather. A larger navigation kit, extra ammunition and knives, something to sharpen the knives with, a tent, and sleeping bag. Simple enough, easy to grab and go when on the run.

Harley's ears popped to attention as Amaia walked over, bending down to squeeze around her body, causing her to squirm and pant out of her mothers' arms. She laughed, kissing around the sides of her face, then up and down her forehead to her nose.

"Good girl baby, you know momma loves you. Right?" Harley licked the side of her face in agreement. "Oh my sweet girl, you're the prettiest, bestest, smartest, baddest bitch in all of Monterey, okay? You listen to uncle Ril and be a good girl, and maybe a little devil if things get a bit boring around here."

Harley barked, hopping onto Amaia's shoulders and slobbering down her shoulders. Suckerpunch whined from next to me, startling me. My heart clenched. I'd said my goodbyes this morning. More tearful than I'd expected, but hey, that's my kid.

"Papa will be back for ya boy," I winked, tossing him a piece of jerky from my pack. "Give 'em hell."

Amaia mounted her horse, turning to us all, solemn faced as the others let their gazes rest over the wall of The Compound. Prescott and a few soldiers stood in front of the gate, noise starting to hum beyond the wall.

"Ready?" she asked.

Her curls were wrapped in two braids, bouncing as she kicked the horse gently in the side, taking off at a gallop. At that moment, I saw her for who she used to be, who I thought I'd come here to hate, only to find a sorry version of her instead. The woman now in front of me was fierce.

A warrior-like woman on a mission, and God bless whoever ended up in her path.

SUCKERPUNCH AND HARLEY FOLLOWED US THE FIRST FIVE MILES BEfore Amaia gave a final cry for Harley to listen and go back. Harley had let out a loud whimper, and sat in protest with Suckerpunch at her side. They'd howled until we were out of sight. Seth confirmed they'd made it back with Riley an hour later. Amaia and I both letting out a relieved sigh, meeting each other's eyes briefly.

The ride to Hollister was solid. Picturesque, something that belonged in a frame and would sell for an ungodly amount of money in some rich person's house. A memory jogged in the back of my mind, envisioning something similar hanging over the tub in my parents' bathroom. My mom doing her best to make every room feel like an escape from outside the constraints of the home. Her freedom to travel was restricted to my father's business and where it brought them, if he allowed her to go at all.

The terrain was decent enough. Lots of green rolling hills and scattered oak trees that someone would spend a shit ton of time trying to paint, only for it to come out as a fuzzy brown and green blob. We passed a few vineyards, overgrown, but had probably been an ideal tourist location at some point in the past. Amaia had jokingly grabbed a handful of grapes, saying it'd make the heat more tolerable. Reina had chucked her own handful at her, saying the weather was the dictionary definition of autumn and to "drop the contraband."

For the most part, it was quiet, peaceful even. The area hadn't been super populated to begin with, leaving Pansies scattered and far between. Nothing Reina couldn't take out with an arrow from a distance, or Amaia nonchalantly raising a piece of trash from the ground and forcing it through a skull without a second thought.

Seth had noticed the curiosity in my face, riding up next to me, giving me a simple explanation. "If you leave 'em alive, you're only taking another human life."

There wouldn't be any hesitation on my end. Was just glad we were all on the same page.

At our leisurely, but steady pace, we made it outside of Hollister right before nightfall. The only two breaks were for Reina to give the horses some water and a quick treat to keep their endurance.

We'd officially crossed into San Jose borders near the beginning of the day, giving us peace of mind that any troops we encountered out here would either be soldiers Amaia sent out to help, or friendly faces from San Jose. But there was always the risk of running into trouble, so Amaia had determined a spot out the way would be best for the night.

It was a decently sized city. Steering clear from the edges of town was probably the safer option anyway, be it from the living or the undead. We left the horses near a vacant rundown roadhouse, tied up near the back with enough lead to lie down for a night's rest. Amaia and Seth led the way as we walked down the road, stopping between an old facility and some trees.

"Reina, Moe, you two in Seth's tent," Amaia directed, curls popping out through her braids from the wind during the ride, exhaustion taking over both her posture and her face.

Reina's energy, to no one's surprise, remained high. "What? Seriously, come on, don't make me share with these two!"

"Hey what's wrong with us?" Tomoe's head tilted up from her position, dust from the ground coating the knees of her black jeans crouched on the ground, rumbling through her bags.

"Yeah Reina, I stink?" Seth said mockingly, pretending to care. His face said *please go anywhere but with us*.

She caught on. "Okay, see case in point. Look at them. No way they're gonna respect my presence."

"What kind of friend would I be to make you fall asleep to that?"

Reina eyed Tomoe earnestly. "Aw really, Moe?"

"All offense, sister"—Seth looked pointedly to Amaia, the pink and orange from the sky making his red hair appear to be made of flame—"but is there a reason she can't set up her own tent?"

The blood under my skin turned hot, my fists clenched. "She still doesn't trust me."

"That's what this is about? Make him set up his own tent. Reina can stay with you. Matter fact, since we're on the subject, if you don't trust him, now's a good time to make him turn back around, or this whole thing is pointless."

"It's not that I don't trust him. I just trust you more to protect the two of *them* if something happens in the middle of the night"—my eyes narrowed, vision honing in on Amaia's mouth, daring her to keep it up—"And yeah, maybe I do only trust him as far as I can throw him. At least for the first night."

It was an insult that only I would get. She'd tossed me to the ground during our first spar. Caught me off guard and embarrassed me, had enjoyed it too. It was the first, and only time I'd seen life in her eyes for the first few weeks I'd entered The Compound. Once I'd been assigned to Riley, I'd watched them move weightlessly around in The Ring.

In hindsight, the light in her eyes I'd accused her of when around Riley had likely been about the sick trauma bond they had going on. I'd fought Riley too. They both struck to kill and intended for their opponents to do the same. Pain made them happy.

Pain had made my father happy too, one of the many things I hated him for passing down to me.

I rolled my eyes, feigning boredom instead of instigating a fight. "Again, two of the three people you are talking about, I went out of my way to save."

"Okay, I wouldn't call it out your way. You were there. The only way to get out was to fight. What were you gonna do, let us all die?" I hadn't taken Seth to be one with a small ego, *noted*.

"Point stands."

Amaia wasn't buying any of it. "As does mine. Reina? Moe? Any objections?"

"Uh, yeah," they chimed in unison.

"My objections don't count?" Seth grumbled, face red and eyes lethal.

"They do, but yours take less hesitation to overrule."

Another thing I'd noticed, if Seth wasn't fighting with his sister, he was fighting with Amaia. Never taking the same tone with Riley or Moe. Tomoe was assertive, blunt with her words, but not cold. She meant well. Gave me hope that she at least tried to stand up for herself with Seth behind closed doors. The way my mother had failed to with my father.

I hadn't held any issues with Seth myself, hell he'd advocated for me to come along, but Amaia's choice to make him her second was ... questionable. Despite her own internal struggle, I'd come to find each move she made calculated. She'd let me accompany them, but under her watchful eye. Perhaps that's why she'd left Riley in charge.

She walked to the furthest part of the little square we'd decided to reside on for the night, taking inventory on the items in her pack and writing in some notebook. Reina and Seth started bickering. They snatched a larger tent from Seth's pack back and forth, debating on the way their father had taught them to pitch a tent leaving me and Tomoe staring face to face.

Her eyebrow arched, and she laughed sarcastically under her breath, shaking her head.

"Sake reveals the true heart, huh?" I mumbled.

Her jaw went slack, and for once her eyes focused as she studied me skeptically, recognition sliding over her features before fading away quickly.

"My father made sure I was quadrilingual. 'Good for business.'"

More curiosity. "The business of?"

"Nothing good." I scoffed, leaving it at that.

"Hmm."

"Hmm."

With nothing else to say, I started to walk away, a soft hand wrapping around my forearm stopping me. "I've known Amaia for a few years now, you two are more alike than you think."

I tilted my head, her fingers answering before I could ask what she meant, pointing to my own. "Hellbent."

"More observant than you let on."

"It's the eyes, huh?"

Her sense of humor made me feel at home. If I was open to friendship, she'd be the type of friend I'd want to have. *I think.*

"The losing consciousness didn't help."

"Happened once."

"Twice." I tossed up two fingers. "Technically you were passed out that first day I arrived at Amaia's door."

She bit down her lip, eyes going somewhere else, lost in thought before finding my own.

"If you could both pull your heads out of your asses, you'd be able to do some good together. Make a good team. From what I heard about your assessment, a power to be reckoned with."

My fingers found my rings, sliding them up and down out of habit before I forced myself to stop. "I didn't come here to be on her team."

"Then why did you come here." She wasn't asking, not really.

Silence followed before she made another attempt. "I'll try again. Why come on this mission then, if you had no intention of being a team?"

"Because I've got people to do right by."

Without missing a beat, she took a chance, feeling confident she could trust me too. "Then do right by them. Because I have a feeling, we'll probably need that in the future."

She'd been having visions since we'd left for Reno. Visions she hadn't told anyone else about. Visions of war in the future. She hadn't told Reina, or Seth, and by her words, certainly not Amaia. Hoping that this trip could help change the outcome, she didn't want to burden Amaia with the different versions of their future reality. Didn't want her to become unfocused and make the wrong guilt-wrecking mistake. Scared for her to fall victim to her own mind and abandon them all again.

"You don't feel guilty? Taking that choice from her?" I asked.

She smirked, bumping my shoulder. "See, already going to bat for your teammate. But no, the future always has the ability to change, and I hope that it does. Putting the weight of the future on her shoulders, knowing that every choice she makes can directly lead to the loss of thousands … I can't put that on her, won't."

Leaving me with that last thought, she gave offered another playful shove before heading to break up the now full-blown argument between Seth and Reina over a fucking tent. *Children.*

Amaia had just started pitching our tent when I made my way over, helping her in silence. When it was finished, she'd left towards her friends' tent, offering no words as I headed inside. The sky was a few shades from pitch black. Soon there would be no natural light other than the soft glow of the stars. Since Amaia was adamant about not being 'dumbasses to let their target see us before we can see them,' a fire was out of the question. Officially making doing anything outside the tent pointless.

She joined me a few minutes later, eating our food. Small smacks and slurps of water were the only sound, the others keeping their voices low inside the tent. We were hidden between enough brush to be out of eyesight in the dark, but too much noise would cause anything out there to start investigating the cause.

Neither of us slept that night.

The tent was stiflingly quiet as we lay there, our sleeping bags overlapping in the cramped space. I could sense her eyes on me, even though I couldn't see them in the dark. Both of us reluctant to turn our backs to each other in such close quarters. Every little shift or rustle brought us closer, our limbs tangling together. It was hot and stuffy, a night I'd usually strip down to nothing and enjoy the kiss of the damp air on my skin. When I'd stopped moving long enough and she assumed I'd fallen asleep, she wiggled out of her sleeping bag, her skin brushed against mine, sending a shiver down my spine. Her shirt was lifted just enough to reveal a sliver of her stomach, shirt slightly lifted against my arm.

Neither of us moved again, and I woke up not knowing who had truly fallen asleep first.

"I AM *NOT* DOING THAT AGAIN."

Amaia sat legs crossed, reviewing the map as she smacked on nuts and bread, waiting for the others to awake while leaving me to pack the tent away. She'd said nothing as she unzipped the tent, had merely sat up, grabbed her belongings, and scanned the perimeter, gun drawn.

Reina emerged from the tent resembling a walk of shame stumbling in a hungover state across campus, ended up in the city, and left at a bus stop for her friends to show up three hours later, asking for the details. Her hair was tangled in a knot at the top of her head. She wore a shimmering night gown of all things, her skin blanched and pink near the corners of her eyes as if she'd been rubbing them incessantly.

"What happened to you?" Amaia asked, trying to contain a laugh. "Look like you've seen a ghost."

"More like listening to these two swoon in each other's ear all night and make *disgusting* noises. And then Moe did this thing with her—"

Tomoe slid out the tent glaring at her friend and pulling on her jeans from the day before, handing Seth his cotton button up shirt back. "First of all, we thought you were asleep."

"Second of all, shut the hell up," Seth chimed in, *like clockwork*.

Tomoe worked to nip it in the bud before it began, elbowing him in the gut as he let out a grunt.

"Moe, you promised, you weren't gonna do it in my presence!" Reina said, her voice loud even as she attempted a hushed tone.

"No, I said I wouldn't make you fall asleep to that. You're usually a solid sleeper. You slept through Amaia rage, lighting the bed on fire last summer!"

"We were drunk. That doesn't count! Doesn't matter, not doing that again."

Reina walked behind some bushes in the distance, mumbling about needing to tend to the ladies' room before directing her energy towards me and Amaia. "By the exhaustion on y'alls faces, your tent ain't much better!"

A mix of confusion and contained laughter filled the awkward silence of the campsite. The lack of her voice meaning nothing, knowing she wasn't yet finished.

"I'll just cowboy up and do my own damn tent," she yelled from her outdoor bathroom. "I'll be just fine, thank you very much."

Amaia tossed her hands up in surrender before pushing herself off the ground and announcing to pack it up and be at the horses in twenty.

THE RIDE TO STEVINSON WAS SMOOTHER THAN THE PREVIOUS DAY, the further inland we went, the more desolate the area became. Nature reclaiming what rightfully belonged. Reina had kept her word about setting up her own tent, compromising by squeezing it in between ours and Seth and Tomoe's. It only made for a tighter squeeze inside as the edges of Reina's pressed into Amaia's side of the tent, causing her to inch forward to keep it from poking at her back. It was her idea, after all, to post up in the narrow gap in the coverage of the overgrown fields.

The heat of the day lingered, making the night unbearable. Sleep was elusive, even after two restless nights, her constant turning and shuffling throughout the night, telling me she wished for the same.

Her breath brushed the side of my neck, tickling my throat as she breathed in and out. I could feel the heat emanating from her, the closeness of her body sending my primitive senses into overdrive, but my mind resistant to give in. It was a strange feeling, almost electric, as I turned my head towards her.

"Hard time sleeping?" she asked.

"Yup."

"Yeah," the word, little more than a sigh.

It was like we'd been transported back to that day down by the water again, watching the waves crash, capturing our words as they left our mouths, making it feel as if they're gone forever, weightless.

The feeling both freeing and unsettling. "You ever wonder if that one thing never happened. Never broke you. Where you'd be now?"

"All the time," the words came out as a bite, hesitant, not knowing if she should keep her walls up or not.

"You just can't be nice to me, can you?"

"Rich, coming from the guy who called me a bitch for doing my job, trying to protect my home, my family. The very same thing you're protecting now. But you're not going to tell me *why* are you?" She let the words weigh on me for a moment before snorting. "Of course not."

"I have people to protect too, people I want to keep safe."

"You mean the guy you met in the middle of the night like it was a drug deal?"

My veins burned against my skin, fire flowing through them, consumed by anger. "You followed me?"

"Please, if I'd been following you, I would've at least gotten a name."

I remembered the late-night runs she'd been on and decided to offer her something to work with. I did have people to keep safe. But if I told her who I was keeping safe, then she'd ask how

I know him, which would only lead to other questions. Questions that might only cause problems for this mission, and that would defeat my purpose in being here.

The day we met flashed before my eyes for a moment. She'd understand. She'd been in self-destruction mode when I'd arrived. I knew that mode because I'd walked that path for a long time. When you lose the people you love the most, and then find something, someone worth living for again, only to have them taken from you, too.

"How many did you lose before you got here?" She knew what I meant. Everyone had lost someone, didn't know a single person who had everyone they loved make it out.

"Too many," she said softly.

"We were coming from a funeral." The words were out my mouth, flowing before I could convince myself to stop, to keep it all in, keep it to myself. "I was on my bike, not too far in front of my family. Father insisted we all ride together, but … I was out drinking the night before, partying. Showed up late and ended up needing my own transportation."

I cleared my throat, masking the shakiness of my breath. "The alerts were going crazy on my phone, but, I didn't wanna take it out while riding, we were going over a bridge and my mom is … was, always nervous about me owning a motorcycle. She'd freak if she was watching."

Her breath was even, listening, as her hand found my own, letting it all come out.

"I heard the tires sliding across the pavement first. Took me a second. Damnit, the bike was too loud, I couldn't hear. My brother had told me their neighbors had complained. Pissed my father off, the extra attention. So I'd made it louder out of spite." I chuckled at the memory. "Spite is a funny thing. Usually ends up biting you in the ass later. By the time I turned the bike around, the car had rammed into the one next to it, made it on top somehow. Impact broke part of the barrier. Car was halfway over the bridge. Driver had started to turn. At the time, thought it was just a seizure, medical emergency, or something. First thought was to get to my brother. He was sitting in the back, driver's side, easy to get to. Easy to get out."

I needed another moment. This story had been told only once before. To Tiago.

"I went for my mom next, had her hand and everything but the son of the bitch, as much death as he caused, he couldn't face it himself. He was a coward, down to his dying breath. Tried to scramble out before her, pulling them both back. The weight was too much, they went over."

She said nothing. There was nothing to say. Everyone who's lost someone close to them could tell you the same thing. *No words make it better. Just listen to them, be there, your presence is enough.*

But something about the weight of her silence felt genuine, real. Like she gets it.

It's not that those words aren't true, nothing anyone says truly makes it better, but I've found that on the other end of the presence, is the need for them to feel better. Feel that their job as that supportive person is done, but it's not. Real support is understanding the pain and feeling the suck with them.

When you lose someone you love, you don't *want* to feel better, because if you feel better, you might feel happy. And if you feel happy, you might forget what it feels like to be happy *with* them, and learn to be happy without them. And when you love someone, you want to feel that happiness with them, to feel it without them is to acknowledge their absence.

For me, there would never be the desire to live happily without my people I loved, my family. I couldn't give a shit about my father. But my mother, my brother, Tiago, I'd die so they could live again. Everyone grieves differently, sure, and I chose to hold on to the pain. I deserved it.

"My brother, well. I wish I could say we had much longer after that, but I'd be a damn liar." I shook her hand from mine. "He was sixteen when he died, a baby in the grand scheme of things. Life hadn't even begun for him."

There were plenty of habits of hers that I detested, but speaking without thought wasn't one of them.

"Sammy was my best friend," she started, her breath now shaky, in match with mine. "We started this together, us and Harley. I was so naïve, insane honestly, thinking we'd camp out at her place until the government got a handle on things. I mean, shit, I'd seen all the zombie movies. Just didn't think it would be a reality. They killed her," she said simply, "and I had to kill him."

I gave her a moment, letting her settle with her thoughts.

"I was engaged in The Before. Not to Jax, but a sweet, sweet man," her voice had gone soft, gentle. "Xavier. He was kind, always helping people, always trying to make people happy. Make me happy. Smart too. This world would have eaten him alive. Stained him."

"I know what you mean."

Her head shifted, leaning forward in curiosity, not realizing there wasn't much space left. The soft whisper of her lips brushed against my ear as she spoke.

"We were planning our wedding when it happened. He was like your driver. Turned instantly. I didn't know what was going on, but he tried to attack me. It was a fight to get out the apartment, but I ... I didn't want to hurt him, so I grabbed Harley and ran. It wasn't until Sammy died that I went back out of necessity, the key to where all my guns were stored were back inside. Where I'd trapped him. Didn't have any other options. Going to a gun store would be a moot point, and going unarmed for scraps would be stupid. I thought I'd be able to out move him, grab them and go but. Harley was just a puppy ... she wanted to defend me but ended up in his ..." She shuddered. "Her cry was agonizing, I just wanted it to stop. Then he turned on me, got my leg. I was scared, didn't know you couldn't turn back then, well wouldn't."

It wasn't a contest, but relieving a burden.

"Death changes you, ruins you. It happens immediately, but you'll deny it. The things you have to do, and part of you wants to justify it. Say you did it because you had to, out of necessity, for survival. Then after you're responsible for so many, you begin to wonder what about you makes your survival more important than theirs."

And then it clicked. She wasn't just talking about the undead anymore. Her friends hadn't said anything, they knew. I'd seen them watching her the way a mother watches her child in an expensive furniture store for weeks. She'd come close, the smell of alcohol hinting on her clothes as she passed by, as if she'd dropped a splash on accident, but never from her mouth. From what I could tell, she hadn't had a drink since I'd arrived. Despite her friends' reactions, and her abhorrent appearance the first few weeks, she seemed to have a pretty good handle on her drinking. Well, was coping in other ways, which is what had shocked me the night before we left.

Reina had offered her a drink, promising to cut her off before it was no longer appropriate. She'd hesitated, babysitting it until we'd gone around the room a few times refilling our glasses, before closing her eyes and downing it. Indulging, downing one after the other, a sad, tortured empty look in her doe eyes. I'd been fairly confident she wouldn't drink. She'd appeared troubled enough over the decision that I'd started to assume the worst in her against better judgment. That was before she'd lost herself and ended up flailing around the bar and relying on Riley for support through their dancing.

In an instant, it clicked. She drank that night because she didn't plan on making it back. The familiar feeling of guilt crept in, hating myself for caring.

"You mean Jax."

"Jax, yes. Amongst others."

"You don't plan on making it back, do you?"

"No," she whispered, "I don't. But *they* have to. We don't get along, you and I Alexiares, but I think part of why I can't stand your presence is because I see part of myself in you. I know you'll do what it takes to survive. I need you to promise me, on whoever it is life you're trying to save, don't think I've forgotten, to please, make sure they do too."

Too close, I've gotten too close. I reacted without thinking it through.

"To ask me, of all people, after the show you've put on is hilarious. I'm not Jax. I'm not the good guy you can count on for favors. Ask someone else, whatever you're trying to do, right here. Connect with me. It's not happening. We're here on a mission, nothing more. Take care of your own family. Move over."

Amaia scooted back abruptly, taking part of the tent with her, realizing how close our faces had been. "If you stopped being such a dick, you could find your own family here, too. Riley and Moe really like you. Don't let them down."

"Or what?"

It came out as a joke but we both knew it wasn't. "Or I'll add you to my list of people to feel bad about killing."

"My families dead. I don't need another to mourn."

"Can't mourn if you're dead."

CHAPTER
THIRTY-TWO

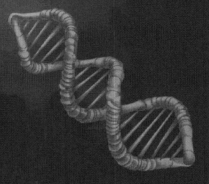

AMAIA

S tevinson to Snelling was uneventful, despite the blistering heat. The further inland we went, the further away the wind-break from the Pacific Ocean was. Ninety-degree weather on top of a sweating horse, was miserable.

Snelling was one of those cute towns you'd see in some *Hallmark* Christmas movie, but slightly less charming. It truly was in the middle of nowhere, surrounded by farmland and water. Merced River made it easy to cool off. The horses drank while we all splashed, enjoying the frigid, rushing water. We caught a few fish, munching as we took advantage of what was left of daylight, letting my fire roast them into a flaky bland, yet satisfying meal. As evening came, Seth and I agreed the town was small enough to go straight through and find a place to hunker down for the night. Settling for a modest home that was somewhat well reserved.

I'd started to become skeptical. The further out we went, the more I'd wondered where The Pansies were coming from. We'd encountered a few, but nothing dense enough to pose a threat to any respectable unit or community. And none had moved with the cadence and competence of the ones we'd faced near Monterey, nor what our neighboring settlements had either.

Thoughts that had come too soon. Halfway to Buck Meadows, Moe collapsed, hitting the ground hard from atop her horse. If her eyes hadn't glazed over, unseeing, I'd have checked her body, searching for signs of physical trauma.

"Oh shit," Seth said, whirling his horse around at the thud and galloping back towards us.

I was off my horse in an instant. "I got her."

Seth marched over, practically diving onto the ground and sliding her from my lap to his. Reina and Alexiares were at our side, blocking the sun with their shadows a moment later.

The next few minutes passed painfully slow. Her eyes went from unseeing to frosty white, body trembling as tears ran down her face.

"We have to run. We have to run. We have to run. No. Go! No. Run. Run. We have to run," she muttered over and over again.

Reina slid a hand over her body, trying to relieve some of the stress from her to no avail. She shook her head. *It's beyond me.* It went beyond her magic. Moe's magic would block her out in this state, forcing Reina to wait until after it delivered its message, fighting to remain in control.

Slowly, her eyes returned to their usual inky brown. Sweat beaded on her nose, lip quivering as she pushed herself out of Seth's lap, face angled.

She turned to me slowly, voice tremulous. "There's no way out. Every path we face trouble."

My heart dropped, making me take a pause before asking, "What's our best option?"

"To stick to the path, we're on." Her eyes flickered around at the group. "Can't say it won't be hell, though."

She went on to describe us, *trudging through a forest, hearts pounding with fear. Wolves toying with us. A cat with a mouse as their bloodcurdling howls chased us. We were running, clothes caked with dirt and sweat. She wasn't able to keep track of time or day, with no clouds on the horizon, rain wasn't likely and the day tomorrow would probably resemble the weather of today. Our clothes were re-worn, several days at a time*, making the next bit unable to be time-stamped. *A herd of Pansies headed for us, situation after situation beating down on us without mercy, making us question our existence.*

Suddenly, she'd found herself transported to The Expanse, *a desolate and barren place with a blonde woman standing before us. Her hair whipping around her face and her sharp features making her look otherworldly, powerful. Cold air cutting through our skin, making us shiver uncontrollably, even me.* She'd realized with horror that *our magic had been cut off, hands bound behind our backs and helpless.* Vulnerable and defenseless, two of my greatest fears. Then she saw me, *tears streaming down my face, fire blazing around me and earth bending to my will, becoming a weapon.*

We gave her a moment to collect herself. Reina checking her for any injuries after her fall and clearing her after a nurse's fuss. No one spoke for hours, all lost in thought, jumping at every rustle behind a tree, birds flapping past our heads. Being on edge was easy when you knew possible death was looming around every corner.

The plains gave way to the towering mountains of Sierra Nevada; the elevation getting steeper, taking a toll on everyone's lungs, including the horses. I found myself taking in the view. Another place I'd foolishly left on my bucket list, thinking I'd had all the time in the world to get here. To see it all.

"We're close," Moe said, slowing her horse, causing us all to stop, awaiting her next words.

The way the words left her mouth had everyone's hands reaching for their weapons.

Alexiares spoke first. "The terrain is the same for the next sixty miles, which is about the distance for the next safest place to stop."

Everyone shifted in their respective space, deciding whether we should voice our opinions on moving forward.

He understood that, adding, "It's more dangerous to move through this place at night than it is to set up camp. We won't be able to see the terrain, down at ground level the moon won't be able to penetrate through the trees. There isn't even a way to use Amaia's fire without letting everyone within twenty meters know where an easy victim is."

"Good enough for me," I said, though everyone else was still skeptical. "We can leave the horses behind one of those buildings up there, then set up camp a decent bit away. Gives us enough room to bail if we need to, but also stay hidden from any danger."

I led the way, heading down the road and stopping in front of an old lodge. We tied the horses up, given the risks and circumstances, it was best to keep them where we knew we could find them and not let them wander off.

After some back and forth and scoping around, we settled on heading across the road into the forestry for cover. A few minutes into the walk, we'd stumbled upon another old building, this one unmarked. The structure appeared far from sound enough to go in without risking a collapse, instead we chose to set up off to the side.

"Shit," Moe was freezing in place, and taking in her surroundings, reaching out for objects of similarity.

"What?" I said, looking around.

"It's time."

Alexiares drew his knife, planting his feet while his eyes scanned the perimeter. "Now?"

Moe turned impatient. "Yes, now."

"Well, which one?" Reina's face was blanched as she reached for her pack of arrows, slowly pulling them around her back.

"What do you mean, which one?" Moe hissed.

We moved into a circular formation, fire singeing in my fingers and drawing my throwing knife. No guns for now, too loud. Seth called out a series of instructions, helping Reina and Moe fill in the gaps between Seth, Alexiares, and me. A broken formation was a weakness.

I quipped, "Does it really matter, Reina?"

"I'd like to know what I'm preparing for!"

"Shh! Quiet." Seth demanded, "I hear something."

He could hear better than we could. His eyes landed on mine, wide with fear as if he'd seen a ghost.

"Run," he said.

"Which way?" I asked through my teeth, wanting clarity.

Reina whimpered, "I'd still like to know what we're running from."

"That," Alexiares said, pointing to the woods in front of him, a series of clicks and groans filling the air at the same time.

A herd of Pansies dashed towards us with preternatural speed. Focused directly on us, moving between the trees. Wraiths, gliding towards us with intention.

"Got it, so that way I assume," Reina said as I threw up a wall of fire. She grabbed me by the waist, pulling me forward and taking off in the opposite direction.

"The horses are the other way," Moe panted between strides.

Alexiares leveled with her, "We don't stand a chance going through that. Did you see them fucking running?"

"We could try, use y'alls magic," Seth turned around briefly, taking in the scene behind us, "Never mind. Good point." He could outrun us, leave us behind, but he didn't.

Branches scratched against our skin as we shed the extra weight of our packs.

"Over here," I said, pulling their attention towards another small building. There were no doors. We couldn't stay here, but it could buy us some time.

The herd moved past us, lingering a few feet ahead, trying to figure out how we had disappeared as quickly as we did. We watched as they huddled in small groups, moaning and groaning as their limbs flailed around. They went still, listening to something, someone that was not present before spreading out their search in coordinated efforts.

I let a few minutes pass, studying their habits and the way they systematically crossed paths, trying to cover as much ground as they could, but headed in the wrong direction back towards the horses.

My lips were painful, dehydrated, and burned from the sun. I brought my finger to them, making sure each of my friends faced me as I mouthed, "Be quiet, this way."

We made it a few hundred yards away before the natural quiet of the forest took over, the noises of The Pansies fading away into the distance. Our movements were slow, purposeful, but the sound of our boots crunching against the fall leaves betrayed us.

Reina whispered, more of a soft yell than anything, "Hey guys, are we actually being quiet or are we just making noise more slowly?"

I glared at her, daring her to say another word.

"We can probably cut through here and loop back around, grab the horses and try somewhere sheltered, abandoned. If we guess right, we won't have to clear it," Seth's voice was low, offering her an example on where to level hers at.

It was my turn to speak. "Find shelter where? It's a gamble. We're in the middle of a national park."

"There's bound to be a cabin around here somewhere," Reina responded, offering words of optimism.

"No harm in trying," Alexiares shrugged, sweat dripping down the sides of his face. His hair had grown out on the sides, covering the tattoos that decorated the nape of his neck.

"Whatever," I said, sure to bump his shoulder as I walked in the direction he'd pointed to.

We didn't make it far before howls rang out from behind us. They were distant enough to give us time to react, but close enough to understand they'd caught on our trail long before we'd realized they were present.

"You mean to tell me you saw none of the little details?" Alexiares directed at Tomoe.

"Nope," she answered, offering him little more than a haphazard smile.

You cannot run from wolves, not for long anyway. I realized that. But wolves were simply undomesticated dogs. If you give them a better option, they'd happily redirect. The game of switcheroo was simple enough.

"I've got an idea. Follow me," I said, sprinting back the direction we'd just come.

Their howls were on our ass just as Moe had described. The sound of their heavy paws pounding on the ground beneath them, getting closer with each passing second. Nervous laughter escaped my lips as I recalled that the moment you hear a wolf howl, they're a hell of a lot closer than you think.

Reina and I were in agreement, both not wanting to use our magic against the creatures we both loved and respected, not wanting to hurt an animal whose territory we'd pranced into. We tossed out small tokens of our power, enough to cause a yelp and create some distance. Just something to buy us time.

"Keep going, don't stop. Just stay with me," I shouted over the passing wind.

The Pansies were within view now, *if I could see them* ... Heads snapped up, eyes lasering in on us. *Perfect timing.*

I hopped over tree stumps protruding from the ground. They'd turned to run right at us, and I prayed my plan would work, a classic monster versus monster. At the last second, right as I was within grasp, I cut in between a narrow parting between trees. The movement was too quick for their uncoordinated bodies but not my friends.

As The Pansies tripped up at the turn, the wolves intercepted them, a series of yelps and long groans filling the forest air. We left it behind, running as far as we could until the air in our lungs burned from the speed and elevation.

We regrouped in our defensive circle as I checked in, making sure everyone was okay. No one was hurt, but we needed water and a moment to figure out where we were. Reina sat on top of her bag, opening her canteen and chugging it down.

Seth pulled his compass from her pocket, moving towards Alexiares as they debated which way to go. Moe had joined Reina, motioning me to follow. The moment my knees bent, something flew over the top of my head, pulling a few of my curls, stunning me as drops of blood landed in my lap.

"What was that?" Reina asked, peering up from the noise before gaping at the blood gushing from my head.

"What is with these woods? You gotta be shittin' me," Seth groaned, scrambling to pull me to my feet.

Two more arrows whirled past, landing cinematically in the stumps of the trees behind us. I felt dizzy, looking at the blur of the world and seeing the others scan the perimeter, desperately trying to spot the perpetrator.

"We're in Yosemite. Feral people hunted these lands long before the undead. I imagine the situation has only turned more dire now." Alexiares mumbled a cryptic explanation.

The next arrow sent the group diving into two, splitting off into separate directions, a group of wild men coming from the brush. Seth, Tomoe, and Reina one way, Alexiares and I in the other.

Adrenaline took over, my vision becoming crystal clear once more. Alexiares kept my pace, one step behind me as we shouted off warnings of danger. An extra set of steps thudded at my rear, risking a glance behind me as Alexiares growled angry words of encouragement not to look back.

"There's two on us," he signaled for me to make a sharp left.

It would have worked, had they not known the woods better than us. They split off, pushing us towards a downed tree large enough we'd have to take effort to move over.

We'd have to fight our way out.

Weak bursts of flame flew out towards me and I grinned, letting my flames encase my body, showing what I was capable of. Remembering I could start a brush fire, I dimmed them. The distraction giving them the advantage as I felt an arm close in on my throat from behind, cutting off my air supply. Under normal circumstances, I'd have a little under four minutes to fight my way out of this, but the air at this elevation served as a disadvantage. I risked my flames again, desperate only for them to be doused by the water flowing from the arms tightening around my neck.

I felt my eyes go wide, darting around frantically. Alexiares was caught in his own battle, a feral man lunging at him, teeth snapping, somehow more savage than Pansies themselves. He dodged him, emulating the very move I'd used to take him down during our first spar.

Hands tugged at the waist of my pants. Throwing my head back, my skull connected with the jaw behind me. A man's voice rang out in pain, as my head lightened from the effort. The man didn't let go. He sought a tighter grip as the man in front of me drove a fist hard into my torso, limiting my air even more. Forcing my body forward.

I hooked my leg behind his, using all the momentum I could to throw myself forward, wiggling free from the aggressor in front as I reached for the ankle behind me. He let go for a moment. With his balance gone, I was pulled down with him.

His arms re-secured around my neck, the man in front pulled, tugging my legs straight again. His long nails on his rough fingers met the skin under my shirt, scraping the skin as I let out a guttural yell. Blood seeped to the surface from the raw scratches on my stomach down to the lower part of my waistline.

I felt helpless, thrashing like a fish out of water. You can be a great fighter all you want, but the angrier a man gets, the more their adrenaline takes over. Each passing moment is precious, valuable, if you want to get yourself out of the situation. And my window was closing. I had to fight not one man, but two.

I gave up trying to take on both at once, opting another method and putting my energy on one at a time. My hands reached out, grabbing what I could and using my magic to send a twig into the eye of the beast behind me. He didn't give up, but his grip loosened a bit. *Good.* Suddenly, he went limp. My eyes darted to where Alexiares had been fighting, and took in the slumped, unmoving man. His body twisted into an unnatural position.

A wet slush rang through the air. The man behind me gurgled, choking, warm liquid flowing from his mouth and dripping onto the part in my hair, resting on my scalp. He sunk towards the ground as my hands found the soil. Using the momentum, I tossed out a kick, pushing it into the neck of the man in front of me, his windpipe crushed as he gasped for air. In one motion, I moved to straddle him, my own knife moving swiftly across his throat.

"Piece of shit," I spat at him.

Alexiares watched me, wiping off his knife and trying to take in my injuries in the shadows of the dark forest. The small clearing a few feet from our right side being the only grace of light from the moon now high in the sky. I glanced down, taking in the now disconnected fingers from the attacker who'd grabbed me from behind.

"He did not deserve to die with his hands intact. Not for what he had planned."

"I didn't need your help," I grumbled, shaking his hands off that had somehow wrapped around my arms without me noticing. "I had that."

"Didn't look like it from where I was standing. We need to go. Can you run?"

I nodded, though my vision had gone blurry from several head injuries.

"Here, hang on to me," he offered, sticking his arm out.

"I said I've got it."

We kept along the clearing, not daring to pass through it in fear of being spotted. There wasn't a way to retrace our steps and find our way back to the others under the darkness of the forest. Everything looked the same. Alexiares boosted me into a tree, deciding it was our best bet to stay hidden until we could figure out where the others were.

"You're hurt," he said, lifting my chin with a finger, touching the bleeding wound at the top of my head.

I moved my face away. "I'm fine." Shame finding me for not being able to defend myself, then shame for feeling the shame.

"Your idea earlier. Nice job."

"Thanks," I said skeptically, picking at my nails and scanning what I could see, pointlessly searching for signs of my friends. But the forest had gone quiet once more.

"I'm sure your friends are okay."

As the words left his mouth, Seth's voice entered my mind. I listened, not wanting to interrupt and miss important details. I nodded in understanding, Alexiares' attention fixated on me expectantly.

When Seth was done talking, I answered, "They're fine. They're in a tree too. Said to try to meet back at the horses in the morning. Looks like we're up here for the night," my words slurred. I was exhausted, the adrenaline leaving my body and taking a toll.

"I've slept in worse."

I yawned. "Of course you have," tossing my leg over the branch.

I straddled it trying to find my balance. I leaned forward, hesitating at the feeling of metal inside my sports bra. Reaching my hand in, I pulled it out. *A ring? Where'd that come from?*

Right, right, Alexiares ring. *I should give this back to him.*

"I'll keep the first watch," he said, pulling me onto his shoulder.

I tensed before realizing his arm was the only thing securing me to this tree if I were to move into my sleep. The movement caught me off guard, my hands now feeling awkward as I tucked them into my pockets. There wasn't much room where we were sitting and with two of us on it, it could be dangerous.

"Thanks," I whispered. Mind slipping, before losing myself to sleep.

I awoke the next morning to sounds of hyperventilating in the distance. The sky was turning orange; the sun making its first appearance for the day. He'd let me sleep through the night.

Panic rushed through my body. He was no longer next to me. Shifting to take in my surroundings, my gaze fell to a figure beneath the tree. He was pacing; the leaves surrounding the tree disturbed by loose dirt and various sized holes.

He'd moved me to lean up against the tree. With him gone there was a good chance I wouldn't fall. A good chance, but not a one hundred percent one. *I'm gonna kill him.* I angled myself, preparing to climb down and scold him for playing with my life, but changed my mind once my feet hit the soil.

The closer I got, the more disheveled he appeared. His hair was tousled, fingers shaking as he muttered to himself.

"Hey," I said, reaching out to touch his shoulder, and he jumped, eyes bloodshot and red rimmed. "Hey. It's okay. It's me. What's going on? What's wrong?"

"It's ... it's gone. I can't find it. I had it on yesterday while we were running, and now it's gone. Fuck, it's gone." His voice shook.

I reached into my pocket, handing him the ring that must have fallen down my shirt as he'd killed my attacker. Placing it into the palm of his hand, I winced. Pain shot down my side at the movement.

"I'm sorry. It slipped my mind last night. I was exhausted. I think it fell off when you ... ya know."

His face softened, and he chuckled in both disbelief and happiness.

"I'm sorry," I added again, feeling guilty for causing him this much distress.

I'd been there. Understood the draining, numb feeling that consumed you after. His breathing finally slowed, and he looked at me like he'd never seen me before. My head tilted in response, realizing I'd never really looked at him either.

The eyes that usually focused on me hard and cold, also had the ability to be kind, and soft. His hand moved to the crusted blood that pinched the corner of my forehead, my hands moved up in the same motion, wanting to hide the blemish. A battle scar I wasn't proud of, his hand brushing against mine.

"Thanks," he said.

My curiosity piqued. "What are they? Your rings? You play with them when you're nervous, but I've never seen you *not* wear them. Except once, during the elemental part of your assessment."

He studied me for a moment, the internal battle on if he should open up to me again showing on every part of his face.

"Working with my old settlement, there was an incident." His voice was hollow. "I lost control, and it ended badly. Learned the hard way that power is nothing without structure, without self-control. A scientist, or *Tinkerer,* as you all call them, pitied me. Made these siphons to help cut back on some of my power. Make me normal."

A dead laugh escaped his lips. "I told you once, and I'll tell you again. I don't need your pity. I lost myself for a second, thank you. Let's go find our packs."

"I can help you," I offered, stopping him in his tracks. "Learn how to control your magic. I've had ... similar issues in the past. It's hard, takes effort. But I can help. You won't need the rings anymore."

His arms moved and though I could only see his back, I knew the rings were now sliding up and down his fingers. He stopped, hands back down near his side, and started walking again. "I don't need your fucking help."

I followed close behind; the trees looked different at night. It took us a while to find our packs, but there were no signs of the wild men. We checked our belongings, making sure we didn't lose anything.

Hesitantly, I decided to try another approach. "I don't pity you. But I understand, when you cause destruction for something outside of your control, it changes you. I just want you to know that someone else gets it, and ... you're not alone."

I don't know what I expected to see, but it wasn't the hard death glare that I received.

"I know," he said.

As soon as the path cleared to the horses, I spotted them. Happiness taking over, pushing out the thoughts running rampant in my head.

"There they are," I said, my side ringing out in pain, a reminder of the night past, as I jogged towards them, grimacing on impact of our group hug as Seth desperately tried to pull away.

Everyone was okay. Reina was more excited than anything. Claiming she felt like a badass, and detailing their night. Moe and Seth lackadaisically watched on as she chatted away, rolling their eyes in exhaustion.

I'd imagined it'd been a team effort trying to get her to be quiet for the entire night, keeping their position in the trees undetectable. There were three of them, and two men that had followed. They appeared to be oblivious to what the group had been capable of. So I kept it that way. Daring Alexiares to say more as he kept his distance, eyes shooting to the hand that rested at my side causing me to shift under his watchful gaze.

I'd thought mounting would be the most painful, but I'd been wrong as we rode the next three hundred miles, the pain had only gotten worse. Stepping away and using the excuse of going to the bathroom to hide my retching, flinching with every gallop or thud.

The days and nights following Yosemite were uneventful, but we wouldn't be caught off guard again, stopping only when we needed to, minimal rest or breaks. By the time Elko graced our horizon, our appearance suggested we'd been through hell and back, *at least* four times.

Alexiares rode at my side, not having left it much since our talk in the woods. He didn't say much, outside a few grumbles and sarcastic comments under his breath, but he watched me all the same. Most nights I'd fall asleep, recognizing the alertness in his breath as he listened to my own. When I woke up in the mornings, he was up too, volunteering to pack our belongings away and take down the tent when we used it.

I wondered when he slept, how he'd been able to keep going. Wanting to check on him too, but not wanting the fight. This game we were playing was exhausting, and I found myself not having the energy to want to engage. I was fine with having a new team member to rely on, to trust, but that worked best when we kept our thoughts to ourselves.

CHAPTER
THIRTY-THREE

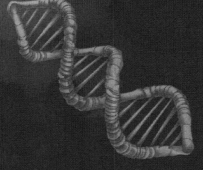

AMAIA

E lko's the kind of town I'd expect Seth to thrive in, even in The Before. The history of the small town was still present in its current purpose. It'd been founded as a stop on the Pony Express, and later became big with mining and ranching. The terrain simultaneously rugged and beautiful, the mountains towering over it as we descended towards their front gate.

Scanning the settlement's defenses from what I could see, I squeezed the reins, fighting with my mind to focus and keep my body atop the horse. They'd made the decision to utilize a natural barrier instead of solid infrastructure. Elko was known to have talented blacksmiths and plenty of horses that earned them a spot within Salem Territory, keeping them protected and a sought-out alliance. Though the blacksmiths were talented in making well-balanced weapons, wielding them and infrastructure was not on their list of talents.

The final ascent to their gate was brutal, my body hunching under the strain, agony pulsing through every nerve. Alexiares reined in his horse, hearing my labored breathing. This trip had allowed me to see landscapes that I'd logged away on some backlist of to-dos that I would never get around to. Now I was just thankful I'd seen so much. Could die knowing I'd lived and seen things I'd thought I'd only read about.

Bile rose in my throat as I bit down into my tongue. At least they had someone to get them there. Alexiares knew the route and could keep them safe. Riley knew the plan. Knew what to do.

"Hands," a guard said, coming from behind the thick, green bristle of the tree line, gun raised and pointed at Seth who'd been leading the way down the narrowing path.

"Kind of hard to do while riding a horse," Seth snickered.

The guard fired off a shot, skimming the top of Seth's hat. "Something tells me you can manage, cowboy."

Seth's body stiffened as I rode to his side, his hat now in his hand as he slowly turned towards me. His pupils were dilated, the stormy blue eyes staring back at me almost black, the wildness in his eyes unnerving.

I cleared my throat, keeping my face neutral, biting back the pain. "Stand down soldier, General Bennett," I introduced myself, "Monterey Compound."

An older woman with frizzy hair and russet skin came out from the right, joining the soldier who'd had his gun trained on Seth. Another man around mid-thirties came from the left. They didn't surprise me. I'd spotted them the moment I realized protocols had in fact, been set in place leading up to the gates. I cursed myself, disappointed in my inability to think clearly.

"Yes, and I'm the Queen of England. Everyone, hands up." Her British accent caught me off guard. Obviously, people had been stranded outside their origin country when things happened, my parents included. That didn't stop it from jarring me every time. A reminder that there might still be a whole world out there trying to rebuild, too. Or ignoring us. Shit, I'd ignore the US too.

I snorted in derision, throwing my hands up my hands in surrender if only to keep Seth under control. The others followed suit, slowly moving their weapons away, their gaze still wary. It'd take me less than a thought to send their bullets through the unintended side of their guns, but I couldn't muster the energy.

"Good. Now, we're not open for visitors. You'll have to turn back around," the man said, finally tearing his glare from Seth and back to me.

"We're not going anywhere," I snarled. "Where's Garcia? Lee?"

Doubt laced his voice. "Still running with the General story, are you?"

"Hardly a story when it's reality," Seth countered.

The man continued in disbelief, "You're—"

"I'm what?" I asked, begging them to be specific.

"A girl. A kid. Not to mention you look like shit. One would think a general could handle herself out there. 'Specially a notorious one." It was the woman this time.

So much for women supporting women.

Moe wasn't having it. "You mean similar to how your troops have been handling things?"

Seth let out a low laugh. All three guns were raised, aiming at her in response. Instead of cowering, Moe smirked, deciding to call their bluff.

"Just show them your papers," Alexiares sighed, tired of the play.

"Planned to," I said, "but I wanted to see how much they'd put their foot in their fucking mouths before doing so."

I grunted, moving to pull the pack strapped behind me and offer up the only piece of paper recognized across the territory. It was signed by all leaders in acknowledgment of my role. It'd taken six months for them to sign it after I was sworn in.

Reina's head snapped in my direction, and I sensed Alexiares creep up to behind me. Her magic trailed over my skin, probing for the cause of my groan. I met her gaze shaking my head. *No.* She obeyed, her magic ebbing away as quickly as it had appeared.

The soldiers leaned in towards the one in the middle holding the paper, perusing its contents. Their faces and necks flushed a deep shade of red, before they abruptly straightened at attention.

"Sorry ma'am," the one to the left said, speaking for the first time, "friends here have been on edge lately, considering the circumstances. We weren't expecting to host you here, hadn't received word. Are more men on the way?" His eyes glanced over my shoulder towards the top of the mountain.

"No. And after that display, you'd be lucky I'd even consider future requests to do so." I wasn't in the mood for niceties. I was tired, my eyes were heavy, wanting to close for a few moments. "My companions and I are stopping through for the night, planned on getting some reports from out this way. I'll be sure to tell Garcia and Lee how their guards treat their superiors. Now open the gates."

Seth threw a mocking salute in their direction, as they pointed us towards the Stables. We'd be able to dismount there, the horses would be taken to the ranch not too far off for some grooming and rest. Keeping your horses outside your community wasn't the smartest planning as far as I was concerned, but what did I know.

Seth, Moe, and Reina dismounted quickly, but I needed a minute to catch my breath. The pain shooting through my side the way my body needed to contort in order to dismount.

"I'm coming. Give me a sec. Just wanna check the saddle," I said, pretending to inspect the perfectly maintained leather.

"You're hurt." Alexiares said, coming up swiftly behind me and latching onto my arm.

I snatched my arm back, not enough power left in me to pull free. "Stop. I told you the other day, I'm fine."

The others turned, wondering what the commotion was.

"Everything okay?" Reina called.

His eyebrow rose as he met my eye. He was going to snitch.

"She's hurt, Reina."

"Am not." I muttered hopelessly.

It was pointless. Once he'd brought it up, Reina wouldn't leave me alone unless I let her check me over. Alexiares elbow flew into my side, and I buckled over.

Reina rushed over. "Maia, why didn't you say anything?"

"You need to conserve your energy, your magic. I was just going to find someone here," I said, giving a weak attempt to push back.

A familiar warmth and tickle ran up the length of my body, pain slipping away as Reina's magic took over. I welcomed it, my body fighting my mind, begging it to let it survive.

"Nonsense, here. You're simply badly bruised. That would explain the wheezing coming from your tent," she glimpsed between Alexiares and me. "I was afraid to ask."

She chuckled, offering me her arm in support as her, and Alexiares guided me towards the gate. I only made it a few steps before darkness took over, and my body gave out.

My eyes shot open and I took in the unfamiliar surroundings, panic creeping in as my flight-or-flight kicked in.

"You're awake," Alexiares' raspy voice came from right out of view.

I jumped, attempting to hop out of the bed on instinct. "What? What's going on? Where am I?" My body flailed.

Where *were my friends? What had happened? How much time did I lose?*

He dropped to his knees at the edge of the bed, gently pressing me into the mattress, only causing me to panic more at the restraint.

"Hey, you're fine," he said, rough hands gripping the sides of cheeks, forcing me to meet his eye, recognize him. "We're in Elko. Look at me. I'm right here." His rough fingers traced the outline of my jaw, stopping on my lower lip.

Tears streamed down my face as I took in the beauty of his face, appreciating it for the first time. The dead eyes I'd been accustomed to looking at, were now soft and filled with worry. I stopped fighting, body now calm as his hands pushed back my loose hair from my eyes. Everything felt gray, the lines of right and wrong blurring as I found comfort under the touch of someone who'd I claimed an enemy only weeks before.

"What happened?" I asked, my breathing returned to normal, exhaustion weighing me down.

"You passed out before we hit the gate. Everyone else is fine. Lay down. I'll go get Reina," he said, getting up and striding towards the door, stopping on his way, eyes trailing over my body, examining me once more. "Glad you're not dead."

Minutes passed. I rolled to my side, registering how I could move without pain for the first time in days. I was in a normal bedroom, likely inside a normal house from The Before. Elko hadn't been damaged the way Monterey had in the aftermath of society crumbling. There'd been no reason for them to start over, only maintain.

"Thank all good and glorious!" Reina's voice echoed around the room, startling me from the power nap I'd taken during the wait. "I was headed to come check on you. You should've been awake hours ago. Was starting to get worried, but Alexi promised to come get me if you started to look worse."

I tried not to be insulted. "Alexi?"

"Yeah, he said that's what people usually call him, but that you're stubborn and told everyone to call him by his government."

My eyes rolled. "How long was I out?"

"One day," she said as if it were no big deal. "You had a crazy infection. Renal contusion."

"English please?"

"Bruised kidney, that turned into an infection since no one knew to watch for further damage," she scolded.

"I'm sorry. I didn't want to scare you." I shifted up in the bed, the desire to lie down and rest gone.

"Scare me? Amaia, I know I joke a lot, but I'm a big girl. More importantly, I care about you. I just want to make sure you're okay girl, I'm literally here to keep you safe. Healthy as a peach. You have to tell me these things, okay? Gotta let me do my job."

Reina's mouth curved into a smile, eyes shimmering earnestly. Her body language indicated she was doing okay. No sign the use of her magic had taken a toll. Her coloring was still good, her pale skin now permanently rosy from the days in the sun. The day of rest had done her well.

I couldn't help but oblige. "Okay."

"Good. Now that that's covered. Let's talk about how Mr. tall, dark and grouchy hasn't left your side," she teased.

My top lip curled at the insinuation. "First of all, ew. Second of all, and you let him stay?"

"You literally share a tent every night, so yeah, I did. Also, let's not play blind. I don't even like men, and I know he's delicious." Her face held nothing but genuine confusion. I couldn't even be mad.

I smacked her arm weakly. "Reina, come on. Seriously though, it's ... it's too soon to move on. Love is the last thing on my mind right now. That's two fiancés. I'm practically twice widowed and I'm not even thirty. And if I *was* ready to try again, the last person would be the man who can't decide if he wants to kill me, or be my friend. Honestly, the feelings mutual."

"Who said anything about love? I just said he's delicious," she teased, eyebrows wiggling as I buried my head into the pillow. "Lust and hate can go very well together. Remember that one girl who—"

"*Anyway,* where's everybody at?"

They'd been given two rooms; I'd been placed in one of their healing homes. A place where the injured could go to recover without taking up space in the hospital. Alexiares had stayed here through the night. Reina had slept in luxury in a king-sized bed, making sure to inform me how comfortable the mattress was compared to what we had back home. Alexiares was now with Seth and Moe in their room, deciding on our next move.

Seth had met with Garcia and Lee last night, briefing Alexiares this morning to help him start thinking about possible routes. For now, Elko's territory was secured, but it'd been a rough couple of months, things could change quickly.

They'd agreed with Alexiares. Best to loop around Salt Lake. There hadn't been any official conflict between them or anyone living in their borders outside their walls, but they'd noticed most of The Pansies had come from over that way. The settlements in Idaho had been facing the same issues from Wyoming as well.

Alexiares and Seth were ready to brief me the second I felt up for it, but Reina insisted I ate first. The sun blinded me, brighter than I'd expected as I raised my fingers to the sky, a quarter to three in the afternoon. It'd truly been almost a full twenty-four since I'd lost consciousness.

She escorted me to a modest house. Seth, Moe, and Alexiares' heads jolted up as I entered the living room before continuing their debate. I settled onto the couch, nibbling on the sandwich Reina had provided, listening to the pros and cons of each path ahead. *Turkey,* Reina had said in warning. It wasn't something I'd choose to consume in my own time, but food was food. That didn't stop every bite from being choked down.

I watched Alexiares in his haughty, infuriating glory. Gone was the gentleman who'd calmed me not even an hour before. I'd become accustomed to Seth's larger size having been around him for so long, but Alexiares took up nearly the same amount of space, without the help of magic. They glowered at each other, protesting each option the other spoke of, frustration simmering off the both of them. The sharp angles of Alexiares cheeks pointed like daggers as his emotions lined his face.

Reina *could* help ease the situation, but that would be a waste of her magic, and it was low-key entertaining to watch their pissing contest. Moe had joined me on the couch, staring off into the distance, here but not here all the same.

An hour later, they'd arrived at a decision. After Montello, we'd cross into Utah and immediately round north. Twin Falls was still too far out the way, but we'd trail along the Idaho/Utah border until around mile eight-hundred, move through the mountains and pass through Lewiston, Utah at a campsite. Laketown would allow us to stop and get in a good protein meal for the night before pushing into Wyoming.

"You good with that?" Alexiares asked, pulling my thoughts back to the present.

What he was genuinely asking, and the question everyone had in their eyes was, *Are you okay to keep going?*

"Yeah, I'm good. Nothing a night's rest can't fix. There's too much light lost for us to make any meaningful ground today. We'll leave at first light." I meant it.

I was extremely fatigued and my body was stiff but I could keep going. Reina had done a good job healing me. Her power still kissed over the surface of my skin, helping with the fatigue and joint pain from laying in the same spot for over twenty hours.

The morning air was brisk, dawn guiding us back out the pathway we'd come. Garcia instructed the soldiers to redirect us to a shortcut through the mountains to cut down on some of the mileage of the day. I felt good as new, stopping to advise Garcia and Lee on improvement points to their structure, to which they happily took to my surprise. The horses seemed well fed and rested as we crested through the mountains, pain in my side no longer.

To Reina's mortification, we spent her twenty-fifth birthday on the run through Montello. We'd made it ten miles from dropping the horses before realizing the random herds we'd seen off in the distance could no longer be considered random if we kept stumbling across them. Ultimately deciding it was best to jog out the final eighteen to a mile marker on Emigrant Trail Road.

A week later, we arrived outside Laketown, exhausted, dehydrated, and covered in filth. If we weren't running from Pansies, we were running from straggling units, patrolling the mountains and wilderness beneath it. Alexiares hadn't exaggerated.

It appeared they'd chosen to use most of their human resources to protect their homes. I wasn't privy to their numbers inside the city, but if it reflected anything like their numbers on patrol, they were a force. Seth had been checking in with Riley every other day and I'd made sure he'd relayed the message to add to our records.

It'd been tough making it to each marker night after night, but we'd made do. We hadn't come across anyone, dead or alive in over a day, deciding to take advantage of the daylight and risk a fire to enjoy any fish we'd caught. I sat around the fire, belly full and thankful for the protein, as Alexiares sat on a stump less than a foot away.

Reina had gone downstream to bathe and Moe and Seth disappeared in the other direction, though they'd all kept short of a shout away.

"Can I ask you something?" I asked. A fleeting moment of boldness taking over.

The tone of my voice caught his attention. His mouth parted, opening for the flaky flesh of the fish, his stare fixated on me as he licked the flavor off his finger before sighing.

"Been waiting for you to say something."

"About Elko?"

He nodded. "Ever since we left, you look like you want to word vomit every time you look at me. You want to know why I stayed with you that night."

"Yes."

"I stay with you every night."

"That's not an answer."

"I don't know," he shrugged, brushing me off.

"That's the thing," I said. "I don't believe you. I think you know exactly why."

"Then why ask if you know I won't tell the truth?"

I pondered his question for a moment. "Because I want to hear you say it. I want to know why you hate me? Why you treated me like some worthless drunk and now you're not only saving my life but waiting at my bedside, promising my family you'll look after me?"

The words bit out. Months of frustration flowing in a series of questions I knew he'd likely not answer.

"You hate me too. Does it really matter?"

Another moment passed as I decided on my next words. "I don't hate you. You're an ass, and you trigger the hell out of me, but you're not a bad person, Alexi."

His brows furrowed in response to my choice of name before breaking my stare, pretending to scan the perimeter for danger. My cheeks flushed, a warm feeling flowing through my body as I worked to push it away.

"I am," he said plainly, insinuating it was fact. "And you shouldn't act like I'm not."

The way he'd said it, a definitive. I waited, letting him decide where the conversation would go.

"I came here to kill you Amaia."

A chill passed over, but I scooted closer. Ignoring the words of warning echoing in my mind. *He wouldn't hurt me.* The trusting innocent girl who'd disappeared the moment the world went to shit, rooted in my head, letting me know it was okay.

"But you didn't," I replied.

"I could. I've got nothing but time left and an open road to do it."

"You could try," I teased him, "but you won't."

He chuckled. "Yeah. Probably not."

"Why?" I asked.

"Odd thing, you know? You don't seem the least bit phased." He tossed back.

The answer was simple enough for me. So much of my world revolved around me single-handedly determining the fate of other people I didn't even know. "Because I probably did something to deserve it."

"You did."

"Yet here we sit."

"Because I don't think you're that person anymore," he said. "Or the person I thought you were, or whatever. You're not who I expected."

"Oh yeah, and what did you expect?" My voice had grown wary, nervous that the next words would send me back down the hole I'd worked to pull myself out of.

He tensed up. "I should find a place to rinse off, too. I'll be back." He wiped his hands along his cargos, standing to walk away.

My fingers curled around his wrist, pulling him down.

"No. Please, stay." I pleaded.

"Or what? You'll pull me back with a ring of fire?"

I blushed at my behavior, guilt creeping forward in acknowledgement of how I'd treated him those first days.

He sat down on my stump, motioning me to scoot over. "You killed my best friend."

A little over two years ago, the country had been at war with itself. Different settlements had stabilized, borders were being drawn, trade networks had begun to establish. History has a sick, fucked up way of repeating itself. And during the most pivotal times, greed destroys all things good.

Settlements around the country protested borders, wanting more people, more land, more control. Choosing to target trade networks they weren't able to successfully reach agreements with. Sure enough, conflict followed, allies were pulled in, and war broke out.

Salem Territory had already established its borders through settlements in our trade network, operating similarly to what had been NATO. The settlements in Idaho had rather neutral relations with its neighbors in Montana and Wyoming, making them allies of our own.

Most of The Expanse had allied with us, out of fear and dealing with the aftermath of the ambitious Covert Province. Monterey had been responsible for leading that fateful battle. Resources limited, some of The Expanse's military had reported under our leadership. Yellowstone had been a mess, the terrain hard to navigate even under the guidance of locals in the area. Pansies, wild animals, human-mage threats, and apparently feral men. It'd been chaos, lines had been blurred in the mix of it. Soldiers were fighting, and no longer understood who was friend or foe. Panic setting in.

Alexiares had stood out within the rankings of his own community's military, his magic plenty, fueled by a never-ending well. They'd used him to their advantage, instructing him to expend all the power he could in order to end the battle, relieve some of the men and help retreat. The details of his role were specific, and he was told to not divert from the plan. He'd let his fire unleash in its entirety through the tree line, what had been determined to be an entry point of battle for our enemy. After his flames had burned out, he'd followed with water to prevent further spread. Flooding the valley and killing over two hundred soldiers. His best friend included.

I'd been there through most of it. The rest of the day had been fed to me a week later, as I'd recovered hundreds of miles away from the scene. A third of the soldiers that'd been lost had been mine, under my control.

"I ... I was dying during that battle." I started, "It is my fault, but not in the way that you think, and you deserve to know the truth."

He shifted, slouching a bit to meet my eye, wanting to catch every word that left my mouth.

"Jax and I had decided to split control of the battlefield. We thought it'd make it easier, more eyes over the entirety of the field. We were supposed to check in, find a moment to debrief and re-evaluate. I never made it to our rendezvous." My body shuddered, not remembering the moments myself, but from the distraught recount Jax had given me over my death bed. "He was worried, waited, returned to his part of the field and came back half an hour later. I still hadn't arrived, and he didn't see my magic flaring up in the area ... he panicked. Left his post to search for me. I'd been stabbed through and through."

I motioned towards the space between my torso and pelvic bone. "I was bleeding out, almost gone. By the time he found Re-ina, I didn't have a heartbeat. So it *is* my fault you see. If he hadn't left his post to save me, our soldiers would've had someone to an-swer to instead of having to decide things for themselves. They'd changed course, that's what brought them into your path. Bringing any soldiers they could identify as being on our side with them. We lost sixty-two soldiers that day. I knew each of them by name. Compound was only half the size it was now. I knew everyone."

He sighed, taking it all in. Silence consuming the passing minutes as I waited for him to speak.

"I think I couldn't kill you, because deep down, I knew if you'd truly been responsible, it would've eaten you alive. There wouldn't have been a general for me to come for. A compound to take down. That was my plan, you know? Take down The Compound, make it crumble around you, take everything from you that you took from me, then kill you." A stark laugh escaped his lips. "Funny thing is, I'm actually the villain I accused you of being."

"I don't see that as being true," I offered.

"After that battle, the Tinkerer I told you about. The one that took pity on me? She's my wife." He paused, gauging my reaction before continuing, "Her father is in charge, like Prescott. Their military works different up there, government and military all in one. Took me under their wing. Magic like that, like what I have, what you have. It's dangerous. Gets people killed, a weapon of mass destruction. But you can't have a weapon of that extent that you can't control. She chose to encourage her father to take advantage of my pain, the loss of my friend, Tiago. He'd been the reason I'd ended up there to begin with. We'd come from Chicago with each other. My brother too."

His rings had been given to him on the condition that he continue to work for them, but in a more specialized capacity. They'd used him to spy, dispatching him to other settlements within their territory, using him to gather intelligence and find information they could use against others. Encouraging him to take out anyone they deemed a problem, or when the fuss they made about living conditions posed a threat to the unity of their home.

He'd been miserable, felt as if he'd become the father he'd sworn to be nothing like, and launched into self-destruct mode.

Each mission taking longer than the last, unable to leave whatever room he'd been staying in, fighting with himself to not move forward, to stay in bed. The guilt that had consumed him, a feeling I knew too well.

The last straw was the moment he'd come home early, unable to do what needed to be done, wanting to seek comfort and advice from his wife. She'd been the last thing he'd had left to hang on to, had started to despise her for it, but had hoped she'd be willing to leave. Start over and see what life had to offer them away from the place he'd grown to hate. Her hands and mouth had been full when he'd walked in, occupied beneath one of his fellow soldiers.

They'd argued. She'd told him he should be thankful she'd even been able to stand his presence after the monster he'd become. No matter the fact that she'd made him that way. He'd lost control, his fire taking out their corner of the city. There'd been no deaths, but the damage was extensive. Immediately, he'd gone to speak with her father. Begging him to release him from his duties, hoping he'd show him a rare moment of mercy and reflect on the man he'd chosen to work under before his daughter's vision of the world had taken its grip. He'd understood the tiresome feeling that came with dealing with his daughter. Realized Alexiares could serve him no good without a desire to live, and had told him to go, and go fast. Wishing him a better future.

In the days that followed, he'd become even more disgusted with himself. Realizing he'd let not one, but two people turn him into the person he'd worked his entire life to not become.

"And who is that?" I asked delicately.

"Do you know who Alexander Drakos is?"

My breath caught in shock. There *had* been a reason his face had been so familiar, just hadn't been able to place him with the years between the now and the last time he'd been in the media.

His father, Alexander Drakos, had been known as a ruthless businessman. His name constantly swarmed the media for alleged drug and gang ties. A different, new accusation every day. Dozens of people had gone missing in connection to him, but the police had never been able to find solid evidence to put him away. He had two sons, Alexiares and Evander.

Not much was known about Evander since he was a minor, but Alexiares ... TMZ had a field day with him. Captured falling out of bars in a drunken, drugged up state. Fighting inside clubs, sporting black eyes and busted lips as accessories. The last piece of media I'd seen was about him and his father. Alexander Drakos had been caught on camera, beating him. Brutally.

A drone hovered over their backyard capturing it all. He'd stepped in between his father's fist and his mother's frail body. His brother pushed to the ground as his father walked away, leaving Alexiares blood splattered across the pavement, crawling to cover their bodies with his own should his father come back for more.

My fingernails dug into the skin of my palms. I'd seen the video and gone about my day. Not thinking twice of it. One of the many videos that would circle around social media for a day or two, only to be followed by something worse, taking the attention and making people move on.

"He forgot his wounds, his hunger and thirst, and became fear; hopeless fear," I muttered under my breath.

His body stiffened at that. "Lord of the Flies."

"I see you have good taste," I said, taken aback by his ability to place the quote. "You became what you feared because you had to. But that doesn't mean you're out of time to change. We don't have to remain the person that was molded by others forever. This fucked up world is a breeding ground for the loss of innocence, of all things good. Has been for a while now, even before this. The only thing that will make it better Alexiares is if people like us, fight for the good ones to survive. There's still good that can come from our souls, even when we feel they've been damned to hell."

My fingers grazed over the tattoo on his knuckles, closing around them hesitantly, then releasing at the uncertainty. His hand locked around my own.

"I'm damaged, Amaia." Pain brimmed the lines of his eyes. "There is no saving someone like me. No turning this around. After I destroyed The Compound, that was gonna be it for me. The last thing I did. But then there were children, laughing and playing. *Being kids*. The Kitchens, the normalcy of it all, the people there aren't savages. Some type of moral code exists in Monterey that doesn't exist anywhere I've been the last few years. And it reminded me of why Tiago had asked me to stay with him at St. Cloud. He'd felt that at the beginning, before my wife had gained a seat at the table, made her father ruthless. But your attitude, man ..."

I shoved him playfully. "What about it?"

"It's a fucking nightmare to deal with." There was no harshness in his words. "But I decided that it might be worth sticking out. Seeing if what I saw around The Compound was bullshit or not, and if it wasn't ... maybe a fresh start wouldn't be the worst thing in the world."

"You're not the easiest person in the world to deal with either," I chided.

"Yeah well," he huffed, "I felt guilty. Like I was betraying Tiago by trying to start over, find happiness in the place responsible for his death. But one night I went for a stroll, couldn't sleep. I thought I was hallucinating when I saw him. They look so alike. Identical doesn't even cover it."

My memory brought the night he was speaking forefront. I'd watched the interaction unfold and had been suspicious of it, accused him of lurking around in the fashion of a shady drug dealer. I feigned innocence, tilting my head letting him finish his story.

"I knew you saw me. Just wanted to hear you say so yourself that day."

I gaped at him. "How——"

"How would Riley know?" he angled his head to meet my eye, and I nodded, *fair point*. "I remembered he'd spoken of a twin, never was able to get in touch with him that day the cell towers had come back up. Had assumed the worst since he'd been in LA when the bombs hit. It was too much of a coincidence, so I approached him, asked if he had a brother named Tiago. Monterey ain't exactly close, but it's not too far to be out of the question. He'd been out on a hiking trip in the Redwoods with some friends, and made their way down here after the war, rumor spreading about Monterey being stable. Took the news about Tiago as any brother would, had been hoping for the best, but deep down had felt the tether had been cut long ago. Tiago, had a little girl, made him a bracelet before she turned a few months in. I've carried it with me ever since he died, but felt right giving it to his brother. Could tell he needed it. The same way he knew to tell me that Tiago had sent me as a sign, a way to always keep each other close. He didn't have much friends in life before all this, and I'd been his only friend after. Call it fate or a higher power, whatever. I just know he sent me here, for redemption or to keep his brother safe. I don't know and I don't care. I just know I'm here to make him proud. And killing you would hardly make the list."

I rubbed my face, not caring about the dirt and grease that smeared as I took it all in. "That's why you volunteered to come."

"Partially, yes. I needed some sort of control in the situation, plus I really do know the land." He gestured towards the lake and trees surrounding us. "And you."

My heart stopped at the words. The silly, school girl flutters faltered as he added in, "Couldn't trust someone in ... your condition to wander out here with cowboy wonder, kill bill, and a girl who packs lingerie to sleep in on a two-thousand-mile journey and expect you to make it there alive."

"Ha, couldn't have that, could we?"

His eyes lowered, landing on my mouth before hovering over the rest of my body. My breath caught. I crossed my arms over my chest, feeling self-conscious in my filth under the weight of his stare.

"I'm glad he saved you," he whispered.

His face was now less than an inch from mine. I lowered my head. Guilt consuming me at the mention of Jax.

Gravel crunched under a pair of boots, stopping just out of my peripheral, we jumped back, turning to the source.

"Uhhh … what's going on?" Reina said, hair wrapped atop her head in a dirty towel she'd gotten from who knows where.

CHAPTER
THIRTY-FOUR

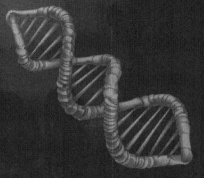

AMAIA

It took sixteen days to cross through Wyoming. The landscape of Kemmerer changed dramatically by the time we arrived outside Moorcroft. What had started as gentle slopes gave way to steep and jagged mountain peaks, rising into the sky like jagged teeth. Reina had taken up the habit of healing us each night, the painful shin splints becoming unbearable around a thousand miles into the journey. The first six hundred on horseback were a breeze compared to the last five-hundred we'd covered on foot, with still nearly a thousand to go.

The air grew colder, and the sky darker earlier as we continued. Trudging through icy streams as the wind howled through the valleys and gorges, forcing us to huddle together for warmth, taking turns sleeping in the only tent made for three. We'd made four work, with one person claiming watch throughout the night. Everyone needed the rest for the miles we'd face the next day, night watch was done in two even shifts.

Between the crowded tent at night, and the exhaustion of constantly moving, dodging, and running throughout the day, we'd never spoken of what Reina had walked in on. It felt like a fever dream, and I'd started to believe it'd never truly happened with Reina never bringing it back up. After a few moments of awkward silence, she'd simply come to take a seat next to us at the fire, picking at her fish and engaging in polite conversation. Which had only made things more awkward. There was only so much polite conversation you could have with someone after being around them 24/7 for twenty-three days straight.

Alexiares volunteered to take first watch most nights, and the nights he didn't Seth or I did, quickly falling into a natural schedule. As we pushed further into Wyoming, Seth and Reina had reminded us to keep our food away from camp at night when we'd slept. With only one person on watch, it wasn't worth the risk of facing a bear. Seth had no elemental powers. Alexiares may burn or drown us in an attempt to turn the bear away. Moe's katana would barely leave a paper cut, Reina's arrow would do no good up close, and a gunshot would only draw attention direction.

The reminder had likely saved us a lot of trouble. A little over a month from the day we'd departed Monterey, a bear had ravaged through our food packs in the middle of the night. We'd placed them about four hundred feet away, and Moe had prayed for her life, holding her breath and hoping that whatever she'd heard rumbling in the darkness of the night wouldn't come sniffing our way. It'd taken the last of our food. We were left with only the few pieces of nuts and dried fruits we'd each kept stored for emergencies in the packs we'd slept with at our sides. A local airport had been a lucky next stop, we'd found a few expired canned goods, two twinkies, and a pack of ramen. We couldn't complain, it was better than nothing.

Things only became more difficult from there. We were hungry, cold, and tired. With little food, and the frigid air, anything that was available to hunt was too quick for even Seth to catch. We didn't have the time to set up traps and wait it out. We tracked what we could, but couldn't drift too far off our route. By the time we reached plains as far as the eye could see, it'd been decided that scavenging through small towns and homes we'd come across would be our smartest move. It would make for more dangerous travel, but we wouldn't do much traveling if we were dead.

South Dakota tested the sanctity of our group. Hunger had taken its toll on us all. God forbid someone breathed too hard while walking, World War IV risked breaking out. The temperature had dropped below freezing. My fire magic warmed the blood in my veins, but my friends didn't have the same luxury. Reina and Seth had grown up in worse, and could tolerate it to a certain extent, but Moe shivered, teeth clattering most waking hours, and those while she slept.

I wondered if Alexiares had enough control over his fire to warm himself too, though I doubted he did. It didn't feel right asking, or even teasing him about it at this point. We'd moved from hating each other, to feeling responsible for the safety of the other, to now avoiding one-on-one interactions. He'd become distant, rigid and closed off again. His behavior of a soldier fulfilling his duty and no longer a friend. If what we'd had for that short time could be called that.

Around day forty-six, I asked myself when his friendship had started to matter, noticing the absence of his body from my side. When we'd shifted to squeezing into a singular tent, he'd made a point to sleep at the furthest point from me in the nights our sleeping hours aligned. Even if we were hunkered in an abandoned home, grateful for any mattresses that were usable and able to be dragged to a central room, he never ended up next to mine. We spoke only out of necessity and he was careful not to meet my eye.

Under normal circumstances, it'd be an awkward situation for anyone present, but our group was in shambles. Moe and Seth had been bickering back and forth parodying a married couple, trivial quirks, setting one another off. Him walking too fast; her walking too slow, the way she held her katana, him moving too much in his sleep.

She'd claimed he'd shut her out, no longer confided in her or sought out comfort. That fight had been one for the ages. Seth had berated her for being worried about such a 'ridiculous' thing considering what was at stake. She'd doubled down and said her feelings were valid. She'd be damned to spend her last days tied down to a selfish idiot. Reina, Alexiares, and I were subject to hearing it all.

Reina had been acting weird too, a little more than two weeks shy of reaching Duluth she'd gone quiet. Originally, I'd assumed it was a mix of the intensity of the travel and the constant use of her magic finally taking its toll and her wearing down. But the first snow of the season had forced us to find somewhere to wait it out for a few days, allowing her to recover and rest. We'd even been lucky to find some food, yet still she was lost to herself. Secluding into the other room, lost in her gaze out the window, watching the snowfall.

The snow had disoriented Alexiares, setting us back half a day before anyone had noticed the Missouri River off in the distance. That'd been the straw that broke the camel's back. Seth had been livid, a list of insults rolling off his tongue. They'd circled each other. Fists raised, breath visible in the cold air, quick and fast, making each breath a dancing ring of smoke and ice. A few seconds passed, and neither had moved, their frustration and anger simmering just below the surface, the cold and fury coloring the little exposed skin on their faces red.

Suddenly, they both lunged forward, colliding in a flurry of fists and kicks. The sound of their bodies meeting thunderous as they fought with fierce intensity. They looked like idiots. Jack rabbits squabbling in ill-fitted layers, Seth's fur pelt latched over his neck as his hat fell into the snow. Part of me wanted to let them fight, see who'd come out on top, too tired to break it up, but the General in me said enough was enough.

I drew my knife, flipping it in my fingers and swiftly moving to knock them both on the head with the pommel of the knife. It'd take too much effort to talk them down, and I found myself wanting to go with whatever the easiest option was.

Team morale was non-existent in the week that followed. Artichoke had been a blessing, the lake there not yet frozen, the carp and minnows plenty. We'd feasted that night, a few fish each until our bellies were full and spirits were lifted. Alexiares and Seth had taken off to clear the perimeter as Reina and Moe helped me curate jerky to carry wish us. It wasn't enough to get us to Duluth. But it would buy us some time, give us some energy, allowing the others to find bigger game to sustain their bellies while the rest of the portions could transfer to me.

We found ourselves delayed another two days for snow as we passed through Clontarf. The small historic town was occupied, but not enclosed. It was interesting, seeing the smoke rise through the chimneys of the Victorian style homes without a care in the world. They either lacked common sense and welcomed death, or had other security measures in place that kept them from worrying about intruders or the dead entering their homes.

Their carefree approach made it simple for us to figure out which homes weren't occupied. The snow made the options slim. We didn't need any questions on the cluster of footprints going from home to home, deciding on a charming one near the corner of town. We weren't lucky enough to find it stocked in any capacity. The home was bare and dust coated the wood floors.

At least we were warm, I'd thought on the second morning. My small fire brimmed in the fireplace a few feet away. My body stiffened at the weight on the other end of the mattress, shocked to find Alexiares lying there beside me. He'd likely settled in after his shift, sure to move slow and quiet.

A small tingle of fear crept from behind my ear at the thought of him being capable of moving that close to me without me knowing. This wasn't the tree, or Elko. I wasn't injured. I'd had a full night's rest in a warm house, with a decent amount of food. There was no excuse to not have my wits about me, no excuse except the false sense of safety in the presence of others. And him.

ALBANY WAS LESS THAN IMPRESSIVE, BUT THE DEER SCAT AND SIGNS IN the area had Reina feeling confident she could have us ending the day with dinner. Seth trusted his sister's abilities, opting to search for dry firewood, but we all knew it'd been a ploy to get away from Moe. No one had heard what'd happened, but the silence between them was loud enough. They hadn't spoken since we'd left Clontarf three days ago.

Moe, in turn had insisted on accompanying Reina on her hunt, claiming the feeling of being an apex predator gave her joy while glaring at Seth's back as he'd wandered into the tree line. That'd left Alexiares with me on weapon duty. He'd been less grouchy the last few days, but we still hadn't said more than a few words to each other, and I didn't plan on starting now.

The rhythmic clanking of metal scraping against a sharpening stone filled the air as Alexiares sharpened the knives from each of our packs. The effort had become a routine each night, making sure they were sharp and ready to use the following day. Flesh and bone dulled knives faster than Hollywood would let one think, especially when it was rotted.

I watched him as I blew down the disassembled gun before clicking the pieces back into place. The chiseled contour of his jawline and sharp angles of his face focused and fixated into a scowl. A deep exhale left my chest. Even after all this time, there was something satisfying about cleaning your weapon, knowing it'd be there for you, a working vessel when you needed it.

When I was finished, I returned my gun into my holster, moving to grab Reina's next. The bag scraped against the side of his thigh as I brushed by unfocused, not realizing how close I had passed.

A chuckle escaped his mouth, almost as if the sound itself wasn't quite sure it knew what it wanted to do. Starting out rough and giving way to a strained, uneven rhythm. His mouth twisted into an awkward smile, eyes darting nervously to the ground.

"What's so funny?" I asked, turning back around to face him.

"We just gonna keep on pretending like that day never happened?"

"You mean when you almost kissed me?" I threw back.

He ran his fingers through his wild, overgrown dark hair, eyes meeting mine in challenge. "Correct, also known as the day you almost let me."

Two figures came shooting out the woods at the same moment Seth came up from behind Alexiares. My mind pulled, not knowing where to focus before settling on Tomoe and Reina. Knees to their chest, their weapons flailing loosely at their sides as their arms pumped, pushing them forward.

Seth sprinted towards Moe's side, wood hitting the ground with a solid thud as he let go.

"What did you do?" he demanded.

"Nothing!" Reina chimed in out of breath, while checking over her shoulders on either side.

A howl rang out in the distance, then another, followed by two more. *Hounds, not wolves,* I determined, as if either option meant

I'd walk away from this. We'd faced wolves already, and I wasn't ready to go toe to toe with them again. But hounds had owners, and people were far worse than whatever we'd faced this far out in the wild.

"Okay, we may have committed just a tiny act of war," Reina admitted, drawing our attention away from the trees and back at dumb and dumber standing before us.

My eyes shot to Tomoe who was a bit *too* quiet. I took in the blood on her shirt, reaching to grab her hands, raising them to show Alexiares and Seth. "Is that blood?" I asked.

She looked at me, cheeks red from the sprint here and a bit of guilt, as she meekly smiled. "Don't worry it's not mine."

"That's supposed to reassure me?" I exclaimed as I turned to grab our belongings and go.

"I thought they were Pansies!" Reina said defensively. "I was closing in on a deer and he got in my way."

Moe wiped the blood off Wrath, sheathing her. "And after the first arrow, we couldn't let them squeal. It's fine. Think they were alone," she justified.

The handprints around her throat indicated there'd been more of a fight than they'd let on. *What the fuck were they doing out there?*

"The *one* time you two go off alone, this is what you do?" I scolded, tossing Reina her pack, trying to speed up our departure.

Alexiares let out a deep groan. "Do you know where we are?" he asked, as if it were basic knowledge.

Before the words had cleared his pink lips, a group of hounds dashed into the clearing and seven soldiers in their wake, guns drawn. They were in terrible condition. If it were different circumstances, I'd be congratulating my friends for putting up a good fight. A few of them had obviously been involved in the altercation, their eyes and frame of their noses purple and badly bruised. Their black uniforms shredded through.

I lifted my hands into the air and glared at my friends. "No Tomoe, I'd say they were *not* alone."

"Let me handle this," Alexiares muttered under his breath, taking a step forward and placing his body between the armed men and our group. "My name is Alexiares Drakos, and it's in your best interest to take me *directly*, to Caelon Thomas."

A soldier with fiery hair snarled at him. "We know who you are, *traitor*. Thought we wouldn't switch up our patrols with your running free in the wild?"

"And Cael Thomas isn't here to save your ass this time," another rasped. The tight coils of his hair peering from beneath his hood.

"And why is that?" Alexiares challenged, rings sliding down his fingers one by one, as he worked each hand at a time behind his back.

"Slide another one down and I'll blow her fucking head off." The voice making me jump. I'd assumed it'd been Moe or Reina coming up behind me. A gun stabbed into the crown of my head as four more men came out the brush, flanking our sides.

The man pressed the gun against my skull for emphasis. "Cause he's dead."

"Died not too long after you left actually," the one with curly hair teased.

"Got real sick, real fast they say," another chimed in. The group clearly enjoying the game of telephone they were playing.

He closed his eyes, his chest rising as he took a deep breath. "Who's in charge."

Not a question, no. He knew the answer, just needed it confirmed.

"Finley. Your wife." The soldiers chuckled, but made no further movement.

My bones stiffened and my blood went cold. She was here, had to be. They were stalling, waiting for their true leader to arrive.

"Really, like what she's done with the place if I'm being honest," the one with fiery hair said, tossing his head in signal for the group to move in.

The guard behind me slapped a metal cuff around my wrist, pulling it down and behind my back. Commotion rang out behind me as Seth tossed his head, head-butting the man who'd attempted to cuff him as Moe brought her boot down onto his skull. A shot rang out and Seth went down, grasping at his knee as blood poured out the wound.

My ears rang from the shot, hearing nothing but muffles as time slowed down. Reina's face came into frame. She used all her strength to drag the smaller woman soldier who'd managed to cuff her, tears cascading down fueled by the water magic that lay beneath her skin. Kicking and screaming, trying to get to Seth and Moe who had now locked her legs around the soldier who'd stood over Seth, attempting to get the cuffs around his hands as he grasped his knee in shock.

It was chaos. Alexiares stood to my left, trying to reason with the soldier who still had a gun trained on the back of my head. A plea telling them he knew how to get us to stop, to call his men off. I slapped his gun away, lunging for my friends, wanting to put my body between them and the wicked men digging into them.

The soldier ignored him.

My knees gave out from under me, and I was down too. Blood gushing from the wound in my thigh, an attempt to get Moe and Reina to calm down. It hadn't worked, only fueled Moe more, put her in survivor mode as Reina kicked her feet out towards anyone who came close. Alexiares pressed his hand onto my thigh, trying to stop the blood, shooting out bursts of flame at anyone who attempted to pull him away.

His rings were gone, yet he remained in control.

I felt his body tense. The pressure remained on my wounds, but he'd frozen in time, eyes wide. I turned my head, wanting to see what had spooked him as a strikingly beautiful woman strode from the tree line. Her face defined by sharp cheekbones and a prominent nose, her eyebrows dark and thick in contrast to her wavy light hair.

Her blue eyes settled on Alexiares, then down at me. The woman from Moe's vision, just as she had described her.

"Finley," I whispered weakly to Alexiares, seeking confirmation.

It was her that answered, "In the flesh."

She grinned as she tossed a metal ball towards us, green fumes leaking from the sides. A pungent, sweet scent filled the air, and the world faded to black once more.

CHAPTER
THIRTY-FIVE

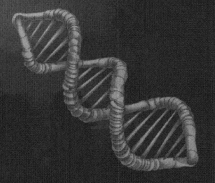

AMAIA

My eyes opened, my head heavy though my cheek rested on a cold hard floor, hands still pressed behind my back. Rays of sunlight filtered, illuminating a moldy cinder block room. I kept my breathing still, my stomach pressed into the floor. There were other quick, rushed breaths behind me. I wasn't alone.

"You're awake," a haughty voice said, dripping with malice.

I used my cheek as leverage to push my body up, a wail escaping my lips as my leg throbbed, a reminder of my last few moments conscious. Adrenaline pumped through me, my feet locking onto the floor and pushing me forward. A chain yanked me back before I could rise, my tailbone singing in pain, my hands unable to break my fall.

My body shivered, the air in the basement biting into my skin, the chains keeping my fire from warming my skin. They'd stripped me to my last layer, all of my weapons removed. Moe lay immediately on my right, the red mark around her neck now bluish-black. She was awake. Her eyes are puffy, shoulders slumped in defeat. Seth and Reina lay further down, still unconscious, but shifty. *Alive,* I thought, *but where is Alexiares?*

"No independent settlement nor representative of another party should engage in any form of espionage or trespassing on another party's territory"—Finley crossed into view, a piece of paper in her hands—"including, but not limited to; its independent borders, waterways, and any facilities within. If one party suspects another party has engaged in such activities, the matter should be brought to the attention of the other party through diplomatic channels and provide evidence to support its claims. The offending party should be held responsible if it's found that they've engaged in said activities. Any disputes arising from alleged violations of said rule should be resolved through means of negotiating, mediation, or execution."

A rifle bounced against the back of her long coat as she finished summarizing the most important law in the treaty. Her arms fell to her hips in disappointment as she looked up at me. "You signed that treaty, were there actually. That's your signature, isn't it?"

She shoved the paper in my face, too close for anyone to read properly, my head turning defensively. Alexiares sat in a chair near the door, his eyes meeting mine, staring ahead as if he didn't recognize me. He leaned forward, hands resting on his knees as he watched.

Unchained.

"I see you've done your research," I said, nodding towards the piece of shit in the corner. A knife similar to Alexiares' now in her hand as she strode over.

"Ooh, honey. I know all about you, *General Bennett*. Had three days to catch up on what I'd missed, too." Her knife pushed into the soft skin in the center of my neck. "He despises you, you know? Dreamed about slitting your throat. Even made jokes of burning you to ashes, giving you the ending that you deserve."

The pommel of her knife connected with my jaw, sending me on my back. Her long legs wrapped on either side of my shoulders, the weight of her body pressing into my chest.

"I know all about San Jose, Redding, *Monterey*."—her top lip curled in disgust—"The entire fucking Salem Territory. You people are delusional, living like nothing happened. Behind your walls and rules, pretending that the last five years never happened. It's pathetic."

I spat, blood hitting her in the face as Finley laughed, wiped my spit off her face, and licked it as she turned to Alexiares, weight shifting over my right rib.

"What's that stupid fucking quote you used to say?"

He smirked, eyes piercing at me as he recalled, "Which is better, to have laws and agree, or to hunt and kill?"

Lord of the Flies.

"Ah, yes. That's right." Finley said, thick brows raised, lip curled downwards, mocking me, as she pulled me back up off the ground, "I choose hunt and kill."

Her free fist balled and swung into my face with force, the impact landing with a thud, and my head snapped back, blood spraying from my mouth. A smile pulled over her thin lips, eyes filled with joy as I coughed, choking on my own blood.

"Lucky for you, Alexi drives a hard bargain." Disappointment clawed at my insides and my expression fell, a different pain setting in. Finley burst out laughing. "Oh. You stupid little girl. You *actually* thought he cared about you? I remember being just like you. Stunned, wondering what went wrong. Why he'd betray my trust after everything we'd been through."

With her back turned to me, she sauntered over to Alexiares, her slender legs carrying her with a purpose. I pushed back upright with my feet, not liking the vulnerability of laying on my back as she climbed onto his lap, straddling him and taking hold of his face.

She kissed him with an intensity that left no room for resistance on his part. He surrendered to her advances, his hands firmly grasping her hips as he drew her in closer. As our eyes met, he opened his mouth, allowing his tongue to entwine with hers as he groaned in pleasure.

Despite the rush of blood to my cheeks, I refused to look away. Determined to not allow her to use him as a tool to unnerve me. As she leaned back from their kiss, she tapped him on the face with an air of dominance, as if he were nothing more than a loyal canine. Without breaking contact, she turned around, still seated on him, and gazed back at me with a smug grin that betrayed her true intentions.

She was insecure.

"It hurts, I know," she said, "Turns out it wasn't a me thing, and more of a him thing. My poor husband was dealing with so much and I missed the signs. Made it about myself. Guess we'll have to work through that in therapy."

Reina yelped from the other side of the room, coming to and startled. From the corner of my eye, I noticed Seth awake too, shuffling on the ground towards her. Moe, no longer shell-shocked, scooted forward to cut off the view from the brother headed to his sister's aid.

"Something tells me even therapy can't save this," I taunted, trying to keep the attention on me and off my friends.

It worked.

Finley jumped to her feet, knife back at my throat in an instant. "Shut your mouth, *whore*. I should kill you right now for even thinking about putting your dirty little lips on him."

"Finny." Alexiares' voice was rough as he called her off. "Get to the point."

Her eyes rolled, annoyed with his pestering. "See, Alexi just needed some time to himself. Grieving can be a ... delicate thing. So he went off to do the one thing that would help him sleep at night. *Kill you.* Instead, he found a sorry, drunk, despicably weak shell of a general and realized there wasn't much left to destroy. I mean, where's the fun in that? Can't take everything from someone who can't even care about themselves. His words, not mine."

She looked me up and down, scoffing as she continued, "Once it was clear someone else was as passionate about your death as he was, the long game made more sense. Though I gotta say, Duluth was never in my playing cards. An opportunity presented itself. You see, our people here are struggling. Winter can be a bit tough on food supply when you don't have enough air magic to warm the livestock *and* keep the greenhouses happy. Even worse without the connections."

"I can't fathom why that would be," I mumbled.

She ignored me. "A favor from Duluth could go far. The resources they have could make my job here a lot easier. Turning you in could solve half of my life's problems right now. But then I got to thinking, why stop there Finny? I mean, the world is your oyster. Why not think bigger? We *could* help another settlement, form connections, gain access to more resources, use it to our advantage. A trade for a trade. Or we could help ourselves."

Her steps were slow, methodical as she moved down the line. Sizing up each of my friends before stopping in front of Reina.

"It's a freaking one-stop-shop, you know? The cream of the crop right here at my fingertips. He didn't even have to tell me about this one,"—she kicked Reina in the ribs, eliciting a pained groan—"the bitch started to heal herself the moment we switched the cuffs out. Wasn't even conscious."

I bit back a scream. She was baiting me.

Seth glared at her, growls emitting from the base of his throat. Her body now towered above his. "Don't know what this can do, but his stature and attire tell me enough to know he'd be handy in more than one place." She grabbed his cheeks, winking at him, positioning herself for him to headbutt her in the gut, her knee driving into his nose on instinct.

I yanked at my chains, dust crumbling from the walls under my strength. "I'll fucking kill you." My voice was unrecognizable, even to myself, the threat coming out animalistic. A promise.

It was as if she hadn't heard me at all, stopping in front of Moe who sat there, unmoving and giving her a death glare. I could see each slice my friend was envisioning upon Finley's body as she crouched down to be face level. "Your sword is very pretty. But something tells me what happens up here is more valuable."

Her fingers tapped the side of Moe's head, who snapped her teeth at her in response.

I glared at Alexiares, his smug expression infuriating me more. *How could he work with someone, love someone so cruel?* The words spilled out of my mouth, hot and bitter like bile rising from my gut.

"I'll die before I ever subject my family to working with you." The weight of my words hung heavy in the air as his expression turned pleading. It vanished from his face quickly, making me question if I'd had too many hits to the head.

"Thought you might say that," she said, tsking at him in sign to get up.

He was clean, skin clear as if days' worth of dirt and blood hadn't been caked there in the moments before things had changed. I blinked. He was in uniform now. Black cargos tucked neatly into matching black boots. His black shirt nestled inside the waist of his pants, covered by a matching black cargo jacket with various symbols on the lapel. *St. Cloud* was etched into the pocket above his chest. The dog tags sat tilted against his chest. My eyes narrowed. A bullet-proof vest lay beneath his shirt. A soldier.

A knife shimmered in his hand, fire gleaming in the other. His rings were off. His jaw tensed as he dropped to his knees in front of me, eyes searching mine, sweat collecting around the tip of his nose.

With a guttural cry, Seth gritted his teeth, struggling to get to his feet. His wounded knee buckled under pressure. He refused to back down, the furious determination and tugging sent chunks of the wall crumbling under the sheer force of his strength.

His magic had been cut off, but his size and human strength remained. With a primal roar, the chain bounding his left arm sprang free, hurtling through the air and straight towards Finley's face. His movements were sluggish, body not used to moving after being down here for days. She dodged his attack, ordering Alexiares to start with him instead. Alexiares throat cleared. Four steps were all it took for him to drop in front of Seth, weight grounding onto the loose chain and burn him.

A low whimper rang out, as the smell of burning flesh filled my nostrils, but was quickly stifled as he bit back his lip.

I thrashed against my chains in protest. "No! Stop, please."

My cries were desperate as Finley leaned against the wall, smiling, only turning her head back to Alexiares, encouraging him to continue. Reina sobbed, her cries of agony as if she felt what her brother did. Moe had retreated back into stunned silence, watching Finley and not Alexiares.

Marking her.

Alexiares flames lit the room again, this time a cry in agony escaped Seth's mouth, the knife sliding down to his uninjured leg. A red tinged drop of sweat raced down his face, his dark red hair wild as he jerked back at the pain.

Alexiares' knife plunged deep. "Know what that is, Seth?" he asked. "That's your sciatic nerve. You feel that? That pinch going up your spine? One quick movement and—" Seth crumbled as the blade pulled away at his flesh, the pain so intense, no sound came out. His body going into shock. Alexiares wiped the knife on his pants, a thin sliver of Seth's skin discarded as if it were nothing.

He lit the tips of his fingers once more, body shaking, trying to constrain his power, but Finley grabbed his wrist, whispering something into his ear before kissing the top of his head and calling him off.

Alexiares' face was emotionless, eyes trained on the ground as he stood, moving back towards the door, back to us, and body tense.

"Hmm, you were right, Alexi. Some general—doesn't take much to see her fold. See, the difference between you and us is we don't care who has to die to get what we want. You'll die before you'll work with us but, how about them?"

I said nothing, which was answer enough. I wouldn't let my family die from my stubbornness.

"I'll let you sleep on it for a night. Think it over a bit. Decide how complicated you want this to be, but let me be clear. You either work with us, or they die. Choose wisely," she said, as if it were a real choice. Alexiares opened the door, and she strode past. He lingered for a moment before exiting without looking back.

DIM LIGHT SEEPED INTO THE BASEMENT FROM WHATEVER WAS LIGHTING up the street outside. It was late, hours had passed, but I couldn't be sure of the time. They'd removed the bullet in both my and Seth's legs and stopped the bleeding, stitching us up, but no other healing had been done. *55515*, I repeated to myself over and over. The focused pinched expression on Seth's face told me he was doing the same. With the extent of his injuries, I wasn't sure it would do much to relieve his pain.

I'd used it for years in The Before, The Monroe Institute had done research in the seventies or eighties on the human body's pain perception gene, 55515. The idea was if you repeated those numbers and focused on the area of pain, then the pain would subside. It'd come out in some CIA document and I'd tried it, mostly for period pain or minor aches and bruises. I was shocked when I'd realized it had worked. It didn't totally erase the pain, but it sure as hell made it subside enough to function.

So I'd taught each one of my soldiers the same. That and the fact that the human body can do anything for thirty seconds if you put your mind to it. Tell yourself *just thirty more seconds* enough and you can push through more than you think.

My leg throbbed. No pain medication and no access to Reina's powers was going to be a major disadvantage on getting out of here, which is exactly what they'd intended. Sitting here around my friends, battered, bruised, and hopeless, there was nothing I wanted more in that moment than a bottle of liquor. It wouldn't make everything better, but I'd at least forget for a bit.

I'd failed them. I'd trusted Alexiares and led them right into this trap. I should have sent him back to where he'd come the moment he arrived at The Compound, but I didn't. My gut had told me to, but my family had led me to believe I was being harsh, emotional, and irrational. Denying someone a new home and possible happiness because I'd been void of it myself.

At that moment, I was angry with them too, then angry at myself for being angry with them. It'd been weeks since I'd thought about the bitter taste of homemade tequila burning the back of my throat. I'd had a purpose then, a goal.

Now I didn't have one, and we'd likely all die because of my mistake. They'd be better off without me.

The door to the basement opened and light flooded in. Two guards came in, each with a bowl of food in their hands, sliding them towards us, smart enough to keep their distance. I peered into the bowl. It was too dark to see exactly what kind of meat it was, but whatever it was didn't even look edible enough to feed Harley. *I see why she wants the resources.*

The guards turned to leave as Reina stopped them. "Wait," she said, "you're not going to untie our hands? How are we supposed to eat?"

"Not our problem," one sneered. "Figure it out."

"What about water?" I asked.

They said nothing as they left. There was only one way for us to eat. The water bowls they brought a few minutes later made it clear. Like dogs.

"Someone will be down in the morning," the guard called out over his shoulder.

No one came until the afternoon. I hadn't slept much and had been awake to see the sun brighten up the room and stay there for hours. The windows were thin, and I could hear crowds of people walk by in different waves. Morning shifts, mid-morning shifts, and lunch rush.

The guard from last night entered, eyeing me uneasily before he risked coming closer. I barked at him, grinning as he leaped back, tossing down a battered pink card with a small pencil. *Lucky I can't access my magic.*

Will you be our valentine?

The card was littered with childish hearts and smiley faces.

Love Finley & Alexiares

It was signed, though the handwriting was certainly not his.

"What's it say?" Moe asked, voiced raspy as she leaned over, her first words since we'd awoken.

I showed it to her, reading it out for Seth and Reina who had turned to see for themselves. A collective *no* rang out, saying they too would rather die than work for her. A ping of guilt rolled in my stomach. They hadn't known about Alexiares past, but I had. He hadn't said Finley's name, and I hadn't put two and two together.

Finley was notorious for her cruelty in The Expanse. Gossip had spread across borders over the last few months of a ruthless woman who'd only recently come into power. She was greedy.

Constantly finding loopholes in the treaty and using it to her advantage, seeing how much she could get away with. Pillaging unwalled areas, border towns and forcing them to become outposts of her settlement, trying to build her population. Where others were hesitant to react, still rebuilding and avoiding another war, Finley pushed for one, aiming to use it to gain more land, more power.

We'd discussed her over dinner one night when I'd first returned to my duties. Reina shared whatever gossip she'd picked up from the random person she'd decided to spend an hour chatting up that day. None of them wanted to work with her, but I wasn't willing to sign their death certificates.

I knew my friends, I could sign our lives away at this moment, but that wouldn't guarantee their cooperation once the chains were removed, *if* they were removed. No, I'd have to get them to agree, willing participants, which meant I had to be onboard.

My eyes scanned the room, searching each of their faces. I needed them to see that there was a way out. We could do this.

"Things … things are bad right now, and I know it seems like there isn't a way out, but there is. Our fate has nothing to do with Finley, or Alexiares, or any of these shitheads. No, our fate is in our hands. When I look at you all, I see my family, people with willpower stronger than any motherfucker behind these walls. We'll find a way out, but first we have to play their game."

They nodded, slowly, accepting the truth in my words as I checked off the left box on the card.

When we were escorted from the basement, they removed our chains one by one, forcing us to swallow a pill. Reina had felt her magic recede deep inside her. While Seth had noticed his gifts had also been muted, Moe wouldn't know until she tried to channel a vision, but I already knew what they'd done.

They'd checked our mouths, ensuring we'd swallowed, but I'd managed to hold it in the swelling of my cheeks, Finley's assault playing in my favor. Feigning a sneeze when it began to dissolve in my mouth, I spit it out. Careful to ensure the force slung it across the room, undiscoverable unless they knew what to search for. And by then, I'd hope it'd be too late.

None of their magic came back over the next two days. I'd seen Alexiares only once. Finley had ordered the guards to bring Seth and I to have our wounds healed to a certain extent. Just enough for them to judge our physical abilities as she ran through an assessment similar to my own, but crueler.

Real weapons were used, and her soldiers weren't playing nice. Alexiares had watched me avoid a stab to the spine as I fought off two attackers at once and barely flinched, Finley clapping with joy at my skill at his side.

They'd been all over each other. No sign of remorse in his body language, though there were moments where his eyes lingered on mine a second too long before closing them as he kissed Finley. A weird ping of jealousy swirled through my gut as Seth took his turn. But mostly disgust.

Disgust with myself for feeling jealousy and not having realized when I'd been ready to move on. And disgust for opening myself up to him, someone that would spend time with a woman like her. I'd stupidly let myself fall victim to his con.

Finley had them see to our wounds from the assessment before dismissing us, stating we'd receive a test assignment soon. Something supervised. The guards escorted us back to our rooms as we said nothing to each other, not feeling safe to speak. Nothing positive would come out of either of our mouths in this moment of shared fury. They'd separated us in an old hotel downtown, guards posted outside each of our doors who'd been instructed to follow us each time we left, never giving us a moment of true privacy to talk, let alone plan.

A note was under my pillow as I sank into the bed shortly after arriving back in my room. I knew this handwriting, this language. I jumped up. Pulling on the size too big black pants and shirt Finley had graciously supplied me with, my head spun on what excuse I could come up with in the seconds it'd take me to get to Moe's room.

The guard jumped as I swung the door open, not expecting me to have come out so soon as I rushed to knock on her door.

She opened it moments later, eyes alert, and I wondered what she'd been doing.

"Wanna go for a walk? Not too cold out today," I said inconspicuously. The guards were used to me going for a stroll, my claustrophobia, and anxiety not letting me find peace outside of sleeping in my room.

"Uh, sure," she agreed, not having been included in them in the past two days.

"Great," I said, grabbing her hand and slipping the note as I pretended to eagerly pull her along. She kept her hand in mine, slowly pulling the note into the sleeve of the hoodie she wore.

Walking outside, the guards kept pace behind, where they could point their weapons should we try to take off. We sat on a small grassy patch down near the river. Moe pulled her knees to her stomach, nonchalantly dropping her head to her thighs and shifting the note forward.

I glanced back, pretending to crack my back. The guards remained unaware in their own conversation.

"What's—" she said, pulling her head up too quickly, the note visible in her hand.

"Shh." I mouth, pushing her hand back down.

She read it again, memorizing it before crumbing it. Grabbing a rock and skipping them both into the river.

Αγορά. Τετάρτη. ώρα 16

"Agora, Wednesday. Sixteen hours." Her tone was hushed, translating what she could but not understanding the meaning.

Our eyes locked in recognition. His note had been written to where Moe's translation had been required, but had she fallen short history wise, I'd be able to step in and take her place. I thought back to the documentaries I'd watched with my parents every weekend as a kid. Agora ... a place of gathering in city-states in ancient Greece.

The heart of the city. He wanted to talk.

"I knew not to give up on him." Moe grinned.

Yeah, me too.

CHAPTER

THIRTY-SIX

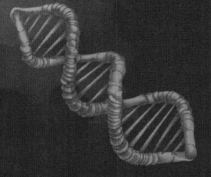

AMAIA

round three p.m. the next day I wriggled my way through the narrow vent in the ceiling, grateful for my small frame that made the task easier. The searing pain in my thigh was but a distant memory now. Our rooms were on the fourth floor, and I only needed to make it to a room around the corner before making my way down the stairwell to freedom.

Peering down from the vent, I scanned the area below for any sign of danger or occupation. Silence greeted me, and I breathed a sigh of relief. Swiftly pushing aside the vent, I braced myself for the impact of the fall, gritting my teeth as the sting of pain shot up my ankles. I pressed my ear against the door, listening intently for any sound.

Every nerve in my body was on high alert as I stepped out onto the street. I struggled to keep my composure, not wanting to draw attention to myself. My heart pounded in my chest as I scanned my surroundings, eyes wide open for any sign of recognition.

We hadn't seen much of the city, just the immediate few blocks from where they'd kept us in the basement to the hotel they had us locked in now. My day shift guard had always been rather lenient, allowing me to get air near the river, and most recently, the building Finley had tested us in. I didn't know where most of them gathered, *if* there was even a space here for that. It was pretty clear to me that they didn't do much of anything here besides work and looked pissed. Their world was tremendously gray, from the pavement down to their clothes.

My best bet was to follow the crowd, allowing it to take me where the masses headed. I stopped where they did, taking in the row of shops where people lingered. Casting uncertain glances, I was taken aback by the stands selling skinned rats and an array of mystery meats, mutated animals. My stomach turned at the thought of what horrors they might have served me in the stew. The river was right there, and it wasn't frozen. Surely there had to be other options.

Further down ale and other liquids sold off carts as people swarmed around them, drinking away the problems of their day. I considered joining them for a second, staring in the direction before a shadow in the alleyway to the right caught my attention.

I cracked my neck, my eyes trailing until they spotted Alexiares. Clad in the same black uniform, he was practically melded into the brick wall behind him. A subtle nod of my head conveyed my acknowledgment before gliding through the crowd, dropping to my knee as if I had stepped over to tie my shoe.

"Look busy. Pretend like you're stretching for a jog." My heart thundered in my chest as his raspy voice reached my ears, the *r* in each word, singing to me as his accent slipped through. It was the first time he had spoken to me since we arrived.

Good thing I'd worn the sneakers that'd been tossed into the room before my physical assessment. Hoping they'd make my movements through the vent silent in comparison to the heavy weight of boots.

He stood just out of view. My face remained straight ahead as his breath kissed the tip of my ear. I grabbed my ankle, pulling my leg into a hamstring stretch, my fingers clinging to the corner of the wall.

"What are you doing?" I asked, wanting him to get to the point.

"Getting us out of here," he said, scoffing as if it were obvious.

I dropped my foot, body stilling before remembering to keep up my rouse, pulling my arms behind my back and leaning forward.

"We don't have access to our magic."

He answered in full confidence, "Yes, you do."

"How do you—"

"You're smart," he interrupted, "there wasn't a chance in hell you'd take it."

I grinned, his faith in me warming my body before forcing myself to bury it.

"Why aren't you locked up with the rest of us?" I deadpanned, remembering the sound of Seth's screams. The kisses. The bruises.

"I'm sorry about that." He interrupted the thoughts before they could get too deep.

A moment of tense silence passed between us as I shifted my body into the next stretch, my eyes scanning the crowd with predatory focus.

"Look, we don't have the time for me to explain anything, just know I lied my way out of the situation. Do you want to waste time talking about why I'm not locked in a dungeon, or would you like to focus on the important things?"

I wasn't about to trust him easily. He'd proven too quick to switch sides. Even though we'd been out for three days as they carted us back here, the ease with which he'd done so gave me pause. "The gas, it didn't affect you as much. You were awake before the rest of us."

"Didn't affect me at all, actually. Finley had us all vaccinated when she first created it. Incapacitating agent."

"Those don't work. Even the military couldn't perfect them. The air, we were outside." I protested. We'd researched them ourselves back at The Compound, a biochemist in the army working with Reina and her colleagues.

"She was smart before, studied at MIT, top of her class. Tinkerer's genes made her into something of an evil Marie Curie."

A gorgeous evil genius plays the villain, the jokes really write themselves.

"You don't believe me?" he asked, noting my silence.

"Forgive me if I hesitate with your little display."

He paused, tilted his head, then looked down, realizing what I was referring to. I turned, pointing my chin up to meet his gaze.

"You're jealous," he accused.

I shook my head quickly. "No."

"I *had* to, Amaia. I need you to hear me. I did what I had to in order to survive, as you would. Because if you survive, they survive." His eyes were harsh, searching mine before adding, "And right now, all I care about is your survival. I didn't think it'd matter, anyway. Not after you pulled away."

"We were interrupted."

His expression turned brooding, and I dropped my head, resuming my stretches, turning my back to him, remembering where I was and why I was here.

"You made it clear you preferred my distance this last month. I gave you space to come to me. I opened up to you and you didn't come." His voice tore, and I stiffened. My back now pressed against him as he whispered into my ear, "Look at me, Amaia. Say it. Tell me. Why did you pull away that day?"

My breath became shallow at the command and I took a step forward, creating some distance. "You mentioned him. Said you were glad he saved me, but because he saved me, you lost someone. Someone that meant everything to you. We both have people we owe things to. People we want to honor. Maybe we should keep them in mind before we make a mistake we can't take back."

The words felt harsh as they left my lips, instant regret washing over me as I took in the stillness of his body. Not having had expected the conversation to take this turn.

"This is about Jax?" His voice was barely audible over the busy street.

"Yes."

He shook his head, clearing his throat. "We don't have time for this."

"Agreed. What's the plan then? I've got about thirty minutes before someone comes and knocks at my door with dinner."

"Don't eat it."

I leaned back onto the wall, attempting to blend in with the others lingering and gathering in the town-like area. My head tilted, waiting for him to continue.

"The pills they gave you start to lose effect around seventy-two hours. It'll be in your dinner for another dose tonight."

My jaw clenched. *Fuck*, we wouldn't have been the wiser, expecting the next dose to be in pill form again. "Copy."

"Give me a few more days. Play along. She's happy she has me back, but she's not dumb. Hasn't given me any worthwhile information. Only reason I'm here right now is because I'm not allowed in their daily debrief. Doesn't loosen the leash much, only time she lets me out her sight. But I'll find a way to get you out. I just need time."

I nodded, grateful to be free of the burden of figuring this out on my own. "Them out too. All of us." I meant him too.

His mouth pulled in a tight grin, pulling me into a tight hug and catching me off balance. My foot tripped a step before he hoisted me up, my back now to the alley, welcoming the embrace. The warmth from his body offered me a pocket of peace in a place where letting my guard down could be a fatal mistake.

"I'm glad you're just a dick and not actually evil." *I'm glad you're safe.*

His arms tensed around my shoulders. "When I let go, get the others and run like hell."

A chill went through my body. Danger laced every word. I grounded my feet, ready to protest, ready to stay and fight. To hell with leaving him here alone.

"Don't look back," he said, pulling me behind him. His rings were off. Fire filled his palms, and I couldn't help but disobey. I wheeled around. Finley stood at the end of the alley, her hair whipping a halo around her face, her sharp features otherworldly as she snickered. Disgust pulling at her thin lips. *Moe's vision.*

"Go!" he yelled.

Finley chuckled. "Oh Alexiares, I was hoping you and your whore wouldn't be so naïve, but alas, here we all are. Well, guess I can't say I don't enjoy a crowd."

His flames were bright, heat hitting the back of my body as I took off.

Finley's next words were nearly lost to the wind. "There's a shield around us, Alexi." She laughed. "You remember Joey from that day we caught you in the field, right? Now that I'm thinking about it, I believe he's the reason you took off all those months ago. Oh, I bet his face has been tugging on you for *days.*"

My heart hurt for him, but for now, I needed to focus on getting to my friends. Her words no more than a murmur in the crowd as I left him behind. The weight of having to choose to save most of my family, or just one, was suffocating, making the sprint harder, my breaths not coming without effort.

The gray of the city was a blur as I sprinted through town. Nobody paid me or the men that now followed in the distance any mind, making me wonder what went on here for them to be unfazed.

I threw open the door; the lobby was empty, no one to stop me from flying up the stairs, taking three at a time until I reached the fourth floor. Easing into the hallway, I paused, listening for rushed footsteps before creeping towards the room I'd dropped into.

My room was untouched when I plopped onto the ground, taking only a moment to catch my breath as I pulled my boots back on, ready to run. I stopped myself short, making sure my breathing had neutralized, greeting the guard at my door, no indication I hadn't been there the whole time.

Smiling, I strolled up to Seth's room unrushed, not wanting to alarm the guards before I needed to. It worked. Seth opened the door showcasing Moe standing not too far behind him, her guard sitting awkwardly on the sink in the bathroom next to the door.

Before either of us could speak, a soldier came running from the stairwell on the other side of the hall. He yelled, demanding me to stay there and put my hands up. The guard in the bathroom jumped to his feet, Seth catching on to the situation quickly and ramming his elbow into his nose. Blood gushed. A red sea caking the bottom of my friend's shoes as Moe grabbed her bag off to the side, ready to go.

Reina's door flew open at the commotion, the guard in front whirling at her as she slammed her foot down atop him in full force. The pain forced him to drop down only to meet her knee, breaking his nose too. Making sure the job was done, her elbow slammed into the nape of his neck, knocking him out before joining us in the hall.

In seconds, we were off running, floating through the closest stairwell and out into the street. I glanced in the direction I'd come from, catching Alexiares running down the street towards us, hair flapping and wild in the wind. He'd have to catch up.

I knew he could.

We turned the corner, my eyes narrowing in on the building ahead. We'd taken our assessment there. Finley's insecurity had left room for a weakness to be exposed. She'd been so set on latching onto Alexiares that she'd failed to notice me scoping out the rooms, moving a step too slowly, pretending their display made me uncomfortable.

It did, but it'd also played to my advantage. Our weapons were in there, a pile that had been sorted through and left out to rust. Who needed basic weapons when you had a mad scientist with gas that could not only take you out but also produce invisible shields?

At least one of the two had appeared to be left behind as she'd rushed from her meeting to corner us. Catch us in the act.

"Here!" I yelled, my friends in tow.

Throwing the door open, the dice the guards had tossed onto the counter rolled and then exploded. The tiny shards of resin shot into their necks as they gasped for breath, blood pouring into their lungs. Moe hopped over them, teeth shimmering as she reached for Wrath. Reina cheered as she found her bow and arrow as Seth opened up a bag tossing whatever was on the counter inside. We didn't have much time, could only grab what was in our faces before turning to run.

Ducking for cover, my hands fired off small flames, Alexiares' defensive magic at my side. He'd caught up in time, our steps now in sync, following after Seth who'd headed towards the river.

Reina's water magic sputtered in her hands, the seventy-two hours coming to an end, but the effects still held her back, not completely out of her system. I scanned the horizon frantically for a boat, a piece of wood, anything, but we were trapped.

"You guys have to swim across," I said, eyeing the distance between me and the water, then back at the soldiers cresting over the hill down towards us.

"We could die in that current, not to mention the temperature." Moe reasoned, the water rushing loudly, forcing us into a shout.

Small bursts of Reina's magic shot past my head. They barely had power left. Exhausted from the little back and forth in the streets.

I'd only begun to touch the surface of mine. "It's our only shot. You need to go now. I'll hold them off."

"No! We aren't leaving you here to die alone." Reina protested.

"Seth," I commanded, motioning him to move towards his sister. He studied me for a moment before nodding, accepting his new mission.

He pulled Reina and Moe back, his preternatural strength kicking back in. Reina's blue eyes resembled the storm of her brothers challenging me. She wouldn't be leaving me.

"She's not alone," Alexiares said, walking over to grip her face, trying to calm her. "Go, please. She won't be able to focus with you here. I won't be able to focus. Is that what you want?" She shook her head no before he added, "You need to channel your magic right now. Focus. Drag it to the surface. Dig deep."

My focus faded as I watched them, admiring his ability to provide guidance and support in an area he had yet to control himself.

The water behind us slowed, then sped back up as she let out a grunt, struggling. "There you go, you can feel that. It's hard to control, but I know you can do it. Now please, go with your brother, get to the other side, and keep running. We'll be over before you know it."

Seth glared at him, business unfinished from the time in the basement, but nodded in appreciation before guiding them to the water. Alexiares moved to my side, our eyes locking, our hands lined with flames.

My gaze fell to his lips, catching them curve into a mischievous smile. A reflection of my own as we pushed our fire into the world, bouncing off the shield of the soldiers now less than half a football field away. It bent, unable to truly contain the force of our power. Understanding washed over me.

That shield could break.

I threw up a wall of fire, covering our exact location, forcing them to aim blindly.

"This won't hold them for long. We need a Plan B."

"Ya think?" he exclaimed, tackling me to the ground to avoid the now wild array of bullets.

Finley yelled, indistinguishable over the wall of flames. Stealing at glance over my shoulder, I searched out into the river, my friends just now making it to the other side. Reina's magic propelling them faster than any of them could swim.

I pressed my fingers into the ground. "Okay, Plan B."

He looked at me, face pale from the use of his magic and contorted with confusion.

"Dig deep like you said. Throw everything we can at those shields until they shatter."

His mouth opened, then closed, coming up with no better idea. "You're insane."

I smirked. "Not the first time I've heard that."

We jumped to our feet, fire slamming into the shield before he pulled back, channeling the water from the river instead, forcing it to stay to the right at his side. He was careful to keep it in control, his entire body trembling. The water dropped overhead, and I threw my flames again, the water fizzling into steam, screams erupting as it baked their skin. We were cooking them from the inside out.

The shield broke.

Rocks, pieces of concrete, anything that was willing to answer the call of my magic rose into the air.

I grinned. "Duck."

He dove to the ground just in time for fragments to fly past his head and land where the shield was no longer protected. The crunch of human bones and cries for help filled the air. Jogging over to him, I grabbed his ringless hands and yanked him up.

"When we get to the river, I'm going to give it everything I've got."

"I'll take care of the rest," he said, knowing where my mind was headed.

We backed up at the water's edge, a scream releasing from the depths of my chest. Orange, and white flame emerged from the palms of my hands, encasing the nearest buildings. Finley rose to her feet, blood gushing from her head, her mouth slack before dashing up the hill towards the city now roaring with flame.

"Let's go." Alexiares tugged, his body heavy as we entered the water. The river was still until we were halfway across. The water rushed, my ears and nose filling with reddish orange water, the fire ahead making it glow.

No, I realized, *not fire, blood.*

"Alexiares!" I screamed, kicking my feet to move behind his unmoving body.

I grabbed his cheeks, trying to stay afloat as I shook him. His body remained limp, red seeping from near his chest, though I couldn't be sure through the darkness of his shirt.

Securing him to my chest, I kicked onto my back, the desire to make sure he was okay, alive, pushing me to the shore. My friends were nowhere in sight. *Good.*

Flames licked at the shoreline we left behind screams echoing in the distance. I grimaced, swallowing hard before lifting his shirt. Scars flecked the tattoos on his stomach and chest, a story of his life before we'd met. I searched, eyes falling on the small hole in his chest. He'd been shot. I lifted his shoulder. There was an exit wound, at least.

My body swayed, memories of Jax threatening to take over. Holes in chests weren't good, people didn't survive those kinds of injuries.

Alone. I would always be alone.

"Fuck, fuck, no." I scrambled, pressing my fingers to his neck. He still had a pulse, but it was weak. I removed my shirt, thankful it was too large, stretching just enough, as I tied it awkwardly around his broad chest to stop the bleeding.

We needed to go. I couldn't linger without risk of them attempting to cross, better yet using the bridge to catch us on the rear. Adrenaline pumped through me. I hoisted him up to his knees, squatting down to latch my arms between his legs and draping him over my shoulders. He was heavy, but I was strong. And I could do anything for thirty seconds.

I made it past a few buildings on the street closest to the river before a door popped open, my friends jogging over to help. Reina was nearly out of magic. Her fingers brushed over his chest just enough to stop the bleeding before Seth tossed him over his back, taking on the weight and insisting we hustle.

At mile ten we stopped to take a break. Seth needed to catch his breath. Alexiares came to, adamant about being able to walk and settling on getting support from me and Seth.

Low on magic, and with only a few weapons with limited ammo, stopping in Foley logistically was the best choice. We hadn't seen anyone chasing us, making the decision easy enough. Alexiares had made clear that just because we couldn't see them, didn't mean nobody was.

It was an eerie enough warning to raise caution, but none of us were in any shape to continue and he had started to fade in and out of consciousness. Likely still bleeding on the inside without Reina being able to do a clean job.

But as we settled into our makeshift camp in Foley, I couldn't shake the feeling that we had just traded one danger for another.

CHAPTER

THIRTY-SEVEN

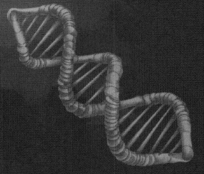

AMAIA

Sitting on the floor, leaning against the side table, my eyes closed from exhaustion. The couch ruffled, shaking the floor gently as Alexiares stirred. He rolled over, flashing me a grin. He winced as I pressed my finger into the recently healed wound and he yelped, muscles still sore.

"You idiot," I scolded, "I thought you were dead! Shot? And you seriously said nothing, just started swimming across a *river* like it was nothing. Oh yeah, leave me with the floating dead body to drag out, real team player of you."

Seth, Reina, and Moe were arguing in the kitchen, voices raised over trivial things. Two of the three hadn't said more than a few words to me in the hours that had passed. Their anger still tangible about the choice I'd taken from them at the river.

He chuckled, wiping his face and taking in my expression.

"What's funny? I want to laugh too." I asked defensively, arms crossing over my chest.

"You. This. Me here. Everything."

I wanted to slap him. "And that's funny to you because …"

"This dysfunctional band of misfits you've got here." He threw up a thumb to a now rowdy kitchen. "I see why you're so scared to lose everything, to lose it all. Realized it the moment we were all caught. Why it's worth fighting like hell."

The words tugged on a piece of me, a tiny string buried deep inside me. "Why?"

"Because family ain't who you're born with, it's who you're willing to die for."

WE MOVED HOUSES THE NEXT DAY, OPTING TO FIND A MORE SECLUDED location a few miles down. We'd recovered enough to find a better spot to keep our cover, but not enough to make any real dent distance wise. It would be another day before we'd be recovered and could continue on, figure out what to do next. We had no resources.

No real food besides random items that'd been left behind. More times than not, having tough luck when it came to gathering food not toxically expired to the point it'd likely kill us if we ate it. Our bodies healed slower than usual from malnourishment. Reina healing us had meant she'd healed the slowest, any magic she'd replenished quickly going to use.

I surveyed the trees that occupied the overgrown lawn; my body tucked into a corner of the porch just out of view for the first watch when Alexiares plopped down next to me. The color back in his face, his body springy for someone who'd been half dead the day before.

Words flew from my mouth, not stopping as I told my brain to shut up. Wanting to explain myself out of panic, from the thought of losing another to the war I'd been losing against death.

"Jax … Jax was my everything and nothing all at once. My heart and soul, but not in the way most would think." He bit down on his bottom lip, not having expected anything but company when he'd taken his seat. But I forced myself to continue. Yesterday hadn't been the time, but if not now then when?

"I've never met someone who connected to my soul the way he did. Not Prescott, not Moe, Reina, not even Riley. With him, everything was simple. Every breath I would take, he would mirror and vice versa. Every truth I hid, he knew and accepted me for it. He pushed and shoved; he challenged me. Our loyalty went so deep I couldn't possibly put it in one category. Not my friend, not my lover, not even family. When he died, part of my heart died too."

"You two shared a room though? A bed?" He didn't look away as he asked, searching for a tell of me lying.

I didn't falter. "No. I mean, yes, but not in that way. Not for some time."

"Then why did you let everyone think that it was?"

"Compound over everything." I sighed. "Prescott thought a marriage at that level would help build morale."

"Stop." The words were automatic, not having realized he'd said them out loud.

My voice turned hard, unwavering. "Stop what? It's the truth. It created a united, hopeful front when our home needed it the most. Prescott's their beloved little king, and to the people, Jax and I the prince and princess. A royal family, a baby … it would have shown them all it was okay to settle in. To find peace. Joy. I loved him, and he loved me. But neither of us were fooled for one second that we would have been anything other than best friends in The Before."

He shook his head, not liking where I was headed. "Why are you telling me this?"

"Because I need you to understand." The rest of it unsaid. I couldn't bring myself to say the words.

He shifted in his spot, distancing himself a bit. "Ah, here I was thinking it was the tattoos." He chuckled, making light of it recalling one of our first conversations.

"Not *just* the tattoos," I teased back.

"Tattoos tell a story," he said.

I chuckled. "Yes, that we can agree on."

He was serious, eyes focused on the tattoos on my own arm, focusing in on one.

"I'd like to hear about them sometime," he said, closing the gap between us as his finger circled over the words on my forearm, *Memento Mori.*

I tilted my head up, allowing my eyes to lock on his, trying to find the words but landing on none. My fingers slid to the nape of his neck, pulling his face towards mine, my lips stopping at the skin right next to his own. I let them hover for a moment before pressing in. His head nestled into the cusp of my neck, breath tingling down the center of my body. A few silent, hesitant moments passed between us before I planted my feet, pushing myself up and headed towards the door.

The words found me before I went out of view, stopping briefly with my back turned. I was scared that if I faced him, they'd stay unsaid forever. "I'm not sure if I can give my heart to someone again, but I know that, right now, it's too soon. But if I could, I wouldn't mind it going to you."

Moe sat in the rocking chair in front of the window, looking on to the spot Alexiares still sat. She'd been listening, still not saying much from the day before. I moved to walk past her towards one of the rooms in the back, not in the mood to work through our problems, or the ones I had with anyone else.

"He would want you to move on, you know." Her words were quiet, but felt like they'd been amplified through a speaker, reverberating through my mind.

I turned back to her, deciding to listen to what she had to say, surprised to see her smiling. Not at me, but out into the distance, recalling a vision in her memory. "I've seen it, you know, in my visions. You smiling and happy. Unburdened."

"Moe, please," I interrupted, not wanting to hear more. We both knew the future was never set in stone, not when it came to trivial things.

"You don't want to hear it now, aren't ready to hear it now, I know. But one day you will be ready, and I just want you to know that you do deserve it. You deserve happiness." She let out a breath, head swiveling back towards the window, dismissing me before I had a chance to do the same.

I knew it was true. Knew that Alexiares may not have been the type of man I would have chosen Before, or even immediately in The After. But that didn't mean he wasn't what I needed now, what worked for me now.

The world was different; I was different, and if I were going to keep my people safe, I'd need to embrace that the old me was gone forever, in every aspect.

As a child, I wanted a hero. Someone to swoop in, take care of me. Make my life easier. A man to lead. Xavier had been that perfect man. Kind-hearted, a great listener, ambitious, handsome. Things that were good on paper.

Jax was perfect in his own sense, too. Had been there when I needed him, helped save me from myself. Held me and kept me steady through the turmoil over the years. Made me see the light, the opportunity in starting fresh. That there was *always* good to find within the bad. He'd given me a second chance at life.

There wasn't anything inherently wrong about any of it. But those things were wrong for me now.

I didn't need a hero, or a savior. I needed an equal. A partner. Someone who had seen the dark and embraced it. Decided it was worth suffering through for the greater good.

The good guys couldn't stay good if they actually wanted to make a difference. I'd hated Alexiares because I'd started to hate myself. When I saw him, I saw the guilt, the disgusting self-pity, the trauma. The lines of his face that let me know it had changed him and he too, would never go back to who he once was. It wasn't possible when you knew that you lived at the expense of others lives.

But I would never be that little girl again. I was a woman who would forever live with burning rage and a pang of pain that simmered away at all things good. At happiness.

The line between me and Finley was clear, I was pained. Burdened, but not ruthless. Evil. And to fight against a Finley, I'd need someone who could think like Finley on my side, but know when it's time to turn it off. Someone not afraid to face the ugly with me in hopes of keeping the future beautiful. Someone who accepted that our souls would be tainted and lost forever. Was okay with it.

Because to keep the people we loved safe, we could not kill our beast, only embrace it.

CHAPTER
THIRTY-EIGHT

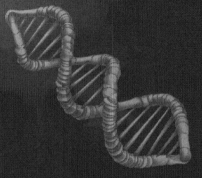

AMAIA

Freezing rain trapped us in Foley for another day, which was fine, considering we still hadn't come up with a solid plan. I wasn't sure what to do; it was possible Duluth hadn't heard of the ruckus we'd caused. Probable actually, given that Finley had indicated there wasn't a solid relationship between the two yet. Which also meant that even if they had been made aware of the situation in St. Cloud, there was a decent chance they wouldn't come running regardless.

Backtracking home would be a struggle in this state, making the decision to tough it out to Duluth and recover while playing emissary sounded like the more appealing option to everyone. We could make it another two weeks until the messenger arrived announcing our presence. But over a month back to Elko or Twin

Falls in our condition, and without weapons was questionable. Out of any real option, another four or five days on the road won in the end.

With no real supplies, we'd had to find homes to hide out in each evening increasing our risk for trouble. It was too cold to risk sleeping outside, even using fire magic to keep myself warm wouldn't prevent hypothermia from taking me in the night. Nature had to have balance that way, you couldn't cheat the system too much. Using your magic to start a fire and increase your chances of survival, acceptable. Using your magic to replace a much-needed coat, well there were worse ways to go, I guess.

The only benefit being the sweaters, pants, boots, and other items left unclaimed in the closets of the homes we'd ransacked. Food was always the first thing people took, medicine was second, but clothes, it appeared outside Salem Territory, clothes were only taken when they were needed.

Ogilvie, Hinkley, and Moose Lake were all the same. The walks each day were quiet, everyone speaking in hushed tones, not wanting to draw attention to ourselves as we passed through and around towns. Seth and Reina spoke quietly amongst themselves once we'd located a safe place to stop each night. Often finding them in corners when they'd gone missing from shared spaces. The behavior was strange.

Their body language indicated they'd been arguing, but they'd never been private about it in the past. I grew concerned, wondering if I'd exposed her to too much, stolen that part of her that made her *her*.

"What was that about?" I asked.

We'd found an inn in Moose Lake in good enough condition to rest for the night. Despite all the space, we'd opted to find a room with two beds, not wanting to be too far from the others in case of an emergency.

Reina jumped, not having heard me approach as she sat on the bed, peering out the window down at the parking lot.

"Nothing, everything's fine," she said. "Just Seth being Seth."

I nodded, understanding her frustration, having had my own when working with her brother.

"He's just insensitive ya know? Like nothin' ever bothers him." She laughed. "Well, except my presence."

"Talk to me, how can I help?"

"It's nothin' important. Just, as kids we spent a lot of time out here. Have," she paused, face scrunched, catching herself. "Had? Not really sure. Family lived in the area. Seeing how it all turned out, seeing it all abandoned, nothing left but a shell of the beauty it once was ... it's hard. Don't even know how our family turned out, their house is too far to check."

She knew we'd reroute if we had to, but I understood, she didn't want to know. Didn't want that certainty weighing on her if it wasn't the outcome she would have wanted. It was far easier to pretend your loved ones made it out, somehow, someway.

I sat next to her on the bed, resting my head on her shoulder. "You know you can talk to me about these things, right? The situation will never be too dire where you can't talk about how you're feeling. I'm here for you."

The others feigned distracted around the room, Alexiares pretending to be busy in the corner reading some book he'd found on the tv stand. Moe made small talk on the other bed with Seth, who pretended as if he weren't currently a topic in this conversation.

"I know, it's not that," she said definitively. "My memories here, they're best kept in the past. No point in focusing on something I can't do nothin' about."

The sound of galloping hooves clacked against the pavement outside. Seth and Alexiares were at the window next to me within moments, taking in the small group of men now gathered outside the inn. Searching for someone. Searching for *us*.

How did they find us?

I glanced back at the table, our two pistols, a single pack of ammo, a few knives, Reina's bow and arrow, and Wrath. "There's not a chance in hell we'll be able to outshoot them."

"There's magic," Reina offered from behind us, peering over my head.

Alexiares considered it before leveling, "Nah, we won't be able to get a clear shot on them without making ourselves an open target."

He was right, a man now stood near the horses a few feet from the door. The rest of the men spread out, starting at the ends of the lodge making their way towards us, thuds rang out around us as doors were kicked in.

I looked to Reina. "How much magic you got locked and loaded?"

"Enough," she said, grinning.

"Good, I need you to target your magic directly at them, I want them to feel like they just ate three Thanksgiving turkeys with extra dressing." I directed, falling into General mode. "Stay tucked in this corner and don't move." She'd need to focus on them through the window to target them efficiently, careful to avoid it from putting us at risk.

Reina moved behind her brother, shrugging him out the way. "Got it."

"Moe"—her head swiveled to face me, eyes determined—"behind the door. Make them feel your Wrath."

She grabbed Wrath off the table, unsheathing the katana, aura of an assassin encasing her.

Seth stood at attention but his gaze kept flickering towards the movement outside, I snapped my fingers, drawing his attention back towards me. "Hey! I need you on it right now. Behind Moe. Grab whoever comes in next, knock 'em the hell out. Don't care

424

how, just do it. The quieter we are, the more time we'll have to take 'em out one-on-one."

"This is a stupid plan," he grumbled, his words made everyone pause, waiting to see if my orders would change.

I stepped to him, what would be chest to chest if he didn't hover a foot and a half over me. "And why is that?"

"We're not just outgunned, we're out-manned. We're hungry, we're tired, we're barely healed." He moved his fingers, counting bullet points. "We can just make somethin' up, get us all out of here and not risk any of the bullshit."

My eyes narrowed in response, everyone would get out of here, I'd make sure of that. "I don't know if you missed everything that happened less than a week ago Seth, but you see how ill-received treaty violators are. And we are, in fact, treaty violators."

"I'm not going down without a fight." Moe said, opposing her partner, no hint of remorse for doing so in her posture.

"Me neither," Reina's singsong voice was firm, sure, though she wouldn't be engaging in any hand-to-hand.

Alexiares watched me, a lazy smile on his face, waiting for me to give him a command.

"Looks like you're overruled. Again." The voice of a commander grasped onto my tone, ignoring the protest and continuing on. "Alexiares and I will stand center bait, draw them into the room and take out whoever makes it past you two."

"We can always say our first messenger didn't make it, that our next one is a week away. It's partly true, it'll be an easy sell," he pushed, taking another approach to convince me.

I turned my back to him, not interested in hearing more. "Do you really think men would come here, heavily armed and kicking in doors if they were interested in any of us walking out of here? Let's not be dense."

My point drove home as he huffed, walking behind Moe, careful to keep distance and avoid the reach of her swing.

The second we got into position, chaos erupted as two armed men rushed into the room. Moe swung her katana down wildly, the first unfortunate head falling to the floor with a wet thump.

Reina pushed herself further in the corner near the window, doing her best to keep each armed prick at bay. The heightened emotions and fear around the room started to wear her down. Her magic wasn't accustomed to taking on so many emotions at once. *There's only one way to make it easier on her then*, I grinned to myself, waiting for the next victim to cross under the threshold.

Seth took on a man of similar stature, finally meeting his match. He flipped him, pulling him into a chokehold, Seth's icy eyes bulging under the pressure. I had to focus, he could hold his own. I trusted that. For now I had to keep my eye on the door, not allowing too many souls to pass at once.

Finally, it was my chance. Two men rushed in, both twice my size as I rushed towards them, leaping. My legs locked around one of their necks as I slammed him into the ground, using him to trip the other.

My fists flew, not stopping until he could no longer be recognized as a man. The magic in me pulling the sheets from the bed to wrap around the neck of the other, air squeezing from his throat.

As the chaos continued, a figure entered the room, my head snapping to watch with horror as their attention narrowed in on Reina who was unaware of the incoming threat. Her body gave out against her will seconds before the man made contact. Before he could strike, Alexiares stepped in. Crossing the room swiftly, he swiped his knife across the man's throat, turning to engage with the next who'd come full speed from behind. He fell too, Alexiares' knife plunging into his torso instinctively, twisting it as he dragged it clean across, gutting him without having taken his eyes from Reina.

In a fit of rage, Moe charged towards the last attacker to enter the room, killing him with a swift blow. Seth narrowly missed the flying head as he managed to get on top of the man who'd had him in a chokehold, wrestling him out the room. The air was now silent except for the sounds of heavy breathing and a small whimper of pain as Reina woke up, grabbing the part of her head that had hit the wall when she fell. Her eyes were wide with fear and shock as they moved from Alexiares, then back at me.

Alexiares wiped his knife on his pants, a wild shimmer in his eyes, sparkling as he surveyed the carnage around him. Slowly, he examined my face, gauging my reaction to his savage display.

I took his knife, wiping the rest of the blood on my own pants before handing it back to him. "Red's my favorite color."

THERE WASN'T MUCH FOR US TO GRAB AS WE SCRAMBLED FROM THE room, sprinting down the center of the road not caring as the darkness of the night closed in. I thought I was hallucinating the first moments of hearing it, kept running thinking the blood was rushing through my ears. It wasn't until he looked back at me that I knew we were in for some shit.

It'd been years since I'd last heard the sound of a truck. The roads hadn't been cleared enough in California for you to get anywhere far without being stuck. Vehicles became an endeavor to worry about years down the line as we'd gotten settled.

Two headlights shined less than a quarter of a mile away, there was no running. There wasn't anywhere else to go, and if the cluster of armed individuals on the back were any indication, running wouldn't matter. You can't outrun a bullet.

"My God," Reina mumbled, slowing to a walk.

My heart thudded against my chest. "I think it's fair to say our luck has run out."

The truck skidded to a stop fifty feet away. A group of six masked and armed men jumped out, weapons raised and trained on each one of us. Not counting the driver and passenger who had two pistols each pointed at my and Seth's heads. They knew who we were all right.

"Hands stay up! Drop the weapons!"

There were no weapons to drop, we hadn't had time to raise them at the speed the truck had barreled towards us. And by the time we realized the situation we were in, we'd quickly understood magic would make no difference. We could blaze our way out of this one, but what happens when they send the next.

My eyes squinted as I peered into the distance, another vehicle headed this way confirmed my thoughts. The butt of a gun smacked into my temple and I tried not to laugh at the irony. It was the same spot that had marked the shit show this journey would end in.

My vision was blurry but I understood whoever stood behind me was talking to me, "If I see even a tinge of magic in your hands, I'll blow their fucking heads off."

Someone stopped in front of me, powder blowing into my face. I knew what it was before Reina whimpered, "It's gone, my magic's gone again."

The headlights became dark as a black hood yanked over my face, a needle pinched into my back, and time became non-existent.

CHAPTER
THIRTY-NINE

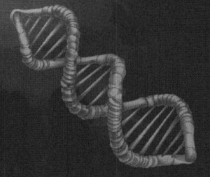

AMAIA

They'd tossed us into the back of the truck, stuffed in close, guns pressed into my side. Assuming I would be dumb enough to try something in my current condition. *Where could I go?* I laughed, wanting to ask them out loud, a jab in my rib telling me I best not.

My eyes burned as the hood was removed, and I blinked rapidly adjusting to the blinding light. *When did we get here?* I couldn't tell. We'd been driving for awhile, but it had to be Duluth. It was the only thing that made sense. The truck had come from the opposite direction of St. Cloud. There had been no uniforms.

St. Cloud soldiers always wore uniforms, Alexiares hadn't taken his off once he'd gotten there. They were expected to wear it each time they left their homes, he'd explained. It'd been part of his initial shock at The Compound. Everyone wore what they pleased as long as it didn't hinder them from their work.

Sure, my soldiers had a standard uniform when they left our walls, but inside, when they trained, practicality was key. I only encouraged what they trained in to be similar to what they'd be expected to fight in. Most had caught on. Anything they wore outside of their duties was none of my concern.

The care of the holding room they'd kept us mirrored nothing in St. Cloud, either. It wasn't anything fancy, but the fear of keeling over from black mold no longer existed. We were all here, unharmed and alive. The hoods had been removed and now, we were left to wait. The blinding lights and no windows, left us unable to determine what time it was or how much had passed. Intentional, for sure.

It became clear that no one would be coming anytime soon, sleep claiming us all one by one. I awoke to Seth pacing, his boots separating from their sole, jeans ragged. The faces of Moe and Reina defeated. If my own appearance resembled theirs, I found it surprising we'd been recognizable at all. Had I seen us from their point of view, I would have shot first, questioned if we were Pansie or a person later.

Moe's braid was matted with blood, hair bunched at the top tangled in guck. Dirt caked around her eyes and her pants had sliced open at the knee as she leaned against the wall. Reina's condition wasn't much better, long gone without a hair tie. Her brown hair resembled a nest made of straw, cheeks stained red from tears that had stopped falling hours ago.

Alexiares stood a few feet away, picking at his nails, his eyes unreadable. They hadn't taken his rings, not that it mattered without access to our magic. Seth stopped pacing, frozen in his steps, watching the door. It opened. A woman my age walked in followed by an older man in his midforties, salt and pepper hair flaking his harsh features.

I rushed forward, fingers wrapping around the bars, yanking them with significant force. "What the hell is going on?"

Her wavy red hair framed her delicate face, the dark circles beneath her eyes betraying the youth that lay beneath. She unlocked the cell doors, unafraid to approach and press her hands into my chest. "Settle down. You're not exactly in the position to make demands."

The man who'd entered with her stood under the threshold. I looked around at the walls. Without windows there'd be no way to tell, but something told me we were heavily guarded.

I smacked her hand away, pushing into her space. "We had a deal, Sloan."

"Deals change." She tossed her hair over her shoulders, turning her back to sit atop the table in the center of the room.

"Deals made to friends? I didn't even know you were in charge. What happened to Morgan?"

Her familiar blue eyes went cold. "Dead."

"You've changed." I shook my head, backing up towards the wall in disbelief.

"As have you, so I've heard."

We'd gone to the college together, bonded over growing up with fathers in the military. I hadn't moved nearly as much as her. After a while my mom had put her foot down on Seattle, wanting me to have some stability. He'd come home when he could, since I'd be off at college in a few years.

Sloan had moved back to stay with her parents after graduation. Content with getting a taste of the small town feeling she'd grown up with in the summer when her mother would bring her and her siblings back to their family home. I'd known she was here, seen her the last time I came. She'd merely been an advisor to Morgan, their leader who was now dead.

Reina's head remained down, chin tucked as she pressed into the corner, not wanting to be seen. I couldn't blame her. She wasn't a soldier, yet she had seen so much. Things were only going to get worse from here, Moe knew that, she'd seen it. I could tell by the lost expression painting her face.

"There's a messenger on the way. We just made it here before them," I tried, deciding to test how much she knew.

"You think you can lie to me? I know you Amaia, you've changed, but not that much." She sighed, frustrated. "Don't forget who was there with you. Your vision of the world got you in trouble then and it's going to cost you lives now."

It was true, military parents raised rowdy kids. If there was trouble to be found, we'd find it. We'd run from campus police many times after organizing protests and trying to encourage local franchises to unionize, always finding a way to support whoever needed it. Her college boyfriend had even bailed us out once. Arrested in downtown Seattle for disturbing the peace. The peace to be disturbed, being protesting what was happening to the homeless encampments in the area.

"What are you talking about? How did you even find us?" I asked, hoping it was Finley mixed with a bit of luck and not what my gut had been feeding me since the day Jax died.

"Finley's been trying to get my attention for the last six months," she said, giving me a moment of reassurance. "Not to mention you royally pissed her off with that building you blew up. Offered me a favor just to kill you herself." She pushed her body around, facing my friends who sat on the floor. "Good thing I don't need or want her favors."

"Don't forget Seth." The man who had entered with her grinned, instigating.

"Oh yeah, can't forget about my cousin here. Well, both of them I should say, but honestly I didn't expect Reina to be along for the journey. Seth's played a very important role in this whole ordeal."

My heart sank. Reina's head popped up, eyes shooting to mine, nothing but sorrow looking back at me. She didn't know. Moe scooted to her left, shaking her head at Reina in disgust, then rising to her feet backing into the corner. Seth refused to meet her stare.

I clenched my fists. Two steps and I could be connected with Seth's jaw. I'd made a promise at Jax's funeral, one I'd spent months hoping I wasn't cursed so much that I'd have to end my brother's life from stealing one of our own. Alexiares stepped between us, his head raised, eyes focused, trained, and willing me to stay calm.

"Stay out of this." I ground out.

He didn't step back. "Relax." His voice was hard.

I wouldn't have to lift a damn finger if I didn't want to, but thing was, I did. In fact, there wasn't anything in this moment I wanted more than to beat Seth to a bloody pulp.

It was the confirmation I needed, but dreaded. My heart had sunk the moment Caleb had focused on Seth before they'd fought in The Pit, a look of disgust filtering it. I'd forced myself to attribute it to the situation at hand, to Seth's ruthlessness and the threat of falling victim to execution from the accusations flung his way. It hadn't been Harley he'd been afraid of that night, it'd been Seth.

Sloan taunted, "Anything to say, cousin?" I glared at her, wondering what had caused a woman who was rambunctious and carefree in The Before to become the shell of a woman that she was now.

I only needed to stand in front of the mirror to find the answer to that.

"Eat shit," he spat at her, like he hadn't played a role in his own demise.

The man who'd entered with Sloan was enjoying this, feeding off the turmoil that unfolded before him. "Now that's not going to get your daddy back, is it?"

"What did you do, Seth?" Reina powered across the room, grabbing at his shirt as he shook her off. She moved her face, forcing him to see her, snot dripping from his nose, his face now completely red as he shoved her back. "What on Earth did you do?" Sobs filtered from her.

She slapped him across the face, the sound reverberating around the room. No one moved, not even Seth.

"Reina, we used to be so close, thought you'd be more excited to see me." An expression of genuine interest passed over Sloan's face before she pushed it away, forming her soft face back into a scowl. "You see, Elliot here has been talking to Seth for months. Mind to mind obviously, feeding us drops of information here or there. Letting us know the best places and times to strike, our names left out of it, keeping you vulnerable. Open to receiving outside help. Didn't take too much convincing on my end, just had to let him know Unc was alive and kicking. But *only* as long as he gave us what we needed."

Seth grabbed at the side of his face that inevitably stung, grumbling as he spoke. "Where is he?"

"Not here." She smiled menacingly, pushing off the table she strode towards me. "You kind of dropped the ball there a bit. Shutting down for months after Jax died, thought I wouldn't even have had to finish the job. I mean, *seriously* Maia you made it pretty damn easy. You put Seth in charge, for fuck's sake. But Covert Province is pushy, and you setting out to save the world didn't help your case."

I angled my head, intrigued. "Covert Province, the hell they have to do anything?"

"You're working with them?" Alexiares asked, not having heard anything about them during the few days we'd been stuck in St. Cloud.

"What kind of self-respecting woman put herself in the position to work with Covert Province?" Moe's voice was fierce, her words intended to sting.

The Covert Province had formed under the belief that people needed to be segregated by their innate powers, that some were by natural law, better than others. More valuable. Useful. They'd been known to arrange marriages, ensuring that if magic was in fact passed down genetically, each line would be stronger than the next.

Their society was highly patriarchal, men holding all positions of power, and women falling into more subservient roles. If their gifts were extraordinary, they'd use information provided, sure, but similar to The Before, what they had to bring to the table didn't matter.

Not when a man could just take credit for it in the end.

So we'd heard. Dissent wasn't tolerated. Verging from the status quo would likely end up with you dead in the center of town.

There were rules for living there though we didn't know exactly what. Having a respectable amount of power was one. Rumors of families rushing over the border roaming through Transient Nation hoping for a new start, running from whatever they'd left behind, was a hot dinner topic at the beginning. It was mostly rumors because if you asked them what they'd seen, what they'd lived through, you would never get a direct response. Like they'd been programmed to avoid the question or answer honestly at all costs.

"You do what you have to do to survive." Sloan's eyes held a ghostly expression.

"They came here first," I muttered.

Her red hair fell forward as she nodded, her pointed nose twitching as the man at the door peered out, checking our surroundings for someone eavesdropping.

One detail stuck out in my mind. "Show me your neck."

"What?" Her voice croaked, not expecting my request.

"Show me your neck, or I'll swipe you from your feet and see it, regardless."

"He'll kill you." He wouldn't. She would've killed me long ago if she truly wanted me dead.

I smirked at her, challenging an old friend. "Don't threaten me with a good time."

She grabbed her hair, lifting it up to show the tattoo on the nape of her neck. It matched.

Anger boiled in my blood, disgusted at her abuse of power. "Those were your guys, your people. Why would you let—"

"I didn't *let* them do shit. They killed Morgan for resisting, killed half of our army. Women and children too, to prove a point. He left me in his will. I wasn't even working with the leadership anymore. He wanted me home, off the field, make sure there'd be someone left to raise Violet. Our daughter. I had no choice Amaia." Her eyes were cold, but also pleading for me to understand.

Amaia coming out like my friend from the dorms. The girl who stayed up late into the night, trolling corrupt politicians on social media while eating leftover pizza we'd smuggled out the dining hall.

I nodded in understanding. There's no way for me to feel her pain, know what she was going through. Grief looked different on everyone, but I could understand. Her fear for her people, the responsibility now laying at her feet, robbing another soul from their innocence.

I'd met Morgan once. He was an older man, about the age of Prescott. I hadn't known they'd been a couple. That's what happens when the only mail that goes back and forth is important, not wanting to risk lives or waste resources. But what I did know was that Morgan had presented himself as being a fair man. And from what Sloan had disclosed, this fair man had died for standing by his beliefs.

She added, barely audible to anyone but me, "My options were to do this, or have no place for Violet to grow up at all."

"I don't get it. What's the end goal?" Alexiares asked, still trying to put two and two together, make sense of it all.

"They want it all." She explained, "The same shit they've been after since the treaty was signed. They think it's better to go back to how things were, but perfected this time. They've been experimenting with DNA. Seeing if he could influence how children are born, using genetic testing and using people who he deems having 'undesirable magic' to run experiments. See if he can change their genes. It's easy, running a controlled experiment in a lab, changing willing volunteers one by one. But it's faster to change *everyone* through contamination or a bite. His first step is to take one settlement at a time, but he wants them fully functioning so the fallout won't be too bad. Thinks if he takes out leadership, leaves the future of the settlement at risk—"

A chill went down my spine. Eugenics. I knew how this story could end. "Then everyone will fall in line under his leadership. Who is *he*, Sloan?"

She turned to Seth, then Reina. "Their father. He's not a hostage. He's in charge of the whole damn thing. It was his idea to reach out to Seth, but you cost him time, time he doesn't think he has. And now, he wants you dead. All of you."

CHAPTER
FORTY

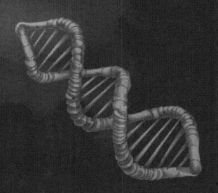

REINA

I broke.

My father is alive. My brother had betrayed me. My father didn't die. I had left him to die.

My brother is a liar. Now, it was my father's wish to see my brother and I dead, and it would happen by my lost cousin's hand.

Each breath was rapid. Sharp. I couldn't breathe, I couldn't find air. *No. No.* I couldn't take this, I couldn't face this. I had nothing. No one. My brother, he didn't just hate me; he didn't care if I ended up dead.

Blood rushed through my ears. My heart was pounding. *No. What? How? Why?* I'd spent all this time protecting him, just for

I was dizzy. The room—*Is it spinning? I want to sit down.* My legs gave out. Water, there was water on my face. It was salty. No, those are tears.

Has my entire life been a lie?

A sharp pain shot through the left side of my chest. Sloan walked past me. She said something to Amaia, but I didn't understand. Couldn't make out the words. *What's wrong with me? Why can't I breathe?*

I heard the clank of the door and then a lock. I'm trapped. *No, I want out! Let me out!* I was up on my feet, sprinting, charging towards the door. My body banged against it, over and over again. Amaia stood behind me, hugging me. Pulling me onto the floor, rocking my body back and forth, her hand running through my hair. My eyes burned and I couldn't see anything, everything was blurry.

Something moved in my peripheral vision, catching my attention. My brother. I couldn't stop myself, wouldn't even if I could. I knew it didn't hurt. I didn't care.

I don't care about anything.

I pushed free from Amaia, my palm stung as it connected with his face, his chest, anywhere as long as it was him. He stood there, letting me. The eyes we shared pleading silently for my forgiveness. My understanding. *I hated those eyes.*

"I hate you!" I screamed, pointing my finger in his face as he smacked it away, turning his nose down.

Not this time, not that easy. "No! You look at me and you look at me now, Seth. I'm your *sister*. How could you? I hate you."

Unable to find any oxygen, my breath refused to bend to my will. He held his chin high, tears threatening to fall. A pinch formed in between his brows, his mouth opened, considering his next words, the expression of a concerned brother, the brother I'd run to Monterey with.

I was reminded that version of my brother did not exist, not anymore. The look faded, the cold, unforgiving brother I knew now returned. "You lied to me first. Said he was dead."

"He is dead." I said, teeth clenched.

"Except he's not."

"She's lying!"

"She's not Reina. They have proof. The emissary they sent around December, he asked me about The Duke and if I'd finally learned my lesson."

I backed up a step, body numb. *It can't be.* A testament to my brother's lifelong lack of control over his emotions. The Duke had been Seth's first horse. Our father was adamant that if we wanted to claim one of the ranches horses as our own, that we'd have to break it in ourselves. Easier said than done. Even as a child, Seth had been hard to control.

Months passed by and he was nowhere close to being tamed. Both Seth and The Duke. Seth's impatience got the best of him, his frustration driving him to throw a fit, kicking sand in our father's face. He'd stormed into the house, the gate left wide open. My father had left it that way, deciding to teach Seth a hard lesson.

The Duke took off at his first opportunity. Our father rode Seth out to him, handed him some gear, and took back off towards the house. My brother was left there to figure it out himself. He was only eleven.

"The kid needs to learn some patience," my father had said as my mom cried, worried he wouldn't make it back before dark.

Our mother was a docile woman. She'd loved her kids ferociously, but at heart was kind. A patient and generous soul, my father had claimed to fallen for her for those exact reasons. He'd spent months courting her, convincing her life on a ranch could be just as enticing as life out on the coast where she was from.

That had been the core of his frustration with Seth's lack of restraint. It wasn't that our father hadn't loved us, he'd just held us to a higher standard. Expected perfection.

Even as a child, Seth had been wildly unpredictable, and since my father hadn't been able to breed the trait out of him, he'd break him like a horse instead.

"Impatience is an unfavorable trait to have," my father had told me, using the opportunity to teach me a life lesson, too.

I'd sat on the porch waiting for him to come back. Night had fallen but there was no sign of him. My father went after him, finding him in the same spot he'd left him, The Duke long gone.

None of that mattered now. I'd done what my father had asked. "You don't understand," I said to Seth, horrified.

"Don't I? You lied, you robbed me of choosing a life of my own. Of making a choice. Family, the thing you claim to be damn happy about finding, what you're glad to be a part of? We had that Reina, still do! But you hated us. You never wanted to stay on that ranch. Never cared about Dad telling us to stick together. That was clear the second you stepped foot in Monterey. You got what made you happy, a life away from the ranch. The friends, the clothes—"

"This isn't productive—" Alexiares started. He stood next to Amaia, still treading in the space between her and Seth. Her eyes were daggers, boring into his and silencing him. It wasn't his place to speak, not right now.

"No," I growled, putting my hand up. "Let him finish."

"We *had* a family to go back to Reina, we coulda found it. Dad had a plan, told us where we should all go if shit it hit the fan."

"It was hardly a plan," I tried. We'd never gone into specifics, but the topic had come up during odd family dinner conversations that formed around books we'd read or shows someone had watched.

"It was!" he shouted. I flinched. "We had a place here, and you tricked me. Lied, tricked me, and then trapped me at Monterey. Kept me from coming here, from seeing if Hunter made it out."

I grasped at my chest, holding steady on Amaia's shoulder. The words caught on the tip of my tongue, so badly wanted to creep out. I'd never let them, never let myself replay those moments in my mind. If I didn't say them out loud, then they weren't real.

"Seth."

"What, Reina?"

The memories were still fresh in my mind. "It wasn't Pansies that got Hunter. It was Uncle Harris. I saw him." My lip trembled. "He … he came after me, too. I wasn't sure what I was seeing, didn't wanna believe it. Hunter didn't see it coming. He was walking away! Had his back turned. But Harris was awfully angry—I never learned what they'd been arguing about, but Harris was drunk."

He'd been through Desert Storm, tours in Iraq, Afghanistan. If Uncle Harris was sober, that meant it was time for work. "I screamed. There wasn't time. I didn't think, just ran. I made it down to the pond, was outta options but Dad was there. Stopped him, raised his rifle and shot five times. Twice in the chest, once in the stomach, through the neck, and last one in his head. Like it was nothin' too. Just grabbed me, told me to try for the sake of the family to forget what I saw. That it would already be hard for momma to take another loss … after James."

Our other brother, he'd died years before we left the ranch. It was a touchy subject. Even after all this time. It had been Seth's fault after all. "If she knew that Uncle Harris had been the cause of Hunter's death. A man she'd grown close to, called a brother herself. Well, he didn't think she'd ever recover from that. So he took care of it himself. Hardly flinched when he did it too, like he'd wanted to do it for some time."

Seth's eyes glazed over as if he were recalling a memory. I glanced down, noticing he held onto Moe's hand. Her eyes glazed as well, sharing what she could to help her family. This was the secret she and Seth had kept these past few months.

Our magic is back.

My body reacted. Grief filled the room. Amaia and Alexiares fell to their knees, buckling under the pressure as I fought to bring it back. To center myself.

Another tear dripped down my cheek. "He told me Uncle Harris wasn't well, that he hadn't been for a long time but now he'd taken care of it. There was no reason to worry, that there was no place left in this world for the irrational."

"A new World Order Cycle is coming."

"Exactly." He'd rambled on about it in the days after the world fell to ash.

That it'd been predictable. If we'd paid attention, we'd have seen the signs. Our father had spent his entire life on the ranch, but had immersed himself in a world full of conspiracies, politics, following theories and forming some of his own. It was one of the things that kept me distant from him.

There were certain things I knew we'd simply never see eye to eye on. While a lot of the information he'd read was based on fact, there were always embellishments. White lies that inspired negative reactionary emotions instead of logical thinking.

"He was *calm*, Seth. Like he'd done this before. Covered for him. Remember all those newspapers we saw in the attic that summer? In Sloan's family house attic? About all the strange unsolved murders around town in the '80s that suddenly stopped one year. The year uncle dodged town. Now think about how he didn't come back until everything went to shit. Why'd we always have to go to their house? Why'd they never come back to the ranch? We were out by the pond, arguing about it, when one came from the water, pulled him in, and was attacked. It was so early. Dad had thought if he were bit, he'd turn too … so he made me shoot him. I missed. My hand was shaky, and I missed. Got him near the shoulder. I couldn't pull that trigger again. He said he'd take care of it, when the time was right. Would keep us from having to hear it, to tell mom it had been swift. I—"

My voice broke, sobbing uncontrollably now. "You admired Dad. A lot more than I'm willin' to bet you'd admit—Uncle Harris too, at times when we were younger." The relationship between them had been rocky at the best of times, but Seth had always chased after our father's approval, respect. "I didn't know how to tell you. Didn't have the heart. Didn't know how to ruin that image of them you had in your head. Yeah I redirected, and redirected. Yes, I got us lost a few times until we were too far to double back. The only person waiting for us here would want an answer, want the truth on what happened to her father. I couldn't lie to both of you, but I also couldn't tell you the truth. You'd lose everything, then you would have nothing at all. And for a while, I thought I meant enough to you to stop the rest from mattering at all."

The gunshots had drawn every Pansie in our area our way. Being a ranch in Montana, we didn't have many. Lands were wide and people were scarce. But that didn't mean none were around at all. It just took them a minute to get there, and the promise of food was an enticing offer. Seth had been out riding, came back just ahead of the herd.

Our mother had been in my room, trying to get the words out of me. She'd figured out what was wrong when movement grabbed her attention out the window, seen them all and realized Hunter and our father weren't with Seth. She loved us, would do anything to protect her kids. Was out the door in an instant, shotgun in hand, picking off Pansies hot on Seth's tail.

A shotgun was not enough to defend yourself against a herd. We'd learned that the hard way that day.

"We have family here, Reina! Cousins, blood we grew up with, you turned your back!"

My brother had broken my heart. Wanted to trade me for a family he didn't share nearly as many memories with. Hadn't celebrated birthdays with, didn't fight over what to watch on Saturday mornings. They hadn't been on the other end of his flying elbows or WWE re-enactments. These people hadn't tolerated his morning breath being blown into their cereal for giggles.

He'd traded me for people who didn't love him the way I did, and for a man who had never accepted him for who he was.

"I was scared Seth! I couldn't lose you, too. You hated me, but I couldn't lose you, so I accepted that. Accepted you would never love me like you loved them. As long as you were alive ..."

We wouldn't see eye to eye on this. I no longer cared. He'd chosen to betray me. Had subjected me to death. I'd come on this gore filled, traumatizing journey to keep him safe, and he'd come to seal my fate.

I looked around. The room was quiet. Moe had let go of Seth's hand, moved back over to the table watching but saying nothing. Silent tears matching my own. Alexiares let out a loud breath, inflating the tension in the room.

It dawned on me. Amaia had said nothing at all, had hardly reacted to the revelation, but towards my grief instead. I could feel her guilt from here.

CHAPTER
FORTY-ONE

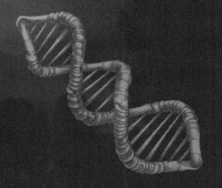

AMAIA

R eina's voice echoed through the room, her eyes wide with emotion. "You're not even reacting. Why aren't you upset? Why doesn't she seem upset?" She motioned towards me.

"You knew?" Seth asked, his voice laced with fury as he slowly turned to face me, eyes still glancing back towards his sister. We all felt our magic slowly returning, and he was smart enough to know now would be a terrible time to turn his back on her.

Reina let out an exasperated sigh, filling the eerie silence that had settled around us. Her eyes bore into mine, and I thought I saw a glimpse of understanding. Her face twisted with betrayal as she stepped forward. Fists curled at her sides.

I braced myself, expecting her to strike me, preparing myself to take it. Instead, she stopped short of me. "Why?" she hissed, her voice low and dangerous.

Taking a deep breath, I met her gaze, trying to convey the sincerity of my words. "Because I had to protect you," I said, barely above a whisper.

"You didn't *have* to do anything, Amaia. You chose to. That's the thing about you, you always think you *have* to do something. But you constantly confuse the words want and need," she ground out, closing in on the space between us. The ferocity in her voice fierce, the sound of it a slap to the face.

Alexiares had been hovering nearby, inching closer, ready to step between me and whatever he assumed was an immediate threat, even if it meant his new family. The tension filling the room.

My hand found hold on his arm, halting his advance. I didn't need his protection. Didn't want it. He grumbled, shaking me off and pacing towards the corner of the room, glowering as he watched the scene unfold.

"I had my suspicions, but no concrete proof. As a general, everyone close to me was a suspect at some point. *My family*. What was I to do? Throw you all in jail? Resort to interrogation and torture? There's six of you, three with high clearance and one of those people is already dead. My options were limited."

Tomoe stepped forward, anger seeping in every movement. "The kind that gets us in this situation to begin with. You put the whole damn Compound in danger, letting him walk around and gain intel. Making plans and orchestrating entire missions!" Her words echoed as if speaking for both her and Reina. I looked at them, their faces contorted into expressions of betrayal and anger.

I sighed. "I did what I had to do, with the information that I had on hand. And now we have to deal with the consequences, for that, I apologize. Truly. No one at The Compound was in any real danger. I had my suspicions, but the only way I'd ever get the truth was if I let him show me his ass himself. I couldn't tell you Reina," I turned to my friend, my sister. "Because even through the bull-shit and fighting, no one knows you better than your brother. No one knows your tells more than him."

The words hung heavy in the air, the room now silent. Reina's anger was palpable, radiating off her like heat waves on the sweltering summer days we'd grown accustomed to. "Seth was responsible for routing half of those men you sent out to assist the others. *San Diego* went down because of him."

"I couldn't ever ask you to keep something like this from your brother, your own flesh and blood." I said softly, her anger dissipating as quickly as it had come. "After all you two have lost … If I was wrong, your own suspicions would have broken you, Reina. Would have undone every beautiful, and pure thing about you. And Seth was *not* responsible for that. Riley was. Though something tells me his men allowed him into their minds and that's what damned them all."

A shiver ran through Seth's body in confirmation, his heading drooping in shame.

"And Tomoe," I said, grabbing her shoulders, forcing our eyes to connect.

"You weren't wrong. It wasn't just you. I saw things too. Signs," she whispered.

I looked at her with a heavy heart. "No, this is my burden to bear."

There had always been a connection between them beyond friendship. They'd kept their feelings to themselves but it had been painfully obvious to everyone around them. No one had understood why, not until now.

"I had to keep my suspicions to myself." I explained to Tomoe, my tone heavy with regret. "If I acted on them prematurely, I might have jeopardized your chance at happiness. It's not that I don't trust you either, Moe. Don't think that for a second. But you love him. Love can be a powerful force, and in the worst of circumstances, it can blind us to the truth. He knew that," I spat at him, "He knew we love him, and let it blind us all."

Her expression was unreadable as she listened to my words. I could tell she was struggling to take it all in, to process everything. It was a lot.

"Loved," she said finally, her eyes cold, unyielding. She glared at him as he stepped near, outreaching a hand, to comfort her. She let it hang in the air.

I could feel her disappointment. It was like a knife twisting in my gut. I'd let her down, and there was no denying it. But I knew what I'd done had been best, even if it meant keeping the truth from them both.

"Love. And more than anything Moe, I wanted to be wrong so bad. So fucking bad. Desperately, but I wasn't. I know I should have told you, but I thought I was doing the right thing."

"This would have been his pick." I saw the reflection in her eyes as she focused on pulling a vision of our initial argument over my decision.

Tears welled in my eyes as the memory of him in those last moments flooded my mind. He would have been the one to give Seth a chance to prove himself, to extend the benefit of the doubt. He'd valued their relationship, would've hoped, prayed, even though it had been his brother to be the one to betray him.

I also knew he would've argued bringing him with us on such a journey would be the safest bet. It didn't feel that way at the moment, but it was true. If he was here, with us, then he wasn't there gathering intel to share, or risking more lives. Compound first.

He was here, under my watch. And now Alexiares' watch too. We could keep Reina and Moe safe if we had to.

"This would have been *his* pick." I confirmed. The results of which would haunt me for years to come.

My attention shifted to Seth, the brother I'd chosen. My stomach churned with unease at his distraught appearance. *He doesn't have the right to be upset.* So many lives had been lost because of him. Families torn apart that had thought they'd a chance of life again in The After. He'd let us all down, but most of all he had failed Jax. The reality of that was crushing.

"And you," I hissed, my finger pointed mere centimeters from his face. "You proved me right. You shattered the trust we had in you. Destroyed our family. I will *never* forgive you for what you've done."

Seth pleaded with me, dropping to his knees in defeat. A sight I never thought I'd see. A remorseful Seth Moore.

"You have to believe me, Maia. I never meant for Jax to die. It's torn me apart—"

"Quite honestly, I don't want to hear another word." I injected firmly, "I believe you, but I've heard enough from you for a very, very long time. Maybe more than one life can account for. You're lucky I don't take your life right here. Oh," I chuckled. "How I'd like nothing more than to drive my fist through your chest, and feel that last beat of your heart clenched between my fingers. If you think I'm not tempted to leave you open on the floor the way you left my Jax … well then you're poorly mistaken. You should probably hug your sister for that blessing. Don't think she'd ever forgive me for that, despite the anger and pure disgust seeping from her damn pores at the moment."

I turned to face my friends who'd always felt more family. Like blood despite all the pain we'd been through. Though I hated Seth, would never forgive him, wanted him dead at the moment … I still cared for him deeply.

"No one was in real danger," I said confidently. "Riley's my true second and has been from the moment I walked up those steps and entered The Arena. He knows it. He's been my eyes and ears for months. Nothing classified ever crossed Seth's desk, only tests or menial tasks. And even then, nothing made it to his desk before it crossed Riley's."

I waited for them to challenge the trust I'd put in Riley. Ask why he hadn't been someone I'd suspected, withheld information with. But none came. Riley's loyalty was clear as day.

I turned my gaze back to Seth, narrowing my eyes, daring his temper to unleash. "Which is why Riley stayed behind. Not to man the gates or serve as my temporary second, but as my lieutenant. *General,* should something have happened to me. He has specific orders to debrief Prescott if he doesn't hear from Seth with particularly specific phrasing in the next three days, a messenger within the month. Should we have been unsuccessful in our travels." He'd arranged all the details down to the halfway point for his men to meet, nothing left to chance.

Tomoe slammed her palm into the table before sitting down, putting her hands on her head in disbelief and exhaustion.

"Unbelievable," Reina mumbled.

I felt terrible. I'd betrayed them too by taking their choice away. Again. My intentions had been good. I didn't regret my decision. If I had to do it again, I would. They'd had those last few months of happiness, not having to carry this heaviness around with them. All the memories they'd made between then and now would go untainted. There would be no guilt on their end.

"I can sit here and tell you how sorry I am all day. None of you would accept it." His words weren't bitter but conscious-stricken. "But that's not gonna get us out of here. I stopped giving them information five-hundred miles back … didn't seem right."

He glanced shamefully around the room. "My father, *our* father, has chosen to have us executed. I'm no longer useful in this, and that's what we need to focus on."

"Good thing I don't need you to be Seth. I wouldn't expect that from you, anyway." I rolled my eyes and let my repulsion for him show. "I need a minute to think through what we have to offer. But we're getting out."

EVERYONE HAD MOVED INTO SEPARATE PARTS OF THE CELL. IT'D BEEN hours since anyone had spoken. Reina had since fallen asleep, sniffling quietly, while Seth paced back and forth at the door, occasionally mumbling to himself and pulling out strands of his hair.

Alexiares sat opposite of me, still watching, but saying nothing. Not wanting to be silenced again. Part of me wondered what he was thinking, of the mess I'd made. I doubt he'd pass judgment, we'd both done far worse things in this life. But seeking comfort in his presence didn't feel right. I needed to sit with this. Deserved to.

Tomoe approached me, fists clenched in anger, her expression fierce. "I saw it. He fucked with my mind. I *saw* this, and he convinced me it was nothing."

She'd channeled him, but received more than vague memories, instead receiving a jumbled play-by-play of his life. Unable to determine when most of the memories were from or if they were just options of the future. She'd felt as if she *were* him, and not just a vessel receiving moments, bits and pieces.

He'd reacted similarly, though she never learned what exactly had occurred on his end. Seth had insisted they'd kept it to themselves, dodging the conversation every time she'd brought it up. She'd thought he'd just been spooked. She'd been spooked too. Wasn't sure what to make of it. But now she had a theory, vulnerability.

It'd happened in a moment of vulnerability, and now she'd wanted to understand why no one had come forward with it before. There had to be some trick to it. We just didn't know what. But that didn't mean we couldn't leverage it.

Alexiares whistled. "Power-sharing. Never saw that one coming."

Seth's guilt was laid bare, stopping his pacing as he glared at Tomoe's back, frozen at the revelation.

"This changes everything."

CHAPTER
FORTY-TWO

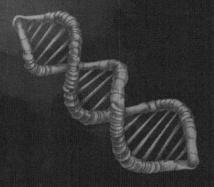

AMAIA

"A deal?" Sloan gave a curt laugh. "There is no deal to be made when our citizens' lives are at risk. They expect information from us every week. If they don't get it, our guys die. Ten for each network that doesn't have anything to offer."

There were dozens of independent trade networks. Each settlement could develop trade with whomever they wished, though there were four main ones running through what once was the continental United States.

Powder had been expelled through the vents, firing off loudly, echoing from the compressed air, stabilizing our magic before she'd stepped foot into the cell. She'd left a disaster in her wake the night prior and knew it. I hadn't known why she'd returned.

Didn't give her so much as a moment to tell us, proposing a deal the second she entered.

Welp, five-hundred miles was a few weeks, Seth's body count was truly racking up. I wanted to rub it in a bit, let this betrayal smack him in the face, hurt him as much as he hurt us. But one look at his face showed he'd done the math.

"Then we'll give them information," I cooed. "Perhaps it would be advantageous for me to inform you that there's a way to become more powerful. *Without* having to resort to unethical experiments."

Her wildfire hair fell in front of her face as she considered my offer before angling her head back up, her face brightening. "I'm listening."

I am too, and now I know I've got your interest.

"Oh, no. It doesn't work like that. You see, now you know that I have information that can change the game. You also know me well enough to know that you're not getting it out of me unless I so choose. Meaning, let us out." I said, face hard with determination, "In order for this to work, we'll have to work together, as true allies. You need me if you give a shit about your people. Yeah, you know me from before, but my reputation precedes me now. That war wouldn't have been won without me."

There had been others, people possessing greater knowledge than me, more expertise in warfare and battle tactics. But there was value in those with a fresh perspective and the unwavering determination to protect what's yours. They knew more than me, but my ideas saved thousands of lives. Two things could be true at once.

"I need more than just an empty promise of more power, Amaia. There's lives at risk. You have to give me something tangible, something to work with."

I studied her for a moment, ready to call her bluff. This was the one leg up we had, I needed it to work.

"You'd be a fool to pass up what we're offering," Alexiares said, his head tilted to the side, danger seeping off him. "What other option do you have besides offering yourselves up on a silver platter? If that's your idea of helping your people, you're an ill-matched ally to have anyway. Weak." The last word ground out, repulsed.

"You think I don't know who you are, Alexiares? What you've done in this life and the past, *Bloodhound*. What you deem as weak, would likely be acting in my best interest." Sloan's hand went up, eyes assessing him.

It was an effort to keep the surprise off my face at the name, another connection I'd failed to make. He'd told me he'd had a past, had acted of sorts of an assassin. Their settlements weren't too far apart, and he'd noted he'd been here in the past.

Sloan's gazes locked on my own, challenging each other, my intensity driving her to drop her stare in submission and I smirked. *I win.*

"How many soldiers are in your command?" I asked.

She looked at me skeptically, trying to decide whether she wanted to answer, knowing a response would seal the deal. "Down to eight-hundred," she replied.

"That'll do. And how many citizens are also trained to fight?"

Alexiares watched me intently. I struggled not to smirk at the smug grin of respect plastered on his face. His eyes slowly tracing each of my movements. *If only I could snap a photo and show him.*

"None," she answered, expression confused at the given option.

Stupid. There were fifty-thousand of them, and they relied on eight-hundred men. "I can fix that."

"General's not the brightest either," she added, reflecting my thoughts. *Negligence and small-mindedness also come to mind.*

"Can fix that too," I assured, "We'll work *together*. I can get the word out through Salem discreetly. They won't stand for this.

I'll head our army, work with other allies, whatever you need. Between the both of us, we can rally the power to fight back."

We'd named Salem in hopes its meaning would be enough to start over. It meant peace, security, safety. Free. While that was the goal, every leader and general within would burn shit to the ground to keep their freedom, to protect their vision of the future.

"That'll be a hard sell for some, especially those who have already lost so much," Sloan responded tentatively.

"It won't be, because it's our only option for sovereignty. We've all lost a lot. Tell them to get over it. This doesn't stop with you. With us. You know that, right? This is headed towards war."

Seth shifted on his heels, the action drawing attention causing him to settle at once.

Sloan's eyes tore from Seth, the warning of further action against him at the tip of her tongue. "Go on."

"It'll take time. We'll need to set up a base location, allocate resources accordingly, but if we all work together and organize correctly, we can do this. I know we can, and you know what I'm capable of. He has no idea that we know. It's an advantage. Imagine what we can accomplish together." I saw an old spark flicker in my lost friend's eyes—the rebel that lay beneath all the sadness.

It made sense that she and Reina were cousins. Sloan was simply just a darker, grittier version, but that base layer of them was the same. That passion for life, to live and to love, to enjoy the moments given, that still remained. It'd just been buried deep down.

"It would be nice to not lose men to your ranks." She smirked, contemplating for a moment. "We'll need more than that though. If we're caught, my men will die. I'll bear the weight of that, not you."

"If we fail, my people die, too. If we fail, we fail together, Sloan. Is your freedom not worth your death?"

Sloan groaned, remembering the saying I used to say to her, convincing her whatever protest we were organizing was worth the overall risk of trouble. For all great empires were founded on pillaging, violence, and conquering.

It was time for that to change.

"Open the door," she commanded, determined.

"Magic too?" My fingers wiggled optimistically.

"Don't push it."

"Fine, we'll talk about magic tomorrow."

"Tomorrow," Sloan agreed, turning and leading the way for us to follow.

CHAPTER
FORTY-THREE

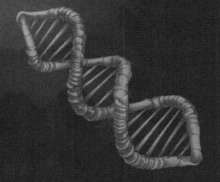

TOMOE

I t had to be below freezing out. My bones felt stiff as we walked
through the city, the snow blinding my adjusting eyes. At least
six inches covered the ground, the liquid seeping into my boots,
too low to keep the unplowed sidewalk out. It must've started not
too long after we'd arrived, or maybe before, couldn't remember
shit from that night.

Where St. Cloud had been bleak and gray, Duluth was just
brown. The buildings were brown; the clothes were neutral, various tones of the earth covered in variations of animal fur to keep
them warm. Traveling through the different territories had been
a continuous culture shock. We had it good in Monterey. At least
people there were happy. Moved with purpose.

Every person we passed was either lost in thought, angry, or looked like they'd spent the night crying. *You and me both buddy*, I laughed to myself. The wind carried from Lake Superior, biting against my skin. I fought the urge to chatter my chin. *Could Sloan walk any slower?*

She'd said the walk to where we'd be staying wasn't far, apparently arranging for us to stay in apartments on the edge of their city. We'd have to remain out of sight in order to pull off our ruse. At least long enough to make contact with the others in Salem and other allies. Then we'd have to find Riley's contact.

It'd only be a matter of time before it got out that we were not, in fact dead and were now plotting. From then it wouldn't be long for things to get out of control. I'd seen that version play out enough to know I didn't like the way it'd end.

There were still options, happier endings, but the future felt bleak from where I now stood. One future that I'd seen had been wrong. A lie. I'd been stupid, willfully blind. Rage crept from me and I found myself wishing Reina had her powers. To take it all away, make me numb.

That was the problem with seeing the future. It gave you false hope.

Sloan had placed a few guards she could 'spare' outside the rundown apartment building she'd dropped us at. Amaia had insisted it was a waste of resources, that they could be of better use. But Sloan had denied, stating it was for our safety against Covert Province and any spies they may have.

I call bullshit.

Reina entered her room at the end of the hall first, announcing the further from Seth she was, the happier she'd be. He'd barely acknowledged he'd heard it. Head hung low. Amaia went next, leaving a room between her and Reina. The look on her face as she entered saying she was giving me an out if I needed one. After making sure Amaia's door had closed and the locks had clicked, Alexiares lingered, eyeing me and Seth hesitantly.

Seth barely noticed, but I nodded. *Thanks, man.* His door clicked, but no locks sounded.

"Answer me honestly, please. For once." I asked, voice brittle, "Was any of it ever real?"

He reached for my hands, his movement quick, causing me to leap back with a hiss. "I need you to trust me. Just once, one more time," he said softly, arms raised, before slowly taking hold of my hands one at a time.

The tension eased throughout my body as I dropped my guard, letting him in with the realization of what he was doing. Selfishly, I wanted to see what he was offering. My subconscious told me to cut the bullshit, to use this as an opportunity to gather evidence or a glimpse at his intentions.

I wasn't given a chance as he locked down on my power, taking the reins. In the distance, I felt two tears racing down my cheeks. It was beautiful. I saw myself, memories of the two of us going for rides through the coastline of Monterey. The day he'd asked me to spar for the first time, recognizing the need to fill the void that had unexpectedly opened in my life. Laying out in the green space, he stared up at the sky as I read, straining my eyes to finish the story despite the lack of light from the moon.

When I'd tripped over the clutter in my study. The embarrassment I'd felt as he watched on, feeling judged, how he'd pushed my hair from my face, telling me he'd be happy to have a home filled with my clutter one day. That it added to the ambience. Told me I'd felt like home. I love you slipping from my lips in response. The shock, then happiness that fell upon his face.

Then there were glimpses of the future, or what had been. What he'd hoped, these were ... daydreams? *How was this possible?* We were living outside The Compound, but still in Monterey territory. He'd passed on his position, opting to retreat to a quieter life but still accompanying me to our true home so I could visit the rest of our family. Reina, Amaia, Riley, Prescott, Luna, even Alexiares were there.

His shifted gears, him and Reina as kids. A boy his age who resembled Reina at his side, a girl with red hair ran into view. *Sloan*, I realized. They were playing hide and seek, an older boy who resembled Seth, with a booming voice, told them to hurry and hide, that they better be ready soon. Reina giggled, grabbing onto his arm, telling him she wanted to hide with him.

Time jumped before my eyes. It was Reina's graduation. Seth turned, facing an older version of the younger boy from earlier. The one that favored Reina. I realized it must be their brother, Hunter. Hunter had patted him on the back, said it was good to see him back home. Reina was happy to have him here, and had talked about him all the time. Seth beamed at the reflection of Hunter's glasses. A proud brother. Their faces, happy, grins pulling ear-to-ear.

Another memory, Seth pulling Reina close. She was sad. Crying, Hunter was dead. A tear fell onto Reina's head. It was his.

It was him and Amaia, riding free through the territory, racing towards San Jose. Amaia's smile was bright as she teased him. He joked that he'd let her win, not wanting to outshine a superior. She'd pulled up next to him, the humored expression gone, sincerity crossing over.

"We'll always be equals, Seth," she'd said.

Riley was there now. They were in Amaia's study. Jax walked in, trays of food in his hand, complimentary Elie he'd rejoiced. They all cheered, stacks of paperwork and plans laid out around them for the long night ahead. None of them looked exhausted though, happy again. Just glad to be in each other's presence, to feel safe inside a home.

The last visions were of his father. A man who read to him every night as a kid, but lectured him with adult expectations by day.

The father who'd driven four hours overnight, just to check on the son who'd had a tough week. Who'd learned how to use social media, just to connect with each of his kids, to stay in the know to figure out how to converse with teens of the times. His protector, his friend, his mentor. His biggest critic.

"It was all real, all of it. I did what I had to because I had no other choice. I don't regret my choice, Moe. But I regret hurting you," he reasoned.

I wasn't convinced.

Alexiares' lock sounded. He'd stepped away from the door, giving us some privacy. Just the two of us now.

"The gate. Did you plan to be there with me?"

His face flushed, shame framing his handsome features. "It wasn't supposed to happen that way, but yeah. I wanted you near-by to make sure nothin' bad happened."

"Nothing bad? Seth, people died—good people died. Riley's friend died. *Our* people died."

Had I laid with the devil?

"Duluth lied dammit!" I jumped as his palms slapped against the wall, voice still a harsh whisper, "It was supposed to be just a few of 'em, not fifty-one. I didn't know. You gotta believe me."

"And Jax, did you know they were going to kill him?"

The silence was louder than any admission could be. His thick brows scrunched, as he thoughtfully chose his answer. "No. They said he'd be … incapacitated. I'd then step up and fill his role—"

"Oh my God," I breathed, horror crossing my face.

"See! That look right there, is *exactly* why I gotta go. I don't belong here anymore. Not sure I ever did." If he wanted my pity, my understanding, he wouldn't get it.

He could write his own story, make everyone else the villain. But he was responsible for his own actions, and actions had consequences.

Wait. "You're leaving?" I asked.

He stepped forward, fingers itching to graze my lips, but I smacked it away. "Moe, please, don't yell. Listen to me," he pleaded. The threat in his eyes kept me quiet. "I love you. Okay? I meant that, I still mean it. I never meant for this to happen."

His fingers curled through his hair, the nerves demanding to find release as he paced the hallway, stopping to grip my shoulders. I let him. Love and the lingering fear of what he was capable of freezing me in place.

"I thought they had my father. This had nothing to do with you. Or even the rest of 'em. I just wanted my family back—"

I shook my head. "I thought we were your family."

"You are, but not like that," he said, brushing me off, all of us off, "not like my dad. My cousins." *And Reina.*

"Not like what? Your blood?" He remained silent. I stifled a laugh. "Right."

"Wouldn't you do anything you could to have your family back together if you found out they were alive, too?" His eyes narrowed, challenging me.

I looked down guiltily. I would. "So you'd just leave Reina behind? Sloan?"

A flash of determination crossed over his face. "I'll come back for them. When they're ready."

I didn't know what that meant. Didn't appreciate the way it sounded. But what could I do? I couldn't stop him from leaving. I had no weapons, no magic of value. *Ha, magic of value. I sound like his father.* I could alert Alexiares, the sound would draw Amaia and Reina from their rooms.

But then what?

Would we become more trouble than we're worth? Seth sent to execution, or Amaia, or shit, all of us? Or worse, they would fight each other, an outcome I never wanted to envision having to choose. But it seemed like that would soon be a reality, just not today. *Please, not today.*

"There's nothing that could convince you to stay?" I tried.

His hands dropped from my shoulders, shaking his head. *No.* His eyes dropped back towards the ground, refusing to meet my eye and say the words to my face. *Coward.*

I brushed past him. "Then I have nothing to say."

"I'll come back for you too," he called after me as I passed him, so quietly I thought I'd imagined it.

Don't bother.

I CLOSED THE DOOR BEHIND ME, LOCKING IT AS SOON AS I ENTERED. Chest panting as I listened, waiting to hear where his footsteps would lead, but I heard none. Minutes passed, but I heard nothing. *Is there another exit?* Amaia had spent over a month instructing us to ensure a house was cleared before doing so much as setting a bag down.

A hard head makes for a soft tissue dead girl.

It was a simple apartment inside. It had obviously been someone's in The Before. The basics were there, a couch in the small living room, no tv because for what use? The bedroom had a bed and a vanity, and the kitchen had cups and plates. Some slices of bread and jam were in a cabinet. I wanted to stress eat my life away, but there were bigger tasks at hand.

Securing all exits didn't take long given the size of the apartment, making the next hour pass by painfully slow as I leaned against the door, still listening. The clock on the coffee table hit six p.m. An hour had passed. I hadn't heard anything, but that meant nothing with his training. Peering through the peephole, I slowly opened the door. The hallway was clear.

A tan piece of paper was placed on the mat in front of the door.

Reina,
I'm sorry I couldn't be the brother you deserve. You've always seen the world different from the rest of us. Don't let this dim your light.

Amaia,
I wish it didn't have to be like this. You've been a great friend. You don't have to forgive me for Jay, because I'll never forgive myself. See you out in the   eld. Give it the best you've got.

Moe,
there's still a future there, I know you see it.
Until we next meet,
Seth

I CRINKLED THE NOTE IN MY HAND MARCHING TO AMAIA'S DOOR. Alexiares door opened at the same time as hers. The urgency of my knock drew his attention. She glanced at him, brows raised before both of them looked on curiously, wondering what I needed so soon after going our separate ways.

"He's gone."

EPILOGUE

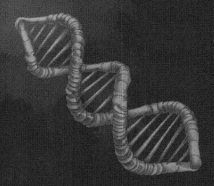

RILEY

'*m not comin' back. They're okay, Amaia is okay. They are all okay. Can't say it's been a good ride, but it's been a pleasure to have known you. Good luck.*

It was no surprise to me; we'd known for weeks. Suspected as much, at least. Either someone had a spy network better than my own or, our chains had been pulled from the inside. Amaia had wanted to give him the benefit of the doubt. Her heart got in the way more times than not. But that was okay. That's why I was here. To protect her. And now, them.

I wouldn't believe that disloyal bastard's words until I heard from Amaia herself. Which could take months. The messenger with our codeword would have to satisfy my desire for confirmation for now. Seventy-three days. I'd been away from my sister for seventy-three days, and now I'd have to wait weeks to hear of her safety. My heart pummeled in my chest. No, that was the adrenaline.

Harley and Suckerpunch were geared up at my side, heads low, crouched down. Drool dripping down the slick snout Harley, Suckerpunch's mouth full of teeth exposed as low growls escaped their lips. I scanned the horizon, the sea not far off crashing against the shoreline, not foolish enough to bring myself closer to the cliff.

We'd been lucky enough to have fishermen out that day, paddling along the coast and noticing the herd headed right in our direction. A soldier had sprinted to Amaia's office, temporarily mine, with urgency. I'd only had time to gather the men who rallied in the courtyard. Any longer and we'd miss this chance.

The sound of crumbling rocks made me freeze, listening. They were uncharacteristically quiet, but that wouldn't fool me. Wouldn't fool us. I raised three fingers, motioning forward twice. They obeyed, Harley taking one side of the cliff, Suckerpunch on the other.

An ear-piercing howl rang out, followed by one in agreement. Hand after hand, finger after finger, clenched onto the wild grass on the edge of the cliff side. I swung my ax side to side, battle cry ringing through the air as fifteen of my soldiers and thirty Pansies sped towards each other in a frenzy of fury. Ready to die to protect our home.

Without knowing the details of what happened along their journey, what the true outcome of it was, or if my sister, my family, were safe. One thing was clear.

War was coming, whether we were ready or not.

AUTHOR'S NOTE

To my readers,

I just wanted to take a moment to say thank you from the bottom of my heart for taking the time to read my book. As an indie author, every reader means the world to me, and I am truly grateful for your support.

If you enjoyed my book, I would be honored if you could take a few minutes to leave an honest rating and review on Amazon, Goodreads, or your favorite review site. Your honest feedback not only helps other readers find my work but also helps me level up as an author.

And if you want to be in the know on my latest releases, promotions, character origin stories, and exclusive content, please consider subscribing to my newsletter. You can sign up using the link below:

https://www.authornellenikole.com/

Seriously, thank you so much for your support. It means more than you could ever know.

Nelle Nikole

ORIGIN STORIES

GET READY FOR AN UNFORGETTABLE JOURNEY WITH RISING: Origin Stories, a collection of three short stories that will leave you feeling inspired and empowered. Join Amaia, Reina, and Tomoe as they share their stories of struggle, survival, and strength.

Experience the thrill of Amaia's story as she flees Seattle and teams up with Prescott to outrun their past. Follow Reina's escape from her Montana ranch and her determination to rebuild her life on her own terms. And be moved by Tomoe's heartbreaking journey as she tries to find solace after the loss of her family.

These three women will captivate you with their courage, resilience, and unbreakable spirit. So why wait? Get your copy of RISING: Origin Stories today and immerse yourself in these powerful and inspiring tales. Download your copy now and discover what makes Amaia, Reina, and Tomoe such unforgettable characters.

ACKNOWLEDGMENTS

I think it's fair to start by saying I never thought I would be publishing a book. Writing is the easy part (for now), everything else in between is harder than I could have possibly imagined, but oh so rewarding!

Ben, you have been a true rock during this entire process. One random winter night I walked downstairs and told you I was going to write and publish a book. Your response was everything, "I can't wait to have a bestselling author wife!" You've filled in the gaps for everything that had to slip by the wayside to make this dream of mine happen, and for that, I can never thank you enough.

Mom and Dad, I never thought I would say this but … thank you for grounding me as a child! Seriously, the emphasis you both put on education and staying true to my values has made this book possible. My passion for reading and exploring the "what-ifs" in life is rooted in the childhood you gave me. You've always encouraged me to write, from being an author to a journalist, the support has always been there. I love you both so dearly.

Cierra, my little sister, the romance reader, thanks for always keeping it real! From reading the roughest version of my draft to letting me know how far I've come with my origin stories. I love you very much and thank you for holding to the highest of standards and expectations.

A very special thanks to Michaela B. From day one, you offered so much support and encouragement. You did some real magic with my Pinterest boards, but more than that, you've always brought that "#1 fan" energy, and it meant so much during the times I became discouraged.

My first degree is in Anthropology, thus, I am huge on representing cultures with sensitivity and grace. I'd like to take a moment to thank Alexandra D., a high school friend that came to my aid when I needed her. Thank you for helping with the Greek translations, you did not have to, yet you chose to. Always a beautiful person both inside and out!

I have to get a bit sappy here for a moment. My editor Emma Jane is a freaking rockstar. Without too much of the personal details, Emma Jane handled my edits with such elegance, during a time where many of the scenes and topics discussed in Rising could be ... triggering. Thank you from the bottom of my heart for taking the time to read and work through my story. Another thanks for the non-editing related chit-chats on music and wedding planning. I am truly looking forward to working with you again.

Jolee at Satisfiction, thank you for taking a chance on little 'ole me. From a Tiktok video, now to your book boxes, you've already helped a large portion of my dream come true. I appreciate you and everything about your business. You deserve all the good things!

My ARC team, you guys are f*cking awesome! There are not enough words to thank you all. The enthusiasm to read Rising filled me with so much joy. I am blessed, thankful, and lucky ... like I said, really no words. Being a debut author is honestly terrifying, but you all made me so comfortable in sharing, and for that, there is no thank you that encases the gratitude I feel. You all believed in me from Day 1, I'm so damn lucky.

To my alpha and beta readers, the confidence you all provided, while still keeping me honest is so appreciated, and you've challenged me to be a better writer. Thank you.

My author support circle on Instagram, Tiktok, Discord, and Reddit has been tremendous. Thank you all for the laughs, encouragement, tips, and overall good vibes. I appreciate you so much!

The support system I have in my personal life is insane. My friends, Nana, coworkers, former classmates, and everyone in between, thank you for being here.

Thank you to you, wonderful readers! For reading. For taking a chance. For reading this far.

This book is a lot of things to me. Writing a story like Rising was a bit therapeutic for me. I am not any of the characters, but each of the characters is a piece of me. We all love and lose in this life, and my journey of grief has not been an easy one. But for me, there were three years where death seemed…to be working its way closer and closer to the ones I loved the most. Grief is a journey, and there are always going to be bad weeks and great days. Without getting too tearful, this book is for them. Drew R., I love you forever, and this book would have made you so damn proud.

Papa, this final thank you is for you. We talked about so much those last few days, and there's so much that I've accomplished that you'll never get to see. But thank you for believing in me, always. Down to that last day.

ABOUT THE AUTHOR

NELLE NIKOLE WAS BORN IN CORONA, CALIFORNIA, SPENT TIME IN the battlefields of Virginia, and now lives in Atlanta, Georgia with her fiancé and their furkid Sophie. A lifelong reader, she began writing thrilling stories to share with her classmates as early as elementary school. Having lived a little bit of everywhere, Nelle decided to take her studies international and completed her Anthropology degree by researching abroad in Rio de Janeiro and throughout Cuba. Driven by an insatiable appetite for knowledge, Nelle pursued a Master's degree in Public Policy, specializing in Global Affairs. After nearly wasting away in corporate life, Nelle decided to pursue her lifelong goal of becoming a published author where she is inspired by all things fantasy, apocalyptic and anything in between.

RISING, her debut novel, speaks to the soul while tackling grief, hope in humanity, and the consequences of betrayal. She uses her real life experience of living amongst a variety of lifestyles, cultures and over-active imagination to blur the lines of reality and fantasy in her magical post-apocalyptic version of The United States seen through the eyes of a powerful female main character and her chosen family.

Find her on:
Tiktok: Author.Nelle.Nikole
Instagram: Author.NelleNikole
Pinterest: Primal Instinct Publishing
Facebook: Nelle Nikole

Printed in Great Britain
by Amazon

32694338R00264